Return To Earth 2: Final Journey of the Cassiopeia

Dennis Calloway

Return To Earth 2:
Final Journey of the Cassiopeia

Copyright ©2025 Dennis Calloway

ISBN 978-1506-915-28-9 PBK
ISBN 978-1506-915-29-6 EBK

August 2025

Published and Distributed by
First Edition Design Publishing, Inc.
P.O. Box 17646, Sarasota, FL 34276-3217
www.firsteditiondesignpublishing.com

Many thanks to my family, friends, co-workers and classmates who read my first novel, Return To Earth. Your feedback over the years was invaluable and went a long way into the chronicling of the Cassiopeia's last journey!

Thanks to the team at First Edition Design Publishing for their continued professionalism and expertise.

And a special thanks goes out to my classmates, Glenn Schoonover and Chuck Cavin. I've known them for years and they were kind enough to take this daunting challenge of reviewing my first draft, prior to publication. Their feedback was priceless, as is their friendship – CNQ!

A final thanks to all of my Dedicated Readers – those of you who read Return To Earth and waited patiently (I hope!) for me to finally finish the second book in the series. I hope it was worth the wait!

CONTENTS

DAY 2

BEGINNING OF THE END

1

Oh God, I wish they would shut up! Nola screamed to herself. She shut her eyes tightly and covered her ears with the palms of her hands, but it didn't matter. The cries and screams of her hapless compatriots were deafening. No matter what she plugged into her ears, she couldn't keep out the brutal slaps and punches of the guards, nor the plaintive whimpers of those around her. Each had its own way of penetrating her eardrums and rolling around in her head until finally coming to rest on her aching psyche. She had an unsettling feeling that if hell existed, it would be just like this – a lot of wailing and gnashing of teeth.

The moon was only eighteen hours behind them, but Nola felt as if she had never even *been* on the moon, or if the moon even existed. To her tortured mind, everything that was happening *to* her and *around* her was nothing more than an elaborate cosmic joke designed to squeeze out any sense of sanity and normalcy.

The faces of Tess and Kyra and others seemed to float in and out of her subconscious mind like ghosts in a dying dream. The thought of them plagued her with tremendous guilt, as much as she tried to deny it. She fancied that in another reality, she would have just seen these women only a couple of days before, but in *this* reality, she began to doubt that they were even real. *But what was real?* She thought. Earth? A broken planet wracked with immense earthquakes and barely holding itself together, was damn near gone or would be soon. The moon? A dying waystation in deadly lockstep with Earth and with an eccentric orbit that will take it so far away from the sun, that by the time it returns some three years later, it'll be a frozen rock – at least until it passes so close to the sun on its return orbit, that it gets burned to a crisp. Europa? A pipe dream that *might* support life if one could make it there. Here on the *Cassiopeia* – *this* was real. This was *her* reality. Here, in this floating powder keg was a reality that was being driven by a madman and his mad lackeys. In Nola's mind, this was her entire existence; her past, her present *and* her future.

She thought it interesting that not once since the ship left the moon, had she thought about how her life would be on Europa. She already knew from Soren's mad ramblings, how glorious, *to him* and fucked up, *to her,* the new world order was going to be, but she never saw herself *there.* She had always been an intuitive person and her intuition now was razor sharp: she would never live to see Europa.

2

"I just don't understand why we need to be out here again!" the dark-haired woman sitting next to Nola cried out piercingly. "Is Soren making *another* speech?" This, she spat out as vehemently as if she were spitting out rotted food.

"I'd watch my tone if I were you, Allison. We've got a long way to go to Europa and a lot can happen between here and there." Nola just happened to glance up at the guard walking toward them and the look in his eyes told her everything she needed to know about him, his agenda, and the new world order waiting for them on Europa. She shivered at the thought of it. Allison must have seen it too, because she abruptly shut her mouth and tried to melt into her seat. Satisfied, the man walked up the aisle, lazily swinging his makeshift baton in one hand, while his other hand rested lightly on the modified medical laser nestled closely to his hip.

When the man was safely out of earshot, Allison turned toward Nola and whispered, "God, Nola, I'm really scared. I wish I was back on the moon with the others." This idea wasn't entirely foreign to Nola. Every day since they left, she had wondered if she had made the right decision in joining Soren's crew. No...that wasn't correct. She wasn't even *part* of Soren's crew. She was part of the spoils, along with everyone else on board. Soren's crew called them, *the passengers.* It made her wonder if she even had a choice in coming.

Some men onboard came willingly, enticed by Soren's patriarchal vision of a new life on Europa, but a fair number resisted and were compensated with black eyes and broken arms for their troubles. The men and women whom Soren deemed key to his survival and his plans, had no choice in coming. Those were the good men, the decent men, but they were crucial to the operation of the ship, so Soren's guards forced them onboard against their will. Many of the men Soren chose as guards were respected men in their fields, but their greed, base desires and ultimate weakness of mind, turned them into lackeys and dangerous footpads in space. These *guards*, as they described themselves, were nothing more than Soren and Rey's henchmen, always ready at a moment's notice to do the bidding of their tin-pot dictator. She thought of some of the worse autocratic nations in the world and realized with dismay that the only way those corrupt and evil dictators stayed in power was through the willingness of their henchmen to brutally suppress any and all opposition. Nola thought it would be an interesting anthropological study to understand just how quickly people shed years of stable civility in the face of greed, desperation and maniacal leadership. In their situation, the men who willingly sold their souls to Soren were men who expected to partake in Soren's mad fantasy of being the *First Father* of a new civilization. Most of the women on the moon were well aware of Soren's misogynistic leanings and would not have gone willingly. Unfortunately, many of them were either drugged and kidnapped or threatened and coerced into coming. Allison Sampson was one of the former. Right before they departed the moon, two of Soren's bodyguards dumped her flaccid and unconscious body into the seat next to Nola and told her to buckle the woman in. She'd had a bruise on her face which was only now starting to fade. Nola looked back at the woman. Her features were hard and looked etched on her face. In another world and another time, she would have been very attractive. Now, she looked like a cornered rat.

3

This was Nola's second time in the Commons. When the ship left the orbit of the moon, Nola and a few others were taken to their cabins and told to stay there until the others – the *recruits* as one guard put it – were properly oriented as to their purpose on Soren's ship. Nola had been relieved she wouldn't have to witness whatever brutality Soren's guards doled out to the ill-fated *recruits*. Now, they were all gathered together in the Commons, nervously awaiting whatever guidance their demented chieftain thought they needed to hear. Soren indicated that he wanted to set everyone's expectations on their trip to Europa, but Nola felt he did it to keep everyone off balance and in line.

She glanced around at the folks seated near her to get an idea of who was here. As her gaze moved across the Commons, it fell upon Doctor Burt Stone. He had an ugly purple bruise on the side of his face that looked fresh and still painful. When their eyes met, Stone held her gaze steadily and then turned away disgustedly. She winced at the hatred she saw in his eyes. On the other side of the Commons, she recognized Larry Drucker, one of Henry Webber's team members. He was cozying up to the guards in a perversely subservient manner. From bits and pieces of information she picked up from Soren and Rey, Larry was responsible for hiding the detailed information the Pegasus satellite was sending back regarding Europa. If Henry had had accurate information on Europa, Soren's plans to steal the *Cassiopeia* and abscond from the moon might possibly have been halted.

She continued scanning the room. She saw the big guard who stood watch outside of Soren's cabin during their last few days on the moon, intimidating a group of men and women on the far side of the Commons. She didn't recall his name but remembered that he was one of the survivors from the United Nations' compound back on the moon. A German security chief or something like that. She remembered that he spoke broken English, but that didn't matter here; intimidation is a silent game.

She thought about the guards again and realized as she glanced around the Commons, that there seemed to be a lot more guards here than on the moon. It was clear now that most of the men who came with Soren freely, were now acting as guards. She counted almost twenty guards here. There were also men like Larry Drucker, who threw whatever morals he had straight into the shredder and decided to get in line with Soren's new world order. She was disgusted. As she had heard it, those men would be first to receive the *human spoils*, as Rey once said. *Human spoils*, she thought disgustedly. Since when did humankind slip back into the prehistoric age where warring tribes decimated the enemy men, only to take their women? To forcibly take the *human spoils*?

She always knew that there were a lot of men on the moon who supported Soren's twisted views but never realized that she'd be in a situation where she might have to submit to Soren or Rey or any of his ignorant goons as if she were some kind of *Handmaid*. And as if from another plane of existence, her memory of Margaret Atwood's *The Handmaid's Tale* broke into her psyche with the force of a mental hurricane. She understood painfully that the women on this ship were in fact living, or would be living soon, the cloistered and controlled lives that Atwood's *Handmaids* lived. And to make matters worse, she helped facilitate this impending fucked up society, to her own detriment.

It hurt her heart to accept the fact that so many good people died on earth, while these morally bankrupt and evil men were given a new lease on life on a new world. She realized, forlornly, that all it took was a catastrophic event and the right mix of bipolar, obsessive-compulsive and dissocial disorders, for their relatively civilized society on the moon, to morph into this precarious and potentially deadly authoritarian space opera.

There was a time when she believed that she was special because she slept with Soren occasionally. She laughed at herself, but there was no humor in it. At first, she actually thought she might be able to use sex to get what she wanted from him, but Soren was not the kind of man who allowed sex to cloud his efforts and divert his attention. She considered he probably didn't even enjoy the sex, but rather the power and control it gave him. She remembered thinking maybe he liked her because she was not only attractive, but smart and held a crucial role in his efforts to deceive Tess and the folks who supported her. It was now painfully clear just how wrong she was and all she did was deceive herself into thinking she was more than just a baby-making machine. She chided herself for being so naïve and understood now, how her actions on the moon led her to the point where she was now – in a truly dangerous situation.

She looked toward the front of the ship and to her chagrin, saw Rey coming toward her, a mixed look of pleasure and pain grafted onto his face, like some perverted carnival minstrel. He seemed to take pleasure in her obvious look of discomfort. She turned away from him, knowing that it would do no good. Next to her, Allison moaned fearfully, having spied Rey coming toward them, and squeezed closer to Nola. "Soren wants to see you...now," was all he said and promptly turned around and walked back toward the cockpit.

4

Nola had been to the cockpit a few times and knew the way, but she followed behind Rey as he made his way to the main area of the cockpit. The Common Area or *Commons*, as some of Soren's folks referred to it, functioned as a central hub for the entire ship, simply because it was connected to most of the main areas of the ship. In the event of a catastrophic event, the Commons could accommodate the entire complement of passengers, and each seat contained secure harnesses. It was also designed to be self-containing in the event other areas of the ship became uninhabitable.

From the Commons, one could go to the passenger sleeping quarters, which were aft of the Commons. One could go to the Med-Lab, which was two decks up, on the port side of the ship. The biosphere section was connected too, but not directly. Nola found herself lost on numerous occasions trying to get to the biosphere section. Engineering and Propulsion was the second largest part of the ship, consisting of three levels. Nola had never been to engineering and had no plans to go there without a guide. The middle level of the Engineering and Propulsion section was connected to the biosphere section by a long walkway. Five hundred feet below the walkway was a cavernous hold that contained huge storage cisterns and machinery that converted and recycled propulsion contaminants, refuse and biodegradable materials. Non-recyclable materials were converted into harmless by-products and released into space. The cockpit was on the same deck as the Commons, but located past several utility areas, common restrooms and crew quarters. She and Rey walked along in silence as they made their way toward the cockpit.

SOREN AND FINCH

The cockpit of the *Cassiopeia* was nothing short of amazing. Huge windows surrounded the entire cockpit, rising from the floor of the cockpit, all the way to the ceiling, giving the impression that one could step right out into space. There were only a few areas where the sleek spaceship controls blocked the view of space. In the middle of the spacious room sat two huge pilots' chairs surrounded by a curved control panel.

The navigation room was an extension of the cockpit, but a huge wall of electronics separated it from the rest of the cockpit, effectively turning it into its own room. It was about a third the size of the cockpit and in the center was a large rectangular view-screen table that offered a three-dimensional view of space and the planets, depending on what coordinates were fed into the Navi-Computers. Anton Finch, who would have been Tess's Third Level Navigation Officer, was working furiously at one of the Navi-Computers. Soren hovered impatiently over the young man, as if his mere presence would make him work faster.

"Are you certain you've tried everything, Finch? The Europa landing coordinates that we received from the Pegasus satellite, puts us in a location that's practically barren and too far from arable land and fresh water. That's why we need to verify this information!"

"I'm trying Mr. Soren!" Finch mewled nervously. When they were still on the moon, Finch had no preconceptions that he would become Tess's First or Second Level Navigation Officer choice. He knew he was the last man at the bottom of the cockpit crew rung, but when Soren asked him to join him, he jumped at the opportunity. The fact that Soren had two huge guards accompanying him when he asked Finch to join their team may have had something to do with his quick decision. Finch knew deep down that he never really had a choice in whether he joined Soren or not, but when Soren said he was looking for an intelligent and solid navigation officer who could operate the navigation controls on the *Cassiopeia*, not to mention someone who could keep his mouth shut, he felt maybe this was the opportunity he'd been waiting for. Before he could respond, Soren had added, "Oh...and Kelly Masterston will be there as well." Finch's mouth dropped open at the mention of Kelly's name and that was all it took for him to be fully on board, no questions asked.

Anton Finch was madly in love with Kelly Masterston. He could count on one hand the number of times they had actually gone out on "dates", but that didn't matter to him. As far as he was concerned, she was his soulmate and one day, they would be married. Fortunately for him, Kelly felt the same way, although he always knew she was a bit more grounded than he was. On the moon, he and Kelly were able to sneak away to many of the secluded areas on the base, where they could be alone and away from prying eyes and running tongues. They were both virgins and swore to remain that way until they were married. However, here on Soren's ship and because of Soren's rules, they would need a miracle to get married.

2

"Look Finch, there must be a way to access those navigation files. The coordinates that fucking twat Drucker gave me are all shit. I should have brought Webber and left Drucker's ass to rot." He huffed angrily and leaned closer to Anton, forcing the young man to slightly turn his head, lest he fully inhale Soren's not entirely pleasant breath. He glanced up at the images they retrieved from the Pegasus satellite during one of its flybys of Europa. "Look at this!" he said angrily. "The coordinates that we have put us right smack in a rocky, mountainous area miles from a significant water source. There's not even any vegetation here!" He looked down at Anton Finch again and said menacingly, "There's some important information in those files that are related to Europa and where we need to land. If a better location has been identified, one that gives us a better chance of surviving, then I want to know about it!"

"I understand Mr. Soren, but these navigational files were meant for Tess and her flight team. Tess, Jack Richards, Dan Melton, Chay…"

"I don't give a shit about that Finch! You just figure out a way to get into those files – your life, *our* lives, may depend upon it!"

Soren roughly swiveled Finch toward him and leaned on the armrests of his chair. Softly, he said, "I know you can do it Anton." Moving his face close to Finch, his eyes seem to scan Finch's face. He moved his face even closer and said lowly, ominously, "Now GET to it!" For a brief second, Finch could only stare at Soren, while a cold and stark realization pierced through him. He realized in one fell stroke, what many on the *Cassiopeia* already knew or were now allowing themselves to believe; that Soren was dangerous and insane. He turned shakily back to the screen, when the door to the cockpit slid open.

3

Soren turned from Finch to see Rey and Nola standing there, looking awkward as if they had stumbled onto an intimate interaction. "What are you two idiots staring at?" Soren leveled at them. And then more softly, "Ms. Sykes! So glad you could make it!"

Nola felt Rey nudge her forward and she took a few reluctant steps toward Soren. He walked up to her and attempted to kiss her, but she demurely turned her head at the last minute, his undoubtedly wet kiss landing on her right cheek. Fighting off the incredible urge to reach up and scrub her cheek with the sleeve of her jumpsuit, she made a mental note to give that area of her face a little extra attention in the sonic shower that night. Rey stared forward impassively, a bead of sweat slowly rolling down the side of his face, past the clenched muscles of his jaw as he grinded his molars furiously.

Soren stepped back curiously and laughed. "Anton, why don't you take a break and do something productive. I need to talk to this beautiful woman. You too Rey." Rey and Anton exchanged glances and then both made their way to the cockpit door and past Soren's personal bodyguard.

4

As Rey and Anton were leaving, Nola glanced around the cockpit. Her eyes fell on the huge three-dimensional display floating above the view-screen table in the navigation room. She could see a three-dimensional image of Jupiter and what was probably Europa, a tiny, bluish-colored sphere set against the huge backdrop of Jupiter. She reluctantly turned toward Soren, knowing that he was probably staring at her. He was.

She felt her insides go sluggish and knew what he wanted. What he had in mind. Nola wasn't a particularly religious woman, but like all human animals caught in a snare, her mind instantly turned to God, *Oh God, I can't do that again. Not again. Please help me.* Almost as if he heard her, Soren said, "Sykes...you have the look of someone needing salvation." He moved closer to her, eyeing her appraisingly as he walked around her, finally coming to a stop behind her. She remained facing away from him, barely breathing, not wanting to see the slack-jawed, grossly lustful look he undoubtedly had pasted onto his face. She was so preoccupied with that look that she almost jumped out of her skin when she felt him breathing hotly on her neck. Goose bumps as large as bee stings, sprouted all over her body. He whispered huskily in her ear, "I think you'd better look to *me,* because *I'm* your God here – you don't need anything else." She stiffened, as if she might run, but run...*where*? His thugs would only bring her back and worse; they may tie her down.

Still standing close to her, he slipped his hand around her waist. She could feel her sanity drying up at the edges as her mind strove unsuccessfully to unmoor itself and just fly off into deep space. He turned her so she was facing him straight on and moved his face close to hers, staring deeply into her eyes. "You know, it's too bad that I'm already spent. I would have enjoyed another romp with you my dear. But our visit today is strictly business." He shoved her away from him.

Although Nola didn't visibly show anything, her relief was almost palpable. The air in her lungs rushed out of her and she didn't realize she had been holding her breath until Soren had turned from her, walking toward a small desk set into the wall of the navigation room.

He faced her again, "I realize this should have been done before we left the moon, but in our, er...haste, we just didn't have time to put together a list of responsibilities." He chuckled at this. "I'm putting *you* in charge of the women. You're smart, you're tough, and uh, persuasive. Most of them were selected because they can perform a useful function on this ship." He saw a quick look of disgust breeze across Nola's face, which was gone before he even realized he'd seen it. *She's good,* he thought. *I'll have to keep my eye on her.*

"I know what you're thinking, but it's more than that. The women on this ship were selected because they are engineers, technicians, computer specialists, architects, and even agriculturalists. And yes, you're all fertile, which will be very important in the new world." He paused for a moment and then added, "It will be very important to *me* as the *First Father* of our new budding civilization."

Nola could only stare at him...stare *through* him. This was really happening. They would land on Europa and Soren would...what? *Breed* every woman himself? It was ludicrous, she knew, but she could see it in his eyes. In the firm set of his mouth. He really meant to be the *father of the new world.* Soren's face doubled for a minute, and she realized that she was on the verge of fainting. She bit down hard on her tongue. A flood of pain and the slight taste of copper filled her mouth, while Soren's image snapped firmly back into focus. I am *not* passing out here, she half-ordered herself. She would not give him the luxury of thinking her weak.

"Don't you know," she stated flatly, "that you can't start a functional and long-lasting society with only one father? It may take years, but the resulting recessive traits would significantly reduce our biological fitness and ultimately destroy our long-term chances of maintaining a strong and healthy people."

Soren looked at her quizzically and then laughed, "You know Nola, you may not believe it, but years before Lycos hit, I was happily married. My career was starting to take off and I was making a lot of money – mostly from the stock market, but from my job as well." He walked over to one of the large cockpit windows and looked out. Without turning back to her, he said, "The only problem with my *great* life was that I couldn't have children. My wife was tested, and she was fine. Turned out it was me." He turned to face her, his eyes like daggers. "They ran all types of tests and gave me all types of pills. I even underwent several surgeries to make sure all the 'tubes' down there were connected, but nothing changed. No, I take that back...the *relationship* with my wife changed. *She* changed. Became distant. I tried Nola, but what did I get for my efforts, huh?" His voice was rising and Nola unintentionally stepped back half a step. "Ridicule. Disrespect. And do you know what happened after twelve long months of painful procedures, testing and swallowing all kinds of shit? My sperm tested positive! Can you believe that? It was like a miracle or something..."

Soren – April 2030

1

Soren weaved through the traffic deftly, quickly, even swerving into the automatic transport lanes. A rapidly speeding automatic transport truck sent out three loud blasts from its horn, as Soren moved out of the transport lanes and back into the civilian driver lanes.

On any other day, he would have been cursing the driverless vehicles, but today, he had gotten good news – no, *great* news. He was returning home after seeing Dr. Moulton, to confirm the results of his latest labs and sperm tests. He had been nervous as hell, because as far as he was concerned, this was his last attempt at becoming fertile. Fortunately, luck was on his side and his doctor informed him that his results were all in the green! In fact, he shared with Soren that he wouldn't be surprised if he and Katherine were expecting this time next year.

And with that bit of news, Wilfred Soren found himself as giddy as a child. He called his wife Katherine at work, right after he left the doctor's office to tell her the good news and that he was coming home early to maybe get started on the *baby-making activities* but was told by her receptionist that she went home early because she wasn't feeling well. He immediately called her personal phone, but the call went directly to her voicemail, which meant that either she turned her phone off or the phone battery died. Soren was willing to bet his life it was the latter.

Almost from the day they got married, Soren found himself regularly telling his wife how important it was for her to keep her phone charged. He bought all sorts of gadgets to make it easier for her, but she never internalized the importance of keeping it charged. "Having your phone on and charged, could be the difference between life and death, Katie!" he tried to impress upon her one evening, but it never seemed to get through. Now, as he waited for the standard greeting to end, he desperately hoped she would get the message and call him back so he could share the excitement with her. He could feel his irritation rising.

Successfully keeping the negativity out of his voice, he said, "Hey honey, I heard you weren't feeling well, so I swung by the pharmacy to get some medicine for you. And I have some great news! I saw Moulton today and it looks like the last procedure worked! I'm fertile! We can have a child now!"

He paused for a second and then plunged forward, "I also picked up some surprises for you! See you soon! I love you!" As he hung up, he glanced at the various sex toys in the passenger seat and could feel himself growing. He smiled, feeling his earlier irritation melting away, and stepped down on the gas.

2

As Soren turned into his neighborhood, he didn't expect a lot of activity. It was the middle of the day in April. Children were in school and the few folks walking around were either old retirees or a couple of stay-at-home spouses enjoying the almost cloudless day.

As he approached his house, he noticed a bright red Corvette Convertible parked in front of the Meyerson's place, directly across the street from his house. *Hmph!* he thought jealously. *Now how is it that John was able to buy* that? *I thought he just lost his job last week.* As he turned into his driveway, he was just able to make out the Corvette's license plates. *A vanity* license plate! With disdain, he thought, *What an idiot. Yeah, you* are *a brute, John...a caveman brute!* He laughed heartily at this but subconsciously began thinking of what he might be able to do to get *himself* a nice new car. Maybe something a little flashier than Meyerson's.

He pulled into the driveway and parked. He looked over at his stash of illicit *Fun with Dick and Jane* paraphernalia strewn about the front seat and immediately felt paranoid. Quickly, he shoved everything back into the black plastic store bag and hurried to the front door, cursing under his breath that he might as well have been carrying a neon sign that said, *super freak coming through!* He tried to make the black bag as small as possible in his hands, but the more he fumbled with it, the more it threatened to spill out and reveal its salacious content to prying eyes. Once inside, he sighed with relief and turned to put his house keys on the wall key-rack and froze. Katie's shoes were in the middle of the foyer, and he could see articles of clothing going up the high wooden circular staircase. The slight sound of music floated down from the second floor. His first instinct was that there was a burglar in the house, but then he remembered his earlier message to her about the baby-making activities, and then his fear and nervousness changed to one of intense excitement. He hustled off to the kitchen, to grab a bottle of wine and some glasses, clumsily stripping out of his clothes as he did so.

3

Tiptoeing up the stairs in his underwear, he carried a bottle of wine in his right hand, with his fingers hooked around two wine glasses. In his left hand and under his armpit, he carried some roses, chocolates and his new sex toys. As he reached the landing, he could hear the music a little more clearly and could hear Katie moving around on the bed. *Oh my God!* he thought. *She's getting ready for me!* He felt himself getting extremely excited and for one terrible moment, he thought he was going to explode right there at the top of the stairs.

Passing one of the bedrooms upstairs, he turned down the short hallway toward the master bedroom. The door was partially open and as he prepared to do his best Jack Nicholson impression, *"Here's Johnny!"* from *The Shining*, the moaning from within increased in its intensity. His initial thought was that she was getting herself ready for him, was replaced by one of concern, because he could hear not one, but two, maybe three voices in the room.

He pushed open the door slowly and as if watching from a distance, he saw himself standing there in his underwear, his partially aroused penis rapidly retreating into itself like a frightened turtle, while watching his wife in a position totally foreign to him. One man was behind her thrusting as if his life depended on it, while another man, standing at the head of his bed, had his hands wrapped in her hair gyrating as crazily as his partner, as he pumped his hips back and forth.

Soren stood there stupidly, unable to move. His eyes were fixated on the entire scene, taking it all in. He felt as if his house had been transformed into some hideous monster's lair, where the scene transpiring in front of him was not his wife with two strange men, but a writhing three-headed creature copulating with itself as it simultaneously purred and snarled on its strained breeding hutch.

He wasn't sure how long he stood like that, but what snapped him out of it was when the bottle of wine slid from his hand and smashed on the wooden floor. The three of them jerked their heads toward the door so quickly, Soren thought their necks would snap. The man standing on the bed, dove onto the floor and snatched up his pants lying crumpled there. The other man, to Soren's amazement, turned back to his business at hand, and continued thrusting into Katie, for what seemed hours to Soren, but was only seconds, until he released himself into her with a shudder.

When he finished, he calmly grabbed his pants off the floor and slid them on, all the while keeping his eyes on Soren. Katie, in much the same fashion as the man who was behind her, got up slowly and pulled a sheet around herself. The look in her eyes, Soren noticed, was not one of embarrassment or terror or even contriteness – it was one of clear irritation. "You're home early, Fred." was the only thing she uttered as she reached over to grab a cigarette from the nightstand. Soren, finally finding his voice *and* his indignation, said, *"What the fuck are you doing Katherine!"*

The man who jumped off the bed, having gotten dressed, hastily squeezed past Soren, halfway expecting the dazed husband to strike out at him. He was a thin man, about the same height as Soren. The other man, more of a muscular giant really, looked to be almost a head taller than Soren, maybe more. Moving much more slowly and confidently than his partner, he smirked and mumbled in a fairly passable English accent, "What do you *think* we were doing here mate? Playing knobs and knockers?" Katie snickered from the bed.

Soren was stupefied. In the movies, whenever the *cheating man* was caught with his pants down, he would almost break his neck getting out of the bed, stumble around for his clothes and maybe, if he was lucky, climb out the window to flee the wronged husband's wrath. It was bittersweet to Soren that the first guy knew his part and played it well, but *this* guy...he was sauntering around the room as if he owned the place. *Well*, Soren thought, *he doesn't know who he's fucking with!*

As the man pulled on his t-shirt and walked toward the door, Soren awoke from his stupor and came charging at him, his lips pulled back in a vicious snarl. His movie-trained mind bravely thought that he would jam one of the wine glasses deep into this man's face and while the man was bent over screaming as his eye dangled from its sockets, Movie-Soren would be on him in a minute, kneeing him in the mouth and knocking him unconscious in one smooth act. But Soft-Soren could only swing wildly and widely at the man. And as Soren swung, the man, obviously expecting this, blocked it easily and in the same fluid motion, returned the attack with a solid backhand smack to the side of Soren's head.

Soren stumbled backwards, almost falling. For a brief moment, he saw stars and thought he would pass out from the blow. Fortunately, he caught his balance and glared at the man through an already swelling right eye. The man took a half step toward Soren, who involuntarily took a half step back. He laughed at Soren, trying to decide if he should give him matching swollen eyes, when the first man yelled from downstairs, "Come on Bru! Let's get the fuck outta here! Jonesy's already fucking gone! That's all I need is domestic disturbance added to my record. I'm on parole!"

Bru laughed at this, bolted down the stairs and was out the door in seconds. A minute later, Soren could hear the powerful roar of what had to be the Corvette's engine as it started up. In a flash, he ran to the bedroom window and saw that they were the owners of the Corvette Convertible parked in front of the Meyerson's place. He grabbed a pen and paper from the drawer of the nightstand next to him and squinted out the window at the convertible's license plate. As he started to jot down the plate information, he stopped himself with a disdainful snort. *I don't even need to write this down*, he thought, since he had seen the vanity plate earlier when he arrived, but he did so anyway: *B-R-U-T-O-S*. By the time he finished, the red convertible had sped around the corner and was gone.

4

Soren looked over at Katie, a combination of contempt, anger, sadness and despair washed over him at the same time. "How could you Katie? How *could* you? I know things have been rough between us since I found out that I couldn't have kids, but things are going to be different now. We can...we can be happy now." Katie got off the bed and stepped into the bathroom, locking the door. "*Happy?*" She shouted out. "With *you*? *Please!* I'm leaving you Fred. I thought I could stick it out for at least another year, until I could get myself situated, but hell, I can't even have *fun* without fear of you showing up and fucking it all up!"

Somewhat taken aback, Soren plowed on, "*But we can have kids now!* The doctor said so. It was just some sort of blockage that the last procedure was able to help with. We can be...a family now. Don't you understand that? Don't you understand what that means now?"

Katie was silent for a moment and then Soren heard the shower start. As she showered, he paced the floor, the forgotten roses, now broken and almost completely petal-less, still clutched in his trembling hand. He glanced over at the stain-covered rumpled bed covers and went cold all over. *Should I have seen this coming?* he thought to himself. Things had definitely soured for them since his bad news, but they had been getting better...*right*? He paced the room again and was in the midst of trying to remember the last time they had spent real quality time together, when the bathroom door opened and Katie stepped out, dressed in jeans and a t-shirt...her *traveling* clothes he figured. She went into their huge walk-in closet and came back out with one of her designer suitcases. Plopping the suitcase on the bed, she began to fill it with various articles of clothing and jewelry.

Soren looked stupidly at her. "What are you doing? Are you *leaving*? Did you hear a damn word I said? I told you we can be a family now. With *kids*! Doesn't that mean anything to you?"

Without looking up from her packing, she laughed shakily and said, "Do you think I want *children* with you Wilfred? I don't even want a *life* with you!" She stopped packing and looked at Soren. "You know, my sisters are very good judges of character and they *never* liked you. Sophia actually said that you might be dangerous, in a *crazy* way, and being a psychiatrist, she would know what she's talking about. It's a shame I didn't listen to her."

Soren could only stand there in stunned silence. She must be serious, because he couldn't remember the last time she called him "Wilfred". It had always been "Fred". She finished packing, zipped up her suitcase and headed out of the bedroom, pulling her suitcase along behind her. Following her like a dutiful cuckold, he stopped her at the top of the stairs. Pitifully, he exclaimed, "But everything I've done, I've done for you Katie. For *you*!"

Turning around, she laughed at him and looked him up and down, "For *me*? You've done nothing for me Fred. And the *only* thing you did for me today was interrupt the best part. But at least he *finished.*" She looked at him evenly, "You saw what kind of man he was. If I'm lucky, maybe I'll have *his* kids." She laughed as she bent down to grab her suitcase.

Katie's last comment eviscerated him. Whatever arguments he had formed while she was in the shower, ebbed from him like a dying spirit. He realized, woefully and with finality, that there was nothing he could do or say, that would make her stay. His intense and heartfelt desire to become a parent, a *father*, would not happen with Katie. And in the deep recesses of his mind, he accepted fully and completely, its prediction that he would never father a child. Even as he felt himself being fundamentally transformed by this raw, internal turmoil, he sensed motion in his right arm as his fist swung up from his side and caught Katie's jaw in a solid uppercut motion. He heard her teeth crack and felt her jawbone give under his blow. As if in slow motion, her head whipped back violently, as she started losing her balance backwards. Her eyes wide, she reached out frantically to grab the banister, but she was already moving back, toward the edge of the stairs. Her other hand reached out to Soren, but he was transfixed, mired in his own muddy sucker punch.

As gravity pulled at Katie, she landed hard on her backside and Soren thought he heard a small snap. Her head whipped back and hit the edge of one of the stairs. Her momentum picked up as she continued her downward spiral, rolling end over end down the hard wooden floors. She landed hard on the bottom landing, her body twisted at a grotesque angle.

Shaken out of his motionlessness, Soren stared at his wife's broken body at the bottom of the stairs. Suddenly, he was afraid. What had he done? Surely, this was all a misunderstanding. I didn't actually hit her, *did*

I? She just slipped...right? These impotent thoughts assailed him like rancid mosquitos, birthed from fetid water. No matter how much his mind swatted at them, they still found places to root. Slowly, he crept down the stairs, terrified that his wife would suddenly jump up and scratch his eyes out.

Katie's eyes were closed and she was motionless. Soren could see that one of her arms was clearly broken by the sharp, almost clean, white bone poking through the skin; and the other was most likely broken, simply by the way it wrapped itself under her body. One of her ankles was an angry purpled-colored lump. The shoe on that foot had come off during her tumble and her foot was rapidly swelling. Soren put his hand over his mouth and almost gagged. Her neck was also swollen, with an ugly bruise almost growing before his eyes. Blood oozed through her matted hair and began to pool on the floor underneath her head.

"Oh my God, Katie! Oh my God! It was an accident! I didn't mean...I didn't mean to..."

At that moment, Katie's eyes flew open and Soren almost screamed. Her mouth moved, but nothing came out, but dribbles of spit and blood. She looked at him with pure pain-filled hate. "I'm sorry, I'm sorry! It was an *accident!*" he yelled out. "I'll call 911!" He jumped up and ran to the vid-phone in the kitchen and almost dialed 911, but stopped short of dialing the last digit. Somewhere, deep in his frazzled mind, he made the connection that no matter what he told the police, his wife would say he tried to kill her. He would be tried and jailed for attempted murder. Or if she dies, manslaughter at the least.

He hung up the phone and thought furiously. Incredibly, his mind flew to a number of late-night detective shows, where some unbelievably smart detective finds the smallest of prints on the victim's toenail, but it's enough to put the murderer away for life. He slapped himself. *This is not helping! What's different here, than in those shows?* He stood there in the kitchen for what seemed hours. When he had finally given up and resolved to just pack a bag and get the hell out of town, he remembered that in most of those shows, there are no others in the house other than the true murderer and the victim. In this case, he had had *two* people, maybe three, in his home who did *not* belong here.

As the general outline of his version of the story started to take shape, he began to see how he could survive this. *When I got home from work and saw my wife's clothes strewn about the place, I thought maybe she received my message about my visit with the doctor and was getting ready for me.* He thought about that part and realized that as embarrassing as it may be, it would be entirely believable, because it was true. *When I got upstairs though, there were two men raping my wife. I went to stop them but was knocked down. My wife threw on some clothes and went to help me and they hit her and pushed her down the stairs. I ran down after them, but they ran out through the door. One guy called the other guy "Bru" and said he was on parole. The other guy mentioned that someone else, someone named 'Jonesy,' was already gone. They were driving a red Corvette Convertible and the license plate was B-R-U-T-O-S.*

He was entirely satisfied with the story and had no doubt that the police would find the men's fingerprints all over the bedroom and if that failed, then the big guy's sperm inside Katie would be a dead giveaway. Everything except for the next part was true. He looked over at Katie again and then bent down to open the cabinet underneath the sink. He grabbed a pair of yellow rubber cleaning gloves and a large piece of plastic. He went over to Katie lying broken on the floor in a pool of blood and excrement and looked at her wildly staring eyes. Soren gagged again. Katie saw the items in his hands and immediately knew what he intended to do, but try as she might, the only thing she could do was twitch one of her fingers. Right before Soren's shaking hands put the plastic over her mouth and nose to smother her, she was able to utter a frantic *"No, no, no..."*

5

Nola stared at Soren, a newer, darker understanding of the man creeping into her brain. A lot of killings happened when Lycos started bearing down on Earth. A lot of these killings were probably in self-defense, she thought, but many were cold-blooded murder. She figured that most people were starting to lose their sanity, doing whatever they could to survive. She thought back to that hectic time and shivered. She could only imagine the overwhelming fear that must have consumed billions of people as they watched the huge monstrosity called Lycos, hanging above their heads like the sword of Damocles. But Soren was a murderer, pure and simple. And he didn't even have Lycos to blame. Sure, she could understand his anger and desperation, but it didn't excuse what he did to his wife. Nola shuddered involuntarily. Soren's long-dead wife was right about one thing; Soren was mad...and dangerous.

Soren continued on, oblivious to Nola's wide-eyed and incredulous stare. "I had neighbors who were able to corroborate that they saw a red Corvette speeding down my street with two men in it, but they were not able to identify the men in a lineup." He snorted angrily, "After six long months, the police finally arrested two men in connection with Katie's murder, Buddy Akers and Nate Mason, but they were never able to confirm that the big fellah, Barney *Brutos* Clekman...or *Bru* was ever there." He said Clekman's name with pure hatred. Considering Soren's personality, Nola assumed his hatred of the man must have been borne of pure jealously. Soren saw this *Brutos* character as being everything *he* was not. "Apparently," Soren continued, "Clekman was able to provide proof that he had loaned his vehicle to Nate Mason, the third guy, while he remained at home helping a friend with a project." Soren huffed disgustedly, "His alibi checked out, over Buddy Akers strenuous objections." He looked up at the ceiling and continued on, "They found prints of Akers and Mason everywhere. They found hair strands from Akers, the guy shoving his junk into Katie's mouth, all over the bed. Mason's prints were found pretty much all over the house. I think *he* was the one doing all the robbing while Clekman and Akers had their fun with Katie." He looked off into the distance, "Initially, I didn't know how Katie could have ever come across *quality* men like them, but when I received her computer back after the police were finished with it, there were a lot of things I didn't know about Katie." He took a deep breath and continued on, "In the end, there were no clean prints of *Brutos* and no hard evidence linking him to the murder. Even his jizz inside Katie wasn't enough to link him to the murder because she had douched right before showering."

Nola kept quiet, disgusted by this hideous and senseless death. She almost sighed relief, thinking that he was done, when he added, "Yep, this character was able to totally escape justice. In fact, the two men who were convicted were sent to Harlan Penitentiary in San Antonio, where Brutos was actually the head prison guard! Imagine that! And no one blinked an eye when Akers and Mason died mysteriously in their jail cells within months after arriving there." He paused for a second and then said, "His illegalities and ultimately, the murders of Akers and Mason, were discovered years before Lycos hit and he was sent to the place he ruled over!" Soren laughed heartily over this. "Well," he continued, "if he didn't get pulverized by Lycos, then I'm sure he's nothing but a bloated body now, orbiting Earth like the rest of those sad fuckers. Good fuckin-riddance, I say!"

He looked at her and laughed...almost merrily. "But I digress! I know all about *recessive traits* and the problems with too small a gene pool. I don't plan to be the *only* father on Europa, but every woman on this ship *will* bear a child for me, including you, my dear Nola. And you can take *that* to the bank!"

Nola unconsciously cringed backwards, even though Soren made no move toward her. When she first came in, she noticed a small toolbox on one of the consoles. Surely there was a hammer or screwdriver or something inside it. In her mind's eye, she could see herself vaulting over the table that separated her from the toolbox, like some Olympic gymnast and in one smooth motion, yanking out the screwdriver and ramming it into Soren's diseased brain, ending this nightmare. For a brief moment, she thought she felt her muscles tighten in preparation, but something in Soren's eyes planted her firmly to the floor, with her arms dangling useless by her sides. A quiet, more rational voice in her head told her that even if she were quick enough to make it to the toolbox, Soren would be on her in a flash. Soren's guards were right outside the door and they would be on her only seconds after that. She would be stopped, restrained, beaten, and then what?

Soren looked at her curiously and then went on, "We can discuss the childbearing activities at another time. Right now, I want you to understand that I'm making you responsible for *all* of the women on the ship. The ship's engineers are already doing their part, but the scientists and specialists, who'll be invaluable on Europa, don't know shit about the ship. Those are the ones I want you to assign jobs to. I have Rey doing the same thing with the men." Soren walked over to one of the wall printers and retrieved a sheet of paper. He glanced at it briefly and then handed it to Nola. "These are the people who will populate our new Eden," he said, boastfully. "The highlighted names are *your* responsibility. It's your job to make sure they can become productive members of our, er, little society. Other than being the mothers of our new nation, they have no usable skill on this ship." He chuckled, "Hell, *most* of my guards are in the same boat as those women, but that's why they're *guards* – because that's pretty much all they're good for!" His chuckled turned into a full-throated laugh, which morphed into a hacking cough that caused him to double over. Nola silently prayed he was having a heart attack.

He looked up, red-faced and breathing hard, trying not to look weak. *Too late*, Nola thought, stealing a furtive glance at the small, but growing urine stain in his pants. *Mr. Big Man can't even hold his water*, she thought and almost laughed out loud. Once again, she bit down on her tongue, but this time, to avoid what would have been a deadly mistake. Soren may not be able to hold his water during a coughing fit, but he was deranged and extremely dangerous. He probably would have killed her on the spot.

He stood up straight, as if nothing had happened. He neither realized that he coughed a small urine sample into his pants, nor that she had just avoided a serious mistake of laughing at him. "So, anyway, take this list and get them acquainted with their new responsibilities. Rey!"

Within seconds, Rey was there, looking nervous and happy at the same time. The incongruent look made Nola queasy. It reminded her of those odd, sad-faced *happy* clowns at backwater carnivals that seemed to promise fun in the bright sunshine of the day and exquisite torture if you let the darkness catch you there.

"Nola's got her list. She'll pretty much have free reign within the ship to get these women started. Make sure your bonehead guards don't fuck with her while she's performing her duties!"

"Right Commander...I'll see to it." Rey popped off quickly.

As Soren and Rey conversed, Nola feigned deference by keeping her head down. She took this time to really get a good look at the controls on the bridge. Although she was not a pilot, she briefly dated one and had the opportunity to see this very console in this very ship, but in a completely different lifetime.

Back on the moon, many of the women, and a lot of the men, believed she was a flirt, but she was just the opposite. She was very selective in who she dated, and she never really wanted the affections of Jack Richards, the pilot of the *Galileo2*. The thought of him evoked a momentary sense of sadness at the memory of his death on the *Galileo2*.

Even though he was married when she first met him, she couldn't resist his insistent efforts to go out with him. After the death of his wife, he began to spend a lot of time with her despite his many trips back and forth to the moon. She casually mentioned to him one evening during some late-night pillow talk, that she would love to see the moon and the next thing she knew, he was inviting her to the shuttle base. He had told her to *pack a bag*. At the time, Lycos was still years away, but the government was sending shuttles back and forth to the moon in an urgent effort to complete the moon bases. Jack, Tess and a number of other key individuals became more and more important. So much so, that they were able to do things that would have been impossible for others, such as bringing her along on his shuttle trips and more importantly, getting her a position at the moon base. During their shared trips to the moon, she was able to sit in the jump seat in the cockpit and observe Jack and his copilot pilot the ship. He oftentimes gave her impromptu lessons in piloting the ship. On her first trip to the moon, he gave her a tour of the *Cassiopeia*. She remembered fondly that he loved that ship and couldn't wait to fly it. She knew he was to be Tess's copilot, but the way he talked about the *Cassiopeia*, one would have thought that it was *his* ship, owned and paid for.

That all changed, once Soren got to the moon base. No more tours of the ships and no more back and forth passes from Earth to the moon. Seeing the writing on the wall, Nola had Jack finalize her position in the orbital lab and she remained on the moon from that point on. Unfortunately, Jack's last trip back to Earth was the last time she saw him.

6

She hadn't been to this bridge in over a year and now that she was back on it, she started remembering a few things Jack had told her, like the quickest way from the bridge to engineering or how the water and food reclamation systems worked. Jack had shown her the huge Cargo Container and went on and on about the external access operations in case of problems with the reclamation systems. Sometimes, she would grow tired of his endless explanations of how the shipped worked, but she always listened, mostly because she loved hearing his smooth baritone voice, and she always remembered. Now, as she stared at her surroundings within the cockpit and the navigation room, she wondered idly if she would have been capable of flying the ship if it came down to it.

She was so caught up in her thoughts, that she didn't feel Rey leading her out of the navigation room. "You got work to do Nola, so get to it!" With that, he gave her a slight shove into the hallway connecting the crew quarters. Nola quickly left the area, lest Soren, or Rey, call her back.

Before Rey could close the cockpit doors, one of the crew latrine doors opened up and Anton hustled out, drying his hands off on his pants. "Is Commander Soren finished with Nola? He wanted to meet again to discuss some of the astronomy charts."

"Not yet Finch, he wants to see me...alone". Anton made a mock pouty face and turned toward the hallway that led to the common area. Looking over his shoulder, he said, "Okay, be a good man and give me a shout when he's done. I'll be in the Commons."

With a scowl on his face, Rey watched the young Brit jogged lithely down the hall. Engineering had the ship's gravity set to roughly Earth gravity, but he still felt that it was not 100% accurate. It was off, not by a lot, but still off and watching Finch almost skip down the hall made him certain of it. He shut the door and stepped back into the navigation room, where Soren was waiting impatiently.

7

"Look Rey, if this is going to work, I need every swinging dick to do his part. I don't want you acting like some jealous school whelp! I'm in charge here and everyone needs to understand that, including *you*. Most of these women were selected by me and I mean to have each and every one of them whenever, however, and as often as I please. Do you get me?"

Rey stared stonily ahead. He was in the throes of a massive migraine. Each time he tried to look at Soren, the image doubled and then trebled. Sometimes, the face even changed. At least twice during the last half hour of Soren's ravings, he thought he was looking at Melvin Durhart in Engineering. "Yes sir," he croaked out, barely holding in this morning's breakfast.

"Are you getting *sick*? I mean...*space*-sick?" Soren asked him disgustedly. "What kind of pilot gets nauseous in space? No...don't answer that! It's too bad I couldn't have kidnapped Tess, huh?" Without waiting for a response and not really expecting one, he trudged on, "The great *Tess Robinson*! I'm sure she and the rest of those idiots on the moon are in full panic mode now!" He laughed raucously at this.

Rey was about to respond, when Soren waved him off. "There are some things you and I need to discuss, but that'll come at a later date. Just know that there is some classified information locked in the computer memory files that will be very important to us as we get closer to Europa. Highly classified files that only a handful of people know about or at least know how to access the information. Most of them are dead, one thanks to you. Tess would know too, but of course, she's still on the moon."

Rey ignored Soren's hint at the death of Dan Melton, the only other surviving pilot who would have had access. Rey didn't feel any guilt – he did what was required. "Classified information regarding what?" Rey couldn't imagine what Soren could have been talking about. "Is there a problem with Europa? Air? Radiation? What?"

"No, nothing of the sort," Soren responded nonchalantly. "Especially nothing wrong with *Europa*," he said in an odd mocking tone that Rey found discomforting. "And speaking of *Europa*, I've been thinking about a *new* name for our future world. What do you think of Sorenticus-Giganticus?"

Rey looked at him stupidly for a minute and then asked, "You want to change the name of Europa to *Sorenticus-Giganticus*? Why?"

Seemingly out of nowhere, Soren flew into a rage. "Because it's *my* world Rey! Without me, a lot of you fuckers would still be on the moon with the rest of those wretches! I made this happen Rey. I...saved you...*all* of you from certain death! I am your savior and what I say is law. *My* law! Do you understand me, Rey? Do you understand just what the hell I'm telling you?" At that moment, the cockpit door slid open and one of Soren's guards tentatively poked his head in. Soren waved him off and he backed out quickly. The door slid shut silently.

Rey could only stare at Soren, nodding slowly. He always knew deep down in his gut that Soren was somewhat dangerous, but he felt that somehow, he might still be able to control him. He was starting to understand that controlling Soren was like trying to control a bull in a china shop, without breaking any china. Like Tess, Soren was past controlling. If he wanted to be in charge, Soren would have to be subdued or even killed before they arrived on Europa, or whatever the hell Soren wanted to call it. But before he could make that type of move, he would first have to know what classified information Soren was alluding to. What could be so important that it's got Soren riding Finch for hours at a time in the navigation room?

"I understand Commander," Rey responded dutifully. "I just wanted to be sure I..."

"I don't give a shit what you *wanted* Rey, just make sure everyone knows it or you'll find your ass floating to Eu...*Sorenticus!*" Exasperated, he waved Rey toward the door. "Send Finch back in here posthaste...we have unfinished business."

Rey palmed open the door and standing there with a smirk on his face was Anton Finch. He shoved past Rey brusquely and the door slid shut behind him. Three of Rey's guards were also there, waiting on his orders. "Come with me," he said without fanfare. They quickly crossed through crew quarters, turned down a short hallway toward the tube ladder leading up to the observatory and within seconds, were gone.

DOCTOR BURT STONE

1

Doctor Burt Stone stared out through one of the small port windows in the Commons. All he could see was blackness, save for a few distant points of light. He glanced around the Commons at the men and women strewn about the seating area, each wrapped in his or her own thoughts of despair. He looked back outside at nothing in particular and could feel incredible guilt swelling up inside. For probably the tenth time that day, he wondered how it could come to this. How could he have allowed something so sinister and unholy to happen? Doctor Stone wasn't a religious man, but he was God-fearing and was now seriously wondering how his own story would end and how he would answer for his ignorance.

He looked toward the hallway that led to the crew quarters and the cockpit and saw Nola scurrying past one of the guards. When Rey came for her, not more than ten minutes earlier, she looked absolutely nauseous. Long gone was the smug look she wore when they were all herded on the ship in what seemed like years ago, but was barely hours. To Stone, she now had the look of someone who just realized they were not on the winning side after all. The guard tried to stop her by grabbing onto her elbow, but she yanked it away viciously, as if his hand were a hot stove. "I'm doing some work for Soren, so get your fucking paws off me." Stone could see the split-second mental battle of good versus evil, being waged in the guard's head, where the "good" was really only a lesser form of evil. The guard was about to say something that most likely would have included some form of verbal assault, but held his tongue. Instead, he muttered the only thing that seemed appropriate to him at the time, "His name is *Commander* Soren, little pet, and don't you forget it." Nola ignored him and continued on through the Commons toward the back entrance. She glanced at Stone as she went by, but couldn't or wouldn't maintain the eye contact. She looked scared and probably had reason to be scared, but Burt couldn't care less how she felt. She had aligned herself with Soren, so as far as he was concerned, her lot was cast. She continued past him, toward the hallway leading to the passenger quarters, wrapped in her own personal hell. As for him, he would take each day as it came and do the best he could to help his patients make it through this hellish ordeal.

He let out a shaky breath and looked around at the guards here. They were all unstable and ruthless. He knew the newer guards were professionals before all of this, but eventually allowed this brutality trait to put down roots. It was Soren and Rey's "seasoned" guards who were not strangers to brutality. He wondered how they were selected to be on the moon base in the first place, but remembered that the United Nations' moon base had a large number of international security teams as guards for the United Nations' families. Big, hulking brutes who seemed more like automatons, than real men. Most of them were fairly young, anywhere from their late 20's to early 30's. Ex-military types. None of them were married. Burt assumed that was because of their assignment. They traveled everywhere with their respective UN leaders, so having a family would have been an unfortunate distraction for them. Luckily for most of the guards, and unluckily for the general population of the US moon base, the majority of them were training at the US moon base when the meteorite storm peppered the UN base with basketball-sized meteorites, killing the majority of the people there. If those guards had died at the UN base, Stone thought sourly, Soren and Rey would never have had the "muscle" to carry out their plans.

His thoughts turned briefly to Nola. He didn't really care for her, but was relieved that the guard didn't go further than just correcting Soren's title. No one deserved the treatment that they seem to so easily mete out. His thoughts turned even darker as he pondered what would actually happen once they arrived on Europa. He thought of old Nazi Germany and its slithering decline into totalitarianism and dictatorial rule. The resulting evil that plunged the world into war. They weren't at war on the *Cassiopeia*, but their situation was just as dire. He struggled mightily to understand how they allowed someone as twisted and morally corrupt as Soren, to manipulate them to their own demise. A thought drifted up to him; a years-old saying or quote that seem to capture the essence of their situation; *Those who fail to learn from history are doomed to repeat it.*

At that moment, he heard several voices and looked up to see Rey and a couple of his guards storming into the Commons. Almost like some Pavlovian test subject, he felt himself draw up inside, as if he were trying to make himself as small as possible. Rey stopped as soon as he entered the Commons and looked around imperiously. His eyes rested on Dr. Stone and for one terrible moment, Stone was sure that his part in this hell-story was reaching its last chapter. Instead, Rey turned to face the rest of the group there in the Commons. "This meeting is over. Return to your cabins. Nola will be contacting a number of you women with job assignments and I'll be in touch with a number of the men for work details. If you already have assignments or work areas, then you can go there." And with that, he turned toward one of the exits and was gone.

Shakily, Burt turned to Zoe Addison, Elsa Peyton and Jana Morgan, the only medical technicians on the ship. "You guys head on back to Med-Lab. There's a couple of things I need to check on. You can get started on preparing the refrigeration units for the blood collection. Also, start creating medical files for each person on the ship." They nodded in unison, three young women, their eyes wide and terrified.

Burt got up and headed toward the exit at the rear of the Commons. He was headed back to engineering to have a chat with Jaime Mendez, the chief of engineering. As he made his way to engineering, he could feel the guilt of abandoning Tess and the others, clinging to him like an unwanted shadow. Of its own accord, his mind drifted back to the moon. In his mind's eye, he could see himself talking to Soren, while everyone else enjoyed the lavish "bait and switch" meal that allowed Soren and Rey the time needed to kick their plan into high gear.

2

"This is wonderful!" Sophia said as more and more food was brought out to the meeting hall. She and Burt were close to the front of the hall because they were planning to make a quick announcement regarding the scheduling of annual physicals. They were hoping to make this announcement before Soren got there, when the dining facility staff started bringing out mounds and mounds of food. They stood there transfixed, when they heard Soren call out to them. He was walking directly toward them, smiling a little too widely. "Doc! Nurse Smith! Glad to see you here! You actually saved me the trouble of trying to find you in the room." He looked around at the wide-eyed stares of the folks in the meeting hall. "We should step back here out of the way. With all this delicious food coming out, we're bound to get trampled!" Soren laughed heartily at this. Burt and Sophia laughed too, but exchanged curious glances with one another.

"Oh!" Soren exclaimed, "Congratulations on your engagement!" He leaned forward to kiss Sophia and probably would have kissed her on the mouth if she hadn't turned her head. Burt stared at him, trying to hide the slowly rising irritation he was feeling. When Soren pulled back, the plastic smile he was wearing was gone and he became serious. "Look Burt, I need you and Sophia to go take a look at Arnold Williams. I was told he was working on one of the cargo bay harnesses, when he fell. He's alive, but he's unconscious. Julie's there with him, but I'd feel better if you two were there. Julie brought your stuff, so go straight there. Please."

"Right away!" Burt said and he and Sophia hurried out of the meeting hall. As they half-jogged down the corridor leading to the cargo bay, uncomfortable thoughts dogged at him. Why would Soren allow this big feast, when they've been rationing food ever since they arrived on the moon? He would need to look into this later, but his focus now was on the injured maintenance worker. On their way to the hangar, they saw multiple individuals headed in the same direction. They were carrying small duffel bags and backpacks. At one point, they passed a corridor and Doc was certain he heard someone yelling *get the hell out of my cabin!* He would have to investigate that further, but for now, they had a medical emergency they had to attend to.

They arrived at the hangar, slightly out of breath, eyes already scanning the huge area for Julie. Burt was about to grab the intercom hanging next to the entrance when he realized something odd about the cargo bay activities. The rear of the ship was open and workers were loading supplies. The huge cargo cabin was now mounted onto the ship and he could hear and feel the smooth rumble of the *Cassiopeia's* engines. In a flash, he realized the horrible truth; they were preparing the ship for launch. Since he didn't see Tess in the meeting hall, he wondered if she was on the ship. But there were tons of people in the meeting hall, gorging themselves and waiting for Soren and the others to speak. Something wasn't right here. Sophia turned to him and asked, "What's going on here Bur...?" when her eyes widened. He turned to see what her startled look meant when stars exploded in his head.

When he came to, he was tied down in a seat, next to Zoe. She had been wiping his forehead when his eyes popped open, somewhat startling her. "Doc!" she exclaimed. She hugged him gingerly. "I was so worried! I thought maybe you had slipped into a coma." Her normally pretty face was etched in deep lines of concern and unbridled fear. "What's going on? Two guards from the meeting hall basically forced me to come with them here. They made me get on the ship." She glanced around. "They told me that I would be hurt if I tried to leave the ship." Her eyes started tearing up.

Doctor Stone's head was still foggy and he only caught the gist of what Zoe was telling him. He knew he had been hit by something...by *someone*, but he didn't know who had hit him. His immediate concern at the moment was Sophia. He looked around nervously and didn't see her anywhere amongst the crying and complaining throng of people. "Where's Sophia!" he shouted into Zoe's face. "She was with me before I was hit in the head and dragged in here. *Where is she, goddammit?!*" He struggled in his seat, trying to free his arms, but the zip ties only dug deeper into his wrists.

Zoe looked down at her hands. When she looked back at Burt, tears were streaming down her face. "She fought like crazy when they dragged you onto the ship. She made it to the top of the air-stairs, when one of the guards," she nodded at Dante, "jammed one of those batons into her face." Zoe hesitated, unsure of how to go on. "Finish it," Burt stated flatly, hotly.

Zoe cleared her throat and continued, "She fell backwards down the air-stairs and didn't move once she hit the floor. Rey yelled at him and said she was supposed to come with us. When he finished, he told Dante to take care of her and get the body out of his sight."

Doctor Stone turned toward his window and strained to see if he could see her body anywhere on the ground. He thought he saw something hidden behind one of the workbench platforms, but he couldn't be sure. Just as he was straining to get a better look, he saw Rey jogging over to the maintenance area door. Standing there in his robe, looking both sick and bewildered, was Dan Melton. He knew Dan had been ill the past several days and was surprised to see him up and about. They appeared to speak briefly and then Rey led Dan into the small maintenance office. After a minute or two of seemingly friendly conversation, they both walked over to the desk and then he saw Rey plunge what looked like a small knife or scissors into Dan's stomach. Burt flinched away from the small window, but didn't take his eyes away. Rey stabbed him repeatedly and when Dan slumped to the floor, Rey grabbed his head and slammed it into the desk. A minute or two later, Rey emerged from the office wearing a different jump suit. Burt snapped his attention forward. Burt had never witnessed a murder before and felt sick to his stomach. Rey had killed the man in cold blood. He looked at Zoe and saw that she was as pale as cottage cheese. Apparently, she had been looking over his shoulder at the gruesome scene and was starting to shake uncontrollably.

Burt stared into Zoe's eyes and very calmly spoke to her. "Zoe, don't ever mention this to anyone, you understand? Rey is extremely dangerous and would probably not hesitate to kill you...or me, if he ever finds out that we witnessed this murder."

Zoe stared back, her eyes once again filling up with tears. She nodded shakily and laid her head on Doc's shoulder. He could feel her body shaking as she continued crying. He looked up in time to see Rey come aboard and just before Rey turned toward the cockpit, he glanced briefly at Doctor Stone, the oddly vacillating look in his eyes was compounded by the malicious smile that crept across his lips.

As he sat there, with Zoe crying quietly on his shoulder, he could feel slow despair seeping into his bones, totally saturating him like a dirty, bloated sponge. He leaned his head back and closed his eyes. As his turbulent mind began to drift back to the others, unaware that while they feasted like kings, they were about to be abandoned on the moon, he felt someone kick his foot, hard. The jarring caused both him and Zoe to sit bolt upright in their seats.

Standing in front of them was Dominic Dante, one of Rey's guards. He felt Zoe squeeze into him in a fruitless effort to get away from Dante. He was a hulking brute of a man with a bad temper and equally bad hygiene. Despite the small pouch of a belly, he still towered over Burt by two to three inches and Doc himself was just over 6' 4". "Hey Doc! Looks like you found a new nurse." He smiled wryly and said, "A much *younger* nurse."

Doc froze in place, even though he was seated and tied down. He had been doing his best trying to keep his mind from drifting toward despair and anger, but his carefully structured façade was torn down disdainfully by the man most likely responsible for Sophia's death. He sat there, trying unsuccessfully to keep his body from shaking, wanting so badly to yank those zip ties off his wrists and grab something to bash in this Neanderthal's skull. But even as he thought this, he knew that these very zip ties saved him from certain death. To attack one of Soren's guards would bring immediate retribution from the other guards and he knew that he would be tortured and then killed gruesomely. It didn't matter that he was the only doctor on the ship; Soren's guards didn't seem capable of that type of higher-level, long-term thinking. He could only glare at Dante while a single tear coursed down his cheek.

"You got something you wanna say to me Stone?" Dante hissed under his barely concealed temper. Burt could hear several guards chuckling and knew they were waiting for the sparks to fly. Their blood was hot and they were in the killing mood. *No*, he thought. He wouldn't give Dante a reason to put him in his own Med-Lab. He looked down at the floor and left Dante's taunt hanging in the air like some foul stench. He let out an immense sigh of relief when he heard Dante's contemptuous laugh as he headed back toward the other guards. He thought darkly to himself that the next time something like this happened, one of them will not come out of this alive.

3

Burt snapped back to the present as he reached the aft vertical turbo lift. This lift would take him directly to engineering, several decks below. He stepped out onto the smooth black surface of the hallway and looked around. He was met with total silence, save for the faint humming of the gravity generators coming from the floor and the ceiling. The area was cloaked in a sort of semi-dark gloom. Soren had ordered the lighting for low-traffic areas to be set at lower lighting settings, to reduce power usage. In theory, it made sense, but standing here in the semi-darkness with only the green and red intermittent junction lights to keep him company, Burt couldn't help but feel strangely exposed and vulnerable.

As he made his way toward the lift, the feeling that Burt had on that first day, hung around his neck like a noose. Even now, knowing that he was saved from certain death on the moon, he couldn't shake the inescapable fact that an undefinable darkness was coming for him. Coming for *all* of them. In the depths of his mind, he wondered if *any* of them would make it to Europa. Soren and Rey's apparent psychoses were getting worse and in Doc's mind, would probably be the death of them all. He hustled over to the aft vertical turbo lift, his hand slightly trembling as he pressed the "Engineering and Propulsion Section" button on the lift wall.

DAY 10

THE BIOSPHERE SECTION

1

Nola walked quickly along the enclosed catwalk above the water reclamation machinery. This was her second time down here and she hated it. She looked over the railing through the transparent walls that encircled the catwalk and shuddered. It was easily a 200-foot drop. Even though it was close to impossible to exit from the catwalk and fall over the railing, the fact that she was suspended over all that blackness, chilled her to the bone.

She had just left engineering to check on the two women she had assigned to Jaime Mendez's team. She actually met Mendez on the *Cassiopeia*, but had seen him once or twice in the cafeteria on the moon base. Stocky, with a severe crew cut, he wasn't prone to much conversation and was still fuming that five of his team of eight engineers got left behind on the moon.

2

During the day of the big feast, Mendez and his team had been given orders to have the ship ready for launch. He hadn't spoken directly with Tess about it, but the order came through on their secure mail-link connection, so he had no reason to doubt its authenticity. He ordered his team to move their baggage on board and start prepping the engines for departure. It didn't take much for them to have the ship ready, since they had been working night and day for the past few weeks, so he decided to allow five of his team to head to the "banquet" to enjoy the festivities – it would be a while before they would get to eat like that again.

Just as he was about to send one of his guys to go pack them up so the others could grab a bite to eat, several of Soren's guards showed up in engineering pointing their modified medical lasers at Jaime and his team. A pale man with a heavy German accent blocked his way. "We're leaving. Sor...*Tess* wants you to divert energy to the main drives and bring the engine nodes online." Mendez considered refusing the order, so that he could get confirmation from Commander Robinson directly, but looking at Soren's guards told him that Tess might not be in charge on the bridge.

"Look, I still have five engineers out there. They're probably almost done eating. Give me five minutes to get them. I...can't do this without them. They're essential."

Unconvinced and unsmiling, the guard walked toward Mendez and leveled the medical laser at his face. "You know what *I* think is *ezzential*? If I was to fire dis off in you face from dis distance, not even deine Mutter would recognize you. Do it...*jetzt!* Or..." he looked over at the engineer standing closest to Mendez. "Or...*L. Carter* will be der new Chief Engineer." He stared at Carter intently, his eyes appraising her lasciviously. Under his breath he muttered, *"Du wirst meine Hündin auf Europa sein".* With a wry smile he said, "Was ist dein Vorname, baby?"

Carter stared at the hulking man in disgust. She looked at Mendez helplessly and then mumbled, "Liz. My first name is Liz and I'm First Engineer."

"Wunderbar!" he exclaimed bogusly. "Du sprichst Deutsch! Ich heiße Otto Helmut...at your service!" He clicked his heels together and mocked bowed to her. "Now, Fraulein Liz, how would you like to be der new Chief Engineer?" He moved a step closer to Mendez, his finger sliding over the trigger button.

"*No!*" Carter yelled out. "Jaime, don't do this. We don't have a choice here!"

Mendez stared at Otto Helmut angrily, the back of his teeth grinding. Finally, he turned toward Carter and yelled out, "Initiate main drive core and bring engine nodes online!" As the remaining members of Mendez's team jumped into action, Otto Helmut stepped back toward the entrance and smiled at the other guards. "Engineering coming online," he whispered into the communications link on his collar.

3

When Mendez had shared this story with Nola, she remembered he was still sore about it. All she knew was that they were extremely lucky to have Mendez and his team onboard. They were Tess's handpicked engineering team and knew the *Cassiopeia* very well. And Mendez was smart. He may not have liked the two new additions, but he would have no problems training and utilizing them. Both of the young women were engineering graduates and had worked extensively on the design of the *Galileo* spaceships.

As she walked along the enclosed catwalk toward the biosphere, she couldn't help but feel the weight of the huge ship looming above her. She was essentially at the bottom half of the ship, where the darkness seemed impenetrable and the dim lights offered only a vague outline of the catwalk in front of her. Soren's ridiculous decision to reduce lighting in some areas had already resulted in several accidents, one almost fatal. Although he never mentioned anything in his regular "meetings", she had heard that there were slight energy drains happening throughout the ship and while the jumpsuits kept out the cold of space, the reduced lighting made for slow and sometimes scary work.

She finally made her way to the biosphere entrance and placed her palm on the reader. In most parts of the ship, the palm readers were set for general access, but in certain areas, only a few had access. Of course, Soren, Rey, and his guards, had access to all parts of the ship.

The thick circular door slid open soundlessly and Nola had to squint her eyes. Despite the possible issues of energy loss, this was the one area that Soren allowed the required temperature and lighting settings. She stepped into the biosphere and the door slid shut behind her. She walked down the padded aisle, her eyes wide open. Despite the fact that she hated the physical act of coming here, she was always rewarded by the sheer beauty of the biosphere once she actually made it here. The huge biosphere contained row after row of various plants, vegetables, fruits, nuts, mushrooms, and stuff she never would have dreamed could grow out in space. One section of the huge pod had trees of varying sizes, bushes, and flowers of all types. High above her were huge, reflective panels that gave off light, and to Nola, what felt like warmth.

Something lighted on her head and she jumped, not really knowing what to expect. A beautifully-colored Monarch butterfly drifted lazily in the air in front of her and flitted off into the distance. A laugh from behind her made her start again as she whirled around.

"I'm sorry Nola! I didn't mean to startle you! I swear you jumped a foot when that Monarch settled on your head for a rest break." She chuckled lightly to herself.

Nola couldn't help but smile at the young Botanist. Unlike most of the woman on board, Kelly came of her own volition. When Soren's goons had come for the women and men who weren't aware of his plans to leave for Europa sooner than scheduled, Kelly had been at the moon base's only biosphere. She was determined to find out why all the plants had died and so had ignored the repeated invitations to go to the big meeting banquet. On her way back from the biosphere section, she ran into Allison Sampson, the senior Botanist at the moon base. Allison told her that Soren was taking the *Cassiopeia* to Europa and not everyone would be coming. "He's already agreed to bring you on board," Allison had confided in her. Still, she hesitated. She didn't trust Soren and she didn't want to leave her friends; Nola and Anton.

"They're *both* on board already!" Allison had exclaimed. "If you don't want to get left behind, I suggest you come with me now. You don't even have time to get your stuff!" Although she hated the idea of leaving Tess and the others behind, the thought of Anton leaving her was unthinkable. With both Anton *and* Nola gone, she would be a wreck. She was in love with Anton and Nola was like a big sister to her. "Let's go then!" she shouted at Allison and they both ran toward the hangar bay.

"Hey Kel...how's it going down here?" Nola said, smiling. "You look like you're in heaven."

"It's great down here Nola! Everything is responding nicely to the new biosphere settings, thanks to you." She hesitated for a moment, glanced around and stepped closer to Nola. Lowering her voice, she asked, "Did you get a chance to talk to Mr. Soren about Anton and me?" Her eyes bored into Nola's pleadingly, hoping against hope. As she searched Nola's face, the eager brightness in her eyes seemed to cloud over first, and then finally went out. "*What?* What's wrong?"

Nola let out a sigh, "Honey," she began, but paused. She was having a difficult time trying to put into words what Soren's *new world* would look like. It would be unthinkable, especially for a pretty young woman in love. "Soren was not in a very...*accommodating* mood today." An image of Soren's wife tumbling down the stairs, breaking bones as she went, flashed into her mind. She saw him standing above her, thinking dark, murderous thoughts as his wife lay bleeding out on the floor. "I didn't say a thing to him Kelly because I'm afraid what he may do to Anton...and to you. On the moon, you pretty much kept to yourself and the news you received, was filtered through Anton. He loves you and he didn't want to share the horrible things people were saying about Soren and his *ideas*." Kelly was staring intently at Nola, barely breathing. She waited patiently for Nola to continue.

"Soren has abolished all marriages until we are on Europa. In fact, he has abolished relations of *any* kind. His reasoning is that because the contraceptive patches will be nearing their expiration dates within the next few weeks, the possibility of accidental pregnancies increases tenfold and could hamper operations on the ship." She studied Kelly's face. The girl appeared to understand, but gave no outward sign to attest to this.

"This is what he *said*, but I don't believe it's the real reason. Kelly, Soren wants the first generation of children born on Europa to be *his* children.

After which, he will dictate who is mated together. The reason his guards are so intensely loyal to him is because he has promised that they will be what he has called, the *Second Fathers*, for the second generation of children. And so on, and so on." Nola could taste bile in her mouth with every word. The thought of repeating Soren's psychotic nonsense turned her stomach.

"*What?* Are you serious? People aren't going to stand for this! How can he do such an idiotic thing Nola?" Kelly's eyes were wide and she was perspiring heavily. On her forehead, the few red strands of hair that escaped the antique gardening hat she was wearing, clumped together almost in defiance of Nola's words.

"He can and he will Kelly, make no mistake about it," Nola said. "His guards are armed and the people are terrified. They are hoping he and that ass of a pilot, Rey, can get us to Europa safely. If we can just survive this trip, we'll be alright once we land. It's a large planet and it will be extremely difficult for Soren and his guards to keep us contained. For now, just play along and play it safe."

"But that will mean that Anton and I can't be together." She looked guiltily off into the distance. "And if what you say is true, then by the time Anton and I can be together, I'll have two children by two different men!" She was breathing hard, "I can't do that Nola. I can't. I *won't!*"

Deciphering that look, Nola warned, "Kelly, listen to me and listen carefully. At 26 years old, you're too old to be my daughter, but you're part of my family. If Soren or one of his guards catches you and Anton in the act of doing *anything* sexual, then..." she broke off. She could see Soren's dark eyes contemplating murder. Stuffing plastic into his wife's mouth. But it wasn't the face of Katie Soren that Nola saw...it was Kelly Masterston's.

Laughing nervously, Kelly's face turned bright red. "We haven't *done* it yet, but we've gotten close. You see, I'd like to wait until we're married. Like my parents did." Her eyes dropped as she said this.

Taking her gently by the shoulders, Nola said, "I think that's special Kelly, but please hear me. The world you and I grew up in is gone. The world where your parents were able to court one another is gone. *This* is the world after. It's decadent and it's dangerous. Wait until we land on Europa. Once we land, we'll figure something out. Somehow, we'll get away from Soren and his rabid dogs. Now is the time for strength Kelly. Can you be strong Kelly?"

Kelly looked up from the ground into Nola's steady gaze. "Y...yes," she stammered out. "I can be strong Nola. I can be strong for you and for Anton."

"Yes!" Nola exclaimed. She hadn't realized how worried she was for Kelly and Anton until just that moment. "Just keep a low profile and don't do anything to attract attention to yourself. Anton's been helping Soren with something on the bridge. Make sure you tell him to keep a low profile as well. He's in the lion's den for sure, but as long as he minds his own business and does nothing to provoke Soren, then he'll be fine."

Kelly seemed to consider this and then finally nodded her head. "Yes, I'll tell him that Nola."

"That's great Kel. Also, don't..." A noise coming from the biosphere labs interrupted her chain of thought and she glanced in that direction nervously. She didn't think Rey had been following her, but one never knew with Rey.

Kelly rolled her eyes, "Oh...don't worry about that. It's probably Allison and Larry." She hesitated for a second and then added, "He comes down here...a lot." She smiled coyly at Nola.

Nola looked again in the direction of the biosphere labs and saw Allison and Larry walking up the ramp toward them, hand in hand and wondered how long it would be before Soren found out about them.

"What brings you down here Nola?" Allison asked, probably a bit harsher than she intended, but not really caring if she did. "Trying to spend some time away from *the king*?" she said sarcastically.

Ignoring the bitter edge in Allison's voice, Nola said, "Look Allison, you know full well that Soren has forbidden *any* relationships until we land on Europa. What do you think he'll do if he comes down here and sees you two basking in the afterglow of coitus interruptus, like two nervous kids?"

"Let him come!" Allison cried out, yanking her hand out of Larry's. "I'm tired of having to sneak around like this...I'm a grown fucking woman! For crying out loud, I feel like I'm back in high school! I absolutely hate being here! I was excited at first, but after Kelly boarded, I had a really bad feeling about it and decided I didn't want to come after all. I turned around to leave the maintenance bay and ran straight into one of Rey's goons. He told me to get on the ship and I told him to pound sand. The next thing I know, I wake up on the ship thousands of miles away!" She stared unblinkingly at Nola, a few tears making treks down her cheeks. "I didn't want to come."

While she thought Allison was being foolish in her escapade with Larry, Nola was not without compassion for the woman. She hated the fact that Soren's guards coldcocked her and brought her along against her will, but wasn't that how it was for more than half the women here and many of the men? And where did she herself stand? She wasn't forced, but she wondered if she *would* have been forced, had she changed her mind about going? It didn't matter now. She was here and she was going to *live*. She told herself every night since they departed that she would rather live in this floating banana republic than be stuck back at the moon base, either freezing to death when the power gave out or slowly roasting to death as the moon crawled past the sun on its increasingly erratic orbit. No. She would make it work here and she would live.

"Allison, I don't know what will happen to you and Larry if Soren finds out that you've been sneaking around like a bunch of hormone-driven teenagers, but I can promise you this; it won't be good." She could almost see the bloody spit bubbles in the corner of Katie Soren's mouth, as she desperately, urgently tried to scream. "For your sake, don't tempt him."

"Don't worry about us Nola," Larry Drucker said, breaking his silence. "I'm on good terms with Rey. If it weren't for me setting up the phony server connections back at the moon base, then Henry...and Tess, would have figured out that all of their information had been manipulated. Eventually, they would have found out that I was rerouting the real data directly to Soren. I'm also a damn good navigator, so if Finch can't do the job, I'm a reliable backup. You might even say I was *indispensable*." He smiled smugly, "So, the way I see it, I'm on the winning side!" He put his arm around Allison's shoulders. "Besides," he continued on confidently, "they'll never catch us in the act – we know where all the good hiding places are!" He laughed uproariously as Allison mock punched him in the chest. Nola sighed.

"I've *also* done stuff for Soren and Rey," Nola responded sarcastically, remembering how angry Kyra was when she erased her orbital tracking data. "The problem is, it doesn't matter what favor you do for Soren or what action you take to undermine your co-workers or even if you pretend to enjoy his company. He doesn't reciprocate like normal people do. He just doesn't work that way. *Fascism* doesn't work that way! In the end, Fascism always eats its own...*always*." She could feel herself getting worked up, afraid that even now, Soren was devising some scheme to punish Larry and Allison. "You may have fooled poor Henry Webber and I may have destroyed some important work Kyra was doing, but make no mistake about this; Soren is deadly serious about forbidding relationships on the *Cassiopeia* and he will see through you and whatever flimsy façade you try to wave in front of his face. And he'll make you regret it."

For a second, no one moved. It was completely silent, save for the low hum of one of the moisture machines. Nola glared at them once more, suddenly tired of trying to make Larry and Allison understand the danger of their tryst. Finally, she dropped her gaze and muttered, "Fuck you both. Do what you want."

With an air of defiance and a departing grunt, Allison grabbed Larry's hand and they headed back to the biosphere lab offices, their whispering voices fading off into the distance. She looked over at Kelly, who seemed stricken with fear. She moved close to her and whispered softly, "You'll be fine Kel. Just wait until you get to Europa and then you and Anton can make plans to be together...somehow." Kelly smiled at her, but Nola could see that it was a troubled smile, full of doubt.

As Larry and Allison disappeared into the recesses of the biosphere labs, Nola gently touched Kelly's arm and said softly, "Just remember to be inconspicuous. Make sure you tell Anton." They hugged one another and Nola headed toward the exit at the other end of the biosphere, the one that led to the nearest turbo-lift, her smile quickly falling from her face. She felt guilty for not sharing with Kelly all of Soren's plans. She actually didn't believe him until he handed her a list of 10 people – eight women and two men. She was disgusted and had shown it openly. He had laughed at her and told her to start an appointment schedule. He would let her know when the appointments would start and who the first appointment would be. Nola breathed out a heavy sigh. Their few days of uneasy peace will be shattered when Soren starts having his sexual "appointments." She glanced back at Kelly and at first, didn't see her. Then she saw the old-fashioned hat moving amongst the tall bushes, back toward the gardens. She turned and headed back toward the exit again. Kelly would not be the first, but she was on the list.

She palmed open the biosphere door and headed toward the turbo-lift. She pressed the turbo-lift button and waited, her mind racing. Once they executed the Mars slingshot maneuver, then it would be one, maybe two months to the Jupiter system. *Just hang in there until then*, she told herself. She was so caught up in her thoughts that she didn't see the shadowy figure duck out of sight behind a large banana leaf bush just before the biosphere door closed behind her.

DAY 16

REY

1

Despite his pounding head, Rey enjoyed his little "forays" into the innermost chambers of the ship. Eddie Chin was on duty on the bridge, dealing with Soren and his maddening efforts to access the ship's archive files. Eddie was a capable co-pilot, but to Rey, he was too green and had a nasty habit of second-guessing him. In a couple of weeks, they would be performing the slingshot maneuver around Mars, at which point they would be able to engage the engine nodes and ion thrusters. This concerned him because he didn't think Eddie and the other flight engineers would be up to the task. *Maybe you're worried about yourself being up to the task,* his mind hinted at.

He blinked. *Did I just say that out loud?* he wondered. He grimaced, clutching his head. *I may have to go see Doc again if these migraines don't let up,* he considered. But for now, he would continue "inspecting" the ship. Rey had not been on any generation ships other than the *Cassiopeia*. He spent a little time on the *Orion*, while it was docked at the United Nations' moon base site, but after the meteorite storm blew everything to hell there, he assumed the *Orion* was reduced to a useless, hulking piece of twisted and scorched metal. In fact, no one went there, except for Tess and a few others when they went scrounging for supplies. When Soren finally made the decision to take the *Cassiopeia* to Europa, he considered taking a team to the site to see if there was anything to salvage from the *Orion*, but figured it would most likely end up being a wasted trip.

Tess. He wondered how Tess and the others were getting along on the moon. He had no concern for them. His interest was purely one of curiosity, as if he were observing the breakdown of some microscopic organism in a Petri dish. By now, he figured they were starting to run low on food, but that wouldn't be what kills them. He thought about the primary generator and air converters that they removed from the moon base when they departed. They were probably sucking on moon-fumes by now, if they're not already dead.

He shifted his position in the crawlspace to get a better view of the team in the food reclamation section. The crawlspace tunnels ran throughout the entire ship and were large enough for maintenance teams to access and make repairs, but they were only large enough for the workers to sit and work. The only areas of the crawlspace tunnels where one could stand were the junction points, areas that connected other crawlspace tunnels. He had just passed through one of these areas and was now in the crawlspace tunnel that hovered high above the food reclamation section of the ship.

He had crawled about 15 to 20 feet until he reached an area of the crawlspace that functioned as an air circulation vent. It gave him a complete aerial view of the section. He couldn't have been more than 20 to 30 feet above them, but no one looked up. And even if someone did look up, the lighting was so dim that they would never have seen him. If someone *did* see him, they would say that he had been spying on them, but that wasn't what he was doing at all. As the pilot of this ship and second in command to Soren, he had a right to know as much about the ship as possible. And if they were worried about him spying, so much the better! That would force them to behave accordingly.

2

Scanning the team below, he could see three women working the food processing machines, but he seemed to remember Nola saying there would be at least four, maybe more. He looked near the rear exit and saw the fourth woman. She was flirting with the guard posted there. He frowned and made a mental note. He would have a chat with Dante, about his guards being too friendly. They all knew Soren's expectations and the need to refrain from any hints of favoritism and they knew the punishments. The woman turned from the man and despite the flirtatious way she had carried herself only seconds before, on her face she wore an unmistakable mask of disgust.

As he continued his progress toward the junction point connected to the maintenance areas below the Commons, he stole one last glance at the women below. They were working hard, and from what he heard, putting in extra time. One of his guards had told him that they're all working hard, hoping to avoid Soren's "list".

He laughed and then caught himself. He couldn't tell if he was laughing to himself or if he had laughed out loud. He remained completely rigid, barely breathing, like some overgrown opossum caught in the open road. After what felt like hours, he finally dared to glance back down and saw that nothing had changed. Everyone was still hard at work. Apparently, discussion of Soren's "list" had gotten around and everyone was working hard to *not* be on his list. But no one he spoke with could tell him what the list was actually for. They just assumed it was bad. Rey knew, of course, what the list was for and they had good reason to be wary of it.

He reached the vertical ladder leading to the crawlspace below the Commons and started up. He made it about halfway when a bolt of pain shot across his forehead. He froze once again, but this time in pure agony. His head felt as if it would explode at the slightest movement. He moaned quietly and started mumbling an old nursery rhyme his grand-aunt used to sing to him when he lived with her for a time after his parents died. The old tune had a soothing effect on him though. In the past, it always seemed to help calm him down when he got too excited.

When he started having migraines as a young adult, the tune somehow inserted itself back into his psyche like a friendly botfly. While it calmed him down, or soothed his aching head, what remained terrified him in such a visceral way that he would wake up the next day, his bed clothes completely soaked in sweat and his voice hoarse from screaming. Sometimes, he had noticed, his bed clothes were soaked with more than just sweat.

"Here we go round the mul-b'ry bush, the mul-b'ry bush, the mul-b'ry bush. Here we go round the mul-b'ry bush, so early in the mor-ning." Almost immediately, like a cold draft through an open door, dark unbridled feelings came rushing back at him. He looked fearfully around, half expecting someone, or some*thing,* to be skirting hungrily through the crawlspace toward him. He closed his eyes and pushed forward through the tune, almost knowing that *this* time, he wouldn't get away in time. Knowing that the rest of the tune wouldn't be capable of whisking him away from *it*, whatever *it* was. His tortured mind moved forward in time to a small group of people – Soren, Nola, Doc and several others, standing around his broken, bloodied and ripped body curled on the floor in a death rictus of pain and horror, wondering what monstrosity did this.

"Here we go round the mul-b'ry bush so ear-ly in the mor-ning." And now...the waiting. Intellectually, he knew that this only lasted a fraction of a second, but deep within his mind, it was somehow longer, more permanent. He would either open his eyes and find his migraine manageable or...or what? He didn't know *what,* not really. At one point, he thought maybe he would just...disappear. He waited for the interminable one to two seconds to pass. All of a sudden, he could feel an immense loosening in his head, like giant clamps being removed. The overwhelming feeling of dread retreated from his psyche like dirty water down a rusty

drain. His mind saw a cheap, dollar store plug, half-heartedly covering the drain hole in his subconscious.

His eyes popped open and oddly enough, he felt completely refreshed. His migraine had dissipated to a low-level headache. A minute ago, he was ready to storm Med-Lab to see Doc, but now, he felt Doc could wait, there were more important things to do. He climbed a few more rungs and then opened the hatch leading to the maintenance area below the Commons. He was whistling.

DAY 21

MED-LAB

1

"You're doing great Elsa." Doc whispered from behind Elsa. He and the other "interns" were quietly observing Elsa Nguyen sewing the final stitches in Melvin Durhart's forearm. He was injured in the propulsion room when a power surge caused one of the engine nodes to rupture.

The engineering team had been working overtime to check and double check the ion drives and overall propulsion system to ensure that the ship would be capable of making the slingshot maneuver around Mars without tearing itself to pieces.

Melvin, the only member of Mendez's team qualified to work on the intricate fusion and ion drive components, was removing a wall panel encasing engine nodes three and four. There were three such engineers on his team, but the other two were left behind on the moon. Melvin had already disconnected nodes one and two in order to determine the stress loads on three and four. He was just about to check the stress load readings when he heard the propulsion system being engaged. Durhart's head snapped up and Mendez and Carter stared at each other incredulously. They both sprinted toward the communications wall unit. Slamming his fist down on the engineering-to-bridge communications button, Mendez shouted frantically, "Bridge! Disengage propulsion drive now!" Mendez cursed to himself. He had specifically told Rey and Eddie to simply *monitor* the engine node output parameters while they performed their test. He had said nothing about engaging the system. Engaging the propulsion drive now, with nodes one and two disconnected, could disproportionately spread the power load and possibly cause the remaining nodes to burn out.

He heard Liz Carter yelling at Durhart to get to one of the safety cubicles, when all of a sudden, the wall panel was ejected from its moorings and went rocketing over their heads. He and Carter dropped to the floor simultaneously, staring in horror at the now misshapen panel sailing over their heads. Trailing behind it, like the tail of a kite, was a thick strip of bloody skin. The panel slammed into a bank of computer wall units and cluttered to the floor, just as the propulsion system disengaged. They glanced over at Durhart, who was staring down at his forearm curiously, as if he were looking down at a science project in a lab. Try as he might, he could not move his fingers. However, each time he tried, he could see movement in the ripped open bloody mess in his arm and out of nowhere, his mind conjured up an old scene in the movie *Terminator*, when the Terminator had to perform "self-repair" in some seedy-looking hotel room. As the Terminator moved his fingers, gears and steel tendons moved back and forth. Durhart was so mesmerized by his own Terminator-like tendons, that he almost grabbed one of the moving "things" to see if it would actually move his finger if he pulled at it. Luckily, Mendez was there to grab his healthy hand and stop him. He looked at Mendez and uttered a halfhearted chuckle. A second later, he fainted, his shocked body falling against Mendez.

2

Now, Durhart snored lightly on the Med-Lab bed, while Elsa finished with his stitches. They were able to save his arm, but he would have a nasty looking scar when it healed. Elsa, one of the three woman that were assigned to Doc as "interns", completed the final knot in the stitch, snipped off the excess and then turned to Doc and the other two ladies. Doc smiled approvingly. "You did fantastic Elsa. Next stop; open heart surgery!"

They all laughed and the women hugged one another. Doc looked at them, his smile wavering; *they could have all been in the same sorority in college*, he thought. They had only been with him a few weeks, if that, and already, they were like daughters to him. A sudden image of Tess, her husband Stan and their son Lenny popped into his mind like unwelcomed guests showing up a private party. As much as he cared for Tess and her family, their memory only made things worse, in light of their current situation. It made him feel untrustworthy because he felt he should have been there for her; done *more* for her when things got bad at the moon base.

He tried to be there for her when they found out that Stan and Lenny perished on the *Galileo2*, but she was inconsolable. She refused to see him for a long time. Maybe it was because he reminded her of her lost family. No matter what he said, it wasn't enough. Her actions toward him hurt more deeply than he wanted to admit, back then.

And she had aligned herself with Rey! Of all people! This, he thought, was what hurt him the most because he treated Rey on numerous occasions back at the moon base and knew that there was something deeply troubling about the man. Once, he tried to engage Tess on the subject and she refused to talk about it. When he pressed her, she cursed him and left him standing there, not knowing what else to do.

He had come to determine that Soren was getting out of hand, but he was not a political man at heart, and so stayed out of the moon base *politics*, as he saw it. Now, he realized that he harbored anger toward Tess for shutting him out of her life and so never approached her about the growing popularity – and power – of Soren. He saw the slowly-building authoritarian leadership traits surrounding Soren and his "associates". Saw Rey's increasing apparatchik loyalty toward him. At one point, he interrupted a conversation Nola was having with Rey about something Soren wanted her to do in the computer lab. What little part of the conversation he heard, sounded like tampering with Kyra's orbital data. They stopped mid-sentence when he walked up and actually glared at him until he apologized and excused himself. Still, he said nothing to Tess. When he finally shared his thoughts with Sophia, she encouraged him to take it to Tess. But it was too late...Soren had made his move. And he never imagined – *couldn't* imagine – that this move would lead to Soren abandoning their friends and fellow survivors. He never imagined that after the death of his first wife that he would fall in love with Sophia, only to have her ripped savagely from his life by one of Soren's moronic guards. He never imagined that he would be an unwitting survivor on a one-way trip to a hell that may very well destroy what's left of mankind.

Mendez poked his head into the lab and said, "Doc, can we have a word with you?"

Doc nodded and turned back to the women, "Okay team, please clean the area and place Mr. Durhart in Recovery Room One. By the way, whose long break is it this time? Zoe's or Jana's?"

Elsa and Zoe rolled their eyes and pointed toward Jana, who took a mock bow.

Doc smiled at her. "You can leave Jana, Elsa and Zoe can handle the cleanup. You've earned the next 3-days off. You should check out the observatory at the top of the ship, the views are amazing!" He gave her a red and white plastic chip with the number 3D on it. It was one of two of Med-Lab's "ship passes". Each department on the ship had a set number of its own chips. "Make sure you keep this with you at all times." Doc said to Jana. "You know the rules."

Jana nodded absentmindedly, "Yeah Doc, I got it. For crying out loud, I feel like I'm in grade school."

He looked at her sympathetically, "I know. Get some rest and we'll see you in a few days."

She grabbed her satchel, blew Elsa and Zoe a kiss and was gone.

"Okay, you guys," Doc said to Elsa and Zoe. Let's get this taken care of."
They both nodded and went to work. He turned toward Mendez and led
him to a small office within the Med-Lab. Liz Carter followed closely behind
them.

3

"I'm telling you Doc," Mendez practically spit out as soon as the door to
the office slid closed. "I specifically told Rey and Eddie that we would be
doing our propulsion and engine node testing today and that all I needed
them to do was *monitor* the node reactions throughout the process. You
probably don't know this, but we only need fifty percent of our engine node
power to run at our current speed. When we approach Mars for the
slingshot maneuver, we'll need one hundred percent of the nodes, but they
all have to be in top working order." He was staring intently into Doc's eyes,
almost boring into them.

Doc stared back, waiting for Mendez to continue. Mendez started to
speak up, then stopped himself. He thought a moment longer and then
added, "This was no accident, Doc. Whoever started up the propulsion
drive, waited until the exact point in our testing that would cause the most
damage. Either that, or the flight team is filled with a bunch of supremely
ignorant idiots."

"I would bet money on the latter," Doc said. "It doesn't make sense for
them to purposely try to sabotage the trip." He froze, his glazed eyes
staring through them. Before Mendez could say anything, he seemed to
snap out of it. "Other than your man Durhart escaping with twenty-odd
stitches, was there any damage to the nodes or the engine room?" Doc
asked, glancing back and forth from Mendez to Carter.

Carter answered back, her voice a little shaky, "No significant damage,
Doc, but it was a near miss for us. Our Mars' slingshot would probably have
succeeded, but the nodes would have failed immediately afterwards." She
paused to catch her breath. "We would literally have been a crew of
skeletons by the time we reached Europa's orbit because the trip would
have taken years, *maybe decades.*"

Doc wondered if *all* of them would have been skeletons. He knew how
people behaved when they lost everything; water, food…hope. He was on
the *Galileo1* on Tess's last trip from Earth to the moon. He could have gone
months earlier, but wanted to be there to provide any medical assistance
if needed. He saw firsthand the increasing agitation of the people at Wright
Airfield right before they left. People grew violent in the face of certain
death. If they were to become stranded in space with no hope of reaching

Europa, things would get very bad on the ship. His mind conjured up a number of scenarios on how this brief colonization effort would play out in the end – and none of them were good.

"So what do we do Jaime? Have a chat with Rey?" He didn't intend to sound as sarcastic as he did, but none of them were oblivious to the fact that Rey was highly unstable.

If Mendez detected any sarcasm, he didn't show it. "I don't know Burt. I simply don't know. Our situation here is tenuous at best and if we're not beaten down by Soren and his guards, then we run the risk of dying in space at the hands of imbeciles."

Again, Doc stared through them, his face slightly contorting as he grappled with some internal debate. Mendez and Carter exchanged worried glances as Carter reached out to touch Doc's knee. Just as she was about to pat his knee and asked if he was okay, his hand shot out and grabbed her hand. He glanced furtively toward the large window in the office and then looked from Carter to Mendez. "We need *real* starship-qualified pilots on this ship. We need Tess Robinson."

Now it was Mendez and Carter's turn to stare blankly at Doc. Carter found her voice first and asked, "Are you suggesting we turn around and return to the moon? To go back for the others? For Tess?"

Mendez whipped his head toward Carter, clearly not expecting this line of thinking. He looked back at Doc. "You can't be serious! Is this what you're thinking? We might not even have the *fuel* for something like that!"

Doc looked at both of them earnestly, "Guys, I honestly think that's our only option. I've heard talk of Soren's plans here *and* on Europa. I'd like to think that if I was lucky enough to survive the end of the world, then I owe it to myself..." he stopped and cleared his throat, "...I owe it to Tess, to do everything I can to help us, *all* of us, make it to Europa safely and not be held hostage to some maniac's delusion."

Liz Carter stared at him and then looked back at Mendez, a teardrop slowly rolling down her cheek. Mendez wiped it away with his thumb and looked back at Doc. "I think we can do this Doc, but we have to act now, *before* the Europa coordinates are fed into the Mars' slingshot maneuver. Because after the maneuver, our Gravitic Velocity Drive will kick in and we'll be traveling much too fast to do anything at that point, but slow down. Returning back to the moon would be impossible by then."

Doc was a neural surgeon and could tell you everything there was to know about operating on the human brain, but his understanding of how the starship's velocity drive worked and how they would be able to go that fast without being crushed was beyond him. And he didn't want to know.

What he wanted to know and figure out was how they could pull this off. It was not impossible, but it would take a miracle.

"So, how do you propose we do this Doc? Force Rey and Eddie at knifepoint to turn the ship around?" Mendez asked, not jokingly. "The more I think about it though, the more I believe that fuel will not be an issue. We'll probably burn up more fuel in the slingshot maneuver than in the entire trip itself. After the gravity assist, our propulsion fuel usage will significantly drop because of the velocity drive."

Before Lycos became a threat to the Earth, Mendez worked as one of the chief engineers in the development of the Gravitic Velocity Drive, or GVD as it became known. Even during that time, the prevailing thoughts within the scientific community was that if mankind was to ever truly explore the stars, they would need technology that could significantly reduce space travel-time. The idea was to ultimately travel to Alpha Centauri, but what good would that be if it took thousands of years to travel there. The Gravitic Velocity Drive was the first step in making this type of travel possible and would ultimately enable ships to travel millions of miles in space in only a matter of months. Instead of going into detail why fuel usage won't be a problem once the velocity drive was employed, he simply added, "To put it simply, we can still slingshot around Mars, but instead of calculating our exit vector for the Jupiter system, we'll change it and essentially, retrace our steps back to the moon. The GVD is capable of computing the speeds necessary to go the distance from Mars to the moon. We may use up a little fuel with the retropropulsion rockets as we get close to the moon, but we could be back there in a matter of *days*." Mendez thought for a second and then added, "And when we depart the moon, Mars will still be in position for a gravity assist to Jupiter. Goddammit...we could do this. We could."

Doc had been listening intently, slowly nodding his head. "Okay, I believe you that it's possible to get back to the moon and then to Europa with the fuel we have, but what about Rey and Eddie? Eddie *might* help, but Rey would fly us into an asteroid before allowing himself to be forced to return to the moon."

Mendez looked at Carter and then back at Doc, a slight smile forming at the corners of his mouth. "What if I told you that there is someone here who may not be as qualified as Tess Robinson, but for a young guy, he's pretty damn good."

"Who is he?" Doc asked, his interest piqued.

4

"Anton Finch," Mendez said. "His father was Melvin J. Finch, President and CEO of FINCH AEROSPACE, the English company that was contracted to build both the *Cassiopeia* and the *Orion*. Melvin Finch relocated to the moon long before *Lycos* was a concern – well, not a concern for 99% of the world's population, since they didn't know anything about it yet." Mendez showed visible disgust at this, but continued on. "Finch and his people found out about *Lycos* about the same time as the United States government and he parlayed that information into a long-term contract for his company. I find it amazing that in the face of almost certain annihilation, man will always find a way to get that almighty dollar!"

Mendez got up and walked toward one of the large windows in the office and looked out. After Durhart's surgery, Med-Lab seemed almost deserted. He thought he saw Zoe or Elsa moving about in the main area of the lab. He turned back to the others and continued. "By the time Finch's son Anton arrived on the moon, the UN facility was complete and they were pretty damn close to finishing up the *Cassiopeia*. Anton was in charge of completing the *Cassiopeia* and organizing detailed training sessions for some of the best pilots in the world. In the end, Tess Robinson was selected to pilot the *Cassiopeia* and Skip Masterston was her co-pilot. Her *original* co-pilot.

Eventually, Skip sent for his daughter, Kelly Masterston to join him on the moon, after her mother died of cancer. Of course, Kelly was suffering from severe depression due to her mother's death and had it not been for her budding relationship with Anton, she probably would have killed herself."

"So how did Anton learn how to fly the *Cassiopeia*?" Doc interjected. "Did he have prior training on other ships?"

"No, incredibly!" Mendez stated emphatically. "He's a navigator, by training, but Skip instantly took a liking to him because he had such a positive effect on his daughter Kelly. They spent a lot of time together on the *Cassiopeia* and Skip began including Anton on their flight training exercises. Eventually, Skip became more of a father figure than Anton's real father had been. Unfortunately for Kelly and Anton, their fathers were both killed when the meteorite storm destroyed the UN facility." Mendez looked at Doc, expecting a response. At last, he added, "He's not officially a pilot, but he's spent more time on the bridge of this ship than anyone other than Tess and Skip and I'm willing to bet he knows more about flying this ship than Rey or Eddie."

Doc considered this last piece for a moment. After almost a minute, he looked up at them with a grim expression on his face. "You know, this might work. There are enough disgruntled people on this ship that we just might be able to take it over. Regardless of whom we are able to persuade, there is another who is just as critical as our young Mr. Anton Finch."

Mendez's forehead was furrowed in deep concentration, "Who? Who's just as important as Anton?"

Doc stood up and walked to the other side of the small office. He turned to them, a look of doubtful concern in his face. "Soren seems to have an axe to grind with everyone on this ship, including Rey. We need someone who is not only close to Soren, but who is able to move somewhat freely about the ship. We need Nola Sykes. Without her help, our little insurrection would be stamped out before it even got started."

DAY 23

KELLY AND ANTON

1

"I just don't like it!" Kelly said, exasperated. "It's dangerous and like a…" She faltered, looking for the right word. "Like a *double-cross*. I think a lot of people will get hurt if we do this." She was standing with her back to Anton, staring blindly at a section of small tomatoes that were now just starting to germinate. Anton placed his hands on her shoulders and turned her gently toward him.

"Honey, no one will get hurt if we do this right." He was gazing into her eyes earnestly, as if he were trying to hypnotize her. "Chief Engineer Mendez and Doctor Stone told me everything. I know what's going to happen in engineering. I know what will happen with the guards, and they've explained what will need to happen on the bridge. I know *everything* darling, so really, there's nothing for you to be afraid of."

She gazed back at him for a moment longer and then buried her face in his chest. She felt lost. Anton always had a way of making her feel safe, but this new turn of events was terrifying her. She felt as if she were being pulled in two different directions.

He continued talking to her, trying to soothe her frayed nerves. "Kel…we both know what Soren's plans are for all of us on the ship. And we know what he has planned once we land on Europa. You remember, right?"

He felt her nod her head shakily against his chest. "Well, I'll be buggered if I let that happen to us Kelly! You and I *will* be married. I'll be honest though, I didn't think it could happen until Jaime and Doc approached me and told me of their plans. This is an opportunity for us Kel and I plan to take it!"

She pulled away from his chest, but remained fixed in his arms. "And you're certain no one will be hurt?"

He smiled broadly at her. "Absolutely! I'll make sure of it!"

She smiled back at him and kissed him gently. She trusted Anton completely, but an old quote flashed into her brain quite unexpectedly and scared her to the bone; *The best laid plans of mice and men often go awry…*

She didn't know where it came from, but she had heard her father say it so many times, that she must have absorbed it deep within her psyche. *The best laid plans...* She began to tremble.

DAY 24

THE BLOOD THAT BINDS

1

Nola laid back on the cot with her eyes closed, squeezing and releasing the hard, rubber ball in her fist every few seconds. Her eyes weren't closed because she was squeamish about her life's fluid flowing through the tubing and collecting in the 450mL blood bag hanging from the IV pole attached to her bed. Closing her eyes was her only means of escaping the scared, angry and frantic look on Doc's face. She was lying on one of the cots in Med-Lab, with a large needle in her arm. Soren had ordered that everyone have their blood drawn and stored every two weeks in the event of some unknown catastrophe that might require blood. It was one of the few things that he ordered that actually made sense.

Unfortunately, it meant that she was now Doc's captive audience. The minute Elsa or Zoe – she couldn't remember who was who – started the process, Doc came in, bubbling with what could be space dementia for all she was concerned and ranting on about their plan to return to the moon. Ridiculous nonsense!

"Look Nola, I know you and I have had our differences and we've never really liked one another, but we really need your help to make this work." He searched her face earnestly, "I'm trusting you with this because I really don't think you like what's going on here on this ship. Am I right?"

Nola looked into his eager, tortured eyes. She knew what had happened to Sophia and although she would never tell Doc, she wept about it. She could feel his pain and even empathize with him, but actively participate in a coup against a mad man...that was a totally different story altogether.

"Doc, I've already sworn not to tell anyone about this, but I think it's madness. Soren has an almost preternatural hold over Rey, the guards and many others. Hell, they barely take *shits* without his thumbs up. Your plan will fail and it will fail utterly. Someone in your little ring of spies will talk to the wrong person and Soren will kill you all, but not until after he tortures you and the rest of the ringleaders. After this slingshot maneuver, we'll be within months of arriving to the Jupiter system and Europa. I just want to keep my head down, do my job, *service* Soren if I have to and then get to Europa…alive! I may be pregnant with his child, but I'll make it there. If you and Mendez and all the other crazies want to try and take on Soren, then be my guest. I don't want any part of it."

Doc looked at her disgustedly. "We have close to 70% of the ship on our side."

Nola had been looking at the blood bag filling up and tried to will more blood out so she could extricate herself from this dangerous and suicidal line of thinking. It was filling up, but much too slow for her. When she heard Doc say 70% of the ship's passengers were with them, her head snapped up. "*What?* How is that possible?"

Doc smiled at her. When he wasn't raving like a space cadet, he actually looked, well…handsome. She quickly looked down at the needle in her arm, her face slightly flushed. Doc walked over to where her needled arm was resting by her side to check the needle. Satisfied that it had not moved, he continued, "Yes, in the last two days, half of the ship has come in for the blood drawing and the other half we saw at their stations. Like you, Nola, I have privileges too. Maybe not as good as yours, but better than most on the ship. In my own way, I've *vetted* these people and know who I can trust. They know what's at stake here and none of them are ready to simply hand their freedom over to a mad man without a fight."

Nola considered this for a moment. *My God…70% of the passengers are willing to take on Soren and his guards, just to go back for the others?* With that many people, their coup just might work. It might. She shook her head, as if warding off an evil spirit. "Soren is crazy Burt. And a killer. If he gets word of this, this *uprising*, he may not take it out on you directly, but he'll hurt someone you love or are attached to. His leverage over us is our humanity."

Doc's dark brown eyes turned even darker and Nola could see him visibly stiffen. "He's done everything he can to me already Nola. We've abandoned someone I loved like a daughter, one of his idiot guards, through his carelessness and malice, caused the death of someone I cared for, and I saw Rey murder an innocent man, all because he was in the wrong place at the wrong time. I'm no stranger to death and murder and…" he paused, seeming to take stock of what he was about to say, "I can kill too…if I have to."

Nola could sense the seething anger just beneath the surface of Doc's tightly controlled demeanor. Yes, she could see that he would be willing to kill Soren, Rey, and whatever guard got in his way. Doc and his insurrectionists would carve a bloody path all the way from engineering to the bridge if necessary. The thought of it made her skin crawl.

"I...I just don't think I can do this Doc." She struggled for her next words, almost afraid that simply uttering them would make them come true. "Whenever I try to envision myself getting off the ship on Europa and feeling the new planet's air on my skin, I get cold all over. There's a darkness in place of that hope and it terrifies the hell out of me." She looked up at Doc, tears filling her eyes. "I can't shake the feeling that there's an empty void waiting for me just around the corner. Some dark...*thing* that I can't see. Waiting for me just on the periphery of my perception. I'm afraid I'll never make it off this ship!"

Doc walked over to the edge of the bed opposite the blood withdrawal equipment and looked down at her. His anger toward her was immense and each time he thought of the others abandoned on the moon, he couldn't help but place part of the blame on her. On the moon, she had the confidence of Soren and Rey. They entrusted her with their plans to steal the *Cassiopeia* and knowingly strand dozens of people on a temporary lifeboat. He knew people like her. He knew what kind of person she was, but looking at her now, he was beginning to wonder if she had had any options back then. When he saw her leave the cockpit soon after they departed the moon, she had the look of someone in over her head and drowning fast. He sat on the edge of the bed and placed his arm around her shaking shoulders. She hesitated initially and then leaned toward him and put her head in his chest sobbing freely. He couldn't help but feel sadness for her. A month from now, they could all be dead from a million different things, but Nola had internalized this fear of her death so deeply that it forced her into a state of passivity. He knew she would do nothing that, in her mind, would hasten her demise. And he would not press the situation. He felt strongly that he could trust her not to say anything to Soren or Rey or anyone for that matter.

While Doc sat there cradling her, Elsa entered, checked the blood bag and then removed the needle from her arm. She glanced at Doc with a worried look on her face and then promptly patched up Nola and secured her pint of blood.

Nola's shaking shoulders relaxed and she looked up gratefully at Doc. "I'm sorry Burt. I've never told anyone about what I've been feeling and I guess it just overwhelmed me a bit."

He gave her shoulders a squeeze and stood up. "I understand Nola and no apology needed. You go about your same business, but keep a low profile a day or two before...before we take *corrective action*. No one knows that I'm telling you about this except Mendez and Carter and I'll just tell them that I decided that I couldn't trust you, so I withheld the plan from you. If it goes south, then I'm certain Soren will believe that we couldn't trust you for fear that you would share it with him and Rey. Totally believable."

She nodded appreciatively and slid off the cot. She began to walk away, but turned back to him. "Please don't think badly of me."

Before Doc could respond, she turned back toward the recovery room door and within seconds, was gone.

2

She was floating! She knew it had to be a dream, but she relished in the feeling. She knew exactly what state her mind was in at that moment and she knew that she could somewhat dictate the flow of the dream simply by nudging her mind in that direction. *I want to fly!* she thought and that was all it took for her to be instantly floating above white clouds. She could feel her arms out in front of her as she sailed over the white puffy cumulus clouds. But hadn't it been ages since she last saw a cloud? And that realization was all it took for the dream to rapidly begin to dissipate. The fluffy, friendly clouds turned dark and ominous. She could feel the roiling thunder throughout her body as she began to spiral downward, out of control.

She opened her mouth to scream, but she had no mouth. Her lips had been fused together. She plummeted to the…what? Earth? No, that wasn't right. I'm not on Earth anymore. I'm on the…the…the *Cassiopeia*! This sudden realization was enough to wake her, but she couldn't see and her mouth was still fused together. In a moment of pure panic, she began to think that she was in one of those waking coma states where you lie in bed completely aware of your surroundings, yet unable to move. She forced herself to calmness while she mentally prepared to make an effort to rip herself out of her frozen immobility when all of a sudden, she felt a hand softly caress her cheek. The touch was so light and unexpected, she practically jumped out of her skin.

"Easy now," the hand's voice whispered, almost melodically. "You're okay. The medication is just wearing off and you're slightly crashing. The good thing is that you're okay."

Whatever effort Jana Patterson had made in calming herself, crumbled in an instant. She could feel her heart beating, no *hammering,* in her chest. Fearfully, she now knew that she was awake, but she couldn't see, speak or move. Something covered her eyes and completely snuffed out the light and she could now tell that she had something over her mouth. Her body, however, was dead to her. She could feel, but she couldn't move as much as an inch.

She tried once again to slow her breathing, but she felt she couldn't get enough air. She was only able to breathe through her nose and even then, it seemed painstakingly slow. *What the hell is going on?* She thought. *Where am I? Why can't I move??* She made a herculean attempt to calm herself and tried to remember what she was doing last.

She remembered Elsa stitching up one of the guys from engineering. His name was nothing but a blur on her memory. Doc gave me some time off. Something deep inside clicked and she remembered that it was her long days off. Doctor Stone had given her the chip! She thought furiously for a moment and then remembered that she had the next 3 days off. In her mind, she could feel her brows furrow in deep concentration. It seemed to help because she remembered something else. She was finishing up her jog and returning to her cabin when she heard someone come from behind her. And that was the last thing she remembered.

A chill spread through her like an electric jolt and she could feel herself sinking into a dark pit of intense fear and panic. She wanted to scream and kick, but her body completely ignored her. At first, she thought maybe she was tied down, but she couldn't feel any restraints. She guessed she was lying on a table because she could feel the smooth surface under her shoulders, back, butt and legs. She found that she could move her tongue, but barely. She painstakingly pushed it past her teeth and with great effort, to her lips. Horrified, she realized that nothing was covering her mouth – she just couldn't speak. Her mouth had been open the entire time.

She also realized that nothing covered her eyes because she could feel a slight breeze on her closed eyelids. She stopped exploring with her tongue and focused on opening her eyes. With a tremendous effort, she tried to open them, but it seemed the harder she tried, the heavier the eyelids became. She could feel herself tiring out and made one more exhausting attempt to open her eyes. As she felt her energy begin to ebb out of her, she at last saw a very faint sliver of light peeping through her eyelids. If she could have spoken, she would have yelled for joy, but this was not a joyous moment...no, far from it. She was in trouble and had no idea whose voice had told her to relax. She didn't recognize it and was certain that if she were in Med-Lab, she would have easily recognized Doc's soothing voice. Elsa or Zoe or both would probably have been fussing over her too, if she were in Med-Lab.

A horrid thought came to her, slithering out of the primordial ooze of some of her darkest memories. *What if I'm in hell?? What if I fell over the catwalk between engineering and the biosphere? What if I'm dead?* At this possible realization, a single, distressingly pitiful whimper slipped through the catatonia of her vocal cords and she did the only thing she could think to do; pray.

She felt movement near her and considered trying to open her eyes again, but her heavy eyelids were not what stopped her. It was the insane fear that she would open them to some hideous beast with equally hideous soft paw-hands. She imagined it would smile sweetly at her with jagged, poisonous teeth and an idiot grin right before it ripped her to shreds. She imagined it would devour her as she lay there wide-eyed and incredulous, watching it shove pieces of her into its maw of a mouth, while it still smiled and grinned at her stupidly. Despite her fear, she bravely thought that she would rather face her fears than wait interminably for the slash, or bite, to end her existence. She focused again on opening her eyes and for a brief second, her right eye opened halfway and then closed again. Her heart leapt with terror during that split second her eye was open. A huge face was staring down at her, barely a foot away from her face. Her conscious mind bolted from that image, trying to hide in the relative safety of total darkness. She realized now that she was not dead and not in hell, but in a very dangerous situation. As she tried to rationalize the situation she was in, she couldn't find the words to describe the sinking, desperate feeling she was having now. The huge face, as frightening as it was to be waiting there when her eye popped opened was bad enough; but the hideous, bloody smile that accompanied it was much more ominous. And it was in fact bloody. She saw blood dripping from the front teeth. Despite whatever anesthetic she was on, she could still feel a dull pain in her left thigh. The pain seemed to be telegraphing itself from far away. In her heightened state of fear, she could feel herself starting to shut down – the mind's way of dealing with extreme terror, she realized – and she welcomed it. As her mind begin to retreat into oblivion and the world of unconsciousness, she heard a disembodied voice coming after her, "Hey, don't leave me now...it's just getting good."

DAY 27

LARRY AND ALLISON

1

Nola woke with what felt like hundreds of hands grabbing at her. She flailed her arms uselessly as she crawled out of a murky nightmare. "Alright Nola. Get up! Soren's order!"

In her tortured mind, Nola's fear of being killed practically materialized in front of her. She started swinging her fists and kicking viciously at the intruder. "Get the hell away from me! I'll kill you! I'll KILL you!"

The guards looked at each other stupidly. One of the guards, Jake Sandstone, smacked her hard across the face and grabbed her by her night shirt. "Wake up Nola! Soren is calling an emergency meeting right now! Everyone needs to be in the Commons in 10 minutes. If you're not there, we'll be back to drag you kicking and screaming if we have to!"

Her nightmare finally fading, Nola began to settle down. After seeing her relax, Jake let her go. "You should be happy you get a few minutes to get yourself dressed. Pretty much everyone else got yanked out of bed and dragged to the Commons in whatever they wore to bed." The two other guards behind him started laughing as they all turned to leave Nola's room.

Nola sat on the edge of the bed, still a little shaken up by her own demons. She walked over to the small sink set into the wall and placed her hands under the automatic water faucet. She splashed cold water on her faced and glanced into the mirror. What she saw startled her. Although she felt as if she had begun to relax, her eyes looked haunted and nervous, as if they wanted to jump out of her skull and go racing around the room.

Why in the hell is Soren rounding everyone up now? What could be so goddamn imp... At that thought, her heart nearly leapt out of her chest. *Oh God! Maybe he found out about Burt and Jaime's plot to take over the ship!* Although she refused to join the uprising, in her heart, she wanted them to succeed. She wondered how Soren found out and who might have told him. As she quickly slipped into her jumpsuit and shoes, a quote from George Orwell's *1984* slithered its way into her aching mind, *Big Brother is watching you.* She shuddered involuntarily and made her way to the Commons.

2

Even before she made it the Commons, Nola could hear yelling, screaming and crying. It was strangely familiar to the day they left the moon. She stepped around a small puddle of blood on the floor and her stomach turned. She could only imagine the brutality that the guards were doling out to their fellow travelers. Unchecked, they probably could put someone in Med-Lab every day until they arrived at Europa.

She walked into the Commons and went to her "assigned" seat. Soren had the brainchild that whenever they had a meeting, everyone was to sit in the same seat each time. They even had their names scrawled into the headrests. That way, he and his guards would know immediately who was missing and who was present. She noticed that Allison was not in her seat yet, even though it seemed like everyone else was there, other than the key night shift personnel down in engineering. She looked to where Doc was seated, but his back was to her. Almost as if he could feel her eyes watching him, he turned around in his seat and stared at her. She half smiled at him and he responded with a barely perceptible shake of his head. Something was wrong and somehow, it involved him. She began to feel sick to her stomach at the thought of Soren making martyrs of Doc and whom Soren would no doubt call, the *insurrectionist ringleaders*.

She noticed the seat next to Doc was empty, which meant one of his nurses had not made it yet. Hopefully, Soren won't make an example of her. And where the hell was Allison? Almost as if the thought of her name had power, Allison appeared at the front of the Commons with Soren standing close by. She was totally naked.

3

Normally, whenever Nola saw Soren, he would appear refreshed and well-slept. But now, his hair was disheveled and he looked tired. He also looked extremely dangerous, like some feral animal backed into a corner. His eyes were small black pits in his face and at that moment, reminded her of those emotionless, deadpan eyes of Great White sharks – dangerous, unpredictable and hungry.

"Thank you all for joining me this morning," Soren stated, almost casually, nonchalantly. "As much as I love my sleep, there is some nasty business we need to handle immediately. This is one of those urgent situations that we can't allow to fester or it would infect the entire ship."

At his side, Allison shifted uncomfortably in her nakedness. Her lip was swollen and Nola could see an ugly purple bruise on her cheekbone. She stared at the floor, her lower lip trembling.

"As you all know, space travel is a serious business. Everything has to function perfectly in order to safely accomplish the mission at hand. Engineering has to function at peak efficiency and the crew and passengers all need to work together as a well-oiled machine. *We* need to function like a well-oiled machine. If that doesn't happen, the machine breaks down. And when the machine breaks down, *we* break down. And that, my friends, is when people die."

Nola glanced around the room and could see an almost palpable fear emanating from the faces of the others. They all knew Soren and knew what he was capable of. Their initial excitement of being "selected" to escape the almost certain doom of the moon and travel to Europa withered away on a daily basis until there was nothing left but fear and desperation as the real Wilfred Soren began to manifest itself. Almost overnight, he had turned their somewhat democratic way of life on the moon into a harsh, authoritarian Noah's Ark Police State. She turned back toward Soren and her eyes fell flat on Rey's placid face. He was staring directly at her. He was wearing that same pained look on his face that she'd seen many times. A look trapped in the nether worlds between partially laughing and partially crying, but both in agony. She shivered inside. To her, Rey was a silently ticking time bomb. He had grown more and more morose with each passing day. One day, he's going to erupt and God help us when that happens.

"And I was informed several days ago," Soren was saying, "that someone had been stealing food." He looked around the group dramatically, as if for effect. "Why would someone steal our precious food when we are so far away from our new home? That food has to be rationed carefully. What if it takes longer for us to make it to Europa? Our food reclamators only provide us with a small percentage of our food. And since we have no animals on the ship, we would be a week away from starvation if some unknown calamity should befall us. I, for one, am not interested in being part of some interstellar *Donner Party* mishap."

A noise from the rear entrance to the Commons forced everyone to turn around. Bloodied and bruised and also completely naked, was Larry Drucker. His hands were tied behind him as he was shoved toward the front of the Commons. "We found him hiding in the bushes in the biosphere!" laughed one of the guards as he shoved him forward.

When Nola first saw Allison standing bound next to Soren, she thought that maybe Soren found out about Doc's coup from Allison, that is if she was even involved. But when she saw Larry, she immediately knew what may have happened. Larry and Allison had been fooling around and were finally caught. She had warned them both, but they disregarded her as some old schoolmarm. A deep, foreboding chill ran down her spine as she watched the two standing in front of the group in their nakedness. She felt as if she had been transported back to the medieval ages.

Soren looked at the both of them with disgust as he circled them. "I've tried to be as clear as possible about the rules of our ship. I've laid the ground work for what will be the foundation of our new society once we arrive on Europa. We have a brave new world waiting for us, but we will be a young society and as a young society, there will be certain, ah, rules put in place that many of you won't like. But these rules are for your own good. For *our* own good."

Nola's head was spinning from this kabuki theater and she felt as if she would pass out. She had read long ago about repressive and authoritarian societies like North Korea, Russia and Nazi Germany, but she never dreamed in a million years that she would actually become part of one. Would actually *live* in one. She could feel her sanity slowly drying up at the edges, becoming crinkly and brittle, ready to crumble to dust at the slightest touch.

"And when those rules are violated, the whole system breaks!" Soren yelled, breaking Nola out of her self-induced trance. "These two," he glanced at both of them with malicious eyes, "have broken my most important rule; *absolutely no intimate relationships!*"

Nola glanced around. The silence in the Commons was deafening. She saw a handful of people tearing up, but most wore impassive, almost depleted faces. She cut her eyes over at Doc and could see that he was fuming. She saw Kelly several rows ahead of her, shifting uncomfortably in her seat. Anton Finch was seated on the far right of the Commons looking around nervously. She was immensely gratified to see them sitting apart, lest it give the wrong appearance.

"We also have a crewmember missing." Soren continued. "According to Doctor Stone, Jana Patterson was given a 3-day pass and was due back to her station a couple of days ago. When she was reported missing, I had Rey do some investigating and he found some of her clothing – her *bloody* clothing – hidden in both Larry and Allison's cabins. She probably found out that they were involved sexually, not to mention stealing food, and threatened to turn them in. For that, they attacked her."

Nola glanced at Rey as he stood motionless behind Soren. She saw that he was no longer looking at her, but now seemed fixated on some point that only he could see. All of a sudden, Larry cried out, "We didn't hurt Jana!

We had nothing to do with that! We have no idea how those bloody clothes got inside our cabins, but I didn't do anything to Jana and neither would Allison!" He looked around, pleadingly, "Okay, so we took a little food. My God, it was just a few packages of cheese and grapes! And I know...*we* know, that having a sexual relationship was wrong, but I..." he stared out at the group, seemingly more embarrassed by his next comment, than his nakedness. "I love her. I love her..."

His voice trailed off into a whisper. Part of Nola believed him, but she also knew what he was probably only now realizing; that it didn't matter what everyone else believed. What mattered was what Soren and maybe Rey believed. She looked at Soren and could see that he was unfazed by Larry's heartfelt plea. In fact, he nodded at one of the guards flanking Larry and in one smooth motion, the guard jammed his baton into Larry's unsuspecting stomach. Larry's mouth flew open, but the only thing that escaped was an exasperated grunt. He crumpled unceremoniously to the floor, moaning pitifully.

Ignoring Larry's writhing, Soren looked out at the others. "I've asked Rey to describe for you what he believes happened and what needs to happen next." He nodded to Rey, who stepped forward to the front of the small group.

"Doc came to me the other day and told me that Jana never returned from her 3-day pass. We searched her cabin, but found nothing out of order. Later, I spoke with a number of people quartered in the same wing and found out that she was last seen headed toward the biosphere section. She had been jogging. Most likely, she probably stumbled upon Larry and Allison...having relations." To Nola, he said *relations* like it was a bad word. Something foul and obscene. *My God,* she thought, *what's gotten into this man?*

"They had somehow gotten into the secured food stores and based on what I found, they had been drinking wine and eating cheese like they were at some goddamn picnic." Allison's lower lip began trembling and tears dropped from her eyes.

"I had my guards round them up and detain them, while I checked out their cabins. In both of them, I found bloody clothing." He hesitated a moment, as if for effect and then added, "I also found something else."

Nola stole a glance around the room again and could see that everyone was captivated by this burgeoning horror story. It was a real-life Agatha Christie tale. Rey slumped his shoulders and stared down at the floor, as if what he was about to say was too difficult to voice. He almost waited a full minute before he raised his head and said, "I found Jana's mutilated hands and feet in Larry's wall freezer unit." At that, Allison's head snapped toward Rey and Larry bolted upright as best he could from the floor. Their eyes were wide and infused with some terrible understanding.

Ignoring them both, Rey plowed on, "Since no one else is missing, I assumed that they must have been Jana's, but I had Doc verify them anyway. Jana Patterson was dismembered by Allison and Larry. Whatever the foul reason was, I don't know, but I plan to find out."

Despite her apparent fear, Allison turned toward Rey angrily. "That's *bullshit* Rey and you know it! Why in God's name would we want to kill Jana and why in the *fuck* would we cut off her hands and feet? That's insane!"

"I never said anything about you *killing* Jana. Did you kill her?"

Allison stared at him uncomprehendingly for a second and then said, "What? No! *No!* I liked Jana. I mean, I *like* Jana." She looked desperately out at the group, some standing, most sitting and pleaded with them. "You guys know me. You know Larry. We would never do anything to hurt anyone. You know that. You *know* that! Soren is crazy! Rey and his fucking goons are crazy!" Nola's heart hurt. Allison's fragile hold on her sanity was slowly slipping. It was as if she knew how this was going to end. It didn't matter what they believed or didn't believe. In the end, Soren would win. *"We're all going to fucking die on this ship!"* she screamed before one of the guards came up behind her and rapped her on the back of the head.

Allison's last words before Jake smacked her in the back of the head, pierced Nola like a spear. She found herself thinking of past atrocities on Earth like the atrocious concentration camps in Nazi Germany and the doomed people in the Jonestown settlement in Guyana. She remembered the heinous North Korean Incident in the late 2030's, where peacekeepers uncovered more than five million murdered men, women and children in thousands of dilapidated and ill-maintained prison camps littered across the countryside, during the violent overthrow of the government. She wondered if the people involved in those atrocities, unwittingly or not, could pinpoint the exact moment when their situation slipped into unalterable darkness and anarchy. Her heart almost skipped a beat as the realization dawned upon her that now, at this very moment, their little world aboard the *Cassiopeia*, had taken its first dangerous and inexorable step into a lightless abyss. Watching this little horror show play out, she imagined the *Cassiopeia* floating lifeless in space eons from now, the word *"Croatoan"* carved in bloody scrawls on the outside of the ship.

She looked at Rey, standing next to Soren. They both had a preening look of moral reverence shining in their eyes. It disgusted her. Soren cleared his throat and stood before them once again. A few people were crying, but most seemed to be in shock. He cleared his throat again and spoke out loudly, "In normal situations where there has been a breach of our rules and decorum, we would typically have a vote on what needs to happen to the transgressors, but in this situation, it's fairly obvious what their crimes are; an illegal and distasteful tête-à-tête, stealing much needed provisions from the rest of us, and the willful kidnapping, mutilation, and possible murder of Jana Patterson."

There were groans at this and Nola could see, almost *taste*, the doubt that many of them shared. They could sense that something bad was about to happen to Allison and Larry, but she could see that they were not on board with it, despite the allegations and charges that Soren leveled at them. Her hapless comrades were slowly becoming inured to Soren and Rey's lies. Nola was convinced that Doc and his coup would be wildly successful if they attacked Soren and his people right now. Part of her *wanted* him to. She looked in his direction and willed him to do it. And when Doc stood up, she had to bite her lip to stifle a shout.

As if he were talking to an unruly child, Soren glanced over at Doc and asked impatiently, "Yes, Doctor Stone. What is it?"

Despite her impetuous, almost frantic desire to foment a rebellion, she was relieved when Doc simply stood up to ask a question. She respected him, despite how they started out. The people on the ship would need him. She would need him.

"Thank you, Commander Soren. I'm horrified about what has happened to Jana, but maybe we should focus on trying to find her. Maybe she's not dead. She might be somewhere right now dying from blood loss or infection." Doc's team, Elsa and Zoe, sat huddled together, looking tearfully up at Doc. "We're sort of going about this as if she's already dead and we don't really know that yet."

Rey walked over to where Doc stood, invading his personal space and stared up at him, his seemingly laughing eyes immersed in a sea of painful facial tics. Although Doc's 6'4" frame was a full head taller than Rey, he seemed to shrink back when confronted with Rey's aggressive and unpredictable demeanor. "Are you questioning my methods, Doctor?" he said, flatly. Nola detected no anger or retribution in his voice, but the sound of it still chilled her to the bone.

Doctor Stone stared down at the man. A part of him wanted to destroy that oddly oscillating face. Here was a man who murdered someone in cold blood and caused someone he loved, to be killed. Deep in his heart, he knew that Rey most likely murdered Jana. Larry and Allison were screwing like rabbits wherever they could – everyone knew that. They wouldn't have killed Jana over something like that. In fact, he seemed to remember that Allison and Jana often ate lunch together at the cafeteria back on the moon.

No, she didn't kill Jana and wouldn't have a reason to. Rey was the culprit here, no doubt about it.

Nola could feel her heart hammering in her chest as she watched Rey nonchalantly walk up to Doc and stand in his face, mere inches from him. She wanted to scream at them. Wanted to scream at Rey for being a sadistic freak. Wanted to scream at Doc for being there. For putting himself in the limelight. Couldn't he sense Rey's guards coming up the aisle behind him? She could see their coup failing even before it got started. If Doc were put under guard or worse, killed, their coup would wither and die. Or would it? Maybe it would help their cause if Doc were martyrized. Maybe *this* is what it would take for them to take down Soren.

Still, she didn't want to see anything happen to Burt. A lot of people liked him and trusted him. If anyone could lead them to take over the ship, it would be him. Before her tortured mind could follow this thread, Doc spoke up. "No. Your direction is crystal clear. As you know, my team is willing and able to provide assistance, if needed."

Rey stared at him a moment longer, almost daring Doc to say something else. He shifted his gaze toward Elsa and Zoe. They shifted in their seats uncomfortably and then quickly averted their eyes to the floor. Nola could see them shivering.

Laughing, Soren boomed out, "Alright Rey, if you're done, let's get down to business." Rey turned on his heels and marched back toward Soren. On his way back, he nodded toward Dante and mumbled, "It's time."

As if those words had power, both Larry and Allison simultaneously cried out. Dante grabbed Allison's wrists and pulled her forward toward the rear of the Commons. The other guard, Jake Sandstone, was right behind him with Larry being shoved along.

4

At that moment, it seemed everything erupted at once. Everyone was screaming and the guards were punching and shoving. "Alright everyone! Get up and follow Jake...*now!*" Nola had no clue what was about to happen, but she dreaded it just the same. She stood up and just as Doc neared her, she jumped in line, next to him. "Burt, what the fuck are they about to do?" she whispered frantically in his face.

Doc grimaced as the surging crowd moved him forward. "I wish to God I knew, Nola." They were headed toward the Cargo Hold area toward the rear of the ship. Since it was located on the same level as the Commons, they had a direct route to it. "It could be that Soren plans to jail them in the

Cargo Hold. At least, let's *hope* that's what the plan is." Nola grabbed onto his arm as the noisy throng stumbled forward toward the rear of the ship.

5

It took the entire complement of folks to reach the Cargo Hold in just under an hour. Although Doc couldn't see them very well, it appeared that Larry and Allison had been knocked to the floor repeatedly, slowing down the procession. When they arrived at the Cargo Hold, Doc saw Jaime Mendez and Liz Carter standing near the far wall, huddled close to one another. He looked around at the frightened faces in the Cargo Hold. Some were bleeding and quite a few were holding their arms or sides, where the enthusiastic guards either punched them or whacked them with their batons. *Soon*, Doc thought to himself angrily, *very soon*.

As he turned back to face Soren at the head of the masses, he was surprised that everyone actually fit into the Cargo Hold. Luckily, there wasn't much in the Bay, but a couple of Rovers, some supplies and an air converter. Although there were two levels *inside* the Cargo Hold, there was only one way in and that was through the main doors that they just came through. Soren had ordered the heavy door to remain open because the automatic locking mechanism would become engaged, each time it closed. Opening it was a simple matter of placing one's palm on the reader and typing in their respective Section Number. Although Soren had only been to the Cargo Hold once before, the exercise of gaining access to this area overloaded his patience quota. Since that time, the door was set to *Open*. The only other exits within the Cargo Hold were the Cargo Hold umbilicus airlock on the second level and the portside airlock. It was here where Soren and Rey had positioned themselves with Larry and Allison.

"Gather close, people," Soren purred. "You are here to bear witness to justice-served." He motioned for the guards to turn Larry and Allison toward the crowd. Doc could see that they had been beaten and cut during their journey to the Cargo Hold. One of Allison's eyes were swollen and she had a nasty cut on her abdomen amongst the numerous bruises and whelps on her arms and legs. Larry was bleeding profusely from a scalp wound, the blood covering his entire face and upper body like Carrie White, in Stephen King's *Carrie*, but this was not pig's blood. His groin area looked swollen where he had been repeatedly hit. Several of his toes had been broken and pointed in impossible directions from the rest of his foot. Doc looked down at the floor and closed his eyes. He could feel Nola's fingers digging into his arm and he welcomed the distraction.

Soren stood in front of Larry and Allison. He slowly looked them up and down, measuring them. He spit into their faces, one at a time. "Larry Drucker and Allison Sampson; you are sentenced to death. You lived false lives as lovers aboard our divine ship and so you will die as lovers in the cold of space." At that moment, Rey palmed open the portside airlock. The coldness of space immediately swept in. When Larry and Allison saw what Soren intended to do, they began to wrestle within the arms of Sandstone and Dante, but they were weak and had lost too much blood. Their efforts were in vain. Sandstone forced Allison over to the door and shoved her in. She tripped over the threshold and slammed to the cold floor. Before she had a chance to get up, Larry was thrown on top of her in a bloody lump. As they struggled to stand up, Rey palmed the door closed and engaged the locking mechanism.

Soren spoke up again, harshly, "Now each of you will walk past the hatch and view our lovers before we vent the oxygen. There will be no talking. This is a reverent moment." He nodded to Rey, who opened a panel set into the wall. An interior diode changed from green to red, as he turned off the environmental controls in the airlock. "Let's begin," Soren whispered, barely audible.

6

They each walked slowly past the portside airlock. After briefly looking in through the window, each person went back to their original position in the Cargo Hold. A few of the first ones started back toward their sleeping quarters and were roughly turned around. Nola was still holding on to Doc's arm in a death grip, but let go as she approached the airlock door. She looked in and could see Larry and Allison clinging to each other on the floor. They were shivering uncontrollably and Nola could see the beginnings of frost forming on the walls. Allison turned toward the hatch window, the look of fear and utter incomprehension on her face was so palpable and rich, that Nola felt she would be lost in it forever if she continued looking at her. Just before Doc gently pulled her away, she saw Allison lethargically turn Larry's face to hers. She kissed him on his quivering lips as they both fell on their sides. Nola gasped and buried her head in Doc's arms.

Rey stared at the two, as they went back to the middle of the crowd. His hatred toward Doc was becoming more and more focused. Doc had basically called him a liar earlier, intimating that he wasn't being very thorough in his investigation of Jana's disappearance. And even before that, he seemed to be questioning everything Rey did. And now, right before his eyes, Doc was stealing his woman. *His* woman! Soren had promised him Nola when they arrived on Europa. Of course, she would bear Soren's child first, but then she would be his and his alone. But now this black bastard was interfering with plans beyond his control. His eyes shifted nervously around the bay. If Doc was not careful, he might find himself floating headless in a reclamation tank, despite Soren's orders to let him be. He turned abruptly back to the control panel and pressed the airlock oxygen button. It turned from green to red, but Rey thought it was a moot point by then. Most likely, Larry and Allison were already dead from hypothermia and the dead cold of space. Soren faced the group again. "Do not weep for them. They were sinners and they murdered one of our compatriots. Justice has been duly served. Remember what you have seen here...and abide by it. He turned to Rey and commanded, "Open the airlock!"

Rey palmed open the control panel for the outside airlock door. The button to open the outside airlock door was enclosed by a protective cover. He punched in a series of numbers and letters and the cover flipped open. Underneath was a brightly lit button. He pressed it, but nothing happened.

Soren glared at Rey, clearly irritated by this malfunction. "What's the problem?" He said impatiently.

Rey ignored him and tried to troubleshoot the problem. As far as he could tell, there was nothing wrong with the panel. He restarted the process several times with the same results. Nothing. Angrily, he slammed his fist against the wall next to the panel. "I'll have to check on this Commander. It could be a short in the panel."

Pissed that his banishment ceremony didn't have the full effect he was looking for, he turned back to the group and snapped, "That's everything people. You're dismissed."

7

They walked back to their respective cabins in silence. Doc and Nola walked side by side, each wrapped in their own internal counseling efforts. Nola touched Doc on the arm and looked up at him gratefully. "There's no way I can sleep now. Do you have anything in Med-Lab that'll make me sleep until we reach Europa?"

Doc chuckled grimly. "Sure, come on up. I may just take some myself."

When they got to Med-Lab, there were several folks waiting for them. Like Nola, they wanted – *needed* – something to help them put this night behind them. After an hour of providing the best counseling that he could, only Doc and Nola remained, physically and mentally exhausted.

"Those poor souls," Nola whispered, more to herself than to Doc.

Doc walked over to the couch where Nola sat in his office and sat down next to her. "Oddly enough, that was probably the best death that they could have asked for."

Nola snapped her head toward him. "Surely you can't mean that! That was barbaric!"

Doc gently grabbed her hand. "What was barbaric was how they were abused before they were forced into the airlock. With the airlock environmental controls turned off, it probably got cold in there very quickly. Deep-space cold. By the time Rey turned off the oxygen, their bodies had probably already shut down."

Nola only stared ahead. To die like that. In the deep cold of space. It was terrifying to her. She hoped Doc was right that they didn't suffer long. She was so wrapped up in thought, that she didn't realize she was squeezing Doc's hand. She looked at him and found that he was looking at her intently. "I hope I'm not hurting your hand," she breathed out quietly.

He smiled sweetly and kissed her hand. "You're not hurting me at all."

She grabbed his other hand and looked into his earnest face. "I want to join you and the others. I want to take over the ship and go back for the others. I want to wake up from this unending nightmare and I...I want to be with *you*. I want to wake up with you on the new world. I love you, Burt, for who you are. I love your strength and I love you for making me feel safe each time I'm near you." A single tear rolled down her cheek, as their mouths connected. Nola could feel an intense heat, slowly radiating throughout her entire body as they lost themselves in each other.

DAY 28

SOREN AND REY

1

Rey and Eddie sat in front of the semi-circular flight control panel almost on the verge of fisticuffs. They were working up the calculations of the slingshot maneuver and Rey was adamant against the angle of approach, as recommended by their onboard computer.

"We're simply not going to generate the speed we need unless we get closer to Mars." Rey spat into Eddie's face. "The non-fliers who programmed this system have built in way too many safeguards. At this angle of approach, we may as well double the time it will take to get to Europa." He threw his hands in the air violently and stormed off toward one of the bulkhead windows.

Eddie Chin tried as best he could to keep the disagreement "civil". He knew where he stood and he knew Rey. It would not do him any good to antagonize the man, lest he find himself *sleeping with the space fishes*. "I know this onboard computer system Rey and those safeguards are already *very* aggressive. With a ship this size, if we try to get closer to the planet to increase our speed, there's a good chance that we could either damage one or more of the engine nodes or simply tear the ship apart, your choice."

Rey had still been pacing, until Eddie's last comment, *your choice*. The actual words didn't bother him. It was the *way* Eddie said it – *your* choice. It was full of sarcasm, distrust and backtalk. He stopped immediately and slowly turned toward Eddie. Eddie could feel his insides turn to mush as Rey glared at him through dangerous, passionless eyes. "I'll let that slide Eddie...*this* time. You'd do well to remember that I am second-in-command of the *Cassiopeia* and I will not suffer insubordination. Do you understand me?"

"Yes, sir," was the only thing that Eddie dared to say, and this came out in a hoarse whisper.

"Continue working on those numbers. I need to see the Commander," Rey ordered as he turned on his heels and left the cockpit.

2

Soren sat in one of the large chairs in his spacious cabin. It was the only two-level cabin on the ship and it had its own view to the blackness of space. The upper level was similar to the observatory at the top of the ship, including the retractable bulkhead, giving it an almost 360-degree view of space. Currently, Soren had the bulkhead opened to enable him to see out into space. Looking toward the rear of the ship, he could see that the sun was still quite large from this distance and he thought he could see the misshapen Earth. *Could that be the moon right next to it?* he wondered. He smiled as he thought of that bitch Tess and her troupe of useful idiots. "Good riddance to bad rubbish!" he whispered to the darkness.

Earlier, he had been looking out at the stars, envisioning the slingshot maneuver around Mars. He could see Mars. They weren't close enough for him to make out any specific terrain features, but he could make out the multiple reddish colors of the planet. They were getting close, which meant that they would soon be starting their countdown to the slingshot maneuver.

His mind drifted toward Doc's assistant, Jana. That whole dismember-ment thing was a nasty affair and although he didn't know anything of her disappearance, he had a strong reason to think that Rey may have been involved. Over the past couple of weeks, Rey had become more and more despondent and argumentative. He seemed to question everything and more than once, requested that Nola be bonded to him and him alone. Almost as if he wanted her *imprinted* on him, like some fucking animal. He wanted Soren to exempt her from his harem of *First Mothers*, but he bristled at the request. Nola was one of the best-looking women on the ship and she was smart as hell. Why in the world would he forgo the opportunity for one of his offspring to have *her* genes? He stood up and walked closer to the main window at the front of his cabin. He didn't know Rey before they were all forced to live together on the moon, but he had researched everyone slated to be domiciled on the U.S. moon base prior to his final trip to the moon. He was shocked when one of his investigators, Travis Tinkett, uncovered a treasure trove of unsettling information regarding Rey's younger days, before he entered the space program.

According to Tinkett's reporting, Rey's parents were killed in a house fire when Rey was 10 years old. The cause of the fire was inconclusive, but Tinkett had found out that the boy was a fire bug and had most likely caused the fire. Whether it was accidental or intentional, was unknown. With his parents gone, the youngster was sent to live with his next of kin, his grandmother's sister on his mother's side in some backwater town in Arizona.

Tinkett's information from this point on was thin, but he did uncover that Rey's grand-aunt was found dead in her bed just before Rey's 17th birthday. She had been beaten and tied to the bed, cuts and bruises covering her entire body. According to the police report, she had apparently been left there to die. Unfortunately for her, the assailant left the door open and she was eaten alive by rats and the local wildlife. Rey had an alibi because he was on a camping trip with friends about 20 miles way. They all testified that he was with them the entire time, although they admitted that they were all wasted by the time they fell asleep that night.

Soren shuddered involuntarily. *How in the hell did he pass his psyche test?* Soren thought to himself, as he remembered the details of Tinkett's investigation. The thought chilled him to the bone as he realized that his life was in the hands of an unbalanced sociopath. Soren could hear Rey finishing up his conversation with Eddie and wondered, not for the first time, whether he made the right call in betting all of his chips on Rey. Tess was right in not trusting him, maybe he shouldn't either.

3

Rey tapped lightly on the cabin door and after a moment, it slid open soundlessly. "Sorry to keep you waiting Commander." Rey announced as entered Soren's cabin. Soren motioned for him to sit down. "Eddie and I were just working out some of the details of the slingshot maneuver. What did you want to talk about?"

Soren looked at Rey's seemingly restless face. He felt that if he alternately closed his left eye and then his right eye, he would see Rey first laughing and then crying out in pain, as if he were in some drug-induced nightmare. It was very disorienting. "What the fuck was that about with Doc yesterday? Are you purposely trying to cause problems with the rest of the crew? These people like him and you're playing with fire if you think you can antagonize him without upsetting the others." Rey stared at him, impassively, waiting for him to continue.

"If people think you're trying to cover up something and you take it out on the doctor, then we could have problems. I don't want to give these people any reason to think that they can stand up to us. We might have a few weapons, but they have the numbers. I just hope *they* don't realize that."

Rey got up and walked around the large room. It was clear that he was furious, but when he spoke, his voice came out even and unemotional.

"Doctor Stone needed to be put in his place Commander. They *all* do. I've observed them all – *secretly*. Many of them don't like you and more than a handful wish we could go back and get the others from the moon."

This wasn't news to Soren. He knew that Tess was a *favored child* back at the moon base. If she hadn't been so caught up in her own despair about the death of Stan and her son Lenny, she probably would have been more aware of his plans to leave her and her followers on the moon. He chuckled to himself. With their air supply running out, they were now nothing more than asphyxiated mummies, a look of fear and incomprehension etched into their sunken faces.

The possibility that there may be some *organized* effort to stop the slingshot maneuver was not lost on him either. He knew that the good doctor was close to Mendez, Carter and a few others and lately, they seemed to be as thick as thieves. His handful of spies seem to never get close enough to them to really know what they were talking about. As for Nola, she still seemed to be indifferent, barely threading the line between the past and the future. Despite the fact that he considered the possibility of an uprising inconsequential, he nonetheless tripled the guard detail in key areas of the ship and authorized them to use lethal force if necessary. As far as he was concerned, no one was indispensable.

"As surprising as it might be to you Rey, I'm aware of what's going on. You aren't the only one who provides me with information. One might say that you *validate* the information I receive. And don't you worry about my public image with our passengers, you just make sure that Finch and Chin are ready to handle this slingshot maneuver. Is everything in working order? Is there anything that could go wrong?"

"As I said, Chin and I are working out the details of the slingshot, so there's no need to worry about that. I think Finch is fine too, but he's been seen in Med-Lab on multiple occasions and he's spent some time in Engineering with Mendez and Carter. He also spends an inordinate amount of time with Kelly Masterston down in the biosphere section."

Soren raised his eyebrow at that. "Is that so? And what do you think of that?"

"I believe he has a crush on her or maybe he thinks he's in love with her. He hasn't done anything with her to get into trouble, but it might be worthwhile to have a chat with him. Maybe you can find out if he's aware of any potential *obstacles* that could affect our slingshot maneuver."

Soren was aware that Finch had a schoolboy crush on the Masterston girl, but seemed to adhere to some old nostalgic mores regarding relationships. He seemed to remember being told that Finch was hoping to marry the woman and when they consummated their marriage, it would be the first time, for both of them. He almost barked a laugh out loud at the thought. Finch's wedding night vision was just as likely to happen as him turning the *Cassiopeia* around to retrieve Tess and the others. It just wasn't going to happen. Still, maybe he could leverage the young man's innocence and see what tales were being told out of school.

"Tell you what. Send him to my quarters after you've had your pre-maneuver sessions in a few days. I'll have a chat with him before you begin your final checks."

Rey nodded smartly, left Soren's cabin and headed for the cockpit. Two of Soren's personal guards nodded to him as he left. Rey ignored them as he proceeded down the hallway, a small smile forming on his lips.

DAY 30

THE BEST LAID PLANS

1

"And Rey...that motherfucker's crazy! He scares me." Mendez was saying when Nola walked into one of the small engineering alcoves. It was the one area of the engineering section that was closed off to the main section. Only a handful of guards were currently in the area, but their focus seemed to be on the crew physically working on the engine nodes. Mendez, Carter, Doc, and Melvin Durhart were in the alcove, while several of Mendez's engineering technicians were working one level below them in what they called the "Well", the only area where they could access the components that led to the fusion engines.

"You guys might want to keep your voices down...this place carries." Nola said as she neared them. She smiled at Doc and touched him on the arm, which didn't go unnoticed by Carter.

"Hmmm...I don't think we have to worry so much about our voices carrying, than your barely-hidden PDA Nola," Carter teased. Both Nola and Doc blushed and simultaneously looked at the floor. "You're right Liz, I need to be more careful about public displays of *anything*, let alone affection. But seriously, I could hear you guys the minute I stepped through the hatch."

"No worries there Nola." Mendez interjected. "I have guys posted everywhere and believe me, we would easily have a five-minute warning if any guards, or anyone not cleared by us, happens to come this way. I even have some techs doing fake work up in the crawlspaces above and below us. Apparently, that's where Rey spends a lot of time, when he's not on the bridge. He's like some fucking alien scooting around in a maze of tunnels! God only knows what he's doing in there."

Liz's face turned serious and she looked around at the group. "I'm still having a hard time with what Soren did to Larry and Allison. How in God's name could we allow that to happen? Yesterday it was them, tomorrow it could be you and Burt. Or even Jaime and me." She looked down at the floor.

Jaime rubbed her gently on the back. "It's because Soren holds all the power. We have no weapons to fight them off. Those damn medical lasers they all seem to have, may not be powerful enough to damage the ship, but could melt through damn near anything else, especially flesh."

"I know!" Liz exclaimed. "It's just that I can't believe we've devolved into this. Punishment without so much as a trial? I mean, Larry and Allison were genuinely shocked when Soren accused them of murdering Jana. I don't know. I just don't know."

Doc grimaced and spoke up, "*I* know. Neither Larry, nor Allison killed Jana. It was Rey."

They all stared at him. Although bothered by Burt's revelation, none of them seemed too surprised. They'd each spoken with Rey on numerous occasions back on the moon and always felt that he had a deep capacity for evil.

Jaime found his voice first. "How do you know it was Rey, Burt?"

Doc seemed to ground himself and then spoke quietly to the group. "When Jana didn't show up for her shift, I went looking for her. Of my three assistants, Jana is the most reliable. She's detail-oriented to a fault and is almost neurotic about being on time. She consistently gets to the lab before her scheduled time and she's a firm believer in if you arrive on time, you're already late." Burt took a deep breath and continued on.

"I went to her cabin first and found nothing out of the ordinary. Since Rey's guards are always prowling about the ship looking for unauthorized movement during working hours, I decided to find Rey to express my concerns for Jana. I couldn't find him anywhere, so eventually, I decided to go to his cabin." They looked at him in what could be nothing short of awe. As most of them had already realized, most encounters with Rey invariably turned out bad, not to mention that Rey seemed to have an axe to grind with Doc.

"When I got to his cabin," Doc continued, "the door was open and there wasn't a guard in sight. I called out to Rey, but got no answer." He looked around the group, shuddering. "Believe me, I had no intention of going into his cabin, but I was worried for Jana. Really worried. So, I went in.

"At first, nothing stood out. It was just like all of the other crew cabins, only a little larger. It was extremely neat though. *Unnaturally* neat, if that makes any sense. I didn't touch *anything* and I was sweating my ass off! I just knew he was behind me the entire time in the room."

Nola touched him on the arm, "So what makes you think he killed Jana?"

Burt looked at her and then at the group. "That's just it. His cabin was so neat that everything had a place. Nothing was out of place, yet something was. It's hard to explain because that was the first time I had ever been in his cabin. Something was there that shouldn't have been."

"I don't know Burt," Jaime said. "Maybe you *thought* you saw something that..."

Ignoring him, Burt continued, "Against every fiber in my body, I closed my eyes and slowed my breathing and made myself relax. This was terrifying. I just knew I would open my eyes and Rey would be standing inches in front of me, teeth poised to bite my nose off." He shuddered involuntarily.

"After about 30 seconds, which felt like an eternity, I opened my eyes and looked at his desk again. What I had failed to accurately define the first time, stood out like a neon light in the darkness. The chip that I gave Jana for her 3-day pass was lying on top of a neatly placed writing pad. I know it was one of Med-Lab's chips because I could see my initials clearly engraved on it." He paused and looked down at his hands. They were trembling slightly. "The chip was stained with dried blood on it."

Durhart looked stricken and then his face hardened. Liz gasped and grabbed at Jaime, while Nola stared stonily ahead, as if trying to get her emotions under control. Durhart looked around at the others and then back to Burt, 'Why didn't you grab it and present it to Soren? It would have been proof that Rey is fucking crazy and might have possibly saved Larry and Allison's life!"

Burt turned toward Durhart angrily, "Who the hell do you think we're dealing with here, Melvin? I'm almost one hundred percent certain that Soren already suspects that Rey murdered Jana. Soren is no friend to anyone on this ship, but he'll choose Rey over any of us, if it came to it."

He looked around at the others, his voice quavering slightly, and said, "In the Commons, when I asked about looking for Jana, I wanted to see if Rey would admit that he had her 3-day pass chip. I thought maybe he would admit that he'd found it and where he found it. If he had done that, I wouldn't have suspected him of murdering Jana, but he didn't share that he had her chip and damn near threatened me when I questioned him about looking for Jana."

Jaime slammed his fist on the metallic work table. "Why in the hell would he kill Jana though? It doesn't make any sense! She is one of only four medical personnel on this ship – someone we'll need on Europa. Why would he try to hamstring us *before* we've made it to Europa?"

Before Doc could answer, Nola spoke up, "Because he's *crazy*, that's why! And so is Soren. He's got some sort of *messiah complex* and I have no doubt that he'll do whatever it takes to be this *father of humanity* that he's always raving about.

"I know what Soren is capable of and if we're not careful, we may all find ourselves jammed into one of the airlock portals." She shared with them Soren's admission of the horrific, cold-blooded way he murdered his wife. She thought she was going to vomit halfway through it.

"I was hoping to keep my head down and do what I had to do in order to make it to Europa alive, but I don't want to live in a world where a megalomaniac is dictating how we live our lives, while his henchmen slowly beat us into submission and passivity. I want us, *all* of us, including the people we left behind on the moon, to live in freedom on the new planet." She grabbed Burt's hand and squeezed it. "We need to do what it takes to take over this ship, subdue Soren, Rey, and his fucking guards and go pick up our friends on the moon."

Burt looked at her and smiled, "That sums it up for me. I'm willing to die for this and it may come down to that for some of us. We may have only one shot at this and if any one part fails, then we all fail."

2

"This will be great for us Kelly!" Anton almost shouted as he stepped into the artificial brightness of the biosphere section.

Slightly startled, Kelly snapped her head up and looked toward the entrance Anton had come in. She smiled, even though she was still deeply saddened by the death of Allison and Larry. Anton made his way quickly over to her. As much as he wanted to kiss her, he simply gave her a hug, furtively glancing around the section as he did so.

When they disengaged, he faced her and was about to speak, but Kelly interrupted him. "You shouldn't be coming down here so much Anton. You saw what happened to Allison. To Larry." Her mind went back to the image of Allison's freezing body and blue lips exposed to an unimaginable cold. "I can't allow that to happen to us Anton. I just can't!"

Anton hugged her again, but this time to console her. "I understand Kel, I do. I would never do anything to get us into that type of trouble. Sure, we've kissed, but Soren would never punish us like he did Allison and Larry. I just don't see it."

"*Why?*" Kelly asked incredulously. "Why would he forgive us and not them?" She hesitated for a moment and then added, "I don't think Soren even has the *capacity* for forgiveness."

Anton stood straighter, seemed to gather his courage. "I've had a chance to get close to Soren and you know, he's not such a bad guy after all. Yeah, he's a little rough initially, but when you get to know him, you can tell that he's being that way to ensure our safety and the success of our mission to get to Europa. He's simply playing the part of a hard-driving, mad man, but he really means well."

"But he *murdered* them, Anton!" she shouted, her eyes blazing into his. "He sent them through that fucking airlock and left them there until they froze to death. And for what? Because they were having *sex*?" She stomped off shaking her head.

He walked after her, a little reluctant to put his hands on her shaking shoulders. "Well," he started uncertainly, "they knew the rules, honey. They were having sex in every nook and cranny whenever they had the chance. They knew the rules..." he finished weakly.

"Yes," she continued for him, turning to face him, "they knew the rules and so do we. The only reason *we* haven't had sex is because we want to wait until we're married. *If* we can get married. Otherwise, that could have been you and I sitting on that cold metallic floor, our bodies shutting down, praying for death to come take us."

Anton was momentarily speechless. Of course she was right. Even here in the *Cassiopeia*, Kelly and he had their fair share of sneaking around and making out. They didn't go as far as having sex, but they could have gotten themselves into a lot of trouble. In light of what had happened to Allison and Larry, he almost felt compelled to keep his hands in his pockets or keep at least five feet between them both, lest someone with more prurient interests, misconstrue their actions as unacceptable under Soren's twisted code of conduct.

"Like I said Kel," he started out a little shakily, "once you get to know him, he really doesn't seem that bad. He's shared all sorts of mission-related information with me. In fact, he..."

Kelly interrupted him and asked matter-of-factly, "Has he shared any details about these 'lists' we've been hearing so much about?" Anton began stuttering when Kelly added, "And what about this *First Fathering* thing Anton? Has Soren expounded on his great design to be the father of a new nation...literally?"

Anton found himself speechless while Kelly's earnest eyes bored into him. "I...uh...I...don't know what to say about that Kel." He swallowed hard and added, "I don't quite feel up to asking him about those things...not just yet anyway. I think...maybe he'll share them with me...once he's ready of course." He smiled half-heartedly and she turned away from him, her shoulders slumping resignedly.

Despite this, he turned her gently toward him and spoke softly, "I don't know much about Soren's lists, but I promise you Kel, I'll find out." He gazed into her eyes, hoping he was calming her frayed nerves and then added, "I came down here to tell you that I've talked to the others about our takeover of the ship." He turned his head and looked around the biosphere section. He wanted to be sure that there was no one lurking nearby as he brought Kelly up to speed on the ship takeover.

Kelly was generally aware of the plan to take over the *Cassiopeia* and go back for the others on the moon, but she was not interested in the details of the violence that was sure to come. She only wanted to know what she needed to do when the time came, to keep herself safe. As Anton detailed his role, she could feel her grip on reality loosening. The edges of her normally sharp clarity beginning to blur. She wished she could stay in the biosphere section until the whole bloody mess was over, but that was impossible. She would have to be in the Commons, practically in the middle of the human storm to come.

"Eddie will be seated in the co-pilot's chair," Anton was saying, "and I'll be seated in my navigator's chair. At 1500 hours, I will secure the cockpit door, but not before Melvin and Walt Moore arrive. By then, they will have already taken care of Rey's guards. I will need them in the cockpit to keep Soren and his personal guards neutralized. Eddie is with us, but in case he has some last-minute objections, then Melvin and Walt will be able to handle him."

Kelly stood transfixed, her heart was pumping wildly. She was terrified. If they were successful, then everything would change. They would return to the moon for the others. They would be released from Soren's despot and tyrannical rule. And overriding all of this was the knowledge that she and Anton would be free to get married and to live in a normal world where crazies don't force you into a deep space ice box.

Before Kelly could say anything, Anton gently ran his hands through her red hair. "I can't wait until all this is over honey." His smile faded and he turned serious, "Look Kel, I have to go. Soren wants me to brief him again, but I'll be out to see you when I can." He looked at her intently and spoke quietly, evenly, "When this goes down tomorrow, don't do anything to compromise your safety. Let the others be the heroes. I'm taking this risk for both of us. For you. I don't know what I'd do if something were to happen to you."

She smiled briefly and hugged him tightly. "Be safe Anton. It'll all be over soon and we'll be together." They stood there in awkward silence for only a moment and then kissed each other on the lips. Anton turned toward the biosphere exit and was gone. Kelly stared after him, her heart tentatively daring to dream of a future with him.

"Okay, let's go over this again," Doc stated. They all grimaced, but remained focused on him. He looked at them and smiled faintly, "I know you guys are tired, but we may have only one shot at this. We have to make it work." He took a deep breath and began, "Okay, as you know, there are multiple ways this could play out, but for us, there is only one successful outcome and that's if we are in control of the cockpit *and* engineering. And if we control engineering then we control the engine nodes." He looked around and saw everyone nodding agreement. "If Rey maintains control of the cockpit and we lose engineering to the guards, then we're fucked."

"What happens if we hold engineering, but can't get Rey out of the cockpit?" Nola asked.

Jaime looked at the group and then said, "If that happens or if *we* control the cockpit and they control engineering, then the outcome is the same; stalemate."

"If there's a stalemate," Liz added, "then we still lose.

"Why is that?" Melvin asked. "Having one or the other would at least put us in some type of bargaining position."

Liz looked at Melvin levelly and said, "Melvin, Tess and the others don't have a lot of time left on the moon. I'm not sure if you've already noticed, but there's a generator and an air converter in the Cargo Hold. Those belonged to the U.S. moon base. We can't use those here on the *Cassiopeia* and they would be useless on Europa. Soren took them just to drive the dagger home."

Burt shook his head, "More to drive the dagger into any hope they may have had."

"Right," Liz agreed. "So, you see Melvin, they don't have a lot of time left on the moon before their air is compromised. And with that wasteful banquet that Soren arranged right before we left probably ate up, pardon the pun, most of their rations. I'm certain their food situation is just as dire." Melvin nodded, seething underneath with this new information.

"Well, our goals are clear then," Jaime said. "We need to control the cockpit *and* engineering, if we hope to save our friends." He looked at Finch and Mendez and said, "First, Finch and Mendez will be in direct communications with one another on a secondary communication's link that they've set up. Once Finch and Eddie Chin take control of the cockpit, then they will enable the engine node safety alarms and disconnect the nodes from the main drive. This will unlock the engine nodes and allow for their safe removal. If we have control of engineering by then, we will remove two of the six engine nodes. This is critical."

"Why are we removing the engine nodes so soon?" Nola asked. "If we've commandeered the ship and have control over the engine nodes, then why remove the nodes at all? Plus, we'll need them to slingshot around Mars back toward the moon, right?"

Mendez nodded toward the nodes and said, "That's a good observation, Nola, but we only need four of the six engine nodes to make it back to the moon, whereas *all six* engine nodes have to be in place in order to make it to Jupiter. What I'm trying to avoid is a situation where all six of the engine nodes are still in place and by some unforeseen reason, Rey and his guards are able to reestablish control of the cockpit while we're still within the slingshot maneuver window. If that happens, then we're back to square one and they would be able to execute the slingshot around Mars toward Jupiter." He stopped and wiped his forehead with the back of his hand. "Once the slingshot toward Jupiter happens, then we'll be well on our way to Europa. No do-overs, no take-backs, no timeouts. Our speed toward Europa will have increased exponentially and nothing short of an explosion will stop us or slow us down."

Doc was nodding, but looked concerned. "What about the guards that will be posted here? They probably won't let you or your team anywhere near the engine node section."

"You let me worry about that Burt," Mendez answered with a sneer. "I imagine it'll be the same two guards who are always here." He chuckled darkly, "As it is now, they don't take their jobs very seriously. Always *smokin' and jokin'* when they come here..." He paused for a second before continuing on, "They'll wish they were dead when we finish with them."

Despite the gory image that flashed in Doc's mind, he couldn't help but grin. They had a tough battle ahead. A battle filled with blood and death. He knew that some people might die, but the risk was worth it to him and to the others. He felt as most of them did; that it was better to die now, fighting for a better world, then to slowly waste away in a floating prison, en route to some *Europan* feudal society. He opened his mouth to speak again when Anton Finch burst into the little alcove they had been using for their meeting. His eyes were wide and he was sweating profusely.

"Jesus Finch! You look like you've just finished running a marathon! What's the problem?" Mendez asked.

Doc pulled his handkerchief out of his pocket and thrust it into Finch's hand. "Come on son, take a breather. What's happening?"

Finch grabbed the handkerchief and dragged it across his face, "I just overheard Rey saying that they intend to post extra guards down here. In engineering. In the engine node control room."

The alcove was devoid of movement and sound until Mendez broke the silence, *"Goddammit!"* Mendez shouted and slammed his fist onto the small work table. "I *knew* it! Those sons of bitches are so paranoid!"

Nola looked at Burt and then back at the others. "We should have expected this. We know Soren and we know Rey – everything about them is built on lies and deceit. And of course, they would be paranoid...it's the only way they could have survived this long."

"Nola's right you guys," Doc added. "And this changes nothing. It only means that we must succeed at all costs."

Mendez looked at them evenly and when he spoke, his voice was flat, with an air of finality. "As I said earlier, if we fail and cannot control the cockpit – which is a distinct possibility – *and* if all of the engine nodes are still in place, then we run the risk of the slingshot maneuver being successful. At that point, it would be impossible to slow the ship down – we'd destroy it if we tried. After the slingshot maneuver, we would be completely and irrevocably past any chance of returning to the moon. You see that don't you? This is a one-way trip to Europa. Right now, we have enough fuel to return to the moon and then leave again. But a successful execution of the slingshot will put us past the point of no return."

Nola sighed, "Okay, so let's talk about how we are going to subdue Rey. What's the plan to stop Rey *before* he gets to the cockpit? He might get word that we've taken over engineering, at which point he might intuit what we're doing and lock himself inside the cockpit. And then we're at the stalemate you mentioned, Jaime. How can we avoid that happening?"

"Why don't we drug him?" Liz Carter said, almost as an afterthought.

"What did you say?" Doc asked.

Carter looked at Doc, her eyes shining. "Why don't we drug him? If we can somehow incapacitate him *before* he goes to the cockpit, then Eddie and Anton will have to pilot the ship. Soren is not a pilot and won't know that the maneuver didn't work until it's too late. And what can he do anyway? Since Eddie and Anton are on our side, then Soren will just have to ride along and suck it. At that point, Eddie and Anton can adjust the Mars' angle of approach and exit vector, so instead of slingshotting toward Jupiter, we could slingshot back toward the moon as planned."

They were all silent for a minute and then all of them spoke up at once. Doc's deep voice won out. "Listen you guys! Listen! That could work. That could *definitely* work! I have plenty of drugs in Med-Lab that could be used for just that purpose."

"Maybe we should just kill him while we're at it." Melvin stated flatly.

Again, they were all silent. Nola spoke up once again. "No. We can't allow ourselves to become like them. Once we get back to the moon, then we can decide his fate fairly."

Doc grabbed her hand and squeezed it. "I agree. Let's get him out of the picture for now and if all goes well, keep him confined to quarters until we get back to the moon." He turned to look at Nola, a look of deep concern clouding his face. "Nola...you're probably the only one who can get close enough to Rey to carry this out. You realize that, don't you?"

She looked up at him and nodded, knowing how hard it was for him to accept the truth of his own words. Although she avoided Rey as much as she could, she had no illusions that she would be her own person on Europa. She often heard the guards whispering amongst each other, like school kids sharing a dirty joke, about Rey's plans on Europa. She knew that Rey wanted her as *his woman* and would put up with Soren's madman antics as long as he kept his word about her. The thought disgusted her – not only the idea that she would be his woman on Europa, but that she might have to compromise herself in support of their coup attempt.

"What about the guards?" She inquired. "Rey's guards seem to never leave his side."

"This is where these guys come in," Doc said. "Walt Thompson and Melvin Durhart," he nodded toward Melvin, "will each have a group of five people. Each one has been assigned a specific guard and is responsible for knowing their guard's exact routine. They've already been doing this and have become quite accurate in predicting where each guard will be."

Melvin nodded back to Doc and added, "Right. We've been tracking their rotations and have positioned a number of homemade weapons in strategic locations." He seemed to reflect inwardly for a moment, chuckling. "You should see some of these weapons," he mused. "Each one was designed to maximize pain and suffering and would have been at home on any medieval battlefield! In any case, we'll be ready to take the guards out of the equation. Walt and I will personally handle Rey's guards." At that, his face turned dark, murderous, leaving no doubt what was in store for those men.

"What about the folks loyal to Soren?" Carter asked. "These folks didn't bat an eye when we abandoned the others on the moon. What do we do about them when all this goes down?"

"They'll be dealt with accordingly," Doc stated flatly. He thought about despot regimes in the past. Germany, North Korea, Russia, Hungary and many others were all the same: Dictatorships. In almost every dictatorial society, there were always people who either supported it or pretended it didn't exist, to the latter's own detriment. In Soren's twisted mind, he wanted power over what he saw as *limited resources* – the women on the ship. His guards and a number of other men wanted the same thing and were willing to allow Soren to do the things he did, as long as they were able to partake of the *limited resources*. The thought of it turned Burt's stomach. Despite the anger he was feeling against those people, he simply said, "As much as I hate doing this, I will have to drug them as well. Since most of us will be in the Commons, as per Soren's order, then I will prepare something to help everyone *relax* during the maneuver. Placebos for us, the real thing for the others. Although it won't completely knock them out, they won't be much of a hindrance to our efforts."

"Remember," Finch added, "the slingshot maneuver countdown will initiate at 1342 hours. The window for the maneuver is 22 minutes. If we are not on the correct approach vector by 1404 hours, then we will miss the window for the Jupiter slingshot maneuver and be one step closer to getting back to the moon and to our people."

DAY 31

THE COUP

1

1315 Hours. Nola walked fearfully toward the Commons, as if she were walking in a minefield. Her heart was racing and nothing she did seem to help her calm down. In her heart of hearts, she absolutely knew that the minute Rey opened his door and saw her standing there, he would be immediately suspicious. Her wild, lying eyes, frozen rictus of a smile, and thick wavering voice, would pronounce her guilty before she even stepped into his room. In one fell swoop, their coup would be over before it even started.

As she passed through the Commons, she noticed only a handful of folks already there. A couple were slightly dozing and she wondered if Doc had already given them the *chill pill*, as they were starting to call it. She had both a capsule to dissolve in whatever drink Rey might be drinking and a syringe, in case she was not able to use the capsule. She saw at least four guards here swaggering around the Commons, their bravado oozing out of them like old sweat. She looked at the guards closely. They were the exact ones that Melvin said would be here. She hated the guards. Hated what they stood for and hated their anticipation of the female *scraps* they'll get from Soren's table once they land on Europa. She would gladly march them into the Cargo Hold airlock.

Some of her nervousness melted away when she saw Burt near the front of the Commons. He was talking to someone and his back was toward her. She wished desperately that he would turn around. To see his face would have emboldened her even more, but she had a job to do. Besides, it wouldn't do if one of the guards here happened to catch the two of them making goo-goo eyes at one another.

She made her way to the door that led to the crew quarters. As she headed toward Rey's quarters, she realized that she was no longer nervous. She made a mental note to remind herself that a dose of pure hate will reduce nervousness down to zero. She turned down the hall that led to Rey's quarters and noticed that the guards were not there. She wondered if Melvin and Walt had already taken care of them, but was concerned that it might have been too soon.

And in the blink of an eye, she found herself standing in front of Rey's cabin. She stood there for a moment, almost debating if she should turnaround and go back to Med-Lab, when the automatic door response captured her presence and chimed a note to Rey. Within seconds, his face appeared on the view screen. "Nola. What a pleasant surprise. I have to say, this is a bad time. I'm sure you're aware that we're about to execute a very complex slingshot maneuver and I'm within minutes of heading to the cockpit. What can I do for you?"

Smiling stiffly, she looked into the tortured eyes of his smiling face. "Rey. Hello. Some of the ladies I've been working with are a little nervous about this maneuver and I was hoping that maybe I could convince you to swing by the Commons before you head to the cockpit. You know, maybe give them a few words of encouragement and what they should expect during the slingshot maneuver." She hesitated briefly and then plunged forward, "A lot of people are afraid of you and this interaction could play well for you."

He chuckled unsmilingly, "Is that so? I hadn't realized that people were afraid of me. Imagine that. Are *you* afraid of me Nola?" Without waiting for an answer, he continued, "I'm only kidding. Sure, I'll swing by the Commons. Would you like to come in while I continue dressing?"

Nola wanted to bolt from there. She felt like a rat, whose dumb rat-friends had convinced her to pull the cheese cube from the rat trap. *You'll be fine,* they said. *You're much smarter than that contraption,* they cajoled her. *You'll be in and out before you know it,* they convinced her. Now here she was, practically prostrate over the trap, waiting for the catch to release and break her foolish body.

She almost *did* turn to leave when the door to Rey's cabin slid open. He was wearing his flight suit, but hadn't pulled it up over his arms and chest. The fake smile he wore on the view screen was gone, replaced by a piece of stone with eyes, a nose and a mouth carved into it. Nola could feel her poker-face slowly peeling from the edges, revealing the face of uncertainty and terror. Without thinking, she stepped into the unit, tightening her hands around the syringe that Burt had given her.

2

1300 Hours. Anton Finch practically jogged most of the way to Soren's cabin. Soren wanted to see him at 1PM and it seemed to take forever for him to get from the biosphere section to the crew cabins. He had told Eddie he would be in the cockpit by 1300 hours, but the guard who notified him said Soren wanted to see him before he went to the cockpit. Something about wishing him luck. Before he went to see Soren, he made a quick trip to the biosphere section to see Kelly. They had kissed passionately and he felt rejuvenated. He felt like *Superman*. Unfortunately, the closer he got to Soren's cabin, the weaker he began to feel. His legs seem to way a ton and only moved by sheer effort. His breathing became ragged and irregular. His now numb and hazy brain began to wonder if kryptonite really did exist. His brief meeting with Soren the day before went well, so he couldn't understand why he had such a heavy sense of foreboding.

There was a total of five crew cabins, but for some reason, Soren only authorized Rey to have his cabin here. Eddie and he bunked in the section with all the others, which was fine with him – he didn't like the idea of being that close to Soren and definitely didn't want to be near Rey. As he turned down the hall toward Rey's cabin, he began to feel sick to his stomach. He could feel a heavy, malignant force blanketing the entire area. It reminded him of a trip he had taken to the United States a few years before Lycos was discovered. He had just arrived in New Orleans and while waiting for his transportation to his hotel, he began reading an article published in one of the local tabloid magazines. In the article, a couple talked about a new condo they had purchased in an old, newly-gentrified neighborhood in New Orleans, famously known for being haunted. The couple thought the story hilarious and didn't miss an opportunity to retell it every time they hosted a party.

Their "ghost story" was a hit each time they told it and everyone would laugh for hours late into the night. One night, the couple awoke to their two-year old son screaming hysterically at his bedroom window on the third floor. The child had completely wet the bed and it took the nervous parents several hours to calm him down. The next morning, their son seemed normal and couldn't remember anything that had happened in the night. The same thing happened every night for a week until the couple, so distraught by the incident, decided to take their son to a child therapist. Unfortunately, the therapist was unable to determine what the problem was and could only recommend another therapist.

That night, they woke up to their son screaming again. They both raced to his bedroom and froze at the door. They could see their son being dragged across the floor toward an open hole in the floor. The hole seemed to pulsate hungrily as their son was being dragged inexorably into its mouth. His mother screamed hysterically and then bolted for her son, while his dad stood there transfixed, as if his feet were nailed to the floor. He later reported that he was practically paralyzed and the more he fought it, the stronger the hold was on him. The only thing that broke the spell was when he saw his wife dive onto the floor and snatch her son's hand just before he went into the pit. He fell forward and grabbed his wife's ankles and pulled both them away from the hole. They fled their son's room as angry snarling screams yelled after them. The couple fled their home that night, leaving all of their possessions behind.

In the article, the couple remarked that the latent evil they felt, but ignored, from day one, seem to coat the walls in the entire home. They commented that the malice they felt almost manifested itself as physical entities. At the time, Finch laughed uproariously at the article, but now, walking down the corridor of the crew section, he began to understand what the couple meant. He could almost sense the rancid, cloying thickness of evil practically dripping from the low ceiling. He couldn't help but believe that if a person's soul contained enough evil, then that evil couldn't help but leak through that person's pores like body odor through clothing, affecting everything around it. His stomach lurched at the thought and he fought down the urge to vomit.

Two of Rey's guards appeared out of the shadows and confronted him. "What the fuck are you doing here Finch? Aren't you supposed to be in the cockpit?"

Anton stared at the brutes. He didn't remember their names and really didn't care to. All he knew was that he wanted to get this meeting with Soren over quickly and get to the cockpit. "I...uh...am meeting with Soren. *Commander* Soren. I have a 1PM meeting with him before I head to the cockpit."

One of the guards, a dark-haired fellow, invaded Anton's personal space and said, "I know. I just wanted to see if *you* knew." He bellowed foul breath into Anton's face and stepped aside. They both continued patrolling the area, laughing heartily. Anton felt his stomach roil again and tamped it down. *God*, he thought. *I need to get the hell out of here.*

Rounding the corner at the end of the hallway, Anton found himself standing directly in front of Soren's cabin. He could tell by the layout of the surrounding area that it was a fairly large cabin, but this didn't surprise him. Soren's unit on the moon base was larger than everyone else's unit, so why wouldn't it be the same here? He walked up to the door and it slid open, startling him.

"Anton, my boy, very good to see you!" Soren exclaimed loudly. "Come in, please."

Anton, not really expecting Soren's overt friendliness, stood there stupidly for a minute. Soren only looked at him with a wry smile and waited for him to work it out. Snapping out of it, Anton smiled broadly and stepped across the threshold. "Thank you, sir!"

3

1302 Hours. "Sit down, Finch, make yourself comfortable." Soren said as he headed toward the kitchen wall unit. Anton sat in a large swivel chair attached to the floor. Despite its austere look, it was quite comfortable. Unlike most of the general crew quarters, the first level of Soren's cabin contained multiple separate rooms; a bedroom, a bathroom and an entry area that almost functioned like a living room of sorts and a recessed kitchen wall unit area. In the main part of the cabin, a huge window took up the entire wall. Finch looked upwards toward the second level and could see that this window could be seen from upstairs as well. The chair Anton was sitting in was directly in front of the huge window and with the bulkhead open, he could see a thousand stars. Much brighter and surprisingly closer was the unmistakable reddish-colored Mars directly ahead.

Soren returned from the kitchen wall-unit with two glasses. He handed one to Anton. "Drink up my boy! Just a little *firewater* to get you ready for the big maneuver coming up. Anton stared at the clear liquid in the cup, incredulously. He was about to say something when Soren burst out laughing. "It's only sparkling water, son! You can have the real stuff once the jump is made!" He started laughing again as he took a big gulp of his drink, which didn't look like *sparkling water* to Anton.

"How do you feel son?" Soren asked, searching Anton's face. "Are you ready to do this? This is probably one of the most important space maneuvers you'll ever participate in. And just think of it, you'll be one of the last to experience such a thing...at least in *our* lifetimes!"

Finch took a tentative sip of the water and then looked up at Soren. He certainly seemed to be in good spirits. He won't be in a few hours, Finch allowed himself to think. But still, he couldn't help but think he was being set up for a trap or something. He shifted uncomfortably in his chair and wished he was anywhere, but here.

Soren continued on, filling in the silence. "I know, you're nervous and that's understandable. You want this mission to be a success. You want everyone to see you as a valued member of the team. Well, you *are* Finch. You are!" Anton only stared at Soren, taking another small sip of his water. He felt as if he were breathing through a straw.

"As I said Finch, you want this mission to be a success, because a failure could only mean one thing; disaster. I want this mission to succeed too Finch and you know why?"

"Yes sir. You want to ensure that we all arrive on Europa safely. You want to save the last of the human race. Sir."

Soren chortled and continued on, "That's right Finch! It's my destiny!" He took a sip of his drink and stared at Anton. "Do you know why I banished Larry and Allison?" he asked Anton.

This question seemed to come out of nowhere and Anton was actually unsure how to respond. He felt his interior body temperature jump 20 degrees! His mind raced through each and every single time he met with Kelly in the biosphere section and he wondered if he and Kelly had taken their light petting too far. Like most of the people on the ship, he knew that Larry and Allison were screwing around quite a bit. He felt at most, they should have received a verbal reprimand. And the murder charges leveled against them seemed farfetched. He had his suspicions, but he kept those to himself, lest he find himself on the other side of the Cargo Hold airlock door, inches away from the cold vacuum of space.

To his almost palpable relief, Soren didn't wait for him to answer. "I banished them because they were rule-breakers. I don't give two shits about who's fucking who, but I *do* care if someone is not following my rules. If they don't follow the rules here, what makes you think they're going to follow the rules on Europa? They won't." He paused only to take another sip of his drink. "So, they had to die. Besides, they were both rife with venereal diseases. I couldn't allow something like that to spread in this closed society now, could I?"

Anton stared blankly at Soren. He hadn't heard such a thing. Back on the moon base, there were no reported incidents of *any* diseases that the medical facilities couldn't cure. Regardless of that fact, he kept his mouth shut while Soren continued pontificating.

"But I digress, Finch." He tossed back the last of the liquid in his glass and went back for another. Anton noticed the drink was a different color this time. Soren sat down and looked at Anton evenly. Anton held his gaze, but could feel rivulets of sweat running down his back. Soon, he'd be sweating on his forehead. Just when he was tempted to look away, Soren asked, "How's your young lady friend down in the biosphere section Finch? Kelly Masterston is her name, I believe. How's she liking it down there?"

Somewhat taken aback, Anton spoke carefully, cautiously, as if he were walking in a verbal minefield. "She's great sir. I check on her periodically to make sure she's doing okay. I knew her father and I sort of feel responsible for her. Of course, I'm too young to be her dad, though." His accompanying awkward chuckle fell flat into his lap and he shifted again in his chair.

Soren's eyes never left his face. "Right. You're much too young to be her father, but I'd say you're at the perfect age to be...her *husband*. Don't you think?"

Anton Finch was an avid football player. He had been playing the game for as long as he could remember. He loved the game and played as often as he could. One year, when he was 15 years old, his secondary school football team made it to the playoffs and played a particularly aggressive team from Liverpool, known for taking cheap shots when they felt the referees weren't looking. During that game, Anton was kicked viciously in the testicles by one of their strongest players. In that instant, he felt that time had stopped. He remembered thinking that he had two, maybe three split-seconds before his brained realized that pain was on the way. When his brain finally got the telegraph, his entire body seemed to turn into one giant pain receptacle. The only thing he remembered from that long ago match was writhing on the ground in complete agony. When Soren asked him about being Kelly's husband, his body didn't feel the same *physical* pain that he had felt practically pulsating through his hands as he clenched himself ignominiously on the ground, but this sensation was just as substantial as that kick and was a total shock to his system. He felt as if he had become unmoored from existence and if he hadn't felt the sensation of his butt against the chair, he probably would have screamed.

Even though he was sitting at least five feet away, Soren's entire face seemed to expand until it filled his entire field of vision. A huge Soren-face was staring greedily at him and Anton pictured himself a zebra on the Serengeti in Africa, after having been run down by a pack of leopards, lying on the blood-soaked ground, eyes wide and breathing rapidly, unable to do anything but kick weakly at the snapping jaws. He saw himself staring at the slowly advancing face of Soren on the body of a leopard, waiting for death, even while his guts were being unceremoniously yanked from his insides and swallowed noisily. He could feel himself on the verge of passing out, so he did the only thing he could do without appearing guilty. He bit his tongue, hard. The pain was exquisite and he felt that he damn near bit part of his tongue off, but it snapped him back to reality.

Soren was smiling by the time Anton "reconstituted" himself. "You alright boy?" he asked, not really expecting an answer. "For a minute, I thought you were going to either explode...or disappear!" He laughed chummily without a bit of humor in the sound. He leaned toward Anton and his face seemed to turn to granite. "Finch, I've had some interesting conversations recently and I've been told that Doctor Stone has been preparing some medication to help people relax during our slingshot maneuver. Maybe you're aware of this?"

Anton could only stare at him, not trusting anything that came out of his mouth. Soren continued, "I actually think this is a great idea, however, my associate also informed me that some people will receive much higher doses of this *relaxing* medication, so much so that they may become incapacitated." Soren stopped talking and simply stared at Finch. He was amused to see the young man mentally contort himself into a pretzel, while trying not to show any outward emotion. He almost laughed out loud when the thought occurred to him that Finch may either fart or shit himself if he keeps clamping down on his interior systems.

"One thing you need to understand about me Finch, is that I have a finely-honed sense of survival. I don't ignore coincidences and I thoroughly investigate and evaluate *all* rumors. My instincts tell me that violent events are in the offing and while I don't have all of the minute details, I know enough to get to the bottom of it."

Anton dropped his head. He couldn't believe how happy and excited he was, only 15 to 20 minutes prior, when he was with Kelly in the biosphere section. That seemed like a lifetime ago. He fancied that he was one of the heroes of this *space revolution*. The first night after his meeting with Doc and the others, he envisioned his marriage to Kelly and fantasized wildly about the consummation activities. He saw Kelly and himself on Europa, exploring the new world, hand-in-hand. He saw themselves raising children and growing old together. Now, he sat here in complete terror, watching that ephemeral world crumble before his eyes like a sand castle built too close to the crashing waters of a beach, wondering if he would even live to see his next birthday. The only thing he could do was swallow the dry spit in his throat.

"I take your silence as confirmation Finch," Soren stated matter-of-factly. "But all is not lost young man. No sir, not for *you*. You're in love with this young woman, Kelly, correct? And you want to marry her, right? You don't have to speak son, just nod."

As his resolve slowly dissipated, Anton felt his head go up and down. As his head moved of its own accord, he realized forlornly, that he was at the whim of a master marionettist. A single tear streamed down his face, yet he had no strength and no control to wipe it away, unless the master allowed it.

"Ah! Just as I thought," Soren exclaimed. "Although, I would have known you were lying if you said no, but that's neither here nor there." He took another drink and looked off into the distance, as if pondering a heavy decision. He snapped his attention back to Anton, "I have it, Finch! Even though this goes against my better judgement and the plans I have for Europa, I'm willing to make an exception here." Anton raised his head to face Soren. It felt as heavy as a cement block.

"If you are honest and forthcoming with me, Mr. Finch, then I, as commander of the *Cassiopeia*, will marry you and Miss Masterton *after* we've made our successful slingshot maneuver around Mars. You will enjoy status as one of my senior officers, and you and Kelly will be able to move into one of the crew cabins here. Would you like that son?"

Anton was nonplussed at this new turn of events. What was Soren saying to him? That he could *marry* Kelly? His entire being was driven by the hope that he and Kelly would be able to live their lives together. But even as he thought this, he sensed an even deeper, primal emotion. What would happen to the others here on the ship, if he shared with Soren what he knew of the impending takeover? Soren would round them up and they would most likely be punished, maybe even killed. And their stranded comrades on the moon would be left to their fate.

Instinctively, Anton knew that his best chance for survival was to reject Soren's offer and hope that their coup would be successful; unfortunately, his emotional state of mind was completely and thoroughly saturated with visions of his life with Kelly. From deep within, he could feel a dense, emotion-numbing thought, slowly slogging its way into his psyche. He was a survivor. And Kelly would be a survivor, with him as her protector. He began to rationalize that without him, she would not survive. She needed him and he would do anything to ensure her survival. And with that thought, his last wall of resistance crumbled, as he revealed their best laid plans. As he talked, Soren adjusted the intercom volume linked directly to Rey's cabin.

4

1310 Hours. Doctor Stone walked into the Commons as casually as he could. Despite the nonchalant and almost serene look he had on his face, his insides were a roiling mass of guts and nervousness. Only minutes before, he had been speaking with Mendez and Carter in engineering. They were discussing their backup plan in case Nola was not able to get to Rey in time. Like Nola, he also carried a spring-loaded needle and he would use it as a last resort if Nola was not successful. Unfortunately, if Rey was already in the cockpit, then it would be up to Eddie Chin and Anton to take care of Rey. This would have been the worst-case scenario because Soren might be on the bridge, as well as a couple of Rey or Soren's guards.

Doc looked toward the front of the Commons and saw Elsa handing out the tablets. Once she was done, she would go back to Med-Lab to assist Zoe with those sickened after the slingshot maneuver – *if* the maneuver even happened.

He glanced at his watch and thought, *Nola should be on her way here now*. He told her he would be here too, in case she needed help or if something went wrong. He was trying to position himself as close as possible to the entrance that led to Rey's cabin, when Sarah Smith, one of the young women working in the Reclamation Center, tugged tentatively at his arm. Startled, he snapped his head toward her. The woman must have seen his extreme nervousness manifested in his face because she immediately drew back from him. "I'm sorry, Doc! I didn't mean to startle you!" Burt looked at the woman's wide staring eyes and put his hand on her shoulder, "No, Sarah, I'm sorry. I was a million miles away. Is everything okay?"

"Yes," the young woman said, "I was just wondering if you know anything about the slingshot maneuver. Will it hurt?"

"Uh, no Sarah. It won't be bad at all." He fidgeted there standing beside the woman. He didn't have time for idle banter. He turned around and scanned the Commons. He glanced at his watch again and assumed that Nola must have already made it to Rey's cabin. He silently cursed. He wanted to catch her eyes to convey as much confidence as was possible in a stare. As he stood there, he was just about to turn back toward Sarah to excuse himself, when he saw a harried-looking Anton Finch practically running from the hallway leading to Soren's cabin. Why would Finch be in Soren's cabin now? The plan was for Finch to be in the cockpit with Eddie Chin, preparing to take care of Rey, if it came to that.

In that instant, a premonition hit Burt like a speeding freight train; *Finch sold us out!* He started feeling lightheaded and realized he could no longer feel his feet. He couldn't even tell if he was still standing or not. From a great distance, he could hear someone asking worriedly, *Are you okay? Doc, are you okay?* His blurry vision cleared and he saw Elsa standing in front of him, looking scared. He grabbed her and pulled her close, yelling as quietly as he could into her ear, "Elsa, go to engineering and tell Mendez that Soren knows. Tell him he needs to act now. *Now!*" She stared at him uncomprehendingly for a second and then broke free of his grasp and sprinted toward the rear of the Commons, toward engineering.

Doc turned toward the entrance to Rey's cabin and saw that several guards had arrived and they were all looking at him. They were smiling.

5

1317 Hours. Rey moved aside as Nola came into the unit. The door slid shut behind her and Nola had the fleeting feeling that someone had just locked the door and thrown away the key. She clamped down on her fear and looked around the unit.

This was the first time she had ever been in one of the crew cabins and was slightly shocked at how different it was from the others. The thought, *rank has its privileges*, floated up to her mind, but she dismissed it quickly. It wasn't rank that handed out the privileges here – it was despotism, pure and simple. Behind her, she heard Rey zip up his jumpsuit and a far-off part of her sighed in immense relief.

"So, are you afraid of the maneuver too, Nola?" Rey asked, a smirk playing over his lips.

Nola faced him, her hand tightening around the syringe in her pocket. She knew she wouldn't be able to face him head on. He was too strong for her. She would have to catch him totally by surprise if this was to work. "I'm not afraid of anything, Rey. Like I said, the women that I've been responsible for are feeling a bit nervous about the slingshot maneuver and I thought it would be reassuring if you could speak with them. I mean, you're the pilot, right?"

Rey walked over to a small table connected to the wall and pressed a button. A panel slid open revealing several plastic packages of clear liquid. Nola assumed it was alcohol. She thought it almost comical that here they were, millions of miles from the moon and further still from Earth and somehow, alcoholic beverages have still managed to keep their "favored status" amongst the minutia of much needed materials and rations. She watched as Rey poured two drinks through the plastic tubes and walked back over to her. She took the glass from him and said, "Surely, you're not drinking before we execute this maneuver?"

He glanced back at her, the smirk still plastered on his face. "Well, as you said Nola, I'm the pilot and I'm in charge." He took a small sip and then added, "Of course, what kind of pilot would I be to be intoxicated at the helm? Anything could happen to me, right?"

She chuckled nervously, her hands tightening around the glass in her left hand and the syringe in her right. She downed her drink in one gulp and grimaced as the Vodka stung her throat. She didn't like the idea of drinking at the moment, but figured she needed a little liquid courage if she hoped to do what needed to be done. She sauntered over to the small table and sat her glass down. She hadn't eaten earlier and was amazed that the alcohol was already affecting her. She was so nervous, that she actually wasn't sure if it was the Vodka or just the adrenaline pumping through her system.

"Look Rey," she said huskily, hoping she didn't sound like some B-list actress, "I lied earlier."

He looked at her with one eyebrow raised. Now she knew the alcohol was affecting her because when Rey raised that one eyebrow, she almost burst out laughing. He looked exactly like pimple-faced Donny Templeton when he played the part of Porthos in her middle school play of *The Three Musketeers*. It was the only scene where the focus was entirely on him and when the scene kicked off, Donny arched his eyebrow with everything he had. It brought down the house. She pulled herself back to reality and swallowed the laugh in her throat. When she looked at Rey, she could see the barely hidden smirk. "Oh really? About what? What did you lie about Nola, if you don't mind me asking?"

Okay, this is it, she thought disgustedly. *Time to play the part.* She moved up close to him, removing her hand from her pocket. Luckily, the small syringe fit easily into her palm, so it was easy for her to conceal it. "The other ladies are worried, yes," she said, "but I needed a reason to come see you." She reached up and placed her right arm on his shoulder, partially cupping the back of his neck, and used her left hand to fluff up her hair. She could feel Rey move closer to her as he slid both his arms around her waist. She could feel his excitement as he pressed himself closer to her and was revolted by it.

"I love it when you fluff your beautiful red hair like that," he breathed heavily. He began nibbling her ear and for one terrifying moment, she thought she would scream. She placed her left arm on his shoulder as he sloppily slathered the side of her neck.

She closed her eyes while she endured his clumsy and almost frantic efforts at intimacy, and slowly, deftly, positioned the syringe in her hand that would give her the best shot at using the spring-loaded needle. As she maneuvered the syringe, it shifted in her hand and for one frightening moment, she felt it teetering between her index finger and her thumb. She quickly regained control of it and sighed her relief. Rey mistook her sigh as mutual excitement and continued on more enthusiastically. She mimed her excitement and tried to match his swaying hips. She moved her hand slowly and prepared to jam the syringe into the meaty part of his neck, when her arm froze in mid-air. Her eyes flew open and she saw Dante standing there with her wrist in a vice grip. He was sneering at her as Rey continued on, seemingly unaware of this interloper.

Rey backed away from her and kissed her on the forehead. The look in his eyes told her everything she needed to know. Somehow, Rey knew. The guard twisted her wrist and the syringe fell from her hand into Rey's. He turned it over between his fingers, examining it. Nola twisted in the guard's grip to no avail. In her mind, she could see their coup failing all over the ship. Could imagine Mendez and Carter trying to remove two of the engine nodes, while fighting off the guards. She saw Finch and Chin, forced at laser-point to remain at their stations, while waiting on Rey to start the maneuver countdown. And she saw Burt Stone, bloodied and semiconscious, being dragged to the airlock. At this thought, she struggled frantically against Dante, but he only tightened his grip around her neck and midsection. Lights danced before her eyes and she felt herself passing out, when the guard's iron grip loosened. When her eyes cleared, she saw Rey standing very close to her. Although he was still smiling, she saw no humor in his face.

"What are you doing Nola?" he asked, tiredly. "Did you and your band of *Merry Men* really think that you could take over my ship? With *this*?" He thrust the syringe in her face, only inches away. "Why would you destroy the only future we have by participating in a foolish attempt to return to the moon?"

At that moment, Nola heard moaning coming from one of the rooms in Rey's cabin. Rey noticed her eyes glance in that direction and smiled. "Oh yes. I almost forgot. Let me show you something." He walked toward the door to one of the smaller rooms in the cabin. As he neared it, the door slid open and Nola saw Melvin Durhart and Walt Thompson lying on the floor. Walt was completely still and Nola saw a puddle of blood pooling under his head. It was Melvin who had moaned. He was conscious, but his face was completely swollen. She dropped her head and closed her eyes as she realized that it was over. Not just the coup, but any chance at a real life. If she lived through this, Burt would be taken from her and she would be forced into a life of concubinage at the edge of space. She whispered his name forlornly, unaware that she actually muttered it aloud. Rey's voice in her ear sent a chill down her spine. "Ah yes, Doctor Burt Stone. What are we to do with Doctor Burt Stone?" She yanked her head up and at that moment, could have ripped the tongue out of Rey's foul mouth, but Dante still had a grip on her. Rey walked around her shaking his head, "I hope the good doctor has had his fill of your ginger minge, because when this is over, the only thing he'll have of you is a fading memory." A sharp pain flared in her neck and she realized that Rey had injected her with the syringe. With her resolve now in tatters, she welcomed the slowly advancing darkness and as the world around her faded into the abyss, she could hear raucous laughter following closely behind her.

DAY 33

BETRAYAL

1

"Burt! They know! They KNOW!" yelled Nola. She felt hands holding her. Dante's hands! "Let go of me you bastard! I'll kill you! I'll KILL you!" She thrashed mightily, clawing and scratching at anything that touched her.

"Nola! Nola! Stop fighting! You're safe in the Med-Lab. It's me...Burt!" Slow realization dawned on her and she shakily put her arms down. "I can't see! Why can't I see?" She reached up to her face and head and could feel bandages wrapped around her forehead and eyes. "Burt, help me. Please take this off so I can see you."

Burt and Elsa slowly unwound the bandages covering Nola's head. When they got to her eyes, he told her to close them and to open them slowly once the bandages were off. "That son of a bitch Rey allowed you to drop to the floor after he injected you," Burt said through gritted teeth. "You cut your forehead and we covered your eyes to prevent any blood from seeping into your eyes."

When they were done, he placed a smaller bandage over the cut on her forehead. "I think that'll do," he said. "You can open your eyes now."

Nola slowly opened her eyes and despite the blurriness, she could make out the concern on Burt's face, not to mention the fresh bruises. "Oh Burt!" she cried and reached out to him. They held each other briefly and when they disengaged, Nola looked around the Med-Lab. It looked like a trauma ward. All of the beds were filled and there were bloody rags piled up in one of the corners. "Burt, what *happened?* How long was I out? Was it that bad out there?" She was beginning to shake.

Burt sat on the edge of the bed, while Elsa went to check on Melvin several beds over. "It's after 7am honey. You've been out for damn near 18 hours! Most of it was the injection, but the concussion you received when you fell didn't help." He looked down at his hands. "I thought I was going to lose you." Nola grabbed his hands and squeezed them. He looked back at her and his eyes were fuming. "We were betrayed Nola," he said, barely able to keep the anger out of his voice. "It was Finch," he spat out. "Fucking

Finch! And do you know *why* he did it? He betrayed us all because Soren told him he would be allowed to marry Kelly." He rubbed his eyes furiously.

Nola felt deep despair. She wondered how Kelly was taking this. She knew the girl well enough to know that she would never have allowed Anton to make that deal. She cursed him for his incredible stupidity and selfishness and prayed that Kelly didn't pay the price for his naïve and darkly dangerous pact with Soren. He was a vile man and Anton Finch would bitterly come to know the depths of his mistake.

2

Doc turned to look toward the front entrance to Med-Lab and could see two guards standing there in the hallway talking and looking bored. He turned back to Nola and grabbed her hand, "I didn't suspect anything until I saw Finch practically sprinting from Soren's cabin. By then, I assumed you were already in Rey's cabin, but there was nothing I could do at that point. Several of Rey's guards had arrived and blocked the hallway leading to Rey's cabin. I...I wanted to warn you. I wanted to stop you, but it was too late."

"I saw you Burt, before I went to see Rey," Nola said. "You were talking to someone and your back was to me."

"I'm sorry for what happened to you Nola," Burt said, his voice breaking. "I did the only thing left for me to do; I ran to engineering. I had this feeling that Jaime and Liz would need me, especially if Soren and maybe Rey, already knew what was going on.

"Even after seeing Finch running from Soren's cabin, I had the wild hope that maybe he and Chin would at least be able to lock themselves in the cockpit. I think we could have delayed the slingshot maneuver toward Jupiter if Finch was on our side, communicating directly with Jaime. Instead, according to Eddie Chin, Finch brought two guards with him to the cockpit and ordered them to make sure Eddie didn't try anything to thwart the maneuver. Rey had arrived soon after and that put the nail in the coffin of our insurrection. Unfortunately for us, Finch really bought into Soren's bullshit, hook, line and sinker." He glanced at the guards again and saw Jaime and Liz approach the front entrance. He could hear muffled yelling as Jaime confronted the guards.

Nola could see the anguish and stress on Burt's face. She could see that he was also wracked with guilt. She understood that if Finch and Chin were successful in securing the bridge and if Jaime was able to disengage two of the engine nodes, they would have been able to change their trajectory and return to the moon. But their arrival at the moon base would have been bittersweet. There would have been a brutal and bloody civil war on the ship and she would have been stranded in Rey's cabin, *no man's land*, for all intents and purposes. What Burt might not allow his mind to accept, she understood bitterly; as Rey's "captive", she might have been used as a prisoner of war, but more likely than not, Soren would have ordered her put to death.

Doc paced around the room, reliving the last 18 hours in his head. "I got off the turbo-lift right before engineering and kept to the shadows as I made my way there. It was dark as hell and I could hear yelling and screaming the closer I got." He grabbed a handkerchief out of his pocket and wiped his dripping brow. "What I was really afraid of was getting there too late. The thought of losing you *and* Jaime and Liz would have been too much." He had walked back over to Nola's bed and grabbed her hand. She squeezed it tightly.

"Everyone seemed to be fighting down there. I saw Jaime fighting off two of Rey's guards, while Liz worked at one of the consoles. I think she was trying to place the nodes offline remotely. I ran toward them screaming, intending to throw all of my weight onto the nearest guard fighting Jaime. We held them off for what seemed like hours, but then we felt the unmistakable pull of gravity from the slingshot maneuver, despite the ship-wide damping field and realized that we had lost. I was hit from behind and passed out. When I came to, the guards were in control and began marching us out of engineering. As they were leading us out, an overloaded circuit board or breaker popped, sounding like an actual gun, and one of Rey's idiot guards whirled and fired his laser toward the sound and directly into one of the engine node casings. Uncannily, the laser penetrated the engine node in just the right spot, causing it to overheat. There was a chain reaction and the entire engine node housing unit exploded. We barely got out before the engineering section emergency bulkhead doors slammed down. The resulting explosion not only ruptured our fuel pods, but damaged the ship's reaction control housing system and flooded poisonous nitrogen tetroxide throughout the lower decks. The bottom engineering decks, the biosphere and even the food reclamation center are completely contaminated and we have no control of the ship. We're totally cut off from the lower decks and Soren is so paranoid, he won't even attempt to send a maintenance team to engineering to assess and possibly fix the damage. Now, we're headed directly for Jupiter orbit and we don't have functioning engine nodes to slow the ship down, let alone maneuver it."

Nola could only stare at him, her mind racing. She wasn't part of the flight team, but she knew this ship and she knew the *Cassiopeia's* large shuttle was directly below the bottom of the engineering deck. The idea was that the *Cassiopeia* would orbit Europa and the shuttle would be the primary mode of transferring people and supplies from the ship to the surface. If the shuttle was damaged, she knew that the *Cassiopeia* would be capable of landing, but it would never take off again. Whether the shuttle was damaged or not was a moot point because if they couldn't come to a stationary orbit or even slow their speed down, they would never be able to deploy the shuttle safely and the attempt would probably destroy the shuttle and its entire crew.

At that moment, Jaime and Liz came into Med-Lab and smiled at Nola. "Thank God you're okay," Liz said as she bent down to hug Nola. Liz had a few bruises and scratches on her face and Jaime's left arm was in a sling. "What about you guys?" Nola asked. "How are you doing?"

"As good as can be expected," Jaime stated gruffly. He looked back at the two guards standing at the entrance of Med-Lab. "These two idiots think we're still planning a takeover of the ship. It hasn't soaked into their Neanderthal brains yet that there's nothing we can do now. We're going to Europa whether we want to or not." He sighed heavily and continued on, "We've had another meeting with Soren, Rey, and Finch about our current situation. I tried to convince Soren to let me take a team into engineering to accurately assess the damages, but he's completely against it." He rubbed his eyes tiredly. "I won't sugar-coat it guys, but we're in dire straits here. We're still at least six weeks from Europa and we're venting tons of fuel by the hour, the lower decks are completely unusable, our food stores in the reclamation center are contaminated and there's a good chance the shuttle has been damaged." Nola moaned when she heard the last part. It seemed everything was stacked against their survival. Doc let out an exasperated sigh, "So what can we do Jaime? What options do we have, other than a slow death?"

Jaime looked around at the small group, seeming to gauge each person's reaction. "I think our only option is to make a trip to the Cargo Cabin. There are items there that will allow us to repair the shuttle and most importantly, retrieve enough food to last the trip. Right now, the food we stored in the Cargo Hold will only last us about 2-3 weeks, if we're lucky. Also, there are explosive devices out there." They all stared at him uncomprehendingly. "Those explosive devices were designed to be used in potential mining operations on Europa, but we may need them to somehow set off an explosion in the opposite direction of our travel."

"Ahh, right," Doc said, his eyes lighting up in understanding. "I've read about this. It's the principle of *action-reaction*, right? I assume by setting off this explosion in our direction of travel, it should slow us down, right?"

"Theoretically, yes," Jaime answered, "but if we wait too long, then we may not have enough fuel to course-correct ourselves after the explosion slows us down. It does us no good to slow down, only to be so far off course, that instead of zooming past Jupiter, we simply drift past the giant slowly, teasingly, unable to do anything but stare at the Great Red Spot from a million miles away."

Nola looked at Jaime with concern growing in her eyes, "Could there be a chain reaction that destroys the ship or compromises it even further?"

"That's a good point Nola," Jaime stated. "The only way around that is for there to be multiple *timed* explosions, with each explosion having independent explosive yields. We detonate one explosive grouping, calculate our resulting speed, course-correct and then detonate another grouping. Rinse and repeat. The trick is not to overdo it or we could find ourselves a dead stick in space, with barely *any* forward momentum. *That would be bad.*"

Nola withdrew into herself. *That would be bad.* Jaime's words wrapped around her mind like an anchor, pulling her thoughts down into dark despair. *That would be bad.* She felt she knew just how bad things might get if they found themselves almost motionless, just out of reach of Jupiter. Too far to reach Europa and too close to ignore it. Soren's little fiefdom would collapse in on itself. His guards would revolt. Individual groups would become nation-states, fighting over diminishing resources. Even the "good guys" would resort to some level of brutality, but probably not as quickly as Soren and his people. She couldn't gauge how long life on the ship would continue like that, but she knew the last remaining survivors would be those people who sacrificed the last of their humanity in order to live...at all costs. She shuddered violently and rolled on her side, lamenting the end of humankind.

DAY 40

ANTON AND KELLY

1

"I'd like to thank everyone for joining us on this wonderful occasion," Soren said, with a half-smile on his face. Things were finally getting back to normal. He felt they had recovered as best they could after the attempted takeover of the ship. He had to implement new security procedures and severely restricted movement about the ship, but overall, things were getting back on track. Rey suggested that he start using food as a way of controlling them, so they stored all remaining food in the Cargo Hold with only limited access. Apart from a few isolated incidents, most people accepted this new norm. The moronic guard who singlehandedly handicapped their journey was punished appropriately. Soren glanced over at him standing at the rear of the Commons. The man quickly averted his eyes, absently rubbing at the remaining stumps of his right-hand fingers. Soren looked back at everyone seated in the Commons and sighed. They looked dejected, desperate and scared.

"You all look so *pitiful*," Soren said. "This is a happy occasion! That nasty coup business is behind us and we're well on our way to Europa. If we can just learn to live together peacefully for the next five weeks, then I think we'll be okay."

Nola glanced around the Commons. The atmosphere was so thick, you could cut it with a knife. After their failed coup attempt, the fake veneer of being fellow colonists who survived the destruction of the Earth was ripped from their eyes. Soren no longer tried to pretend that they were all one family, looking for a home at the furthest reaches of space. They were now fully living in an autocratic society. A dictatorial *Robinson Crusoe* adventure. *Everything* was controlled. Food was strictly rationed. Movement severely limited. The Commons was as far forward that anyone was allowed to go. Only a handful of turbo lifts remained operational, which basically restricted everyone to just a handful of levels. Med-Lab visits required authorization and the cockpit was off limits to all non-flight personnel. She felt as if she were living in North Korea. Movement at the front of the Commons caught her eye. She saw Anton and Kelly making their way to the main platform in the Commons. She hadn't seen much of Kelly since they tried to take over the ship. She tended to stay in her quarters most times, now that the biosphere was defunct. Kelly and Anton stood up front, holding hands, both looking extremely uncomfortable. Finch looked absolutely terrified.

2

Finch stood stiffly at the front of the Commons. Even though he was holding Kelly's hand, he couldn't feel it. He felt as if he were wearing a sensory deprivation suit that cut off all sensation. They had been living under Soren's rules for so long, he felt he were doing something very wrong, by holding Kelly's hand in public. He was shocked when Rey told him to hold her hand the entire time.

He looked out at his *former* friends and could see the hate and anger in their eyes. They knew that he was to blame for the failure of their take-over attempt. His overwhelming desire to be with Kelly was his Achilles' heel and the ultimate downfall of Burt and Jaime and Nola's coup. He heard Kelly gasp and realized that he had been gripping her hand like a vise. He looked at her with a pained smiled and eased up on her hand. He almost screamed when he felt a hand on his shoulder. It was Soren.

"So, as you all know," Soren said seriously, speaking to everyone in the Commons, "Anton Finch was instrumental in executing our slingshot maneuver. If it hadn't been for his astute awareness concerning the safety of the ship and all of us, in addition to his keen navigational skills, who knows how things would have turned out." He glanced around the room, his eyes darkening as they fell on Doc and Nola and Jaime. "Because of his...er, heroism *and* loyalty, I am allowing him to marry Ms. Kelly Masterston."

Nola saw Burt's head snap up at this announcement. Jaime and Liz also stared in open-mouthed surprise. Nola was more surprised at everyone's *reactions*, than to the news itself. They all knew that Finch was hopelessly in love with Kelly and would do anything to be with her, even it if meant betraying the rest of them. She guessed that what really surprised everyone was the fact that Soren was actually going through with it. Soren lied about everything else, why not this? She saw Rey moving toward the center of the Commons with his hands raised. "Quiet everyone, the ceremony is about to begin".

The rest of the ceremony consisted of a rambling diatribe where Soren explained how everyone will be valued contributors on the new world. He shared his vision of how their new world will be structured and the importance of establishing a society focused on rebuilding the human population. "We are the new Adams and Eves," he declared. "And every man and woman here will do his or her part". It was sickening. If by some miracle they made it to Europa, she was confident that this little intergalactic shit-show would tear itself apart in less than a year.

She groaned inwardly as Soren blathered on, reciting a hodgepodge of pseudo-religious statements that he probably felt was secular enough to have marrying power. Burt glanced at her, silently groaning as well. "So, ladies and gentlemen," Soren concluded, "as Commander of the *Cassiopeia*, it gives me great pleasure to introduce to you our first married couple, Mr. and Mrs. Anton and Kelly Finch. You may kiss your bride". There was sporadic clapping in the Commons, but Anton and Kelly didn't seem to mind. They were completely lost in one another. They kissed passionately, desperately. Soren wore a furtive, deadly look on his face as he watched the two young people grasping at each other. Eventually, their passion subsided to the point where Soren could continue speaking. Anton and Kelly both beamed out at the others in the Commons. All thoughts of the coup and Anton's role in it, subsided to a distant, forgettable memory. Nola looked at Kelly. She wanted to be happy for her, but some part of her refused to believe that the murdering bastard who just married them didn't have some deeper, uglier plan behind this kabuki theater.

"Congratulations Anton and Kelly! You two make a wonderful couple!" Soren shouted out. As Nola listened to him, she was surprised at how normal he sounded. She almost allowed herself to feel that maybe there was no hidden agenda here. That maybe things *could* be different on Europa. That maybe Soren could make this work for *everyone*. For one insane, dreamy moment, she saw herself with Burt and only Burt –not passed on to him after being seeded by Soren's corrupt sperm. The visions she conjured up were heavenly. They were...she started and almost slapped herself. This was *Soren* and she knew him for the monster and murderer that he was. There would be no concessions in Soren's world. Everything he did, he did for his own good. She watched him saunter up to Anton and give him a fatherly hug. Anton was unsure how to respond at first and then returned the hug enthusiastically. Soren turned to Kelly and kissed her on each cheek. It gave Nola the chills to see it.

Soren turned back to everyone in the Commons, his face more serious...and more deadly. "Effective immediately, Anton will become part of my senior flight team and he and Kelly will be moving into the senior flight staff cabins." Anton gushed and pulled Kelly close to him. He looked out at the people in the Commons proudly, almost to the point of arrogance. Gone was the immense look of terror squirming in his eyes when he joined Kelly at the front of the Commons. He and Kelly had successfully climbed the *Cassiopeia* ladder and he would now be able to demand the respect he deserved. He looked toward Burt, Nola, Jaime and Liz smugly. Soren continued, "He will be afforded the same level of respect that all of my senior flight staff have." Nola glanced at Finch again and could almost see his chest puff out in self-importance. It was disgusting.

Soren looked around serenely, almost reverently. "Some of you may not know this, but I'm a big fan of medieval history." Nola was able to catch Doc's eyes. She saw him shrug his shoulders, his eyebrows furrowing in concern. "The Renaissance Period and the Age of Discovery were fascinating! Life seemed difficult, but it was clean, not complicated. The nobles and highborn overlords were very important figures during that time. They were responsible for vast numbers of peasants under their rule and encouraged land development and other agricultural necessities." He chuckled lightly, "We've come a long way since those days and no one here is a peasant or vassal, but you have to admire the beauty of that system." He licked his lips and looked over at Anton and Kelly, still standing at the head of the Commons. Nola found herself transfixed by this non-sequitur. What in God's name was Soren getting at with this feudal society discourse? He was certainly burying the lede if there was more to this droning story. There were no illusions that life on Europa would be fair. They all knew, or at least suspected, that once they arrived, Soren would somehow hold them hostage to the needed shelter and supplies. But this would only be temporary. Once they left the confines of the ship, Soren, Rey and all those who support him would be brutally overthrown. The seeds they were sowing now would be reaped in a bloody and revenge-fueled harvest.

"What I'm trying to say people," Soren continued, "is that as your leader...your *liege lord*, if you will, is that there are certain *rights* that I'm entitled to." He moved closer to Anton and Kelly. Nola could see the first signs of concern break out on Anton's face, even though he probably didn't fully understand why he should be concerned. "Historians refute the veracity of what I'm about to tell you, however, I've done lots of research on the matter and I believe it to be true. During those medieval times, feudal lords had many rights over their subordinates and often exercised what was called *jus primae noctis* or *'right of the first night'*."

Only silence greeted this statement. Nola frantically rifled through the memories of her grade-school education trying to remember anything of medieval Europe and its barbaric customs. She cross-referenced her formal education with documentaries and old movies and just as she was making the connection, Soren began again. "In medieval Europe, feudal lords had the exclusive right to have sexual intercourse with the women under his domain on their wedding nights." Nola looked at Anton and Kelly and now saw the fear and disgust in their faces. Kelly had told her many times that they were both virgins and were saving themselves for each other. In another world perhaps, but not here. Not in Soren's world. Nola felt dizzy and her heart hurt for Kelly. Whatever touching intimacies Kelly and Anton dreamed they would share with one another on their wedding night, would be shattered after one torturous and shameful tryst with Soren. Whatever Kelly was saving for Anton would be soiled, dirtied and contaminated by Soren's toxic and poisonous touch.

Anton found his voice and with tremendous effort, turned to Soren. "Co...Commander, Kelly is now my wife and, I, uh...we were keeping ourselves pure for one another." He swallowed hard and continued weakly, "I, uh...*we* humbly implore you to grant us this one wish. Please sir, commander..." His voice trailed off. Soren's face remained hard as flint as Anton spoke to him. He turned to face him, while Rey and a handful of guards, walked up behind Anton. "Mr. Finch, you are the *only* person on the ship who is being allowed to marry before we get to Europa. You shared vital information with us and I'm repaying that by allowing you to get married. But it changes *nothing* in the big scheme of things." He glanced at Kelly. The tears streaming down her face had turned what little makeup she was wearing, into a nightmarish shroud. "You will be confined to my quarters for the next seven days. Any attempt at trying to leave my quarters will not only extend your stay, but result in punishment...for both of you." He looked coldly at Anton, "After seven days, *you* will report to my cabin when Kelly is due to be released. You will exchange places with her and be confined to my cabin for the subsequent seven days." He smiled dirtily and added, "You see Mr. Finch, in my world, *jus primae noctis* applies to you too". Anton's face fell and Nola could see his legs buckle. Soren laughed heartily and grabbed Kelly by the arm. "Rey, take Finch to his new cabin and make sure he stays there." He strode off toward his cabin with Kelly in tow. She stumbled behind him, too weak to say anything. All she could do was turn her head to look at Anton, fear and loathing in her eyes. Nola turned to Burt, a tear coursing down her cheek. "Burt," was all she could say. She was so offended by this mockery and Soren's deception that she could barely speak. Burt grabbed her hand and held it tightly, looking at the departing Finch family. Nola looked up just as they were rounding the entrance to Soren's cabin. She thought sadly that Finch's betrayal not only forced his newlywed bride to have extramarital sex with a monster, but landed him in a position to be abused as well. She hated being right about Soren's evil and she was certain that Anton now knew the depths of

Soren's darkness. Once this Greek tragedy played itself out, God only knew what the state of Finch's mind would be like.

DAY 55

TO THE CARGO CABIN!

1

"This is the eighth case of radiation poisoning that I've treated this week!" Doc exclaimed as one of Rey's guards exited Med-Lab. He threw his hands up in the air, "I'm running out of radiation treatment tablets and when that happens, we'll all be in trouble."

Nola had arrived at Med-Lab only minutes before to go through an inventory check of Doc's supplies. Their progress had been interrupted when Rey's guard came in complaining of nausea, vomiting and an acute case of diarrhea. Burt headed over to where she sat and flopped down in his desk chair. He reached out and briefly squeezed her hand. The Med-Lab was relatively quiet this day. A lot of people were getting sick and it appeared to be radiation poisoning. Rey had allowed Jaime and several others to scope out the areas where the radiation was strongest. Those areas were sealed, yet people were still getting sick.

"We're running out of more than just medical supplies, Burt," Nola said. "We're running out of food. They've been rationing the food, but the numbers don't work for us. Even with the strictest rationing scheme in place, we'll run out of food weeks before we get to Europa, provided we're still *on course* for Europa."

Doc's head snapped up from the report he was scanning. "What do you mean *still on course*? Is Finch still working on the bridge?"

Nola sighed and looked out the office window to the dark hallways past the Med-Lab entrance. "Yes, Finch is working, but he is basically escorted to the bridge, eats at the bridge, shits at the bridge and then is escorted back to Soren's cabin." She shuddered as she remembered Finch's hunched and seemingly broken form. "He's different Burt. Soren has broken whatever spirit he had in him."

"Fuck him," said Burt. "He made his own bed, now let him sleep in it, literally."

"I know, I know," Nola agreed, "but I love Kelly dearly and I know she *used* to love Anton, but now...I don't know. The one time I had a moment to chat with her she seemed distant and cold. I tried to bring up Anton to let her know that he still loves her and that they would be together soon, but all she could muster for me was an empty and forlorn smile." She took a deep breath and said, "It's too soon to know if she's pregnant or not, but she *thinks* she is."

Doc rubbed his eyes wearily. "I know honey, it's all fucked up. I mean *all* fucked up. Here we are, the last of human civilization and we're damn near starting out worse than the fucking cavemen. We're running out of medical supplies, food resources and half of the damn ship is off limits to us because of fucking radiation leaks!"

Nola said, "Now I'm hearing that the ship's directional sensors are failing, so we don't even know how far away we are from the Jupiter system. Jaime believes we're about 3-4 weeks away, but it's only an estimation. I've been up to the observatory and I can see that we're getting closer to Jupiter because it's much brighter in space, but I don't have a clue about our heading. Also, Jaime said we're still hemorrhaging tons of fuel and may not have enough for the retropropulsion rockets to slow the ship down when the time comes."

At that moment, Dante rushed into Med-Lab. "The Commander is calling an emergency meeting...*now!*"

2

Doc grimaced as he watched the rest of the crew shuffle into the Commons. They moved slowly and lethargically through the doors leading into the Commons. Whether it was from hunger, lack of sleep or from being overworked, Doc wasn't sure; but one thing he *did* know was that they couldn't go on like this. Soren had started rationing food immediately after the Reclamation Center was compromised, but instead of rationing it evenly for everyone, he allowed his guards to have more than their fair share. Of course, they took advantage of this favoritism and soon they were in dire straits again.

He saw Nola come in and let his gaze slide easily from her face to one of the guards ushering folks in. It wouldn't do either of them any good to let Rey see them exchanging glances. He told her to give him a head-start from Med-Lab to remove any suspicions Rey might have and almost as if the *thought* of Rey had the power to conjure him up, he walked in from the head entrance of the Commons and positioned himself in front of the makeshift podium.

More folks shuffled in. Doc saw Jaime and one of his engineers walk in talking animatedly. A few minutes after that, Liz Carter walked in with several other engineers. He smiled to himself; it was apparent that Jaime and Liz were also being careful not to advertise their relationship or antagonize Soren or Rey any more than they had to. Eventually, all of the attendees found their seats and after prodding from the guards, quieted down to a low murmur. Doc heard a noise at the front and when he turned around, Soren was standing there next to Rey. He was reviewing some documents that Rey had produced for him. Finch was there too. Burt was shocked when he saw the young man. Nola was right; he looked like a poor replica of himself even though he had been with Soren for just several days. His left eye was bruised and he had a nasty scar on the side of his neck that still looked fresh and angry. Despite his feelings for Finch, he couldn't help but feel sorry for him. He looked around for Kelly and found her on the far side of the Commons. Soren had long ago given up on having assigned seats, so she was as far away from the front as possible. She stared vacantly out of one of the small viewport windows closest to her, completely oblivious to everything and everyone around her. He looked back up toward Finch and could see the pain in his eyes. He was desperately trying to get her attention, but he might as well have been invisible, as far as she was concerned. Once the Commons filled up, Soren looked out at the group and then spoke up.

"As you all know," he began, "we've attempted to ration our remaining stores to coincide with our arrival on Europa." He looked around at the group until his eyes fell on Doc. They seemed to smolder. "The direct consequences of your actions several weeks ago, caused the destruction of our Reclamation Center, not only reducing our food stores by almost two-thirds, but the explosion altered our course and we are rapidly running out of fuel. This, of course, affects our ability to slow down to a stable orbit around the planet. We've calculated that at this rate of fuel loss we'll arrive within Jupiter's planetary system with just enough fuel to fire our retropropulsion rockets to slow down enough to orbit Europa."

He pulled his eyes away from Doc and spoke to the group again. "Most of you already knew this. What you don't know is that without the Reclamation Center, we'll run out of food weeks before we even reach Jupiter's orbit." He paused to allow this new revelation to sink in. He was not disappointed. The Commons erupted in a combination of yelling, crying and finger-pointing. As Doc had expected, the finger-pointers included the folks who rejected the idea of taking over the ship. As far as he knew, none of them blew the whistle on him and his group, but they were extremely resistant to the idea of taking over the ship. Doc felt it was more fear and capitulation than principle which kept them on the sidelines.

Rey looked from side to side at the rambunctious crowd with a look of contempt. If it was left up to him, he'd have the majority of them locked up and fed just enough food to keep them in a perpetually weakened state. Then they would be certain to have enough food by the time they arrived at Europa. If not, there were other ways to survive. To not starve.

Soren jabbed Rey in the side, who started. "Shut them up for God's sake man! I'm not done here." A momentarily stunned Rey motioned to his guards, who went up and down the aisle shutting people up. After the first few shoves and punches were doled out, the rest of the Commons quieted down quickly. Soren looked around again. He was practically preening. "So, as you can see, we need more food and other much-needed supplies and there is only one place on the ship where we have those items – the *Cargo Cabin*!

3

Whereas the news that they were running out of food and might possibly starve before making it to Europa brought relative mayhem to the Commons, the news about the food being in the Cargo Cabin elicited quite the opposite reaction – total silence. Even Doc was at a loss for words, although he never would have uttered them aloud had he had something to say.

The Cargo Cabin! Of course! Doc thought. Jaime had mentioned this ages ago, but at the time, it was barely a blip on their radar. Not really an option at the time, but it was more than a blip now. That would be where their Europa supplies would be. Everything from food, water, seeds, shelter, limited transportation and even weapons. It contained everything a new medium-size colony of 2,000 people would need. They had far less numbers, so the supplies would definitely go further, but that wasn't the problem here, was it? Someone – or maybe several "*someones*" would have to actually do a spacewalk to the Cargo Cabin to get the supplies they needed. He thought back to his memory of the huge Cargo Cabin when they were on the moon. There were two entry points on the Cargo Cabin, one at the main entrance and one at the rear. The Cabin was roughly 40 yards long on each side, with a slight cylindrical shape. This aerodynamic shape theoretically aided in its deployment, but that functionality had never been put to the test in a real deployment situation. Next to the front entrance of the Cargo Cabin, there was a massive drawbridge-type door that lowered to the ground, allowing easy on and off-loading. The inside of the Cabin looked more like a small three-level warehouse with individual compartments that contained their supplies, by type and size.

During the early months on the moon, Doc had the opportunity to go inside the Cargo Cabin and was amazed at its size and functionality. He was astonished to find that once inside, he could actually walk the entire perimeter of the Cabin. Each category of supplies was a self-contained unit, so he was able to walk down aisles and corridors of colony-sustaining supplies, nestled in their respective enclosures. Turn left at the first aisle and see the multifunctional rover austerely strapped to the floor with arm-thick ropes and chains. Turn again and he found himself standing next to multi-person shelters. It was fascinating. It even contained space heaters and oxygen scrubbers to provide oxygen in the event work needed to happen inside the Cabin while in space.

He was so caught up in this thought that he hadn't realized that the silence didn't last long. The Commons had again erupted into a hall of confusion. But even through all this, one thought cut clearly through Doc's mind; this operation would require a spacewalk to the Cabin. They had the equipment to make it work, but to Doc's recollection, there was no one aboard, save maybe Rey (and that was a *big* maybe), who was qualified to perform a spacewalk. The only two individuals who were qualified to do spacewalks, as far as he knew, was Tess and Henry Webber and they were stranded on the moon, some millions of miles behind them. He understood intuitively that no one person, or even two, could do this work alone, especially if they planned to bring back enough supplies for the remainder of the trip. No, they would need several people to make the dangerous trek, regardless of experience. He looked around the Commons, to see if there were any folks standing up, ready to volunteer, when he realized that Soren was staring directly at him. He looked away quickly, but the sinking sensation in his stomach told him what he already knew, before Soren even voiced it.

Rey stepped forward and said, "Melvin Durhart, Liz Carter, Anton Finch and Walt Thompson will be our intrepid spacewalkers. The rest of y..." Soren cut him off in mid-sentence. "Rey, I've made a couple of slight adjustments to your list. We're going to replace Durhart and Thompson with Nola and our good doctor."

Rey's mouth dropped open, just as Doc sagged in his seat. He was gobsmacked that Soren would send the ship's only doctor on a relatively dangerous mission, not to mention the fact that Nola had no experience in space, other than being stranded on the moon. Clearly, Soren was exacting payback on the individuals involved in their coup. Missing from this group of "ringleaders" was Jaime Mendez. As the Chief Engineer, he was apparently not as expendable as the rest of them, so Soren went for the next best option – Liz Carter.

Rey's face contorted with rage. He opened his mouth to say something, then shut it immediately. A moment later, after he seemingly calmed himself down, he glanced from Soren to Nola and then back again. Soren stared back defiantly, almost daring him to contradict him. Doc stared at this silent standoff and realized that the two men detested one another. It bewildered him how sycophantic Rey was in his relationship to Soren, but he had always known that Rey would do anything for Nola. Doc could almost sense the heat of rage baking off Rey, but when he finally responded, all he could muster was a strangled, "I'll get them prepped."

4

"What about these?" Finch asked, pointing to one of the thick cables tightly wound around a retracting wheel in the cargo area. "Rey said to bring up the dark-colored cables," he added. Doc glanced at where Finch was pointing and nodded. Rey had sent them both to the Cargo Hold to inspect the cables, ropes and tethers they would need for the space walk to the Cargo Container. The first batch of cables they came across were tangled, rusty and badly damaged. Doc wasn't surprised that these maintenance items were overlooked though. During Soren and Rey's rush to leave the moon, their only concern at the time was getting the ship flight-ready and leaving as quickly as they could – without Tess and the others finding out.

"I believe those will work also Finch, but you need to have Rey inspect them. Sometimes the cable connectors become loose or damaged. If you don't know what you're looking at, have Liz look at them too."

Finch muttered under his breath, but apparently Doc didn't hear him – he was still collecting the CO_2 Scrubbers and Oxygen Generators for the air tanks. Finch was infuriated with Soren and Rey and damn near the entire crew. When he was finally released from Soren's cabin, he avoided the others on the ship as best he could. He was immensely embarrassed and found it difficult to maintain direct eye contact with others. He thought that Kelly and he would have each other to cling to, but she had withdrawn into herself. Their conversations were simple and perfunctory. Another wave of anger washed over him. He and Kelly hadn't even consummated their marriage! As far as he could tell, Kelly no longer envisioned their first sexual encounter as magical, but as something dirty. Something that evil men use to control and destroy others. Since he was a man, he was lumped into the same category as them – an evil man. One of the first things she said to him when he returned to their quarters and tried to be intimate with her was, "You've been with Soren. He's dirty and evil. Don't touch me." Not long after that, she moved in with Nola.

He knew that Nola was like a big sister to Kelly, despite the fact that they uncannily look like they could be real siblings. Whenever he would try to talk to Nola about Kelly, she would tell him that Kelly needed more time. That he shouldn't pressure her. Once, he showed up unannounced and tried to force his way into Nola's cabin screaming, "I just want to see *my wife!* Kelly? *Kelly!*" Nola pushed him out of the doorway, but he grabbed her arm as he fell back causing her to tumble on top of him. They struggled together on the floor until Nola was able to ram her knee into his crotch. He immediately released her and grabbed onto his privates, moaning pitifully. "I just wanna see my wife..." he sobbed. Nola looked down at him and yelled, "She's not ready to see you, Anton!" She abruptly turned and went back inside her cabin.

Doc paid him a visit later that day and threatened to knock out all of his teeth if he bothered Nola or Kelly again. He backed off, but he was seething underneath. He found he was angry all the time at everyone. The only thing that kept his ire in check regarding his fellow shipmates, was the fact that they were all in this together. But were they *all* in this together? He didn't think so. He saw himself as a valuable member of Soren's flight crew and when he helped stop the potentially ship-damaging coup, he just *knew* that things would be much better for him. He used to envision Kelly and himself actually starting up a family on Europa. Their lives would have existed outside the Soren bubble of indentured servitude. But that dream was no more. It was replaced by a dirty cloud of vengeful retribution. He unwound the cables angrily, his mind racing for options, *any* options, to deal with his dire and somewhat embarrassing situation.

"What gives him the fucking right to sleep with my wife, Doc? My wife? *My* wife!" Finch had stopped unwinding the cables and was breathing hard in Doc's direction. Before Doc had a chance to respond, his anger forced out another outburst of indignation. "And then he wants to fuck *me* too? What kind of sick shit is that, Doc? I might as well have been in Harlan Penitentiary! How can we follow a man like that? How can we *blindly* follow someone as dangerous and indecent as Soren is?"

Doc looked over at Finch coldly. He could see that Finch was having some serious internal turmoil, but he had no sympathy for him. He wouldn't have cared if Soren had made Finch his fucking concubine for the duration of the trip to Europa. If it hadn't been for Finch, their coup might have been successful and right now, they would have been on their way back to the moon to pick up Tess and the others. Instead, Finch's selfishness condemned their stranded comrades to certain death and pushed them here on the ship, closer to an uncertain future with a madman at the helm. "I see you're still fuming about your time in Soren's cabin, but maybe you should have thought about that before becoming his lackey," Doc said, daring Finch to say something in defense of his abhorrent behavior.

Finch looked visibly shaken, but held his tongue. After a minute, he said, "I know Doc. I fucked up. I *really* fucked up." After a second of contemplation, he added, "You know, that Rey is a sneaky, crazy son of a bitch. He was listening in when Soren questioned me about what was happening in the ship. He's the one who actually carries out Soren's dirty work. And he's always talking to his cronies about how the women will be divvied up once we get to Europa." He looked around, afraid that he would see Rey standing in the entrance to the cargo area. "He needs to be taught a lesson," he said darkly, barely above a whisper. He glanced at Doc, uncertain how to proceed. "He, uh, has his sights set on Nola, Doc and he's not too keen on you and her spending so much time together."

Doc was somewhat taken aback. He thought Nola and he were being very careful, but apparently not careful enough. He knew that their behavior was just as dangerous as Larry and Allison's, but their almost desperate need for one another seemed to outweigh any possible dangers. When he really thought about it, he understood that living in this despotic and ever-darkening world was driving him, Nola and damn near everyone on the ship to seek out comfort and solace wherever they could find it. He chuckled dryly to himself and mused that by the time they get to Europa, it would only be Soren, Rey and a handful of select crewmembers. Trailing behind the *Cassiopeia* would be a human string of abused and frozen bodies, ejected one by one through the airlock because of forbidden relations. He noticed Finch looking at him curiously. "Thanks for that Finch. We'll have to be...a bit more discreet." He turned toward the container of CO2 scrubbers and headed toward the door. As he pushed the container toward the exit, he said over his shoulder, "Finish checking out those cables Finch and get them over to Rey before he comes looking." He headed out toward the airlock, without waiting for Finch to respond.

Finch snorted and rolled up the cables absentmindedly. As he inspected the cables, his mind drifted back to Rey again, thinking how simple everyone's lives would be if he were to have an accident. For that matter, maybe Soren needed to have an accident too.

THE SPACEWALK

Doc glanced at Nola and then at Finch, as they stood side by side in the starboard side airlock. Doc had never been claustrophobic, but despite the fact that the airlock could accommodate up to six fully-suited individuals, it felt distinctly crowded. This airlock was the exact same size as the port side airlock where the ill-fated lovers, Larry and Allison still lay frozen on the floor. The difference here is that this airlock was not part of a Cargo Hold. To access this airlock, one first entered into a large semi-circular room containing spacesuits on both sides of the wall. The spacesuits were upright, each inside its own cubbyhole, held there by a strong magnet at the back of the cubbyhole. During his first few days on the ship, Doc had gotten turned around trying to find engineering and ended up in this room. He felt his heart had skipped a beat when he entered the room in the dim light and thought he saw several suited individuals standing in front of him, staring him down in the darkness.

He felt Nola's gloved hand grab his as they stood shoulder to shoulder in the airlock. Rey stood directly in front of them with his back to them, silently working the airlock controls. He half-turned toward them and said, "As I said earlier, the ladders that lead to the top of the ship are separated every 100 feet. The ladder closest to the airlock is damaged, so we'll have to traverse about 100 feet along the side of the ship to get to the next ladder. This ladder leads up to the top of the ship closest to the front entrance of the Cargo Cabin. There is a tether bar that runs the entire length of the ship, so as soon as you reach the threshold of the door, hook your tether onto the bar. Once we're on top of the ship, activate your GRAV boots to setting two." They all nodded in unison, but Rey had already turned back to the airlock controls. They could hear him giving controls to the flight deck to disengage the airlock gravity.

Nola was in awe. One minute they were in the brightly lit confines of the airlock and the next, they were floating in total darkness – thousands upon thousands of stars in all directions. Once she was safely tethered to the tether bar, she craned her head around in a fruitless attempt to find Earth. She almost gave up looking when she spied a faint bluish, not entirely circular, point of light. Close by was a smaller bright light – the moon she presumed. The sight of it immediately dampened her initial excitement of being out in space. It reminded her of the others left behind. Of helplessness. Of death.

She turned her attention back to the others. They were all drifting silently ahead of her. Burt was directly in front of her and Finch was in front of him, right behind Liz. Rey moved ahead cautiously at the front, getting closer and closer to the ladder toward the rear of the ship. His voice crackled over the internal headset, "Okay, we're almost to the ladder. You'll have to unclasp your tether from the horizontal tether bar and hook it to the ladder's vertical side bar. Stay close to the ladder and move slowly. Our bodies are moving just as fast as the ship, but if you trip or bounce off the ship and you're untethered, you may find yourself too far from the ship to get back. Remember, the ship has dynamic forward momentum and once you're disconnected from the ship, your momentum becomes static. You'll be left behind."

Rey untethered himself from the horizontal tether bar on the side of the ship and reconnected it to the ladder's vertical side bar. He then slowly climbed the twenty-foot curving ladder to the top of the ship. Liz fell in line behind him, then Finch and then Doc. By the time Nola got on the ladder, she could no longer see Rey. She was concentrating so hard on her footing that she almost jumped when Rey's voice boomed into her ear. "How's it coming Nola?" he enquired. "We're all here at the top. Do you need any help?"

She looked up, but all she could see was star-filled space and the continuing curve of the ladder. For the third time, she pulled at her tether. Although the short tether forced her to stay close to the ladder, it quickly became a nuisance because she was constantly stopping to pull it up with her, slowing her progress. She continued up slowly, frustratingly, until the top of a helmet came into view. Doc and Rey were there to help her up. Finch and Liz had already moved toward the Cargo Cabin entrance.

"This damn tether is too short!" she spat into the small microphone set into her helmet as they pulled her up. "I can barely move."

"Let me see," Burt said to her. Burt examined her tether and said, "That fucking Finch was not paying attention and gave you a three-foot tether instead of the six-foot tether." Nola could hear him breathing angrily through his mouthpiece. "Maybe we can switch it..."

"I got it, Doc," Rey interrupted. "I'll trade her out for mine. You go ahead and join the others at the Cargo Cabin entrance."

As Rey started to undo his tether, Doc and Nola exchanged quick glances. They had not slid their sun visors down, so Nola could clearly see Burt's dark brown eyes. At that exact moment, Nola could almost see the anger and rage of the last few months here on the *Cassiopeia* as a dark, physical entity quivering just behind the irises of Burt's eyes. Sophia, the abandonment of Tess and the others, the failed coup, the death of Jana, his assistant – was manifesting itself into a cold-blooded act of murder. In her mind's eye, she could see Rey unclasping his tether from his belt and hooking it to hers, making her tether longer. In that split-second moment, he would be completely untethered from the ship and during that critical space of time, she saw Burt shove him off the ship. Probably not so much as a firm push – but it would be enough, despite the magnetic connection his GRAV boots gave him. She instinctively *knew* this, but she couldn't allow him to do it. Rey was hard to kill. A human cockroach, skittering through the spaceship looking for human food to defile. Rey would survive, somehow, and Burt would be tortured, mutilated and then shoved out of the nearest airlock in his birthday suit. Some part of her deep down understood that Rey's death was probably their best course of action because it would at least break up Rey and Soren's psychotic and dangerous pairing. Rey and Soren complemented one another's worst intentions and they were both crazy. If anyone needed to be killed, it was these two men. If the roles were reversed, Rey wouldn't hesitate to shove Burt into the abyss...and he would be laughing as he did it.

As Rey clasped his tether to her suit, anchoring her to the top of the ship. The only thing keeping him on the ship were his GRAV boots. She saw Burt wedge his feet under one of the many steel outcroppings on the top of the ship. He was already tethered to one of the many tether bars on top of the ship. And almost as if he were following a script Nola had written for him, he raised his hands to seal Rey's fate and commit him to the darkness. He would have done it had he not glanced once more at Nola. She was slowly shaking her head and practically pleading with her eyes. For a second, she was afraid that he didn't catch her meaning or that he *did*, but intended to do it anyway. To her relief, she saw frustrated understanding dawn on him and he visibly restrained himself from carrying out the deed. He turned toward the Cargo Cabin to join Finch and Liz. Nola imagined she could see him slumping angrily away in the spacesuit as he made his way toward the rear of the ship, pulling his tether along.

2

Finch, Liz and Doc had gained access to the Cargo Cabin by the time Nola and Rey got there. Once inside, Rey closed the door and made his way to the Cargo Cabin control panel, set into the wall next to the door. "The cabin has its own power source, but it'll take a minute or two for the lights and heat to come on," he said. "The oxygen generators will take another fifteen minutes after that to kick in."

While Rey fussed over the control panel, the rest of them wandered down the narrow walkways inside the cabin. They passed the section containing the mobile housing construction items. The idea was that each housing unit could be configured to house anywhere from two people to upwards of eight. He glanced angrily at Rey, still over at the control panel, remembering how they so easily abandoned Tess and the others. The Cargo Cabin contained enough resources to support upwards of two thousand people. Nola walked up beside him and touched his arm, almost as if she knew what he was thinking. She could sense that it took an incredible force of will for him not to shove Rey from the ship. She wished she could tell him that, but they were all on the same frequency and small talk was dangerous.

The lights were slowly illuminating the interior, bathing them and the cabin contents in an eerie yellow light. The interior lights weren't as bright as their helmet lights, but it covered a much larger area. As they continued down the walkway, they passed agricultural containers housing countless numbers of seedlings, atmospheric containers, artic preparation containers, space and environmental suits with CO_2 scrubbers, marine and oceanic containers, and countless others. They turned a corner at the backend of the Cargo Container and saw the container housing long-term food stores.

As Doc stared at the food stores container, he began to frown. "What's wrong Burt?" Nola asked, following his eyes.

Just then, Rey walked up and looked at the container. "What are you waiting for?" he said snidely. This container's not going to open itself."

Burt turned toward him with a look of tired impatience. "This container can't be opened here Rey. It's designed to be opened on the ground. Look." He pointed to the sides and top of the container. "There are no recessed panels or entrance ports – it's completely sealed. At least from the sides. There's probably an access port at the top, but these things are designed to be opened on the ground, with clearance on all sides."

"That's bullshit!" Rey shouted. "How do you know so much about this?" He started walking around the container, looking for any type of opening.

"Rey, I've done a little research on these things. Once the Cargo Cabin is on the ground, the rover can be fitted to lift and move it to a desired location. Once there, it can be opened from the top, but the sides come completely down to the ground. It makes for easy access and removal of the items inside. It's not designed to be kept for storage, where one can reach in, grab a few hermetically sealed crates of dried meat and then close it up. No, once it's opened, everything inside is removed at once. It's the same for the Med-Lab supplies." He pointed further down the corridor at the only other huge container at the back side of the Cabin. It was labeled 'Medical Supplies'.

Rey spent another few frantic minutes looking for an opening. To Doc, he looked like a cornered rat, finally sensing his own mortality. If the situation weren't serious for all of them, he would have laughed. Instead, he turned toward Nola and saw that she and Liz had moved further down the corridor, their attention was focused on a much smaller container close to the back corner of the Cabin. "Look here," Liz said into her microphone.

They headed in her direction and Doc was first to see what had caught their attention. He smiled to himself. Leave it up to Nola and Liz to save their asses. Liz pressed a small button on the front of the container and a small hiss escaped through the top, as the lid slid open. After a quick glance, Liz announced, "Looks like we have overflow items over here! There are individual food containers, Med-Lab supplies, surplus CO2 scrubbers, and..." Her voice trailed off.

Rey hustled over to the overflow container and looked in. Nola had never really seen Rey smile, but when he saw the contents, she would have thought it was Christmas Day. He immediately grabbed the one container that made Nola's breath get caught in her throat. He grabbed the container marked 'Concussion Weapons'. He connected his tow cable to one of the metallic rings attached to the weapons container. "Alright," he said, "let's grab these containers." He pointed to two of the five food containers and to one of the two Med-Lab supplies containers. On our second trip, we'll grab the rest of the food."

3

Nola grunted in disgust. Despite the fact that it was intensely cold out here in space and the fact that they were weightless, she could feel her body heating up with the exertion. She didn't realize just how much work was involved in trying to control the movement of your body in zero gravity.

She glanced at her oxygen display lights and was somewhat dismayed to see that her green light was moving to amber, indicating that she had about 30 minutes of air remaining. While inside the Cargo Cabin, they were able to remove their helmets because of the oxygen generators, but now, here she was sucking up her suits air like it was part of her own infinite reserves. They had been out here for over an hour and were now returning from their third trip to the Cabin. As it turned out, there was a lot more food and supplies available for them to bring to the ship. In the end, they still left quite a bit of food and supplies in the Cabin because Rey decided that they had plenty for the remainder of the trip. He surmised that they could always come back out here if they needed more.

Liz and Nola had already gone down the ladder and were slowly making their way forward to the airlock entrance. Finch was at the ladder and Doc pulled up the rear, having secured the Cargo Cabin doors. Rey had been called to the cockpit because of some *spatial anomaly*, as Eddie Chin had put it, so he wasn't out there to ride herd on them.

"Liz, Nola...how you guys doing?" Burt said when he reached the top of the ladder. He leaned out as far as he could, but was not able to see them. Finch had already gone down and only the light from the top of his helmet was visible as he slowly descended down the side of the ship.

"I'm good Burt," Nola's voice crackled in his ear. "Liz just stepped inside the airlock. She's a pro at this! I'm halfway to the airlock. I'd be there by now if this damn container didn't keep bouncing around in front of me. It keeps getting in the way."

Burt chuckled, "I know. It's hard enough moving around in space by yourself, not to mention having a large container strapped to you. I suggest that y..." In that moment, Doc was transported to Los Angeles many years ago, when he experienced his first earthquake. Although he was a grown man, he remembered feeling very vulnerable and extremely terrified, half expecting the building he was in to collapse in on itself. That impotent feeling of terror was coursing through his veins at this moment, but it took him a second to actually place the feeling with the situation. His head snapped up toward the front of the ship, where he saw a huge meteorite burst into a thousand pieces as it slammed into the forward bulkhead of the ship. In his ears, he could hear hundreds of voices yelling at the same time.

"Get back inside the ship now!" Rey shouted. *"We've hit a meteor shower!"* While Burt scrambled toward the ladder in slow motion, it occurred to him that he had never heard Rey sound as frantic as he did at that moment. Just as he was climbing down the ladder, angrily shoving the attached container to the side of his belt, he felt as if he were hit by a truck. An involuntary grunt escaped him as his world tilted crazily. He could feel himself about to black out and so bit his tongue, hard. The pain was exquisite, but the fog descending onto his consciousness, lifted immediately. He realized that he was floating toward the rear of the ship and instinctively understood that if he didn't slow his speed down, his tether would snap and fling him out into outer darkness. He frantically grabbed at anything that his fingers touched, hoping to get a handhold onto

something. He was starting to despair when his grasping fist closed around a steel bar that seemed to fit his gloved hand perfectly. His fingers closed around it briefly and then his speed pulled him loose. Fortunately, it was enough to slow him down to the point that his tether held fast. In fact, it snatched him back so quickly, he felt it broke his back.

"Burt!" Nola screamed into his ear. When they hit the meteor showers, she had frozen in her tracks and glued herself to the side of the ship, while meteor fragments raced pass her. Her head snapped up when she heard Burt yell out. She didn't know what had happened to him, but the sounds from Burt coming through her earpiece didn't sound good at all. She looked back toward the ship, but couldn't see him anywhere. Finch was no more than a few feet from her, his head pressed tightly against the side of the ship. He was trembling fiercely. "Finch!" She yelled. "Burt's in trouble. We need to get back up there and help him!" She inched toward him and froze when he started screaming.

"No!" he yelled out, still facing the side of the ship. *"I don't wanna die! We'll get crushed by a meteorite!"*

"Finch! Listen to me! We need to go back now. He could be unconscious." She hesitated a second and then added, "He would do it for us."

Quietly, almost peacefully, he said, "I'm not going. *You* go."

"Goddammit Finch!" She said angrily. She moved closer toward him and realized that she would have to undo her tether in order to get around him. Despite the longer one that Rey gave her, it was still too short to move completely around Finch's upright prostrate body. And even if she were able to get around him, he would have to unclip her tether and give it to her so she could tether herself back in on the other side of him. She stared at him disgustedly. He held onto the side of the ship like a man holding onto a piece of floating driftwood in the middle of the ocean. He was trembling so hard, she thought he would jiggle himself right off the ship. No. Finch was in no shape to do that. In a crazy, far-off part of her mind, she saw herself and Finch holding onto the side of the ship as it zoomed toward its landing in Europa. "Finch, I need to use you as an anchor to get around you, okay?" Finch, eyes closed, nodded his head jerkily. She looped her fingers around one of the several connecting loops on Finch's suit and then unclipped her tether. She moved slowly around Finch, pressing tightly up against him. Even through the thickness of the spacesuits, she could feel his entire body vibrating with fear. She was almost on the other side of him when he shifted, causing her body to momentarily lose the tight connection to him. Even though her hand was still tightly wrapped around the connecting loop on his suit, she screamed just the same.

"*Fucking stop moving Finch!*" she yelled into the small microphone in her helmet. "I'm sorry!" he blabbered out. "I just wanted to get a better grip." His voice sounded weak and strained. "Just wait! I'm almost there," Nola said and just as quickly, she reconnected her tether to the bar on the other side of Finch.

"I'm okay, Nola. Stay there…it's a little safer than being up here." When Nola heard Burt's voice, her relief was palpable. "Burt!" she cried out. She could hear him grunting and breathing heavily. "I'm still coming for you. I'll be at the ladder in a minute."

Nola began making her way to the ladder carefully. She could hear meteorites still striking the front of the ship. "Okay," Burt said. "I'll make my way to the ladder and wait for you there."

Burt could feel himself getting light headed again. He bit his tongue, but it didn't work this time. He glanced down at his suit display illuminated in the small panel at the bottom front of the helmet. "Shit," he said, not meaning to say it aloud. "My CO2 scrubber has been damaged. I'm losing air." He paused briefly and then added, "I'm bleeding also."

With no hesitation, Nola said, "I'm on my way, Burt. Hang in there." She pulled herself up the ladder quickly and almost missed the last rung. After stabilizing herself, she looked over at Burt and then toward the front of the ship. Her breath caught in her throat. Apparently, a meteorite had smashed into the ship and left a huge ragged scar along the top of the ship. Burt must have been hit by a piece of the broken ship. Even from where she was, she could see a dark stain marring the spacesuit. He was bleeding and it must have been pooling inside his suit.

She hustled as fast as she could over to where he lay. His eyes were closed and he was breathing shallowly, but at her approach, he opened them groggily. "Hey stranger," he said quietly. "Fancy meeting you here." He tried to laugh, but only spat up a few droplets of blood, which floated around his face on their own irregular orbits.

"Shhh…don't talk Burt. Let's get you out of here." She lifted him up and he groaned, but he was able to move forward with her help. She was immensely grateful for that. Something caught her eye and she glanced up just as a meteorite sailed overhead toward the Cargo Cabin. She half-turned, expecting the meteorite to obliterate the Cargo Cabin, but it shot past it with only inches to spare. Nola groaned nervously and turned toward the ladder hurriedly. "Okay Burt…we're at the ladder. Turn around slowly." She helped him position himself. "Okay, put your foot down. Now the other. Good. Okay, hold on, I'm going to unhook your tether from the top of the ship and then reconnect it to the ladder's vertical tether bar." She quickly detached his tether and connected it to the ladder. As soon as he had taken several painfully slow steps down, he looked up. "Okay, your turn. Quickly Nola."

She smiled at him and unhooked her tether. She was just about to reconnect it to the ladder's vertical tether bar when Burt's foot slipped off the step and his legs flew out slowly behind him. He yelled out, mostly from the pain of his undoubtedly cracked ribs. Nola grabbed at him reflexively. "I got you, Burt! You're connected and are not going anywhere." She smiled at him, but he wasn't looking at her. She followed his gaze and saw that he was looking at her tether, floating freely – completely unconnected. *"Nola...connect yourself now! Connect yourself..."*

4

Now, was what Nola expected to come from Burt's mouth, but at that very moment, his eyes grew much too large for his face. She followed his gaze down and saw her tether floating freely. She stared at it dumbly, while her mind made the connection that she was not connected to the ladder's vertical tether bar. She specifically remembered disconnecting herself from the bar at the top of the ship, but she only had a vague impression of having reconnected it to the ladder's tether bar. She was so concerned for Burt's injuries that nothing else seemed to compute. No rational thought...only *concern.*

She could feel herself moving in slow motion and tried to convince herself that it really was the zero-gravity environment and not some adrenaline-fueled, mind-altering state of mind that always seemed to slow *everything* down in potential near-death experiences. Regardless of the cause, she felt a tremendous vibration beneath her feet as a meteorite slammed into the top of the forward cabin of the ship. It bounced off the ship at an angle and shot over her and out into space. Unfortunately, the top of the forward cabin buckled and then crumpled before being ejected rearward, toward her and Burt. This happened in a microsecond, but what terrified Nola was that something big was coming directly at her and it wasn't moving in slow motion.

5

Nola watched in horror as a large metal sheet rocketed toward her. In her mind, she was dropping low to the ship and then slinging herself over the side next to Burt, him heroically reaching out to her and grabbing her tether before she slipped away into the darkness. But the only thing she felt move were her toes inside her boots as the jagged metal turned end over end toward her. She closed her eyes and her conscious thoughts forced their way through her lips, *"This is it. I knew I would never make it to Europa. Funny though...I actually thought it would be Soren or Rey who would end my life. I'm sorry Tess, I was misled. I love you, Burt. I..."*

Despite the pain in his side and his cracked ribs, Burt moved up the ladder and reached for Nola's tether, knowing that he was already too late. He turned his eyes sharply to Nola and saw that she was staring toward the front of the ship, her eyes closed. Out of the blue, he heard her voice, quiet and eerily calm, *This is it. I knew I would never make it to Europa.* He redoubled his efforts to get to her. To somehow grab her tether or her boot and yank her from the path of debris. For a brief moment, he was able to grab her tether, but before he could fully close his hands around it, she was whisked away. Even though he only had a slight grip on her tether, when the metal sheet hit her, the force of the impact was strong enough to unceremoniously yank him from the ladder. He screamed, as much in abject loss as his body was slammed into the side of the ship. He once again pulled himself to the ladder and climbed up as fast as his cracked ribs would allow him. From his vantage point, all he could see was her and the metal sheet orbiting one another as her body moved further and further toward the rear of the ship.

6

When the metal hit Nola, she expected a second of pain and then it would be over. At least that was what she had always read. The pain was there, but it didn't go away. And she felt movement. Why would she be moving if she were dead? She opened her clinched eyes and almost vomited. She was turning end over end. She would see blackness one second and then the silver-gray top of the ship the next second. She guessed that the debris had hit her straight on. If it had hit her at an angle, she would have been torn in half. It took her a minute to focus on her console display and when she finally adjusted her eyesight, she could see that it showed all green, except for the communications connection – it showed red. She may not be able to speak to anyone, but at least her spacesuit had not been compromised. Unfortunately, her slow somersaulting was pushing her further and further toward the back of the ship. She tried to look for the Cargo Cabin during one of her spins and caught a glimpse of the side of the huge Cabin. She was getting close and understood that she would only have one, maybe two tries to grab onto some metal outcropping on the side of the Cargo Cabin. Her tether, useless and stiff, trailed behind her like a vestigial tail.

As she tumbled toward the Cargo Cabin, she tensed up in anticipation of hitting it. The wait seemed endless. Because she seemed to be drifting in slow motion, she was almost deceived into believing that it wouldn't be so bad when she hit the Cabin. This was a mistake. When she made contact with it, she felt as if she were hit by a truck. The immediate exhalation of air fogged up her faceplate.

Immediately, she began flailing her arms in an effort to grab onto anything. She was lucky that the impact not only stopped her from tumbling, but it was at such an angle that she didn't get expelled outward, into space. It slowed her momentum down a little too, but as she bumped along the corrugated and rough side of the Cargo Cabin, she could see how frighteningly fast the *Cassiopeia* was actually moving. If she didn't stop herself soon, there would be nothing but empty space to grab onto.

She was now facing the front of the ship and the only physical connection she had to the ship were her hands, as her feet were angled up and outward. As she flailed at the hard structures of the Cargo Cabin, she saw her useless tether bouncing and threading its way between and around the protuberances of the Cabin. She knew that she was running out of Cabin and time and made one last herculean effort to grab onto anything, but this part of the Cabin was smooth, solid metal. She screamed desperately as her hands flailed uselessly against the Cabin. Just when she thought all was lost, she felt her right hand close around a small, hard piece of metal. Before she had a chance to register this sensation and direct her hand to actually grab the metal, her head hit something hard and immovable. The pain was immediate and she could feel herself passing out. She understood that if she passed out now, she would be lost. She tried biting her tongue, but felt nothing. A calmness slowly enveloped her and she allowed herself to get lost in that calmness. The last coherent thought to drift into her consciousness was a deep sadness that she would never see Burt again.

Burt stared in horror as he witnessed Nola sliding across the top of the cargo cabin, her hands flailing mightily. He screamed for her, but she continued moving further and further toward the back of the ship. Further and further away from him. He blinked. One minute she was there and the next, she was gone. He called out her name weakly, but was greeted with silence. He laid his head against the side of the ship while tears streamed down his face.

THE LOSS OF LEVERAGE

1

Finch fell to the floor hard after being punched in the mouth by Doc. He looked down at him reproachfully, repressing the urge to smash his boot into Finch's face. "You did *nothing* Finch! *Nothing!*" he yelled hoarsely. "I called for you to help, but you did nothing you son of a bitch!" He looked at Finch with raw hatred in his eyes. In that moment, he could have killed him. The pain and loss of leaving Tess and the others back on the moon, the murder of Sophia and now the senseless death of Nola. It was too much for him. He was overflowing with bitter rage and Finch's inaction during the meteor storm unleased the storm that had been building within him since they left the moon.

He advanced again on Finch, but Rey and his guards blocked his effort. "That's enough Doc!" Rey yelled out. "Finch needs to go see Soren and *you* need to calm the fuck down!" Doc looked at Rey and very seriously contemplated smashing his fist into that *meh* face of his, but knew that he would be overcome immediately by Rey's three guards. He turned and stormed off toward the cargo room exit, grabbing at his side.

Finch got up and rubbed at his jaw. He was angry that Doc hit him, but what infuriated him more was being accused of cowardice. He rationalized over and over that there was nothing he could do to help Nola. *It's a wonder we all weren't killed out there*, he thought.

Rey looked at Finch with disgust. He was just as furious as Doc was. Nola was to be *his woman* once they arrived on Europa. He didn't know how he would have done it, but he was not going to allow Nola to become part of Soren's breeding stable. But it didn't matter now. None of that mattered. He found himself slowly losing his footing. His thoughts were becoming more and more erratic and angry. He thought once or twice that maybe he was getting a case of space dementia, but immediately dismissed that. Things were just getting stressful, that's all. Nothing to be concerned about, right? He was uncertain how long he would have stood there over Finch with mad thoughts flitting in and out of his head, if Dante hadn't interrupted his maladaptive stupor. "Hey boss, what are we doing with the food they brought back from the Cabin?"

Rey started violently and looked at Dante, "Put it all in the Cargo Hold. This is the last of our food and I can't have everyone on the ship with access to it. I'll reset the access codes. Now pick up this piece of shit and escort him to Soren's cabin."

2

"What the hell happened out there Finch?" Soren yelled as soon as Finch walked into his cabin and the sliding door closed behind him. "I heard you froze out there."

Finch hated being here. He was basically imprisoned here for a week and grew to hate everything about the place. The only solace he had was staring out into space through the large, observatory-type windows in Soren's cabin. And now, he was being called on the carpet for something he had nothing to do with. "I didn't do anything!" Finch cried out pitifully. "I...I just didn't think climbing onto the top of the ship during a meteor storm was a smart thing to do." He looked at Soren pleadingly.

He walked over to Finch and placed his hand on his shoulder, causing him to flinch. "Look son, I understand it was terrifying out there, but your inaction caused me to lose someone very important to me." He turned from Finch and walked over to the bar set in the wall. He poured himself a drink and then turned back to Finch. "Finch, do you want me to invite you and the little missus for another weekly visit? Maybe I should have both of you here together." He chuckled at the thought. "One big happy family, eh Finch?" Finch shrank back in horror and violently shook his head. "N...no sir. Please, no."

Soren smiled and said, "Well then, maybe you can make up for this debacle. Since you did so well informing me about Doc and his insurrectionists, maybe you can help me with Rey." Finch looked at Soren quizzically. Soren continued on, "I want you to keep an eye on Rey and his guards. I want to know what they talk about, when they talk and where they talk. You see Anton, being the commander of this ship means that I need to know not only what's happening with the troops, but with the command structure as well. Do you understand what I'm saying?"

As much as he hated his unbridled obsequiousness to Soren, he was helpless to stop the effusive gush of words pouring from his mouth. He enthusiastically shook his head in the affirmative. "Yes sir! Anything you say sir!"

Soren looked at Finch and almost laughed. Finch's unabashed fawning almost tempted him to hold out his hand to see if Finch would kiss the ring on his finger. Instead, he looked at him levelly and said, "Good...and don't fail me, Finch."

Once Finch had left, he walked over to the large window and stared out at Jupiter. They were getting close to their destination and they still hadn't worked out the details of how to slow the ship down to move into Europa's orbit. They still hadn't accessed Tess's files to find the coordinates identifying the most suitable place to send the Cargo Cabin. At the thought of the Cargo Cabin mishap, Soren frowned. With the loss of Nola, he had lost the best leverage he had over Rey. He had promised Rey again and again that Nola would be his *after* bearing his child. He had even considered foregoing his interest in her, just to keep Rey in line, but now that option was completely and totally gone. In one fell swoop, he went from having multiple options to having none. He grimaced and began mentally slotting the guards into two camps; his and Rey's.

KELLY

1

Kelly stared at her reflection in the mirror. She barely recognized the person looking back at her. Her normally vibrant red hair looked dull and listless. Her skin looked pallid and worn and her eyes looked pained and haunted. She rubbed her stomach again. She found herself rubbing her stomach more and more these days. Even though she was on her last remaining birth control patch, she wondered if she were pregnant. She wouldn't know for sure for weeks, but by then, they would most likely be on Europa. What she *did* know, was that if she were pregnant, it wouldn't be Anton's child. They hadn't even consummated their marriage yet. In fact, she refused to move back into her husband's quarters, preferring instead to remain in Nola's cabin.

The thought of Nola brought tears to her eyes. She didn't realize just how much she depended on Nola. Being on this ship under these conditions, with Soren and his crazy guards making life miserable for everyone, was almost unbearable, but she had Nola and Anton to lean on. Now, Nola was dead and Anton was dead *to* her. She had no one and she could feel her sanity slowly drying up and dying at the edges. Soon, she would be a pile of human dust blowing through the vents and out into space.

She sat down on the bed and picked up Nola's diary. Nola had told her about the diary and had even let her read it. She had told Kelly that it was more a story of their trials and tribulations aboard the *Cassiopeia*, and less a personal sob story that most diaries consisted of. They had laughed about that until they cried. As Kelly looked at the diary, she felt she would never laugh again. And as it turned out, Nola's diary had very intimate and tender moments in it, intermingled with her fear that she would never see Europa. She loved Burt and felt very guilty at her part in leaving Tess and the others behind. She felt she should have done more to stop Allison and Larry from their dangerous love affair. But she admitted that she could have no more convinced them to stop, then someone convincing her to stop her affair with Burt. Kelly put the diary back into the cubbyhole in the wall and lay on her side. Her mind drifted back and forth between Anton and Soren and

Nola and as sleep came for her, she wondered if *she* would ever see Europa
alive.

DAY 57

A PLACE TO HIDE

1

"You're lucky your ribs were just bruised and not broken, Doc," Zoe said. "Another few days and you'll be good as new."

Doc pulled on his shirt and smiled at Zoe. Her bedside manner was superb and despite the events of the last week, she seemed to be handling it in stride. Elsa was working in the Cargo Hold inventorying the items they brought back from the Cargo Cabin. Even though she had been gone for several days, they found that they were able to handle the duties of Med-Lab with no issues. It was getting late and he told Zoe to wrap things up for the evening. He dimmed the lights and was about to lock his office when he looked up and saw...Nola.

"What the hell..." he began and then realized it was Kelly. Nola and Kelly had always looked to be older and younger versions of one another, and now that Kelly was living in Nola's quarters, she started wearing some of Nola's jumpsuits. Kelly was so distraught about losing Nola that she pretty much stayed in her quarters. Now here she was. Wearing Nola's jumpsuit and looking eerily like Nola.

"Hello Kelly, I'm glad to see you outside of your cabin. How are you feeling?" Doc enquired.

"Hey Doc. I haven't been sleeping well and hoped you had more of the sleeping tablets." She slumped down on one of the chairs in Med-Lab and looked forlornly up at Burt.

"Sure Kelly, I'll have Zoe grab some for you." He yelled out to Zoe to grab some of the sleeping tablets before she completely closed down the medicine cabinets at the rear of the Med-Lab.

"Doc," Kelly whispered, "I dream of Nola every night. She used to joke that we were like sisters, but she was more than a sister to me. She was like a mother and I miss her terribly." Her head slumped down and she began to cry.

Doc sat down next to her and put his arms around her shoulder. "I know Kelly. I miss her too. She left a few articles of clothing at my cabin and I can still smell her scent in them. This gives me great joy and I guard them jealously. What I fear the most is that one day I'll wake up and I won't be able to smell her anymore. It will be then that I will know she is truly gone."

With her head leaning on Doc's shoulders, Kelly sniffled and said, "Nola was my hero, Doc. She helped me when my dad was killed back on the moon. Everyone thought it was Anton, but it wasn't him. It was Nola. She gave me the strength to endure all of this when I was at my most desperate. I will always remember her."

Doc looked at Kelly and nodded sadly, "I think she was everyone's hero, Kelly."

Kelly smiled and stood up just as Zoe arrived with the tablets. She and Zoe hugged one another tightly and then she turned to Doc and hugged him. Before they disengaged, she whispered in his ear, "Nola loved you Doc. You were everything to her." She turned and headed out of Med-Lab, while Doc wiped away the single tear that coursed down his cheek.

2

Burt walked into the refurbished engineering section. He was shocked to find that there were no guards here to stop and question him. From what he could gather, Soren and Rey felt there was no need to severely limit movement about the ship since there was nothing anyone could do other than sit tight and wait until they arrived at Europa. Even still, Burt felt something was different. The guards seemed to be distracted and oftentimes, he spotted groups of them eyeing the women and talking in hushed tones.

"Hey Burt," Liz said from one of the workbenches located next to the engine node housing section. They had been successful in restoring the filtration system here and were able to pump out the remaining poisonous gases. Unfortunately, areas like the biosphere and the reclamation center were still off limits. When Burt neared her she said, "Our nodes are breaking down, Burt. One is completely burnt out and the other ones are slowly degrading. Once they go, we'll be a dead stick as far as thrust and maneuverability. Not to mention we've uncovered an increasing level of radiation in the forward compartments near the reclamation center."

Burt frowned, "But we always knew that there was a radiation leak somewhere up there. And I thought we contained it."

"True," Liz replied, "but it's been steadily increasing since the explosion and all it takes is a small spark from some of the damaged equipment to set off a much larger explosion. And that explosion will either destroy the ship, push us off course, or slow us down to a crawl. None of those options are good for us."

Burt hung his head. "Maybe we should never have tried to take over the ship. At least we would have made it to Europa alive and in one piece." He paused for a moment and then added, "And Nola might still be alive..."

Liz took Burt's hand and said, "Burt, no one could have expected one of those guards to fire a laser directly into the engine node housing unit. And no one could have anticipated that reaction. It wasn't our fault. It wasn't *your* fault." She reached her arms around his neck and hugged him.

Jaime walked in just then and walked over to Burt and Liz. He placed his hand on Doc's back. "She's right Burt, it's not your fault. We all did what we thought was right. Nola believed in what we were trying to do."

Burt stepped back and looked at both of them, tears welling up in his eyes, "I know...you're right. Both of you." He paused for a moment, wiping his eyes, "I just get so angry at this whole situation. I feel as if we're flying directly into the sun, while Soren and Rey stand off to the side cheering stupidly."

Burt glanced around the engineering bay, almost furtively and added, "I'm starting to hear some unsettling things about the guards. They have always been asses, from day one, but ever since we returned from our spacewalk, they seem to not be paying much attention to us. Have you guys noticed that?"

Jaime said, "Yes! I thought it was me, but there's something different about them. They've totally ignored us and seem to be banding into groups and get this, Chin told me that Finch has been spying on Rey and his guards. I'm not sure what's happening here, but I don't like it one bit. I feel as if we're about to be caught in the middle of a gangland turf battle. What do you think is going on?"

"It was no secret that Rey has always wanted Nola. When she was lost..." he swallowed hard and shifted uncomfortably. Liz patted his arm and said, "It's okay Burt."

Burt nodded at her and continued on. "When Nola was lost, I heard that Rey took it really hard. Apparently, he blames Soren for forcing him to take her on the spacewalk. People have heard Soren and Rey arguing and at one point, the guards on both sides almost came to blows."

"Dios mio," Jaime whispered. "This is bad. It almost feels like a damn movie. Some *West Side Story* space opera!"

"That's not too far from the truth, Jaime," Burt said. "There's some really bad blood between Soren and Rey, and between Soren's guards and Rey's guards and it's starting to spill out into the streets, so to speak. I think part of it is that Soren doesn't entirely trust Rey. He always knew that Rey wanted Nola, even when we were on the moon. He might have been sleeping with Tess, but he's always wanted Nola. Rey has always been unpredictable and dangerous, but with her gone, I think he might be totally losing it." He looked at both of them with a deadly serious look on his face. "I think Soren realizes that he might be losing his leverage over Rey and to stop that, he'll need muscle."

"Are you saying that Soren might be trying to win the guards over to his side in case Rey tries to...what...unseat him?" Liz was trying to control the emotion in her voice and was failing. "What the hell are we going to do if they start a full out war on the ship? We have no real weapons and now that they've retrieved those stun guns from the Cargo Cabin, they're even more dangerous. And there's really no place we can hide on the ship."

"Yeah, I know Liz," Burt responded. "There's a real possibility that Rey will convince his guards and maybe some of the folks on the ship to overthrow Soren."

Jaime laughed, but there was no humor in it. "To what ends, Burt? To what ends? Why in the fuck would they start fighting when we're just weeks away from Europa?" Jaime let out an exasperated sigh. "I can't believe this shit. Here we are, the last survivors of the human race, journeying out to a new home amongst the stars, and we've managed to smuggle in good old fashioned violent regime change. We're supposed to be space travelers, for God's sake! Mankind's last hope, not fucking pirates on the high seas!" He shook his head and rubbed his eyes furiously.

Burt nodded, "I've been giving this some serious thought, though. We're about two, maybe three weeks away from Jupiter's planetary system, right?" Jaime nodded and Burt continued on, "If things began to get really bad, I mean *World War* bad, then we need to isolate ourselves until we land on Europa. I thought about engineering, but there are too many access locations and this is not really an isolated area."

"The Cargo Hold!" Liz yelled out, excitedly. "You must be referring to the Cargo Hold, Burt."

"Yes...exactly Liz!" Doc said. "That's the only area on the ship that can be completely isolated from the rest of the ship. The majority of the ship's complement of food is already there, as well as the medical supplies." He thought a moment and then added, "Somehow, we have to barricade ourselves in so Rey and his people can't get to us. It would be cramped quarters, but we can survive until we come to orbit about Europa."

Jaime looked at him doubtfully, "*If* we're able to control the ship enough to orbit Europa. We've got damaged engine nodes and we may not have enough fuel for the retropropulsion rockets to work effectively." He thought for a second and then asked, "Now that we've retrieved the extra food from the Cargo Cabin, wouldn't they have doubled the guards in that area? Also, the Cargo Hold requires an access code to get inside."

"The few times I've gone down there for medical supplies," Doc replied, "Rey or Soren had to come open it. That tells me that only Rey and Soren know the access code. After several days of having to make the trip back and forth to open it for medical supplies and food rations, they've basically gotten lazy. Now, it's *always* unlocked, but as you said, they've doubled the guards."

"Ah, I see," said Jaime. "Once the guards on the door have been dealt with, we can get inside, but we still have the problem of keeping them out. Maybe we can change the code or something?"

"No," Doc said. "We would need to do more than just changing the access code. We would need to cut off *any* access through the entrance, short of blowing through it with dynamite. We need to thoroughly destroy the mechanism that opens the entrance."

Liz said, "When we were in the Cargo Cabin, I found some chemical supplies that could work. I even found a soldering iron kit if the chemicals don't work." She looked at Burt curiously, "Burt, if we damage the opening mechanism, we would be cutting ourselves off completely. We'll still be locked in if and when we make it to Europa's orbit."

Burt said, "That's true that we'll be locked in, but we have a few things in our favor. If Soren and Rey and their people fight it out, they'll most likely kill off a sizable number of guards. Maybe leaving behind a more manageable number that we can handle. Also, if we do land on Europa, it'll be much easier to fight and run, if necessary. Here on the ship, we have nowhere to run, nowhere to hide. Our survivability on the ship is finite." His eyes turned dark as he looked off in the distance, "Once we're on Europa and have broken free of Rey and Soren, we could then rain down holy hell on them until only Rey and Soren remain." Liz could feel her skin crawl as she listened to Burt and imagined the bloody apocalypse that would happen on the new world at the edge of space. There would be no quarter for Rey, Soren or any of the guards if they made it to Europa.

"But how would *we* get out Burt? Remember, the airlock didn't open when Rey tried to eject Allison and Larry into space." Liz shuddered involuntarily as she remembered Allison and Larry being marched into the airlock. And then watching them freeze to death on the cold floor. The airlock door didn't open then for Rey and it most likely wouldn't open for them once they landed on Europa.

Jaime began nodding his head, remembering some long-lost detail. "Of course!" he said in disgust, not believing he had forgotten this crucial detail of the ship. "We can leave through the umbilicus portal. It can be opened or blown, depending on the situation." He glanced at Liz, "Liz found some explosive materials in the Cargo Cabin that we could use. We get ourselves prepared for landing on the planet by consolidating the food, makeshift weapons and whatever else we'll need to survive on the planet. Once we land, we blow the umbilicus and get as far away from the ship as possible." He hesitated for just a second and then added through clinched teeth, "If the information received from the Pegasus probe was accurate, then we won't have to worry about breathable air. If they were wrong, then hopefully it'll be over quickly."

Burt was nodding in agreement, but then his brows furrowed, "Speaking of explosive materials, what's to stop them from going back out to the Cargo Cabin and retrieving more? They could then blow the Cargo Hold door and we'd be sitting ducks."

It was quiet for only a minute when Liz added, "Then we must bring all of the spacesuits to the Cargo Hold. If the suits are locked in with us, then Rey can't organize another spacewalk. We would essentially be holding all the cards."

"That's an excellent idea Liz!" Burt exclaimed. "We would have most of the food, all of the spacesuits and the majority of medical supplies. They would be completely and utterly hamstrung."

"What about the people who don't make it inside the Cargo Hold?" Liz asked. "I know there's still a little food in the Commons Commissary, but will it be enough for the folks who decide to stay or are left behind?" She didn't allow her mind to consciously envision the madness and mayhem that would occur, but it invaded her mind just the same. She saw a ship of mad and crazy, partially clothed men and women, running throughout the ship maiming, raping and killing one another. A *Mad Max* world in space. It would be hell.

Burt said, "That could be a problem, Liz. Not everyone will come with us. Not everyone who wants to come, will make it. And we'll need to know who we can trust. We don't need another Finch betrayal." He turned to Jaime and asked, "What about your people here? Can you trust them all and will they all come?"

Jaime looked around at the few scant bodies in the engineering section. Ralph Valstok was working in the Node area and Lindsey Murton was checking on the fusion propulsion system. Grace West and Wayne Kesk were already gone for the evening. "I can assure you that there is no love lost here for Soren or Rey. I trust my team with my life."

"Good," Burt replied. "Just like our attempted takeover of the ship, we'll need trustworthy people we can depend on when the time comes. And everyone should be prepared to fight for their lives. When it happens, it'll happen fast. We'll have to be ready to move quickly because once we start congregating in the area of the Cargo Hold, the guards will sense something. Tell the people we can trust to be ready and to know the quickest way to get there. Of course, you can't tell Finch. Unfortunately, we can't tell Kelly either, but I'll do my damnedest to get her here. God help anyone who gets left behind." He rubbed his forehead, "Soren may call it his feudal right, but it's nothing more than plain old medieval kidnapping and rape. What he did to Kelly affected her deeply. I will try to get her here, but I won't force her inside. She'll have to make that decision on her own. I'm afraid that if we tell her what's going on. In her current state of mind, she might let it slip and all of our efforts will be in vain."

Liz looked at Burt and then at Jaime. "I understand, Burt. We all love Kelly and it breaks my heart to see the lost look in her eyes. I don't think she would say anything either, but in a fit of anger toward Anton or Soren, she might say something that she'll regret." She took a deep breath and then said, "Burt, I think this needs to happen now. Not today or tomorrow, but very soon. We can't afford to wait until Soren and Rey's war starts. If we plan it now, then we can save more people. If we wait until things get out of hand, a lot of people won't make it."

Burt and Jaime stared at one another for a moment and then Burt found his voice, "You're right Liz. Damn...you're right. My rational mind agrees with you entirely, but I think my emotional self wasn't quite ready to believe that our only hope to survive this nightmare is to cut ourselves off completely from the rest of the ship. Once we are locked inside that Cargo Hold, we don't come out until we land on Europa. God help us."

Liz grabbed Burt's hand and held it tightly in hers, "I know Burt. I know. It's our only option. We've survived a lot since Lycos and we're not stopping now."

Burt smiled at her and squeezed her hand gently. He hugged them both and turned to head back to his cabin. Dark thoughts swirled through his head as he walked through the connecting tunnels. *This is our last hope,* he thought. *Soon, very soon, Rey and Soren will come to blows.* He let out an exasperated breath. He had been observing Rey closely over the past week and he could see that Rey was at a tipping point. The loss of Nola seemed to have pushed him to the point of no return. And Rey and Soren's *war* will consume them all. Burt was stupefied. He couldn't understand how they couldn't see the end result of their conflict. The aftermath of their stupidity would claim the lives of people who survived against enormous odds to get to this point. He wondered if there would even be any survivors left who could pilot the ship.

This thought stuck with him for a minute. There was something Tess had told him what seemed like ages ago, back on the moon. Something about a failsafe backup plan. Something about a knob or a handle... "A switch!" he yelled, startling himself. Tess had told him that all of the newer model generation ships were built with incredibly sophisticated "dead-man switches". These switches, Tess had explained, were much more advanced than the ones employed on trains and planes even 30 years ago. The ones installed on generation space ships, on the *Cassiopeia* itself, were designed to utilize all available data such as origin, destination, speed, planetary bodies, current spatial location and much, much more. In a nutshell, the ship could land itself if certain functions and procedures were not executed by the estimated arrival time.

Burt felt a glimmer of hope. If they can get themselves secured in the Cargo Hold while Soren and Rey killed themselves off, then at least the ship would be able to land when it arrived in orbit about Europa. But how can he be sure that the system was up and running? He didn't know if it was always on or if it needed to be activated. Disgustedly, he realized that he didn't know the answer to that. He considered going back to engineering to ask Jaime, but he was certain Jaime was already at his cabin by now. He would talk to Eddie Chin tomorrow, but he had a gnawing feeling that somehow Finch would find out and go crawling back to Soren, news in hand. But he had to find out if the system was always on or if it needed to be activated. It did them no good to be securely locked into the Cargo Hold, only to die there as the *Cassiopeia* floated silently pass Europa and Jupiter and out of the solar system. As he turned down the passageway toward his cabin, he thought of an old poem he learned in school. It was a poem by William Butler Yeats called *The Second Coming*. When he first read it, he didn't quite understand it. He laughed and remembered that when the teacher read it to the class, he barely heard her. He was totally enraptured by the thought that he was finally going on a date with Desi Viga, a young woman in his natural sciences class. But as he thought about the poem now, years after Desi and millions of miles away from a world that no longer existed, he shuddered as the real message of the poem pierced him. He couldn't remember the poem in detail, but what he did remember turned him cold all over; *the center does not hold; and what rough beast, its hour come round at last, slouches toward Bethlehem to be born?* He shuddered and thought again, *the center does not hold.*

DAY 62

PLANS WITHIN PLANS

1

Burt! Where are you?? Help me! Why won't you help me?? Burt was slogging through waist high mud straining to reach Nola as she sank deeper and deeper into the quicksand. As much as he strained to grasp her outstretched hand, he just couldn't reach her. The closer he got to her, the deeper she sank. He made a final herculean effort to reach her and their fingers touched right before she got sucked under. *No!!* He yelled, but his mouth was beginning to fill up with mud and he realized that he would soon be pulled under. He could feel the weight of the mud closing in around him, pushing him down violently, crushing him...shaking him.

"Doc! Wake up. Wake up!" Zoe was frantically shaking him. "It happened again!"

Burt's eyes flew open as the end of his nightmare merged with Zoe's frantic pleading. He had taken a nap on the couch in his office and the nap had turned into a goddamn nightmare. He was drenched in sweat and he could feel his heart pounding in his chest. "Wha...huh? Zoe? Zoe, what's wrong?"

"Cindy was attacked by a guard this morning," Zoe said. "She was heading back to her cabin when Jake and Troy snuck up behind her." Zoe looked down and Burt could see her hands shaking.

"Where is she now, Zoe?" Burt asked.

"She's in Room 2. She's really shaken up, so I gave her something to help her relax. I'm scared Burt. This is the fifth time this has happened and no one's doing *anything* about it!" She put her hands to her face and began crying.

Burt hugged her and said, "Let me go see how Cindy is doing. You stay here for a minute and then join me when you're okay." Zoe nodded as Burt turned toward Room 2.

Burt was fuming as he walked toward the room where Cindy was, shaking off the last vestiges of his nightmare. As Zoe said, this was the fifth attack this week. Four women and one man. One of the women was raped and the rest were molested. One was beaten badly. That woman was still recovering in Room 1. Burt had gone to Rey and all but screamed at him that things have gotten out of hand. That his guards and some of Soren's guards, have attacked multiple people. But Rey had changed. He had become more and more morose over the past couple of days. He simply looked at Burt with hate-filled eyes and dismissed him.

Burt knocked on the door to Room 2 and said, "Hi Cindy, it's me Burt. I'd like to come in and take a look at you." Through the door, he could hear Cindy's sniffles.

"Okay, Doc." Cindy replied chokingly.

Burt opened the door and almost stopped in his tracks. A huge purple bruise covered half of her face. Her eyes were bloodshot and she had blood dripping down her forehead from a cut somewhere on her head underneath her disheveled hair. Her jumpsuit was torn and there were red splotches here and there. She was sitting on the hospital bed holding her arm awkwardly. One of her boots was missing.

"I can't go back to my cabin, Doc. I just can't," Cindy said. "They forced me into my own cabin and stayed there for hours. I fought back at first, but they easily overpowered me. And they kept hitting me, even after I gave in to them. They kept saying, *'this is how we like it baby.'*" She let out an exasperated sigh as she continued looking at the floor.

Burt could feel dangerous heat rising within him. He could no longer see Cindy sitting on the gurney barely hanging on to her own sanity. His mind's eye saw the death and destruction that accompanied everything that had to do with Soren, Rey and this ill-fated journey. Listening to Cindy's horrible experience, as well as the attacks on the others, forced him to reconcile his and everyone else's fate; they were doomed. Their lives would end tragically either at the hands of sadistic animals, in a fiery explosion or slowly, as their weakened and withering bodies succumbed to either starvation or cold.

He worked on Cindy's wounds, all the while thinking that this was it. Now was the time for them to get to the Cargo Hold and lock themselves in. They were as ready as they could be. Liz and Jaime were able to secure all of the spacesuits inside the Cargo Hold. It took several days and sometimes odd hours of the night, but they were able to do it without anyone noticing. Now, they only needed to start the process of getting to the Cargo Hold. Burt considered their tenuous situation and understood perfectly that it was only a matter of time before one of the guards killed someone. They had been getting bolder and bolder and neither Rey nor Soren seem to be capable of curbing their destructive instincts. In fact, Soren was becoming a recluse, keeping himself locked inside his cabin. Jaime had told him that he heard Soren was becoming more and more paranoid and mused out loud that he was afraid of being assassinated, this close to Europa. Gone were his phony effusive speeches that he doled out at the head of the Commons. Gone were the periodic visits from the list he had prepared for Nola early in the journey. He had become a rare and enigmatic thing, like *Bigfoot*; rarely seen except when lurching hunched forward from his cabin to the cockpit.

He finished with Cindy's wounds and walked her out to the lobby. Zoe walked up to them and grabbed Cindy's hands, "Cindy, would you like to stay with me for a few days? It might be safer if we're together than walking around the ship alone." The gratitude in Cindy's eyes was unmistakable. She dropped Zoe's hands and hugged her tightly, "Yes! Thank you, Zoe!"

Doc smiled and said, "Zoe, why don't you go with Cindy to her quarters to pack up some of her belongings and get her situated. I'll finish up things here. And take the long way." Zoe nodded as she and Cindy left Med-Lab, leaving Burt to his thoughts of the Cargo Hold. He checked on Emma Pennington in Room 1. Despite her injuries, she was sleeping soundly. He would check on her again in a couple of hours. For now, he needed to talk to Jaime and Liz. The time had come for them to make their move to the cargo cabin.

2

Soren stared at the view screen that allowed him to see the entire cockpit from his cabin. He watched uneasily as Rey and Chin worked the controls on the ship's bridge. Finch walked up and said something about Europa's orbit and Jupiter's gravitational pull. Soren glanced at the time clock on the bridge. The clock displayed the time remaining until they moved into orbit about Europa and it currently read 6.5 days. *Barely a week left*, he thought. He couldn't wait to get out of this cabin and out of this ship. He had been hearing ugly rumors that Rey was making comments to the effect that he would make a much better leader than Soren. Soren chafed at the thought. *Why in the hell does Rey think he would be a better leader than me?* He thought about that for a second and then a more threatening, sinister thought came to mind; *maybe he wants to be First Father on Europa?*

He stepped away from the view screen and pounded his fist on the edge of the small metallic table connected to the floor. There was a subdued, meaty sound and Soren winced at the pain in his fist. He opened up the video control board and activated the other cameras on the ship. There were cameras all over the ship, but like any other multi-billion dollar generation ship, there were cameras that simply did not work. The cameras in engineering, Med-Lab and the Cargo Hold seemed to be out of commission. Long ago, he had planned to have Rey look into it, but had either forgotten about it or decided it wasn't worth the effort. It didn't matter though, not at this point. They would be landing soon and he'd be able to get out of this god-forsaken ship and get to the business of fathering the new world.

He glanced at the camera in the cafeteria and noticed quite a few guards there. What the fuck was this? Rey had told him the guards would be monitoring the Cargo Hold. He began to regret his decision to leave it unlocked, but he was tired of having to go there sometimes four or five times a day. And Rey never seemed to be around when he needed him to go to the Cargo Hold.

It didn't matter that most people avoided the area as if it were laced with the bubonic plague. He still wanted it guarded. By his order, only a handful of folks were authorized to take supplies out, but non-authorized individuals who had no real reason for being there, were harassed and sometimes kicked about. *People learn*, he thought sardonically. He stared at the guards in the camera again, a sense of unease threading its way into his consciousness. Over the last few days, he had been seeing more and more guards just hanging out in the Commons, openly flirting with some of the women. Most times, harassing them.

He considered calling Rey to his cabin to scream at him about controlling the guards and making sure they did their jobs instead of fucking around with the women, but the thought of seeing Rey and the barely hidden insubordination in his shifty eyes, made him reconsider his thoughts of reprimand. It just wasn't worth it. Besides, they were almost to Europa and other than food and medical supplies, there was nothing in the Cargo Hold really worth stealing. He understood, however, that he would have to confront Rey and make him understand that *he* was still in charge and would not have any bullshit slap and tickle going on. His thoughts turned darker as he considered the possibility of Rey having an *accident*. He would have to have a chat with his personal guard, Otto Helmut. Otto was hard and capable and loyal. He turned back to the cockpit camera and subconsciously started biting his nails. *Barely a week left*, he thought.

3

Rey was feeling pretty good. Doc seemed to have come around and stopped moping about Nola's death. He complained here and there about the guards knocking some folks around, but what of it? If he wanted to retain control of his guards, he'd have to cut them a little slack when it comes to flirting with the chattel. Soren was in hiding in his cabin, so he didn't really know what was going on out here. Things would be different once they landed on Europa, but for now, he'd let his guards have a little fun.

He thought about Nola. Like Doc, he missed her too, but his attention was now drawn to Kelly. She reminded him of Nola, but she had a sweet innocence to her. He hadn't noticed before, but he began seeing striking similarities between her and Nola. And Kelly looked a lot like Nola, only younger. First, she started wearing Nola's jumpsuits and then she started wearing her red hair like Nola used to, with the ponytail high up on the back of her head. He shivered warmly at the thought of her hair unmoored from its restraint and flowing over his face and body. But this warm feeling was instantly chilled as the image of Soren dragging Kelly in tow off to his cabin inserted itself into his psyche. He hated the fact that Soren practically soiled the young woman with his fetid touch, but what was done was done. She would be *his* woman now, despite the fact that she was *technically* still married to Finch, who was now a pariah to her. Oftentimes, she was heard saying they were not married, since they had never consummated their marriage, nor would they ever. He thought about that farce of a wedding ceremony. Finch and Kelly might have *thought* they were legally married, but as far as he was concerned, Soren had no more authority to marry them than he had to perform open heart surgery. In this world, marriage was a thing of the past. The old-world customs and moral dilemmas had no place here at the edge of space. It was take...or be taken. Kill...or be killed. Eat...or be eaten.

He made it a point to be in parts of the ship where he knew Kelly would be. More and more, she began to open up to him and even smiled at him once. It was a sweet, blissful smile. One that told him she not only needed him, but wanted him. Wanted him badly and often. Wanted him in ways Anton or no other man could ever provide. Wanted him in every little dirty way he had fantasied since his sexual coming of age. He blinked and realized he was sweating profusely. He looked around nervously and then wiped his forehead shakily, realizing right then and there, that he would not allow her to be *First Fathered* by Soren. This was probably a moot point, as she could already be pregnant after spending that week with Soren, but he would not let that stop him. She would be his. His woman.

Rey walked slowly, confidently toward his cabin. Inside, Dominic Dante and Jake Sandstone were sitting comfortably around the small, metallic table in his quarters. He pulled up a chair next to them and asked, "So what did you find out?"

Dominic said, "We might be able to convince two, maybe three of his guys to join us, but from what we can tell, most of Soren's guards are pretty loyal to him." He glanced at Jake and then continued, "He's promised them women after he's done his *First Fathering* thing with them. That alone is enough to make them pledge their lives to him."

Rey scoffed in disgust, "Well, we'll have no choice but to remove them from the equation. All of them. Soren is no longer capable of leading us. If we leave it up to him, we'll have a fucking gene-pool mess on our hands one or two generations from now, with first cousins and half-siblings fucking one another!" Jake guffawed and then stopped himself quickly, covering his mouth with his hand.

Rey ignored him, "I don't give a shit about his delusional *First Father Jim Jones* bullshit. When we land on Europa, I'll be in charge and every man who has proven his worth will be granted a woman." Jake and Dominic nodded approvingly. Rey's face turned dark and he said, "This won't happen if Soren is in charge. Soren needs to be deposed and his guards incapacitated. If they will not join us, then I'm counting on you to ensure that their ability to oppose us is utterly destroyed." Dominic and Jake looked at one another and then back to Rey.

"What about the others?" Jake asked. "Doc and his people could become a problem."

"Don't worry about them," Rey said. "They'll fall in line once Soren's out of the picture. Believe me, there won't be any love-lost for Soren, but if anyone becomes problematic, bring them to me. I'll ensure they understand the new way of things."

DAY 65

ESCAPE TO THE CARGO HOLD!

1

Jaime jerked awake as the pounding outside his door seemed to get louder and louder. He jumped out of bed, suddenly scared that Liz was injured...or worse. He palmed open his cabin door, half expecting to see Liz bleeding and swollen, but saw Burt instead. He barely got out Burt's name before he pushed his way inside, allowing the door to slide shut behind him.

"Jaime," Doc said breathlessly. "It's time! We need to get to the Cargo Hold now!"

Jaime rubbed his eyes furiously, trying to will away the cobwebs in his head. "Burt, what happened?"

Doc slumped down in one of the chairs in Jaime's makeshift living room, trying to slow his breathing. "Eddie Chin came to my cabin less than an hour ago and said he overheard one of Rey's guards talking about getting his own woman before they even get to Europa. His cockpit shift duty was just about over, but he pretended to go over some details with Finch when he arrived to take over. In a nutshell, Rey is making his move on Soren. Eddie wasn't sure how this was going to happen, but essentially Rey's guards will start rounding up Soren's guards. When Eddie left the cockpit, he said he saw a number of Soren's guards posted near Soren's cabin." He was breathing more normally now. "My guess is that there is no one guarding the Cargo Hold right now."

Jaime thought for a minute. He was fully awake now as a new thought struck him. "Burt, we need to get to the women that are coming with us. The guard talking about having his own woman before Europa is not good. Up until now, the only thing that protected our female comrades had been the fact that Soren wanted to be the *First Father* on Europa, which meant that they were all safe at least until we landed on the planet. But now, I think Rey is only interested in Kelly and will basically hand out the women to his footpads, like some kind of barbaric and perverted reward or something." Even as the words were leaving his mouth, he could feel his stomach roiling. The very idea of someone gifting a person to another person was appalling. It stank of the awful stain of slavery in the United States so many years ago. Despite the amazing social and technological strides made in recent history – the cure for cancer, the development of an exploration habitat in the Mariana Trench, the exploration of Mars and the chance to travel to Europa in hopes of saving the human race – in the end, humanity still failed. In their microcosm of a world here on the *Cassiopeia*, instead of rising to meet the moment, to face the challenges of the new world together, they digressed into shadows of their barbaric ancestors. As he finished dressing, he turned to Doc and said, "Burt, you need to get Zoe, Kelly and anyone else in the forward cabins to the Cargo Hold. I'll get Liz and the rest of my engineering team and we'll round up the others. Hurry. Once we're in the Cargo Hold, it's only a matter of time before the guards realize we're gone and start to descend upon us."

2

Doc and Eddie Chin were half running, half stumbling through the corridors of the passenger cabins area. The lights had been dimmed here for some reason and they could barely see. They were going to Nola's old cabin where Kelly had been sleeping. When they got there, they banged on the door, but received no answer. Doc tried the palm access panel and the door slid open. Nola had given him access and apparently, Kelly never changed it. They ran in but could tell that the young woman was not here.

"Come on Doc," Eddie said, "We need to hurry before it's too late."

"Before what's too late?"

Doc and Eddie whirled around in unison and there in the door stood one of Soren's guards, Lukas Martin. Doc had seen him only a couple of times in Med-Lab. He remembered that the man was very quiet and unassuming, but with his laser leveled at them, he looked very dangerous. He took a step toward them and said, "I asked you two morons a question, but don't bother answering it. We've already caught a few of you trying to make it to the Cargo Hold."

Doc moaned inwardly. If they failed and could not secure themselves in the Cargo Hold, that would be it for them, all of them. At least the men. Their actions might be enough for Soren and Rey to resolve their differences. It would be very bad for them.

"Alright, let's go see what Soren has to..." Martin was saying, when there was a loud crack and he slumped to the floor. Beside him, Eddie screamed and grabbed at his leg. Looking at the smoking hole in Eddie's jumpsuit, Doc realized that Martin must have had his finger on the laser's trigger when he was hit from behind, firing into Eddie's leg.

He immediately dropped to the floor by Eddie. "It's alright Eddie, looks like it just skimmed your thigh. You'll be fine, but we need to get you to the Cargo Hold." He looked toward the door past Martin's prostrate form. "Who's there?"

Finch poked his head through the door, eyes wide. "Kelly! Where's Kelly? I thought Kelly was in here and when I saw Martin aiming his laser in here, I...I didn't know what to do."

Doc saw the lead pipe he was carrying, now dripping with blood. "Well Finch, you arrived at the right time. What are you doing here? Shouldn't you be in the cockpit?"

Finch stepped over Martin and the expanding pool of blood forming around his crushed skull and walked into the cabin. "I was in the cockpit and left to get something to eat. As I was leaving, I saw the guards dragging people into the Commons. They were being quite rough with them." He stopped for a second and then added, "And I heard one of the guards say, 'they're headed to the Cargo Hold'. That's when I left to find Kelly. What the hell is going on Burt?"

Doc sighed and said, "I'm sure you've noticed the tension between Soren and Rey and by default, the tension amongst their guards. Rey is possibly planning on taking command of the ship, but he can't do that until he has control of Soren's guards." He looked down at Lukas Martin and sighed again, "Well, this is one less guard for Soren, which probably helps Rey, but that can't be helped." He looked up at Finch, "I've been trying to get as many people in the Cargo Hold as I can before either Rey or Soren's guards come looking for us, but I believe the cat's out of the bag now."

Finch stared blankly at Doc, a small light of understanding dawning in his eyes. "What about *me*, Burt? Were you not going to tell me?" His face betrayed a slight look of angry hurt.

"Look Finch, you betrayed us when we had a chance to go back and save Tess and the others on the moon. There are a lot of folks who would rather leave you out here and let you take your chances with the wolves, but in the end, I convinced them to let you join us. But we couldn't tell you anything until it was time to move. Unfortunately, our hand was forced and we've had to make our move now."

"What about Kelly? Does she know? Is she already at the Cargo Hold?" He turned, ready to sprint to the Cargo Hold when Doc stopped him.

"She's not there, Finch. That's why we're *here*. We can't find her and she doesn't know because we couldn't take a chance on Rey finding out. He's been spying on her and is always around her, you know that."

"Fuck!" Finch yelled out. "Where the hell is she then?" He fidgeted for a moment and once again turned to leave.

"Finch," Doc said, "I need you to get Eddie to the Cargo Hold. I'll go find Kelly." Finch was about to protest, but Doc held up his hand. "Kelly still hates you, Finch. Even if you found her, she would never follow you, let alone believe you. No. I'll find her and get her back to the Cargo Hold." He thought for a minute and then added, "You didn't turn off the dead-man switch, did you?"

Finch looked at him, not fully understanding Doc's question. "Before you relieved Eddie this morning, he activated the dead-man switch system. I want to know if you turned it off."

Finch glared at him. "I didn't even know he had turned it on. I was in the Nav Room all morning. Eventually, I guess I would have seen that it had been activated." He thought of something, "You're anticipating that there will be no one left alive who can pilot the ship. Is that right? You should have told me Burt. I could have helped."

For a brief moment, Burt saw red, "Just like you helped take over the ship, huh Finch? Or just like you helped Nola during our spacewalk? Do I have that right, Finch?" He could feel his temperature rising and probably would have punched Finch in the mouth, if Eddie hadn't moaned again from the floor. He forced himself to calm down. "That's neither here nor there, Finch," he said. "What needs to happen now is that you get Eddie to the Cargo Hold before some of the guards get there. I'll find Kelly."

3

Jaime was running at a breakneck pace down the corridor that led to the Cargo Hold. His engineering team and close to twenty others were sprinting behind him. When he had returned to engineering, he couldn't find Liz anywhere. When he last spoke to her, she told him she was taking some of the needed compounds to the Cargo Hold. He prayed she was there. His only option now was to get there as quickly as possible with as many people as possible. If she wasn't there, he would go out to find her. He would not leave her to face the guards and Rey and Soren without him. He would rather die *with* her, than live without her.

Jaime and his group turned the corner leading to the waste management compartments and ran smack into Wade Smith and Rich Gebbons, two of Rey's guards, nestled in one of the nearby alcoves. They immediately disengaged from one another and looked guiltily at Jaime and the others rushing toward them. Their look of guilt quickly turned to suspicion and then fear. "Stop! Where the fuck do you think you guys are going?!" Smith screamed at them. Seeing the crazed and snarling looks on their faces, Smith and Gebbons instinctively grabbed for their batons and lasers, but Jaime and his coterie of survivors descended upon them like a pack of wild dogs. Smith was knocked unconscious before he even had a chance to pull out his laser. Gebbons had been a little quicker on the draw, but was so nervous that he fired into floor before being overwhelmed by the rest of the pack. Jaime snatched up Smith's weapons and then turned toward Gebbons. What he saw didn't surprise him, but was shocking nonetheless. He saw Cindy Felton and a couple of other women viciously kicking Gebbons in the head, stomach and groin, while he covered himself uselessly. One of the ladies wearing heavy boots connected solidly with his head and Gebbons went limp. Cindy grabbed his dropped laser and sprinted toward Jaime. Before, they only had homemade weapons made of steel and metal. Now, they had secured batons, lasers and a couple of stun guns. They rounded the corner and turned down the corridor leading to the Cargo Hold when they slammed into Finch. He stumbled backwards, but caught his balance before he went down. "What the fuck!" He yelled out.

"Where are you going Finch?" Jaime yelled back at him and put his hand on Finch's shoulder. "As soon as Burt gets here, we're sealing this place up. The corridors are crawling with Rey's and Soren's goons."

"I need to be with him! He's looking for Kelly and I need to go back and help him!" His eyes were wide and panicky and flecks of spit flew from his mouth as he yelled. "I would have gotten her and been back by now if I didn't have to carry Eddie here!" He shoved Jaime's hand off his shoulder and pushed through Jaime's group, "Now get outta my fucking way!"

"Let him go," Cindy said, as Finch turned the corridor and was out of sight. "If he doesn't make it back, then I don't think there will be any love lost for him. Our concern now is to get inside and be ready for the guards. They could be making their way here as we speak!" She looked behind her fearfully.

"You're right, Cindy," Jaime said. "We can't be worried about him." He thought a second and then added, "I *am* worried about Burt, though. He told me not to wait if things become too dangerous." He sighed heavily as they walked into the Cargo Hold. There were already close to twenty people in there now, all armed with medievalesque weapons ranging from jagged and hooked pipes to what looked like a homemade mace.

"He'll make it," Cindy said. She looked around and saw everyone mentally girding themselves for the fight to come. At one of the cargo room tables, she could see several engineers mixing compounds that would fuse and melt the cargo door opening mechanism, keeping *them* in and the guards out, for the duration of their trip to Europa.

Jaime hastily organized several of the men and women to stand in the Cargo Hold entrance and to defend it tooth and nail if they had to. He handed out the lasers and stun guns that they were able to take from Smith and Gebbons. He quickly went around the Cargo Hold, but Liz was not here either. Cursing silently, he grabbed Ralph Valstok and half-yelled, half-pleaded, "Have you seen Liz?? She wasn't in engineering. I was hoping she was here." He ran his hand through his hair. Ralph blinked and then asked, "She's not in the group that just got here? Shit man...she dropped off the supplies for the door and went back to look for you. I tried to get her to stay, but she didn't want to take a chance on you not making it." Jaime dropped his head, moaning. He looked up at Ralph and said, "When Burt gets here, tell him I've gone back to look for Liz. Tell him not to wait for me. Tell him to close the door and you guys melt that fucking locking mechanism. We can't afford to fail now." With that, he grabbed the mace-like weapon and was about to bolt from the Cargo Hold, when Finch rushed in, breathing hard. "They're coming!" was all he could get out before they realized they could here running feet in the corridor. Jaime cursed and yelled to the others, "It's time people! Fight! Fight for your lives!"

4

Doc had skirted quietly around a couple of Rey's guards standing near the entrance that led to the Commons. They had the supreme air of being on the winning side. He saw Rey yelling furiously at Dante near the cockpit entrance. He guessed Rey was pissed because they couldn't find Finch or Eddie or more of the passengers. He caught sight of several of Soren's guards sitting in the Commons. They were bloodied and bruised and looked as if they couldn't believe that they were now being treated like all the others. He thought he saw a couple of Jaime's engineers sitting there also – Sarah Smith and Wayne Kesk. Shelton Hayes was there too, blood dripping down the side of his face. He seemed to remember that Shelton was always fawning over the guards, almost as if he wanted to become one. He grimaced as he saw Emma Pennington sitting toward the front of the Commons. Her slumped shoulders were shaking and Doc realized she was probably crying. He felt enormous guilt seeing her here. She had been brutalized by Soren or Rey's guards on at least two occasions. He realized forlornly, that there was nothing he could do for her, for any of them here in the Commons. They were now prisoners of war and unless he wanted to become a prisoner too, he would have to steer clear of the Commons.

He turned toward the Med-Lab stairway entrance, but his peripheral vision caught something extraordinary. He yanked his head back and saw

Soren sitting toward the front of the Commons. His entire demeanor had a look of worn-out dishevelment. Burt could see dried blood stains on the back of his shirt as he sat slumped in the chair. *Rey's goons must be winning*, he thought, as he turned toward Med-Lab. At the sight of Soren, Burt wasn't sure how he felt. Part of him hated Soren for engineering this entire charade of human survival. For abandoning Tess and the others to certain death on the moon. For his insane idea of fathering a child from every woman on the ship. For forcing this precarious and uncertain future onto all of them. But with Rey in charge, all of their lives would be in utter danger. He had seen Rey kill in cold blood. He had seen the raw and merciless way Rey killed Dan. And in his heart of hearts, he knew Rey had killed Jana. For what reason, the answer to that lay only in Rey's diseased and corrupted mind. Rey wouldn't make a spectacle of killing someone like Soren did to Allison and Larry. Rey would just kill them outright. He shuddered at the thought as he slowly made his way toward Med-Lab to look for Kelly. He was immensely gratified to not see her in the Commons, but if she was not in Med-Lab, then she could be anywhere on the ship. He began to wish he had kept the laser he took off Martin, instead of giving it to Finch to protect Eddie. Now here he was in the lion's den...defenseless.

As he approached the Med-Lab, he could see that the main lights were out. Only the dim automatic nightlights shone, giving off a pale, ghostly blue hue. This would have been one of the first places the guards would have searched while looking for him and some of the others. Rey would want to get everyone into the Commons to gloat about the regime change. But there were really no places to hide in Med-Lab and the search would have taken all of three minutes to determine if it was empty or not. He slipped in and allowed the door to slowly slide shut behind him. Crouching, he made his way back to the first exam room. Unless the guards had looted the rooms, he should have a scalpel in the nurses' cabinet.

He could hear distant yelling floating up from the Commons. He wondered if it was directed at Soren's guards or if they had caught several more trying to flee to the Cargo Hold. He wondered why they hadn't sent more guards to that part of the ship and realized that Rey probably wanted to gain control of Soren and his guards. Once he consolidated his power, in a manner of speaking, then he would deal with the insurrectionists, as he once called Doc and his people. And in Rey's mind, what would the rush be? What did they think they could do by going to the Cargo Hold? They would have simply cornered themselves. Doc smiled to himself and thought, *Rey's in for a big surprise if he's thinking that.*

He didn't find a scalpel in the first exam room and prepared to go into the second exam room when he heard the slightest of sounds coming from inside the room. His hand practically froze in mid-air as he prepared to open the door. He listened intently, strenuously, desperately trying to isolate the sound in the room from the yammering of blood pounding in his ears. He crouched there for what seemed hours, when he heard the sound again. It was faint, but there just the same.

He still didn't have a weapon, but he began to think that maybe this was one of the passengers trying to hide from Rey. If he rushed into the room and surprised whoever was in there, there might be an initial scuffle, but that would be all it took for the guards to hear and come rushing in. He didn't think it was a guard because they typically didn't have a reason to hide. He decided to take a chance that this was someone he knew. Quietly and in his most reassuring tone, he whispered, "Hey...it's Doctor Stone. Burt. You can't stay here for long. Let me get you to safety. I'm going to come inside slowly. Don't scream or run. If you do that, Rey's guards will hear you and then we're both doomed." He listened intently again. First there was nothing and then faintly, he could hear sobbing. He pushed open the door slowly, but initially didn't see anyone or anything. He crawled around to the other side of the bed and in the dim blue light, he could see Kelly sitting in the corner, partially hidden beneath the large hamper. A thorough search would have seen her, but knowing the guards, they probably poked their heads in here, gave a quick cursory look and moved on.

Kelly crawled out from behind the hamper and hugged Doc fiercely. "Oh God, Burt. Am I glad to see you! I couldn't sleep so I just walked around the ship thinking of Nola." She paused a moment and then added, "Thinking of Anton. As I got closer to the Commons, I could hear a lot of yelling and screaming and crying. I didn't know what to do, so I hid." She looked up at him, her eyes red and puffy. "What's going on Burt? Why are the guards rounding people up?

Doc disengaged from her and saw that she was still wearing one of Nola's jumpsuits. "I don't have time to go into the details right now Kelly, but we need to get out of here and head to the Cargo Hold." He began to crawl toward the door.

She nodded and asked, "The Cargo Hold? How can we hide there? Won't the guards just come there, unlock it and storm in?"

"I promise to tell you on the way, Kelly," Doc replied. "Right now, we need to get out of here quickly. He opened up the nurses' cabinet before he opened the door and sighed in relief. He grabbed the scalpel and they both slipped out of the exam room and out of Med-Lab.

5

Liz skirted through the corridors quickly and quietly. She hadn't seen any guards so far and was thankful for that. She knew Jaime would be very upset with her for leaving the Cargo Hold, but she had forgotten something very important to her. When they were on the moon, Jaime had proposed to her with the ring passed down to him from his great-grandmother on his mother's side. She remembered fondly, the stories Jaime shared with her about his great-grandmother's trek from Venezuela to the United States as a young girl. Of course, he never knew his great-grandmother, because she died before he was born, but everyone swore he had a striking resemblance to her as a young child. He shared with her how his grandmother would always accuse him of being his "great-grandmother's great-grandson" whenever he would sneak home from some wild, teenage adventure in the mountains near his hometown of San Bernardino in California. As Lycos was bearing down on the world, his mother, with tears in her eyes gave him his great-grandmother's ring and told him as long as this ring was with him, then she and all who came before him, would live on in his heart. He had told Liz that was the day he shipped out to the moon, knowing he would never see her again.

Liz cursed herself for the third time since leaving the Cargo Hold. She never took the ring off, but today, as she was preparing the compounds to take to the Cargo Hold, she couldn't bear the thought of accidentally damaging it, so she placed it in a container and put it inside her work table in engineering. In the urgency and angst of getting the compounds ready, she completely forgot about the ring and left it in engineering. Only when she arrived at the Cargo Hold and overheard several individuals talking about Finch and Kelly's farce of a marriage, did she remember her ring. She heard someone say, "I wonder what type of 'ring' he gave her? A flat washer??" And at that, everyone burst out laughing. To her, it was like a dagger to the heart. She snapped her head down toward her hand, hoping against hope, to see the ring there, but it was gone. She screamed forlornly, startling everyone near her. And without another thought, handed the compounds to Ralph Valstok and told him she was going to look for Jaime. He yelled something to her as she was bolting through the Cargo Hold door, but she never heard him.

6

Doc and Kelly slithered along the wall connected to the waste management compartments. There were other corridors that connected to the main corridor that led to the Cargo Hold, but this one was a little safer.

They were about to turn down the corridor that led to the Cargo Hold when they heard fighting up ahead. They immediately flattened themselves up against the curved wall. Doc moved quietly to the edge of the wall and looked out. He could see what looked like a full-blown battle. He could see Rey viciously swinging a baton in the air, a look of mad glee dancing in his eyes. Several bodies lay sprawled on the floor, but Doc couldn't tell if they were guards or passengers.

Beyond the fighters, Doc could see the opening to the Cargo Hold. The narrow corridor was only wide enough for a handful of fighters, so they bunched there, swinging out over the fray when a guard got too close to the opening. Finch, Jaime and a few others were holding their own, but Rey had close to eight guards with him. Doc noticed that several of them were Soren's guards, or ex-guards now. If he and Kelly didn't have to take such a circuitous route, they could have gotten here way before Rey and his guards.

Kelly had moved up next to Doc and had peeked around the corner as well. Doc could hear the breath catch in her throat as she caught sight of Anton getting pummeled on the floor. Her heart went out to him. She detested the fact that his machinations landed her in Soren's cabin for a week. She had tried unsuccessfully to erase those memories from her mind. She had realized soon after she was released, that she would not be able to move forward with Anton until she had forgiven herself. Before all of this started, she felt she was getting there. Getting back to being in love with him. Maybe. She knew they had a tough road ahead, but she was finally ready.

But as she looked at him getting his face punched over and over again, she intuitively understood that things would never be the same. Rey had been relentlessly pursuing her. He was always where she was. Feigning a weird and perverted love interest in her. It was revolting. With Nola gone, she knew that Rey would do anything to get her, which would mean getting Soren out of the way. He would probably use Anton as leverage, forcing her to annul her marriage with Anton or outright divorce him. And in return, he would let Anton live. She would be someone's prisoner again. She screamed in her mind and then screamed piercingly out loud. Doc yanked his head toward her, his eyes wide and saw Kelly with her own scalpel, held so close to her neck, that Doc could see a thin red line showing.

7

Rey was the first to respond to the scream which seemed louder than any of the yelling surrounding him. He looked toward the sound and saw

Kelly standing there next to Doc. They were both holding scalpels, but Kelly had hers pressed tightly to her throat. Rey could see blood streaming over her hand and down her wrist. By then, the fighting died down and the passengers staggered slowly backwards, toward the Cargo Hold.

"KELLY!! NO!!" Finch screamed maniacally. "I love you! Don't do this!

Finch had stood up, but was punched unceremoniously in the stomach. He went down to the floor in an agony of pain. "No..." he whimpered.

"Kelly." Rey said amicably. "Kelly, what are you doing? There's been too much death on this ship for you to take your own life." His gaze drifted over to Doc's face. In an instant, it went from affable to demonic. Doc found himself slightly dizzy as if he were seeing an apparition manifest itself in real time.

Doc looked past them toward the Cargo Hold. He could see Ralph give him a thumbs up. To Doc, this could mean that the compounds were ready and the door could be fused as soon as they were inside. Rey caught his gaze and turned around quickly, but not before Ralph could bring his arm down. He turned back to Doc and laughed, "Do you really think you can hide in the Cargo Hold?" He laughed uproariously, genuinely. "Even if you change the code on the door, we would have it opened in a matter of hours, but hey, whatever floats your boat, right? His faced turned hard again, "Now that I'm in charge here, I might have been willing to do things a little differently, but first your pathetic coup d'état and now this little Cargo Hold hide-and-seek shenanigan, you've forced me to consider some even more drastic changes than Soren had."

Kelly yelled out, but not out of fear or surprise, but anger, "Rey!" He gazed at her again, the smooth look of affability washed over his face. "I know you want me, Rey. Don't you?" Without waiting for him to respond, she continued on, "What if I drag this scalpel across my throat? Then you would have lost Nola *and* you would have lost me!"

From the floor, Anton Finch yelled out again, but he wasn't the only one. Doc had yelled out too. He stood in front of her, tears running down his face, "Kelly...no. Please...no. Don't do this to yourself. We can see a way out of this. Please give me the scalpel."

Kelly looked at him and smiled, but her smile was full of anguish and agony. It was a dagger to his soul. She turned her gaze back toward Rey. "Rey, I will do whatever you want, if you'll allow Anton, Burt, and the others to lock themselves in the Cargo Hold. I'll divorce Anton and marry you, if you want. Let them go...now. If not..." She pressed the scalpel even tighter to her neck and grimaced. Rivulets of blood ran down her arm, which was now completely covered in blood.

Rey looked bewildered. He stood there transfixed. "You're telling me that you will not kill yourself, if I allow Doc, Finch and the others to lock themselves in the Cargo Hold? And what...just leave them there?"

Kelly nodded, tears running down her cheeks, dripping to the floor and some comingling with the blood running down her neck. "Just let them go...and you can have...me." The word *me* came out heavy and wet and full of lost.

If Rey had ever learned how to play chess, he felt right now he would have been on the verge of yelling *checkmate!* He turned to look at his guards. "Let them go, all of them." The few who hadn't gone back to the Cargo Hold, got up and limped and stumbled toward the entrance. Finch reluctantly got up and walked slowly toward the entrance. He turned around and was about to start forward, when someone pulled him back, into the Cargo Hold.

Kelly looked at Burt's distraught face. She smiled again at him and whispered, "This was the only way, Burt. The only way." He was about to say something, when she said, "Go now Burt. Go. *GO!!*" Shocked into movement, Doc moved quickly toward the Cargo Hold. He turned to see Kelly hand the scalpel to Rey, just before the door started closing shut. The last thing he heard before the door slammed shut was Rey, "Now get those fuckers out of there...*now!*"

LIZ AND OTTO

1

Liz could hear a lot of commotion behind her, somewhere in one of the corridors, but she had to focus on the task at hand. She crept up to the primary doors leading to engineering and peeked through the small window set in the door. While it wouldn't reveal anyone hiding in here, she could at least see if there were any guards walking around inside. She saw no one. She quickly palmed the door open, half expecting one of Rey or Soren's guards to snatch her up, but she was alone. Breathing a sigh of relief, she sprinted toward her work floor desk, yanked it open and grabbed the small container containing the ring. She slid it on her finger and breathed a huge sigh of relief. She glanced at a screwdriver she had left on her desk and shoved it inside her pocket, just in case she needed it. Just as she closing the drawer out of habit, she heard the smooth hiss of the main entrance door sliding open.

Her head snapped toward the door, just as Otto Helmut was strolling in. His demeanor was casual, but his eyes danced dangerously in their sockets. He was staring at her, his mouth half-open as he closed the distance between them. Slowly, the corners of his lips curled upward, "Hallo, was haben wir denn da?" he said as he continued to close the distance between them. "Fraulein Liz, you have been missing me, no?"

Liz stepped behind her work bench in a futile effort to put something between her and Helmut. The look in his eyes was unmistakable. She considered making a run for the main entrance, but her path would come too close to him. It would be a fool's mistake and he would grab her before she was even halfway to the door. "Where is Herr Jaime?" he said. "Is he hiding somewhere here like a *verängstigter Schuljunge*?" He laughed uproariously as he looked around engineering. "Herr Jaime! Wo bist du? Where are you hiding?"

Liz thought about her options. She was much more familiar with the engineering layout than Helmut and she felt certain she could outrun him if she had to. Helmut was a big guy and that included his big gut. She was amazed that he could have a gut on him with all of the ship's rationing policies. She thought about making a run for the fusion engines compartment. It was a large, noisy, multi-leveled area that not only housed the huge fusion engines, but the sophisticated equipment controlling the gravitational rings within the ship. If she could make it there, she might be able to slip around him make it back to the Cargo Hold before Jaime and Burt fused the door shut. In her mind, she could sense that her window of opportunity was rapidly shrinking by the second.

Helmut had turned completely away from her looking for Jaime and she took that opportunity to sprint toward the fusion compartment. She heard him yell in fury as he galloped after her. She was shocked when she saw how fast he was moving in an effort to cut her off from the entrance. His protruding belly belied just how agile he really was, but she was faster. She sprinted through the entrance and was about to round the first huge fusion engine when she felt a huge yank on her hair. She had her hair tied in a loose ponytail, but it was just enough for Helmut to reach out his long arms and grab enough of it to yank her off balance and drag her to the floor. As she was falling, an old memory suddenly awakened that caused her to chide herself for her foolishness.

Growing up, Liz had always been a zombie fan. She watched all of the movies. She went on social media and passionately argued the pros and cons of the fast zombies versus the slower, *George A. Romero* zombies. She had gotten into it so deeply that one day she purchased a zombie survival guide book. She marveled at the book's detail and ingenuity in how to survive certain zombie encounters and she laughed at the more ridiculous things to do during a zombie apocalypse. What brought this memory roaring into her psyche at this moment, was the book's suggestion that in the zombie apocalypse, women and some men, should consider keeping their hair short. The book stated that women with long hair were in particular danger because a zombie could easily grab that hair – in her case, a ponytail – and pull them to the ground. And with only a bite or a scratch standing between living or becoming the living dead, one's chances of surviving that encounter, would be slim to none. In that instant that Helmut had grabbed her hair, she understood that there was a good chance she would not survive this encounter.

She fell hard onto the grated floor and could feel herself on the verge of passing out. For one frightful second, she imagined maybe this was how it was always going to play out. Jaime would be sealed behind the Cargo Hold door, screaming himself crazy that she was not there, while she lay used and spent on the cold engineering floor, her throat crushed and her body soiled. But even as those reprehensible thoughts assailed her, she rebelled. She would not give in to this animal and would fight back with every ounce of strength she had.

She felt herself being flipped over onto her back with Helmut straddling her. Agile or not, he was paying the price for his little sprint. He was breathing hard, raspy bouts of foul-smelling breath into her face. Both sweat and spittle dropped onto her face as he sat atop her, pinning her to the ground.

"And now, meine freundin, you will, *how do you say?* Experience love-making, *Otto's way*". He half-laughed, half-coughed, as he made to undo his pants. As the fog lifted in Liz's head, she could feel Helmut fumbling around with her jumpsuit. Since it was a one-piece, he was having difficulty getting it off of her. She feigned unconsciousness, realizing she only had seconds to do something before it became too late. A distant part of her mind remembered an uncomfortable, if not slightly painful, jab in her thigh, when Helmut rolled her over. As her mind furiously thought about her options, she could feel Helmut shifting around on her. He hadn't been able to open up her jumpsuit with his hands and was becoming increasingly frustrated. "Scheiße!" he yelled out. "Where ist the fucking..." He laughed genuinely, "If dis was snake, it would well have bite me," he said as he uncovered the recessed opening of Liz's jumpsuit, hidden under the snug turtleneck collar.

He fumbled excitedly at the collar of her suit, unsnapping it, allowing him to unzip the top, exposing her sports bra. He unzipped it as low as it would go, exposing her navel and the top part of her underwear. Liz's mind was in a frantic now. It was time to fight or die. When Helmut straddled her, his knees had pinned her arms to her side. With her fingers, she felt something round and hard in her cargo pocket and wondered if she had been feeling it the entire time. It was the handle of the screwdriver she had shoved in her pocket as an afterthought. She slowly, cautiously, slid her hand into her pocket, hoping to wrap her fingers around the handle of the screwdriver. At the same time, she could feel Helmut's calloused and filthy hand caressing her navel. She almost gagged. She felt him shift back a little until he was fully on her hipbone. She squinted at him through lidded eyes and saw him working at the zipper on his own jumpsuit. When he did this, his weight lifted slightly off her and his knees loosened up on her arms. As soon as she felt this movement, she yanked the screwdriver out of her pocket and in a high, slashing arc, dragged the screwdriver across his face. She felt the flathead screwdriver take root in his face as he screamed piercingly. She thought satisfyingly that if he hadn't been so preoccupied with getting his penis out of his pants, he might have had a chance to block her slash.

"Scheiße! Scheiße!" he screamed. "Mein Auge!" Liz saw him grabbing at his eye trying to stem the flood of ooze and blood gushing from his wounded eye. He seemed to have completely forgotten about her. "Get the fuck off me!" she yelled and she violently jackknifed her hips upward. The sudden movement threw him off-balance, forcing him to drop his hands to the floor near her head. She snaked her hand around his right wrist and yanked it toward her with as much force as she could muster. He crumpled onto his side in a vain effort to reduce the pressure on his wrist, but not before she heard a slight snap. He face-planted into the floor, rolling slightly to his side. Liz brought her knee up quickly and hard, ramming it into his testicles, bringing a fresh set of screams and whimpers. Although she couldn't hear anything, she would have sworn her knee felt something small and vulnerable pop like a stubborn walnut in a new set of nutcrackers. As he started rolling to his side, she made a herculean effort to shove him completely off of her when all of a sudden, she felt a hard blow to her head. Somehow, he was able to maintain his balance and used his elbow to slam into the side of her head. Her efforts to shove him off diminished rapidly and once again, she could feel herself on the verge of passing out.

"I kill you!" he shouted through blood and spit, his desire to take her by force completely gone. Despite the gaping wound on his face and the throbbing pain in his testicles, he wrapped both his hands around Liz's neck. Liz could feel his fingers digging into her windpipe and realized this was how she was going to die. He would either crush her windpipe or choke the life out of her. From far off, she could hear the sound of a freight train roaring over broken tracks and realized it was her own frantic wheezing and gurgling. Helmut screamed at her as he bore down on her throat, but Liz could only hear muted sounds. She could no longer see him above her even though her eyes were open. The only thing she could feel was the soft rumble of the fusion engines in the floor. She began to feel her body shut down when all of a sudden, her damaged throat seemed to open up and air filled her lungs. Despite the burning in her throat, she gulped the air in spastic fits, coughing and crying at the same time.

"Liz! Are you okay?!" yelled a woman's voice above her. "Liz!" the voice yelled, closer this time. Liz could feel someone cradling her head. She opened her eyes and saw a young woman staring intently at her. She recognized the face, but her brain was having difficulty connecting the face with a name. Just as she was beginning to worry that her near-death experience with Helmut may have burned out some of her brain cells, the woman's name immediately came to her. "Elsa! Oh my God, Elsa!" At the thought of Helmut's name, she sat up immediately, a look of pure panic in her eyes. "Where the fuck is he?? Where's Helmut??" she yelled hoarsely.

"It's okay Liz! It's okay." She glanced off to the side toward a crumpled body. "That son-of-a-bitch won't be bothering anyone else ever again." Liz looked over to where Elsa had glanced and saw the huge body of Helmut lying on his side, as if he were asleep. She noticed a thin curly stream of smoke emanating from his head. "What happened Elsa?" she asked. It didn't connect with her why smoke would be coming from Helmut's body. She smelled what could only have been burnt flesh, but there was another, more acrid smell.

Elsa said, "I was trying to make it to the Cargo Hold, but heard some guards running through the corridors, so I hid in one of the uniform supply room closets until it was quiet. I had almost made it to the Cargo Hold when I was forced to detour here. I only meant to hide here for a couple of minutes when I heard screaming and what sounded like a scuffle." She looked down at her hands and said, almost sheepishly, "I panicked and almost ran out of here when I thought I heard your voice. I snuck over to the fusion room and saw him on top of you. Your legs were kicking wildly and then they stopped." She hitched, trying to hold back tears. "I thought he had killed you. I was so angry, I just ran up behind him and put this right up against the back of his head." She pointed to the medical laser she had strapped to her belt. "I put it up to his head and kept the button pressed until I burned a hole in his fucking head!"

Liz hugged her tightly. This young woman had saved her life. It now made sense why there were tendrils of smoke drifting up from Helmut's head. She sniffed and began to understand what the acrid smell was. She disengaged from Elsa and jumped up. "Elsa, we need to get out of here now!" Elsa stood up also with a look of misunderstanding in her eyes. "He's dead though, Liz" she said. "He can't harm us now."

Liz grabbed Elsa by the shoulders and turned her toward one of the fusion engine exterior casings. "Look Elsa! These medical lasers might be small, but concentrated bursts can do significant damage. The laser not only burned through Helmut's head, but it has compromised the casing for one of the fusion engines." As if on cue, they began hearing a whining sound of energy buildup within the casing. Liz grabbed Elsa by the arm and they sprinted out of the fusion room toward the door of engineering. They scurried up the connection tube leading to the Cargo Hold level. They had just turned down the corridor east of the Cargo Hold when a huge explosion lifted them from the floor and threw them violently against the far wall of the corridor. Too stunned to move, Liz and Elsa lay on the floor clutching one another as multiple explosions shook the ship below them. As they lay there shivering, Liz silently prayed that the engineering bulkhead doors did their job and shut immediately.

SECURING THE CARGO HOLD

1

"Get that fucking compound over here, now!" Doc yelled. They had shut the Cargo Hold door and immediately changed the code, but it was only a matter of time before Rey's people overrode it.

"Wait!" Jaime screamed out. "Liz isn't here! I've got to go back out there for her! Let me out!"

Doc jumped in front of Jaime and grabbed him by the shoulders, "Jaime!" he yelled. "We can't brother! We can't. They'll overwhelm us if we did. We were losing out there until Kelly sacrificed herself. I'm sorry Jaime, I'm sorry."

Jaime struggled in Doc's arms, but much more weakly. At last, he sagged against him, crying. "She went looking for me, Burt," he said through sobs. "How can I leave her out there with those animals?"

"I know Jaime, I know," Doc said, starting to tear up himself. "This is probably the only chance we'll have to separate ourselves from all of them. If there were any other way, I would have been first to look for her. But it's too late now. We must seal this door."

Jaime raised his head toward Burt, his eyes red from crying. "Goddammit!" he yelled. "Goddammit!" He pulled away from Burt and walked off toward the rear of the Cargo Hold, dropping into one of the chairs stored here. Behind him, Ralph and a few others were rushing over to the door to apply the compound when a huge explosion threw them and everyone else to the floor. Almost simultaneously, several additional explosions rocked the Cargo Hold.

Doc lay on the floor with his arms covering his head, waiting for the inevitable destruction of the *Cassiopeia*. He thought sadly that the grand ship had finally had its fill of the monstrous and vile things that were being done on her. In his mind's eye, he saw the anthropomorphic *Cassiopeia* violently vomiting and shitting out its infested inhabitants, one by one, into space.

"Burt!" Jaime yelled from the back of the Cargo Hold. "Those explosions came from engineering!" He ran over to Burt and helped him up from the floor. "My bet would be the fusion engines."

Burt thought a moment and then said, "I can intuit that if those were the fusion engines, then our ability to maneuver the ship will be completely lost. Is that right?"

"Yes, but there's something else Burt," he said. "If the engines just died, then we would lose all power of thrust and maneuverability, but they exploded Burt. Which means our forward momentum may have stopped altogether." He opened his mouth to continue when Ralph yelled out, "Jaime! It's Liz!"

2

Things are gonna work out alright, Rey thought, as he walked toward Soren seated in the Commons. Doc and his crew were secured in the Cargo Hold for the moment. He had no concern that they would not be able to get the cargo door open. It would be a pain in the ass, but he was certain they could get in there. And once they got in, he would figure out how many would live and how many would die. Doctor or not, Stone would have to go. He felt the Good Doctor was just too much trouble and would always be the one to get shit started. Yes, he would be the first to die.

Soren looked up as he approached him. Rey chided himself for being fool enough to follow Soren like a lost puppy. Looking at him now, he looked old, worn and useless, like a spent rubber lying in the bushes. And his guards left him like rats fleeing a burning building. The main question now was what to do with him. He was not worried about Soren reclaiming his prior stature, that was gone forever, but would Soren be a help or a hindrance to him on the new world? Rey himself was not foolish enough to believe in Soren's *First Father* bullshit, but it had a certain rakish attraction to it. He considered it briefly, but decided against it. As part of his *rise to power*, he had promised his men access to the women as long as they followed him and were loyal. Everyone except Kelly. Kelly was his. Kelly was...*his* woman.

Kelly had told him that she would annul her marriage to Finch and then would marry him if he allowed Doc and the others to secure themselves in the cargo room and he had agreed to it. Thinking about it now, none of it mattered anyway. They were the last survivors of Earth. Out here on the fringes of the galaxy, millions of miles away from the birthplace of humanity, nothing mattered but survival. To Rey, mundane things like annulments, marriages, and even God was nothing but bullshit created on a planet that no longer existed. Here, he was in charge. He was the strong one. And he would survive. A line from an old movie called *Cloud Atlas*, floated into his consciousness. He couldn't remember the details of the movie, but one line always stuck with him, *the weak are meat, and the strong do eat.* He chuckled to himself and realized just how appropriate that phrase was out here in the emptiness.

"Just go ahead and laugh," Soren said to Rey as he got closer. "Just like Doc, your little coup is bound to fail. Not now and not here. It'll happen on Europa when you least expect it." He glared at Rey with contempt. "You won't win Rey and Nola is still dead."

Rey stared at Soren blankly. His words about Nola stung him, but he didn't dare give Soren the satisfaction that it bothered him. At this moment though, he was struggling mightily not to slam his fist into Soren's fat, dirt-streaked face. "I would think that you'd be more concerned about your own welfare."

Soren laughed harshly. It turned into a hacking cough. When he had settled down, he said, "I know what's going on in the Cargo Hold. Your guards have loose lips. You'll probably never get them out of there. I'm sure by now, they dismantled access through the main door. So, I'm thinking you'll have to wait until we land before you even have a chance to get at them." He paused a minute and then added, "And I saw you dragging the Kelly woman to the cockpit. Did you kill that fool Finch to take his wife?" He laughed bitterly. "This is almost biblical! King Rey killing Finch the Hittite in order to fuck his wife, Kelly! I'd say you can't make this shit up, but this tragic love story was already written." He laughed mockingly and then added, "When I took her, she believed there was still a chance at love with Finch, but now, you'll have to sleep with one eye open or keep her chained up. She actually is a lot like Nola and she'll fight you forever."

Rey stared at Soren with increasing hate in his eyes. He drew his hand back to slap him when all of a sudden, an explosion deep below the ship threw him violently over several rows of seats in the Commons. Even as he was starting to black out, he could feel the ship canting sickeningly end over end.

3

Burt and Jaime sprinted over to the bank of camera screens. Only a handful were actually working. They followed Ralph's eyes toward the camera pointed down the corridor leading to engineering and could see two figures hugging the far wall closely, carefully moving closer to the junction connecting the Cargo Hold corridor with the main corridor. Jaime sucked in his breath when saw a clearer picture of Liz. She appeared to be limping, holding tightly to Elsa and she was covered in blood. Burt glanced at Jaime and saw him stagger backward a bit. He grabbed his arm and said,

"We'll get her in here, Jaime, if I have to go out there myself and bring her in here." He didn't wait for Jaime's response. His eyes went to the screen of the camera positioned directly above the Cargo Hold door. Rey, Kelly and several other guards had left, presumably going to the front of the ship. There was no doubt that more guards would be returning once Rey made it the Commons, but for now, there were only three guards in the vicinity. Two of them were apparently having an argument, while the third sat on the floor against the wall, seemingly nursing a nasty cut on his head. In his lap lay one of the stun guns.

He turned immediately to Jaime and said, "Look! There are only three guards out there now and one of them is injured. He's got a stun gun, but if we're able to overwhelm them, we have a chance of getting to Liz and Elsa!" He glanced back at the camera and added, "We have about a ten-minute window before Rey's other guards come back." Several of the men in the Cargo Hold moved toward him as he was speaking. After a second of stunned silence, Jaime shoved past Burt and started moving toward the Cargo Hold hatch. "Let's go! Let's show these bastards what we're made of! We need to go out there in force, get Liz and Elsa and God help any of those fuckers who get in our way!"

4

Liz opened her eyes slowly. The red glare of emergency backup lights seemed to fill what little vision she had. She tried sitting up and screamed. Her right thigh was throbbing and felt as if a red-hot poker had been driven through it. She used her hands to explore her leg and could feel something jagged sticking out of her thigh. Her exploring hands felt sticky. Just as she started to survey her surroundings, the power in the corridor began reasserting itself and the bright neon lights flickered for a moment and then remained on. Liz looked around and saw Elsa lying next to her. She was moaning and slowly rolling over to stand up.

Everything that wasn't bolted down or secured was scattered throughout the corridor. Further down the corridor, she could hear screaming. "Elsa," she whispered. "Elsa. We need to get out of here. We're close, but I think they're fighting near the Cargo Hold or in the corridor leading to the Cargo Hold." She grimaced when she moved her wounded leg. "Elsa. I'm gonna need some help. There's something stuck in my leg and I don't think I can walk on it."

Elsa got up and walked over to her. Liz was glad to see that at least one of them was fully mobile, but she spied a nasty cut on Elsa's forehead. Elsa examined the shard of metal sticking out of Liz's leg. "It missed your main arteries Liz, so you're not in immediate danger, but we have to leave it in until we get to the Cargo Hold. It'll be painful, but you may bleed out if we try to remove it here." Liz nodded and clinched her teeth as Elsa helped her to her feet. "We'll go slow and steady, Liz," said Elsa. She put her arm around Liz's waist and they slowly made their way down the corridor toward the Cargo Hold. Intensely focusing on each step, Elsa said, "We'll make it if it kills us."

5

Rey lay on the floor of the Commons looking up at the ceiling. He had come close to passing out after being tossed fifteen feet in the air. The lights had gone out temporarily, but were now back on. Somewhere, an alarm was screaming and the ship's voice-enabled monitoring system was calmly stating over and over again that the hull in engineering compartment number 25 was compromised. He looked over to where Soren had been thrown to the floor. Hid eyes were closed and blood trickled down the side of his scalp, but he was still breathing.

Rey stood up and looked around the Commons. There were only a handful of people in here and they were all getting up from the floor. He saw Jake Sandstone stand shakily near the rear of the Commons. He thought about Doc and the others locked in the Cargo Hold and could feel himself heating up with anger. He was in charge now and he was done putting up with their bullshit. He considered letting them stay locked in until they landed on Europa, but he wanted to hold them to account *now*. He yelled over to Jake Sandstone, "Jake! Get some men and get to the Cargo Hold! I want those fuckers out now! Bring them all to the Commons!" Jake nodded and sprinted out of the Commons, grabbing several nearby guards.

Feeling a little more in charge, Rey headed to the cockpit. He felt an overwhelming urge to assess the damage from the explosions. He couldn't help but feel dread about the state of the ship and was anxious to see ship status readouts in the cockpit. He entered the cockpit and hurried over to the ship's main console, deep down suspecting that his fears would soon be realized.

LOCKED INSIDE

Chad Meyers, one of the *Cassiopeia's* maintenance workers, pushed his way to the front of the men moving toward the entrance. He had been secretly seeing Emma Pennington and when he found out that she had been brutalized by some of the guards, he was enraged. When he started fleeing to the Cargo Hold earlier in the day, he ran to her cabin but she was not there. Unfortunately, when he arrived at the Cargo Hold, he did not find her there either. He attempted to leave, but by then, the guards had arrived and they were in a fight for their lives. Despite their slightly greater numbers, the guards' stun guns and medical lasers were punishing. One of the men died when a stun gun shot hit him so hard that he fell back and cracked open his skull on a metal shelf in the corridor. After Kelly and Doc arrived and Kelly agreed to go with Rey, they were allowed to go inside the Cargo Hold. He wanted to run and find Emma then, but several men pulled him inside and they locked the Cargo Hold door. He stomped off angrily toward the back wall, not wanting to think about what would happen to Emma out there. After the explosion, he got up and walked toward the front of the Cargo Hold where he heard Doc say something about going out for Liz. If they were going back out, he would be right behind them. This was his chance to find Emma.

Burt and Jaime both grabbed the handle of the Cargo Hold door and pulled it open. When they first arrived, the first thing they did was cut the power to the door. It would only open now under human power. Walt stared at the camera showing the main corridor, half-expecting a flood of guards to come swooping into the corridor. The three guards who were left behind, turned quickly toward the slowly opening door. He yelled to the men inside the Cargo Hold who were getting ready to go outside, "Get ready! Two of the guards are coming toward you now!"

Chad forced his way toward the front and as soon as the door was open wide enough, he squeezed through, tightly gripping the lead pipe he carried in hands. He sprinted toward the nearest guard. "Slow down Chad!" Jaime yelled as he and Burt squeezed through the small opening. Several more men followed them, yelling as they made their way across the threshold of the door. The remaining men and women in the Cargo Hold stood at the ready to prevent any of the guards from charging in. Most were nursing injuries sustained during their skirmish with the guards when they first got here, but would give everything to protect what they saw as their last chance at living.

As soon as Chad was in the corridor, he zeroed in on Vince Eckels, one of Soren's original guards. Vince stared transfixed at the man running full tilt toward him. He thought he recognized him, but couldn't quite remember his name or where he worked. Vince could also see others streaming out of the Cargo Hold. He didn't dare look behind him, but he hoped Wade and Rich were paying attention.

Vince was originally a philosophy professor stationed at the United Nations' base and one of the survivors of the meteorite storm. When Soren first started vetting his potential guards, he sought Vince out because he was a mixed martial arts fanatic and Soren felt he could use that kind of strength on his team. Vince agreed immediately, not because of the expected leverage and authority he might have, but because of Soren's offer that he would be granted a woman after Soren's *First Fathering* thing. Looking at the angry men streaming out of the Cargo Hold, he began to wonder if he was indeed on the winning team.

2

Jaime stared at Chad's back as he raced toward the guards. As much as he hated the man's impetuousness, a part of him appreciated the fact that his swift attack would be a distraction for the handful of guards in the corridor. He turned and yelled to the others, "Attack the guards in the main corridor!" He pointed to Burt and two other men, "You guys come with me!" They ran behind the men attacking the guards, but turned right as soon as they made it to the connecting corridor where Liz and Elsa were.

They sprinted down the corridor and nearly slammed into Liz and Elsa when they turned around a curve in the corridor. "Shit!" Ralph yelled as he skidded to a stop, bare feet from Elsa. They had flattened up tighter along the wall and Liz was behind Elsa. Their eyes were wide as they prepared to fight whatever was coming toward them.

"Jaime!" Liz shouted when she saw Jaime. She was so overcome that instead of sprinting into his arms, her knees buckled and she would have collapsed right there on the floor, had it not been for Ralph. He caught her easily and eased her to a sitting position. Jaime ran to her and fell to the floor in front of her, hugging her tightly. "I thought I lost you!" he said through slurring words. "I thought I lost you." She smiled at him, even though her eyes were still closed. "You'll never lose me," she said quietly.

"I foolishly went ba..." she began, but was interrupted by Burt, "Guys, we need to get the hell back...*now!*"

3

As Vince watched Chad move toward him in slow motion, he could feel his muscles tightening in anticipation of the fight to come. He smiled inwardly. He always liked this part. The part where an opponent, or in this case, some hapless fool, rushes him blindly, crazily, all full of piss and vinegar. The part where he knew exactly where and how he would incapacitate Mister P. Vinegar. He relished it because there was nothing holding him back from completely destroying this man. Whenever he participated in training sessions or tournaments, he always knew that he could only go sixty, maybe seventy percent. Any more could do serious damage to an opponent, not to mention get him sued. He had come close to being sued several times because of his "overzealous fighting style" as the fighting commission put it. But now he felt...unrestrained. Now, he would actually see if he had what it took to take the life of someone with his bare hands.

He had never killed a person before, but he had killed many a small animal while growing up. Even as a young teenager, he had gotten very good at building traps and placing them in the wooded areas behind his parents' home in Washington State. At first, he was content with torturing and killing the small animals he caught like rabbits, possums, squirrels and the like. But then he advanced to the larger, more dangerous animals. Once, he traveled deep into the woods and laid a small bear trap with spiked teeth. He left it there for several days and when he went out to retrieve it, found a barely alive black bear cub stuck in it. He saw larger footprints surrounding the cub, which meant the mother tried retrieving her cub, to no avail. She no doubt left the cub for good or to bring it food. It didn't matter to Vince, as he slowly crept toward the whining cub. During that time, he remembered thinking that he would have loved an opportunity to confront the mama bear. But that was all in the past in a world that no longer existed. Right now, he had a fool of a man rushing to meet his maker, but he was okay with that. All he knew was that he liked this part. He smiled wickedly as he unsheathed the blade at his hip.

As the man sprinted toward him, he wondered idly what it would be like to kill a real person up close and personal. Did he have what it took to kill someone with his bare hands? He thought so. He shivered at the thought and despite this running fool coming at him like a wild animal, he could feel himself getting a little excited, dare he say, even a little horny.

He chuckled inwardly, slightly embarrassed, but he steeled himself for the attack. As the man got closer, he could see his wild, crazed eyes and his open, slobbering mouth. The look on the man's face told him everything he needed to know about this encounter – it was kill or be killed.

Chad could feel his chest burning with exertion, but he would not slow down. He wasn't sure which guards attacked Emma, but it didn't matter, not anymore. They were all the same. They all stood against anything good and civil. His Emma was good. She was sweet and she loved him. *Him!* Whenever he was with her, he would grow lightheaded and his heart would swell each time he understood that it took the end of the world for them to be together. And these guards destroyed all of that. Rey, Soren, all of them. He would find her and be with her again, but that journey couldn't begin until he dealt with the arrogant fuck standing in front of him.

His plan was to skewer the man where he stood. The pipe he was carrying was jagged with pieces of sharp metal bent outward on the side, as if some powerful explosive burst through it. It would enter and exit the man's guts violently, totally eviscerating him. As he closed the distance to the man, he could see no outward movement, other than a slight twitching of the man's left eye. He was encouraged. The man would be caught totally flat-footed, not expecting such a dauntless and determined attack. He brought the pipe up and just as he was getting ready for ramming speed, the man pivoted slightly. It wasn't much of a movement, but it was enough to put him out of his line of attack. He realized, foolishly, that he had set himself up for a counterattack. He also realized somewhere deep in his mind that it couldn't technically be called a *counterattack* if he never even landed a strike on the man. As he came alongside the man, he tried unsuccessfully to angle his body so he could swing his pipe toward the man's face or anywhere on his body, but his momentum only carried him forward. The only thing he was able to do was witness the blur of a knee moving toward his mid-section. A microsecond after this, he felt something akin to granite, smash into his rib cage. He barely had time to register this pain, when something exploded into his brain. He was numb all over and could no longer feel his feet. The only thing he could tell was that he had fallen to the floor like a rag doll, while his nose seemed to gush red claret endlessly.

4

Ralph Valstok and Ted Donaldson led the way back toward the junction. They moved a bit slower going back, trying to gauge the fighting happening in the corridor leading to the Cargo Hold. Luckily, Elsa and Liz were very close to the Cargo Hold, so they didn't have to run too far away from the Cargo Hold main corridor. Jaime and Elsa carried Liz between them, while Burt brought up the rear to avoid any surprises from behind. Every few feet, he would yank his head toward the rear, bringing his laser up to the ready. He was clutching it so tightly in his hand, he had to periodically look at his hands to ensure it was still there.

Just as they reached the junction, they could see their people engaged in battle. Burt stared openmouthed. More of Rey's guards had joined the fray and it was starting to look like a cross between some mid-15th century medieval army and a *Star Trek Away Team*. Most of the weapons he saw the Cargo Hold folks brandishing looked homemade, but deadly, while most of the guards there were brandishing stun guns and lasers. Fortunately for the Cargo Hold folks, most of the guards were terrible shots. The medical lasers were design for work up close and not for firing into a crowd from a distance. The guards with the stun guns were having a bit more success in hitting their targets. Since the stun guns were designed more for riot control, the beam spread was wide to maximize its effect. Unfortunately, each time the stun guns were used, there was an automatic reset that lasted from five to ten seconds. The cargo folks quickly learned this and pounced on the guards after each shot of the stun guns. There were no resets with the unique and fearful-looking medieval weapons that the Cargo Hold people were wielding and they drove the handful of guards back mercilessly.

Jaime stopped when he entered the junction connected to the Cargo Hold corridor. He counted about five folks from the Cargo Hold fighting furiously in the corridor. When they left to retrieve Liz and Elsa, there were only three guards there. Now, there were at least seven, maybe eight there now. Burt made his way toward Jaime and looked out at the corridor. "We need to get to the Cargo Hold, but we can't leave our folks out there."

"I agree Burt, but I've got to get Liz back to the Cargo Hold now." Liz was leaning heavily on him and Elsa. Her eyes were closed and she was breathing shallowly. "Maybe you, Ralph and Ted can give us a chance to make it there." Burt nodded as he looked out at the fighting. He spied Chad on the floor at the far end of the corridor. He looked lifeless. There was a guard standing over Chad who started to move toward the fighting but stopped immediately, as if he had forgotten something. He turned back toward Chad and applied a vicious kick to his head. Chad shuddered violently and then stopped. Burt cringed and felt sick to his stomach. If Chad was clinging to life prior to that kick, then it was no doubt ripped away from him after that brutal kick to his head.

Disgusted, he turned to Jaime, "Okay, Jaime, when we go, you guys run like hell toward the Cargo Hold entrance. We'll buy you some time." He turned to Ralph and Ted, "We need to get our guys out there and make it back to the Cargo Hold. It'll be tough, but we can't leave them out there." They nodded in unison and gripped their hand-made weapons tighter. Ralph said, "Let's go fuck up some shit!" Burt smiled grimly at the man and looked out at the melee. "Alright, let's go. *Now!*" They all sprinted out into the corridor junction screaming at the tops of their lungs.

As soon as Burt, Ralph and Ted ran out into the corridor, Jaime tightened his hold around Liz's waist and shouted to her and Elsa, "Come on!" They ran toward to the Cargo Hold door and hoped they could make it before a laser or stun gun stopped them cold.

Burt, Ralph and Ted ran into the fray, screaming. Burt could see the guards momentarily lose their bearings when they saw what looked like an attack on their flank. When their attention was diverted, the cargo folks charged in even harder. Burt glanced over to where Chad lay and saw the guard, Vince or Vincent he remembered, turn toward them, as he raised the stun gun in his right hand. "Watch out!" he yelled to Ralph and Ted behind him as he prepared to dive onto the floor in front of Vince or Vincent.

Vince saw the three men advance toward him from one of the side corridors. He was halfway expecting this, but he was still surprised to actually see it. And the ferocity of their attack, caught him a bit off guard. But as they advanced, he knew what he would have to do. He grabbed the stun gun attached to his right hip and brought it up to the level of his attackers. He knew one of them was the Doc, but the other two numbnuts, he had no idea who they were. He zeroed in on the good doctor. He felt a little guilty at first because Doctor Stone had always been fair and nice to him. Vince remembered that he was constantly sick soon after they left the moon and Doctor Stone treated him respectfully. As he lined up the sights of his stun gun on Doctor Stone, he thought, *if I hit him in the head at this distance, it'll probably start some hemorrhaging inside his brain.* He considered the brutality of it and then shrugged his shoulders, *Oh well...he chose the wrong side, I guess.* He tightened his index finger over the trigger and just as he was about to pull it, felt an enormous pain in his leg. But it wasn't exactly his leg. It was further down. His ankle maybe? He collapsed immediately and for one frightening moment, thought his ankle had been amputated. As he pondered this, he turned around and saw the bloody mess that was Chad – *Ah! Chad was his name!* – lying on his side. He saw Chad take a deep shuddering breath and laid still, seeming to sink down into himself. The jagged blade he was clutching, clattered to the floor as his dead hand slowly opened. Cursing, Vince maneuvered to get up and realized immediately that he had no support or control from his left leg. He looked toward his ankle and saw bloody strips of skin and what looked like pinkish tendons draped over the heel of his shoe. In a distant part of his brain, he wondered angrily why he had decided to wear these low-cut exercise shoes instead of his normal boots. He had long forgotten what he had once learned about human anatomy, but he was certain that Chad had basically sliced through his Achilles tendon. He wrapped his hand around the bloody mess and screamed angrily, "You fucker! Do you know who I am? I've beaten opponents twice as big as you!" But Chad's lifeless eyes only stared back emotionless. Vince fired his stun gun into the body that once belonged to Chad Meyers. Chad's body moved closer to the corridor wall, a string of bloody spittle oozing from his mouth. Vince continued pulling the trigger, momentarily forgetting about the reset time. Frustrated, he threw the stun gun away from him and grabbed the medical laser from his belt. Just as he was about to fire the laser point-blank into Chad's face, he heard a noise behind him. He yanked his head around and saw the doctor standing over him with a laser and some sort of 14th century piece of crap. Vince shifted on the floor, trying to point the laser up at Doc, who immediately kicked it out of his hands. Vince stared up at Doc, who simply glared down at him for what seemed like hours. "What the fuck are you waiting for?" Vince yelled at him. "You're just like all the others! Always whining and waiting for..." And that was the last thing that came out of Vince Eckels' mouth as Doctor Burt Stone smashed his head in with the lead pipe.

Burt whirled around and grabbed Vince's stun gun. The fighting had turned into an all-out donnybrook. A few more Cargo Hold folks had joined the fray and now they outnumbered the guards by almost two to one. Burt saw a couple of guards sprinting toward the corridor exit fearfully. Burt decided this was the best time for them to make a run for the Cargo Hold. He yelled at the top his lungs, "Get back to the Cargo Hold now!" He ran up behind one of the guards still fighting and swung his pipe into the man's back. He screamed and fell to the floor, clutching frantically at the small of his back. One by one, they began to peel off from the fighting until there were only two or three left. The four or five remaining guards started to rush them when another huge explosion rocked the ship. Everyone was tossed into the air and came down hard on the corridor floor. Burt rolled around on the floor dazed. He opened his eyes and could see the cargo folks and the guards still reeling from the explosion. He got to his feet slowly, grabbed Ralph by the back of shirt. "Come on Ralph! Let's get Ted and get inside!"

Luckily, Ted was closest to the Cargo Hold door, but he was still on the floor. Burt could see blood running down his face from some hidden cut on his head. They sprinted toward Ted as the other guards were starting to come to their knees. Dante was the first guard to gain his footing. He could see Doc and another man picking someone up from the floor. He looked around the corridor, his guards looked dazed and defeated. He yelled at them angrily, "What the fuck are you waiting for?! Don't let them get to the Cargo Hold!" They gazed stupidly at the slowly opening Cargo Hold door and at the backs of the three men stumbling toward the entrance. They seemed to snap out of their lethargy when they saw Dante running toward the Cargo Hold door.

Burt and Ralph made their way to the entrance, half carrying Ted. He was conscious and trying to run too, but his legs barely supported him. The Cargo Hold door opened just enough to allow one person at a time, so Burt shoved Ted through. After Ted was pulled inside, he yelled to Ralph, "Go Ralph! Go!" Ralph squeezed through and Burt jumped in behind him. But just before he could get fully inside, he felt a tremendous yank on his right leg. Dante had apparently reached the door just in time to grab Burt's leg. "Get back out here you fucker!" Dante yelled. "Or I'll yank your leg clean off!"

A few more of the guards had reached the door and started grabbing at Burt's exposed leg. They pulled him inexorably toward the outer part of the door and for one terrible moment, Burt thought he would be yanked out of the opening of the door and back into the corridor. All of sudden, he felt someone climbing onto his back. Elsa had grabbed a cup of the mixture they were going to use to burn the Cargo Hold door and dashed it out of the opening. Burt felt searing pain when a drop or two fell onto his exposed back, but it was clear where the majority of it went when he heard guttural screaming behind him. The pressure on his leg ceased immediately and he was yanked into the Cargo Hold. As the door slowly closed, Burt could hear muted cursing and painful screaming coming from the corridor.

Entry Denied!

1

"What the fuck do you mean we can't get inside?" Rey screamed into Dante's face. "Just use the goddamn override code and drag their asses out!" Dante shifted nervously and clenched his teeth. He was in agony. When they were trying to pull Doc out of the Cargo Hold door frame, someone threw some kind of acid into his face. He ran screaming to Med-Lab in search of anything that would lessen the pain he was feeling on his face and neck, but there was very little in Med-Lab that would help. Apparently, over the last few weeks, most of the supplies and meds were taken to the Cargo Hold.

They were in the cockpit and Rey was trying to determine the extent of the damage to the ship and whether the explosions compromised their approach to Jupiter. From the ship's cockpit windows, the huge planet was now so close, that it took up most of the view from the forward cockpit windows. What concerned Rey, however, was that he could no longer see Europa. This meant that their trajectory had been thrown off by the explosions. Another concern was that their forward momentum was practically gone. Whatever had happened in engineering had completely destroyed their fusion engines. And since their forward momentum had stopped, he imagined that there was a gaping hole in engineering where the fusion engines blasted their way into space in the opposite direction of their travel, essentially bringing them to an almost dead stop.

Rey groaned inwardly and put his head in his hands. Dante looked at him with deep concern. He had never seen Rey show any kind of weakness. Whatever had happened, must have been bad. Very bad. He edged closer to Rey and tentatively asked, "What's going on boss? I don't know anything about this technical stuff, but I'm thinking that we're at the end of our journey. Who cares about those folks locked up in the Cargo Hold? We're only just days away from Europa...right?"

For a second, Dante wasn't sure Rey had heard him and was about to speak again, when Rey slowly raised his head and looked at Dante. "Look Dom," he pointed to the fusion engines' status readout on the panel in front of him. "We have no propulsion power. None. Those explosions caused a chain reaction that destroyed our fusion engines, all of them, not to mention the engine nodes. That means we have no power to maneuver." He sighed heavily, "And look here," he pointed to a small screen flashing red. "This shows me that our hull has been compromised and the location of that compromise. Luckily, the bulkhead doors of all of the affected areas closed immediately, but the damage was done. The explosion damn near brought us to a stop." He stopped and his eyes bore into Dante's, making him shift uncomfortably. "There are only two ways this little action story is going to play out for us; we are either going to float pass Jupiter, on our way out of the solar system or we will be pulled into Jupiter's orbit and eventually into Jupiter itself. If I was a betting man, Dom, I'd bet on the latter happening."

Dominic Dante was gobsmacked. He didn't fully comprehend the mechanics of their situation, but to hear that they would eventually crash into Jupiter was utterly overwhelming. And the only option to crashing into Jupiter was to float in space endlessly, slowly starving to death. He was so angry, he hadn't realized his fingernails were cutting into the palms of his balled-up fists. When he spoke up, his voice cracked a little, "So, what do we do boss? There must be something we can do." Deep down he could feel the tiny shoots of despair and panic take root.

Just then, the cockpit door slid open and Jake Sandstone stumbled into the cockpit. He was sweating profusely and gulping lungfuls of air, "The override code is actually working," he spat out, "but there's something wrong with the physical mechanism. It's just not opening the door." He took a minute to catch his breath, "When I was down there, though, I think I smelled something pungent, like burning wires and I think whatever was causing that smell is probably the reason why the door is not working. I think they burned out the interior mechanism."

Rey considered this for a moment. When Doc and his folks rushed into the Cargo Hold for sanctuary, they must have known it would only be a matter of time before he would be able to get the door open. At the time, he was okay with them being locked in there. They wouldn't be around fucking shit up and sabotaging everything they could get their hands on. But now, as he sat here and really thought about why they would corner themselves in the Cargo Hold, the realization hit him like a ton of bricks that they planned to be in there for the duration of the trip. They *knew* they could destroy the door mechanism so that it would never open again. He jumped up from where he was seated and stormed around the cockpit, "Fuck!" he said and slammed his fist into the wall. "FUCK!!" Kelly, who was sitting at one of the consoles at the front of the cockpit, was completely immersed in the huge red spot on Jupiter. She was fascinated. They were close enough now that she could see large bands of horizontal cloud formations moving languidly across the planet. It seemed to fit her mood. The clouds gave the appearance of slow-moving serenity, but underneath there was turmoil and dangerous energy. She was startled out of her reverie when she heard Rey cursing out in anger. She turned toward him and laughed derisively as he stormed around the cockpit. At this, he turned and darted to where she sat laughing. "What the hell did they do in there Kelly? It's only a matter of time before we get in there." He paused for a minute, as if for effect, "It won't be pretty when we do."

Kelly spat out, "You'll never get in there!" Kelly was never big on using what her mother used to say was "trashy-girl language", but she knew or felt, that things were near the end for them. For her. The thought made her sad. All the dreams she had as a young girl growing up on military base after military base would only remain dreams. The inside of this dream-killer ship would be the last thing she would see. She almost started crying, but something deep down stopped her. She felt stronger, more emboldened. She stared Rey in the face and said with bitter enmity, "You'll never get in there...FUCKER! They've had a plan all along. They have all of the food and all of the medical supplies in there. You've got nothing but fucking lent in your navel!" She laughed crazily and almost fell off her chair.

As he stared at her, his anger fell away and he smiled at her wryly, "Well, it looks like you're in same boat as us Kelly. Food won't be an issue because we can always make another trip out to the Cargo Cabin. And if I have to, I'll make a spacewalk to the bottom of the ship to get to the shuttle. If I can't get to the shuttle, then we'll figure out a way to land on Europa and once we do, we'll have all the food and supplies we'll need from the Cargo Cabin." He walked up close to her, his face only inches from hers. She could smell rotted decay in his mouth and rank body odor barely masked beneath some pine-smelling deodorant. She could feel her stomach hitching. She almost willed herself to vomit into this madman's face, but her stomach refused to obey.

"It took me a minute to realize this," he said, "but I think I know what they're planning. They think that they'll be able to escape via the umbilicus portal once we land. They believe they'll be able to pop it open and hightail it out into the good ole Europan wilderness. They believe that they will be able to resist us." He moved back from her, but continued to bore into her eyes. "The problem for them *my precious*, is that when we land, we'll be out there to cut them down as they try to exit." Kelly shivered violently. Something about the way he said *my precious*, filled her with dread. It reminded her of that long ago movie about the creature called a *Hobbit* who was hideously transformed by an evil ring. That was Rey through and through: one day, a somewhat respected pilot and Soren's second-in-command, the next day, a human cockroach, skittering through the vents of the ship spying, plotting, and yes, murdering. She had no illusions that Rey was not Elsa's killer. It was practically an unspoken belief that Rey was the culprit. When Kelly came back to herself, she could see Rey smiling sardonically at her, "I thought we lost you there for a minute Kelly." He chuckled and added, "Maybe once we land, we'll just cut off the power and suffocate them all back there in the Cargo Hold. How does that sound, eh?" She looked at him in disgust and horror. He laughed and said, "From where I'm standing, *lent* looks pretty damn good, don't you think?" He turned away from her sharply and headed toward the cockpit exit.

2

Jaime was looking toward the airlock. It was the only area of the Cargo Hold where one could see open space. He stared intently and then gasped audibly. Burt looked up at him and then toward where he was looking. "What is it, Jaime?" Burt asked him.

Jaime was still staring at the airlock. "We've stopped," he mumbled. "I think we've completely stopped moving."

Burt jumped to his feet and made his way closer to the airlock door. He had just finished removing the shard of metal from Liz's leg. Now, Zoe was bandaging her leg tightly while she drifted in and out of morphine heaven. He looked through the small window in the door, trying unsuccessfully to not look at Larry and Allison's bodies, perfectly preserved in the coldness of space. They were no longer cuddled together as they were when they were first locked inside. The explosion had separated them. Larry's frozen body was propped up against the airlock exterior door, while Allison's body was pushed toward the back wall within the airlock. Burt's stomached turned when he saw broken chips of frozen fingers spread across the floor of the airlock.

He pulled his eyes away from them and looked out into space. As Jaime had said, it looked as if they had indeed stopped. Or they were moving infinitesimally slow. He could see debris floating alongside them. Whether they had stopped or were just moving slowly didn't concern him as much as whether they were still moving in the direction of Jupiter or not. He began to feel a gnawing sense of deep despair roll over him. The fact that the Cargo Hold may be their tomb as they drifted past Jupiter and out into deep space was almost too unnerving to even consider. "God help us all," he whispered under his breath.

DAY 75

THE CAMERAS

1

"It's working!" Jaime yelled out from the back of the cargo room. He had been working on the control access panel, trying to *jury-rig* the audio and video components to enable them to see everything within the ship – at least where the cameras were installed. Initially, they didn't think the cameras worked at all, but after some digging, Jaime realized that in Soren's rush to leave the moon, he had forgone the work needed to complete the monitoring system installation.

There were several workstations in the cargo area and each one contained a monitoring system embedded into the wall above a work desk. They crowded around the monitors to get their first look out at Soren and Rey's world. Other than the occasional clanging on the Cargo Hold door, they had virtually no insight into the rest of the ship. Until now.

Doc was removing the stitches from Zoe's arm when Jaime got the system working. She had been searching for additional medical supplies, when the ship was rocked by an explosion, much smaller than the ones that rocked the ship when they first locked themselves in. That had been almost ten days ago. The vibration of the explosion caused a sharp-edged container to fall on her as she was searching the shelves. There had been several such explosions and each time one hit, Burt would think that this was it. That *this* explosion would be the one that finally destroys the ship that was once proudly called the *Cassiopeia*. Burt thought about the ancient R.M.S. Titanic that once sat in the huge New York Nautical Museum. He remembered there were several deaths associated with the salvage expedition of the ship, but ultimately, the salvage company was able to bring the huge ship to the surface. After eight grueling months of preparation, execution and transportation, the proud R.M.S. Titanic rested in its final resting place at the museum. That is, until Lycos hit. God only knew where the Titanic ended up after Lycos...probably back in the Atlantic Ocean, he surmised. It was incredible seeing the disfigured, majestic ship on display at the museum, but what stayed with Burt were the arrogant, if not blasphemous words, '*Not even God Himself could sink this ship'*. He didn't think that anyone said anything as foolish as that about the *Cassiopeia*, but he imagined that if humanity somehow survives and are able to send ships into space once again, they would come across the celestially *sunken Cassiopeia* and find a bloody husk of a ship, pockmarked with holes and housing some forty-plus shrunken and defiled human artifacts and remains – frozen in celestial amber. It made his head hurt to think of it. Zoe gritted her teeth while he finished up removing her stitches. "I'm sorry Zoe...almost finished." He removed the final stitch and wrapped a clean bandage around her arm. "You'll be fine Zoe. Just be careful the next time you have to pull some items down from the shelves."

"Thanks Doc," she said quietly and then hugged him. She pushed back from him and looked up into his face, "What's going to happened to us Burt? Our food rationing will only go so far."

He patted her lightly on the back. "We'll do what we can to survive. We don't know the future. We just have to make it day by day." But even as the words left his mouth, he began to wonder just how long they would be able to survive. He estimated that if they continued rationing their food smartly, they could survive for maybe one month, possibly two. After that, what then? This wasn't like being stranded on an island where a passing boat could see your brightly burning fire. This was open *space*! And there were no ships out here to even pass by them. This was it. There would be no rescues here. No Mission Control in Houston to report a problem to. If they hoped to survive this, they would somehow need to land on Europa. He almost felt faint at the sheer enormity of their dire situation.

He disengaged gently from Zoe and walked over to the workstation where Jaime, Liz and several others were looking up at the monitors. They were mesmerized. The huge monitors showed the images from all of the cameras located throughout the ship. There were at least thirty, by Burt's count. Burt looked at the camera facing the cargo door and could see a couple of guards furiously, futilely banging at the latch and handle of the cargo door. A few folks glanced toward the cargo door nervously, terrified that the guards would come bursting through at any moment, but short of a military howitzer, they were not coming in.

"Jesus, look at them," Liz shakily breathed out. She was looking at the camera in the Commons. Two guards were fighting, while several more cheered them on. Looking on and laughing, one guard had his arm around Emma Pennington's neck. It looked to Liz as if he were holding her to prevent her from running off, but after looking at the woman's bruised face, arms and legs, Liz knew she couldn't run even if she wanted to. She could see a trail of blood running down the woman's legs as she stood there shaking.

Liz crossed her arms across her chest and realized that she was shaking also. She wasn't worried about any of them coming through the main door. After several fruitless attempts, Rey and the guards gave up seriously trying to get inside. The few out there now looked drunk and happened to be passing by the Cargo Hold. The locking mechanism was completely destroyed and there were no other entry points into the Cargo Hold, except for one; the topside umbilicus portal. Fortunately, of the eight spacesuits that were assigned to the *Cassiopeia*, seven of them were inside the Cargo Hold with them. Nola was wearing the eighth one and she was far behind them by now. She wondered morbidly if Nola were still alive. The suits contained food and water receptacles and if she filled them when she donned the suit, then she would have had enough sustenance for at least one week. Maybe two, if she was careful. After that, she would be left with nothing but her thoughts as her sanity ebbed away in the blackness of space.

"Those motherfuckers!" Walt shouted. "Those goddamn mother-fuckers!" Liz walked over to Walt to see what he was referring to on the camera. She saw two guards, Wade Smith and Rich Gebbons, forcing Wayne Kesk to drink from a container they held to his mouth, booze Liz presumed. About a week ago, she remembered seeing several of the guards hauling the last of their potatoes to the cafeteria to make, what she assumed, was vodka. She had looked at them with disgust. Instead of rationing their food smartly, they were out there making alcohol! They most likely still had some food stores remaining, such as peanut butter, vegetables and honey, but they definitely had a lot of potatoes. All they had now in place of the potatoes, was about thirty, maybe forty liters of vodka.

Wayne shook his head back and forth and clamped his mouth shut as tightly as he could, but to no avail. Gebbons grabbed his nose harshly and when the man opened his mouth to breath, they shoved the container into his face. He drank what looked to be three or four gulps and then turned his head quickly to the side and vomited violently. Gebbons and Smith laughed uproariously, each took a swig from the container and then dragged Wayne off to the passenger cabins area.

"Goddammit! Goddammit!" Walt shouted to the cameras. "It just ain't right!" Liz seemed to remember that Walt and Wayne started showing some romantic interest in one another sometime after the incident with Larry and Allison. It seemed the forced expulsion of Larry and Allison had the unintended effect of bringing more people together. That was how she and Jaime became closer.

Walt was furious. "Look at what they're doing to Wayne! They're fucking abusing him and I can't do a goddamn thing about it!" He paced angrily about the room like a caged animal. Finally, he squared his shoulders and said, "Fuck this, I'm getting out of here!" He ran toward the cargo door, shoving people out of his way.

Several men went to stop him, but backed off almost immediately. It didn't matter what Walt did to the door, it would never open again. The only way to get the door open now would be to blast through it and there weren't enough explosives on the ship to do that, not without blowing a hole in the side of the ship. They couldn't get out that way even if they wanted to. Liz glanced back at the monitor and shuddered. *This is it. Our end. We've killed ourselves,* she thought. The die was cast for them. *All* of them. They were locked in the Cargo Hold with no chance of escape, while their broken ship slowly drifted in space. She had given up hope that it would drift into Europa's orbit, but that didn't matter, because she wasn't sure if the dead man switch would even work now. If they were moving, she didn't know how fast they were going, but knew the explosions couldn't be helping their situation. She was thankful that here, they still had food and water. The ship's auxiliary power would keep the cold out and for a while at least, they would have gravity. Out there in what she now thought of as *the wild*, Soren, Rey and their increasingly desperate guards were probably on the verge of total anarchy. All of the food on the ship was being stored in the Cargo Hold. Maybe there had been small caches of food throughout the ship, but it's been close to two weeks and there were roughly about 20 people out there, plus or minus. How much food do they have now? She looked back at the monitors and wondered how long it would be before they lost what little humanity they had left and how long it would be before they completely turned on one another.

DAY 86

ACCESS...BY ANY MEANS NECESSARY

1

Rey was looking at the guidance and propulsion system readouts anxiously. Shelton Hayes had told him there might be a way to patch the guidance and propulsion systems into the Artificial Gravity Generator. If it worked, there was a chance they could lose fifty percent of their gravity, but the guidance and propulsion system might work long enough to get them to Europa. Hayes had been confident he could do it, but Rey was having misgivings. Hayes had been going over the engineering plans for over six hours and still had not figured out the best way to combine these two systems safely. Rey opened his mouth to yell at Hayes when Dante walked into the cockpit. "Hey boss...you got a minute?"

"Yeah...wait for me outside," Rey said without looking up. Dante nodded and left the cockpit, the door sliding shut behind him. "Even if this works Hayes and gives us just enough power to get to Europa, the real problem will be landing." He looked down at his screen again and added, "Even at full strength, this ship would have been difficult to land. With no retropropulsion rockets to assist in the landing, we would come down pretty hard on the surface." Hayes nodded tentatively, not really knowing what to say.

Rey stood up and stretched. "Hayes, I'm going to step outside for a minute to have a chat with Dante. You need to figure this out, even if it means you go into the guts of this ship and manually splice that shit together. Do you understand me? Don't let me down."

Shelton Hayes looked nervously into Rey's face. He wanted to scream at the man. What did he expect him to do...deliver a miracle? At first, he was confident he could map the two systems together, but after spending hours reviewing the schematics for both systems, he considered that he might actually have to physically tie the two systems together. He didn't feel too confident about that option, but he nonetheless nodded his confirmation to Rey, "Sure thing...boss."

Rey stepped outside the cockpit and turned to Dante, "So, what's the problem Dom?"

Dante took a deep breath and said, "The guys are starting to lose it out here. Wade told me that you authorized them to make alcohol. Alcohol boss??"

Rey rolled his eyes, "Yeah, I told them they could make some. Now that we only have a handful of passengers to look after, there's no need for a strict, *no alcohol* policy."

Dante stared at him and said, "But boss, they took it to the extreme and used up *all* of our potatoes to make their booze. They severely depleted what rations we had left."

"What?" Rey spat out. "I put you in charge of the rations *and* the men. Why would you let them use up *all* of the potatoes Dom? Do I need to put someone else in charge?"

"But...but boss. I...uh, I tried to stop them. They wouldn't listen to me. I wanted to tell you, but you were indisposed, locked away in your cabin, with er, with Kelly." He shifted his weight from one foot to the other. "They're not listening to me anymore, boss."

Rey's mind was racing a mile a minute. Dante didn't know just how accurate his statement was when he said they severely depleted the remaining rations. Their mindless actions reduced their food stores from two to three weeks to maybe seven to ten days – and that's if they rationed the food ruthlessly. Again, his mind went back to Doc's people holed up in the Cargo Hold. And again, he found himself angry all over again. If he had the food they stole, they might be able to stretch their timeline out to two months, maybe three. And by then, they might have figured out a way to connect the guidance system to the gravity generator.

"Dom, round up everyone. It's time we paid the Doc and his crew another visit."

2

"Hey dipshit, are you sure this is the right way? I feel like we've been going around in circles." Dante turned to Tony Hurt or "Big Tony" as his friends called him. Dante wondered why they called him "Big Tony" since he was only 5'7" tall, but since he looked like some prehistoric *missing link*, he figured the nickname was probably appropriate. He stared at Tony coldly, "Do you want to lead the way, Hurt? Or maybe you wanna have your fuckin head smashed into one of these pipes!"

During his extensive forays in the hidden passages in the ship, Rey had found multiple maintenance service tunnels that fed into every part of the ship. Back then, he had primarily snooped around the Reclamation Center and sometimes Engineering, but he had assured Dante that he had no doubt that there were maintenance service tunnels that skirted the Cargo Hold, if not fed directly into it.

Crawling now through the seemingly never-ending tunnels, Dante was beginning to wonder if Rey knew what the fuck he was talking about. Rey had provided them with a maintenance service map, but Dante wondered if there was a way to actually get inside the Cargo Hold. He seemed to remember that Cargo Holds were typically self-contained to allow for storage of potentially dangerous materials that could affect the ship if compromised. But, if they could get close enough, maybe close to an inner wall that touched the Cargo Hold, then they might be able to blow their way through and gain access.

Like Liz, Rey had grabbed some of the explosive materials when he was inside the Cargo Cabin. He didn't know then what he would need them for, but was now glad he had them. Before he sent Dante and his team out to Cargo Hold, he had Hayes create a simple explosive device that would be powerful enough to blast through an inner wall.

After hearing Rey's plan, Dante asked why they didn't just go up to the front of the Cargo Hold and blow the fucker open, but Rey reminded him not too nicely, that if he wasn't a knuckle-dragging dolt, then he would've known that the Cargo Hold was situated too close to the outer walls of the ship. They couldn't risk using explosives in this location because any miscalculation could blow a hole in the ship. The integrity and structure of the ship would be so compromised that it would implode.

He had explained to Dante that the walls of the Cargo Hold toward the inner part of the ship would be the best location to use the explosives, reducing the chance of damage to key components in the area. "Dante," Rey had explained, "these explosives have been sitting in that Cargo Cabin for a long time, subjected to the intense cold. They were designed to be used outside, in large open spaces. Handle them with care and use just enough to damage the wall. If you use too much, you might blow up the entire fucking ship. Do you understand what I'm saying to you?"

"Sure boss," Dante replied listlessly. He had used explosives before, so he didn't need Rey's patronizing directions on blowing shit up. "I know what I'm doing boss."

Rey looked at him coldly, "Be sure that you do. Get your people and get going. I want inside that fucking Cargo Room. I'll make what happened to Larry and Allison look like child's play when I'm through," he had said. Dante could only shudder in response.

"Well?" Dante said to Tony. "Do you want me to smash your head into these pipes here?"

Big Tony looked away quickly and shook his head fearfully. "Naw man...you're good. You're good." Satisfied, Dante, Sandstone, Tony Hurt, and Gerald Noonan continued on to the next maintenance service tunnel connecting junction.

3

The maintenance service tunnels that Dante and his team were connecting to, skirted the edges of the engineering section. When the explosion happened, the entire section was sealed off automatically. The bulkhead doors that closed instantaneously had small hardened windows set into them. When they reached the tunnels above engineering, Dante said, "Hold here boys. I want to check out engineering." They looked at him as if he were crazy and then relaxed against the smooth walls of the service tunnel. Dante glanced at the Geiger counter on his wrist and saw that the radiation levels were still within the normal range. He proceeded down the ladder leading to the first level of the engineering section bulkhead.

Even though the bulkhead activated at this engineering section, his Geiger counter showed no increasing radiation. He placed his palm on the reader and the bulkhead door slid open. He was momentarily surprised when this happened. He had just assumed *all* of engineering was swimming in radiation. Apparently it wasn't. He knew this because the bulkhead door to this particular section would not have opened if the air had been compromised. He walked through this section slowly, his eyes constantly darting down to the Geiger counter. It still registered in the "slightly above normal" range. To his left, he could see the closed off section containing the engine node housing unit. He walked over to the window set in the huge bulkhead door. His breath caught in his throat and his face turned ashen. He had only been to engineering on one or two occasions, but what he saw now in the engine node housing section looked as if this was ground zero for a nuclear weapon detonation. He spied a huge hole in the far wall and anything that was not bolted down had been sucked out into space, including the entire engine node housing unit. Jagged edges of metal protruded from the walls in various angles. Further back where the engine node control room was, he saw a grotesquely bloated and frozen body that had somehow been wedged between crisscrossing arms of metal, effectively prohibiting it from making its sojourn into the darkness of space. To Dante, it looked like a *surprised* Otto Helmut.

"Jesus," Tony whispered under his breath. Dante jumped, but didn't turn around. He had been half expecting someone to follow him here, but he didn't realize how deathly quiet they would be. "Look at this fuckin door. It's bent inward," Tony exclaimed.

"Yeah, I don't like the look of it," Dante replied. "Let's get the hell out of here before another explosion hits. I'm not interested in being sucked out into space."

"There's another section that leads to the fusion engines," Tony said. "Do you want to check them out too?"

"Fuck no!" Dante replied. "Let's get to the Cargo Hold, place these fucking explosives and get the hell out of here! Shit, I may go see the boys making the vodka and get myself a drink after this!"

Tony laughed and said, "After you...boss."

They headed back up the ladder and turned toward the maintenance service tunnel leading to the area of the Cargo Hold. Dante subconsciously picked up the pace. He couldn't shake the feeling that the ship was falling apart, piece by piece. Being so close to this immense destruction completely unnerved him as he shakily made his way through the tunnels.

4

"Do you think it'll work?" Doc asked Jaime again. They had heard Rey talking to Dante about trying to blow a hole near one of the interior walls of the Cargo Hold.

"I don't know Burt," Jaime said. "Theoretically, it makes sense that if they can get close enough, they can cause some damage. The only wall they can possibly attempt to destroy is our eastern wall, but that won't be easy. There are no empty hallways or tunnels directly on the other side of that wall. They would have to get through at least 20 feet of components, metal and steel. They would practically destroy this part of the ship trying to get in here. No, I think we're safe in here for now."

Burt breathed a sigh of relief, "That's good to hear. If they ever get inside, that'll be the end of us. I can't imagine that they would even allow us to live on Europa."

"I agree Burt," Jaime said. "We've only been in here about three weeks and already, they're starting to break down." They were both looking at the monitor for the Commons, where most of the guards seem to spend all of their time. Even though each person had a crew cabin, a lot of them were sleeping in the Commons. Burt had heard Rey order his senior guards to keep everyone in the Commons. His paranoia was supreme. He couldn't take a chance that someone would slip away to some dark corner of the ship and return as revolutionaries ready to take command of the ship.

Burt didn't see Soren in the Commons, but he saw Kelly, sitting on the far side of the Commons. She was still wearing one of Nola's jumpsuits, but now it was dirty and torn, with multiple dried blood splotches. Burt cringed when he saw that. Kelly looked extremely forlorn as she stared blankly out one of the small starboard side windows. She sat awkwardly in the seat and Burt could see her absently rubbing her stomach. He was startled briefly, thinking that she might be pregnant, but realized that even though they ran out of the pregnancy patches, most of the women on the ship would be covered for another three months, at least. He realized grimly that in about three months she could be pregnant and would be forced to give birth in this floating tomb. Sighing heavily, he pulled his eyes away from the monitor and rubbed them furiously. *The center does not hold*, he thought despairingly.

5

Burt was in the throes of a nightmare where he was inside a large box that had no windows or doors. He couldn't remember how he got in there and no matter what he did, he couldn't find any hint of an exit. He wasn't a claustrophobic man, but as he ran around the box trying to get out, he could feel his lungs tightening and it was becoming very difficult to breath. He was jolted awake after hearing Jaime calling his name. "Burt! Wake up! They're here!"

At first, Burt thought that Rey's guards had breached the Cargo Hold. He sat bolt upright, his hands balled into fists when he saw Jaime pointing toward the east wall of the Cargo Hold. Still a bit groggy, he jumped up and joined Jaime and several others standing close to the wall. "It took them a while to get here, huh?" Burt said to Jaime. Jaime turned to him with a confused look on his face. "What? Oh...no. Once they left the engineering section, it only took them about ten minutes to get to this area." He looked at the sleep marks on Burt's face, "You've only been resting for a few minutes, my friend."

Burt shook his head as if to get the last remaining cobwebs from his head. "Where exactly are these guys?" he asked Jaime.

Jaime led Burt to one of the huge containers in the Cargo Hold and spread out the ship schematic on the flat surface of the container. He pointed to a convoluted-looking section of the schematic very close to where the Cargo Hold was. "I think they're right here," Jaime said. "It's the only location where tunnels get them anywhere near our location."

Burt squinted at the area. "That looks pretty far away." There was a distant clang deep within the walls.

"And you're certain an explosion there won't damage our wall?"

"I can't promise anything, Burt, but if they use too much explosives, then they could damage our wall, as well as the surrounding areas where the explosion happens." He pointed to another section of the schematic. "If their explosive yield is too strong, they'll definitely destroy our wall, but in the process, blow a hole in the back of the ship. If that happens, the ship will be damaged irrevocably and might possibly implode."

Burt shook his head. "These idiots. We're basically already dead, yet they seem to be in a rush to get there."

Jaime nodded, "You're right Burt, but if you look at it from Rey's point of view, they will be starving in another two, maybe three weeks, so they have to do something drastic, now. They've been scrounging the entire ship for food and have probably found everything left to find." He looked over at Liz who was on the other side of the Cargo Hold talking to some of her engineers. She glanced up at that exact time and smiled at him. "Burt, it will get quite bad out there. When they run out of food, they will run out of civility...what little they actually have. Humans have an indestructible will to survive and will do whatever it takes to live." He sighed, "We have much more time than they do, but we will get there also. We will eventually run out of food and will come to the threshold of anarchy. We need to prepare ourselves and determine how we will meet this crisis, when it inevitably comes for us."

"Jesus," Burt said, "I've never put that much thought into it, although it has always been lurking in the deep recesses of my mind. I guess I've been hoping, praying for a miracle to happen, but you're right, we have to be prepared to talk about this before it becomes an issue."

Just then, they heard a banging sound that seemed much closer. It was loud enough to startle others in the Cargo Hold. Some of them moved closer to the wall to listen, while others looked fearfully at the Cargo Hold door, half expecting a barbarian horde to come bursting through. Jaime and Burt moved back to the wall as the clanging and banging seemed to get louder and closer. Burt thought he heard screams.

6

Dante and his team were as close as they were going to get to the Cargo Hold. Their route from engineering forced them to move vertically in the tunnels until they reached the tunnel shaft that would most likely be the best place to set the explosives. As they were descending the tunnel shaft,

Gerald Noonan lost his footing and plummeted nearly 20 feet to the bottom of the tunnel. Dante and the others could only watch in horror as Noonan rolled end over end down the tunnel. At one point, one of his legs got caught up in the ladder and they mistakenly thought it would slow his descent, but the sickening snap of his ankle clouded over that hope. He hung there for just a moment before his weight and momentum yanked him off the ladder and then he continued his descent to the bottom, landing hard on his back. If he hadn't been wearing the hard casing containing the explosives, he might have just gotten away with a broken ankle and a sprained back, but he landed hard and awkwardly on the casing and for the second time, Dante and the group heard a sickening crack. Noonan screamed pitifully at the bottom of the tunnel, while Dante and the others looked on helplessly.

"Fuck!" Dante yelled out. "You fucking gorilla! Don't you know how to climb down a fuckin ladder?" He pounded his fist against the wall in frustration. They were as close as they were going to get to the Cargo Hold and only needed to descend about five feet down the ladder, where they could have secured their explosives against the wall. This particular tunnel was a closed tunnel and where Noonan lay twisted and broken, there was no outlet and it was much deeper than where they intended to set off the explosives. They would have to haul him out straight up the ladder somehow, but Dante was no fool. They would turn Noonan into a paraplegic if they tried to haul him up some twenty feet, not to mention traversing the other tunnels leading to an open corridor. He glanced down at Noonan again and knew that he was fucked. This entire mission might be fucked too, he realized. It was possible that the components of the explosives might have been compromised when Noonan fell. This was no state-of-the-art explosive device. It was hastily crafted and could very well have been damaged during Noonan's fall. If that was the case, then even now, it could be very close to detonating. He wouldn't be able to tell unless he saw the explosives himself and he would be goddamned if he went down there now.

"Dante!" Noonan screamed. "Get me the fuck out of here! This goddamn bomb is heating up. I mean, it's getting fucking hot!" He moaned horribly. "I think my leg is broken, but I can make it out with a little help." He tried to sit up and screamed, "Fuuckk! Oh Fuck! My back hurts man. Shit...it doesn't feel right. Get me out of here!"

Big Tony moved close to Dante and said, "That's not a good sign, Dom. If that bomb is heating up, then it's only a matter of minutes before it might explode in our faces."

"I realize that!" snapped Dante. He leaned over the opening again, "Look Noonan, I hate to tell you this, but man, your fucked. There's no way we can get you out safely and if that explosive is actually heating up, then it's only a matter of time before it ignites."

'What? What the fuck are you saying Dante?? You're gonna leave me here? Like a fuckin animal?" Noonan squirmed helplessly, grimacing with each movement. "You can't do that man! Get me outta here!!" His eyes were closed against the pain as he railed on Dante, but when he opened them again, there was no one to be seen. "Dante!! Tony? Jake? Come on! Get me out of here! Get me..." At that moment, he felt as if his back were on fire. He struggled mightily through the pain in his back and his ankle and just when the pain became unbearable, the leather strap holding the explosives case to his back, tore free. Painfully, he lifted himself up and grabbed the bottom rung of the ladder. Half laughing and crying, he used his hands to pull himself closer to the ladder. He had a terribly dislocated shoulder, but his back felt fine, if not bruised and burned. Just as he was getting ready to stand up on his one good leg, he heard a slight hiss and clicking sound. He turned his wide eyes to the explosives on the floor just in time to catch a glimpse of a white, blinding flash before his face melted into his skull and his body exploded into a thousand pieces.

Despite the distance of the explosion, Burt and the others in the Cargo Hold were knocked off their feet. Supplies that were stored in overhead shelves came crashing down and many of them could feel the pressure of the explosion in the air. The entire Cargo Hold seemed to rumble and groan, but as quickly as it came, it was gone.

"Was that it?" Liz asked Jaime anxiously. "For a minute, I thought the walls were going to come down."

Jaime looked around the Cargo Hold. A few folks looked shaken up, but overall, everyone seemed fine. "Yes, I think that's it. The explosion seemed to come from below us, which tells me they fucked up on where to position the explosives."

Burt was looking at the monitors. Gauging from the reaction of those in the Commons, they barely felt the explosion. A few folks looked around curiously, but there was no sense of urgency or fear amongst them. He thought about the explosives that Rey had ordered them to bring out of the Cargo Cabin. After Liz had taken some, there wasn't much remaining. He felt certain that what exploded in that tunnel was all that remained. Burt sat down heavily in one of the chairs near the monitors. As far as he knew, this was Rey's one and only chance of getting in here and they survived it. Now, he and his people will be forced to deal with their final, ugly reality. Based on what Jaime told him, they had maybe a couple of weeks of food rations left and that was it. Before it's all said and done, Burt had the feeling that he and the others here in the Cargo Hold would be witnessing total anarchy and barbarism on the other side of these monitors. They would brutalize one another until only one person remains. And that final person would survive as long as his food and his sanity lasts. Eventually, Rey's world will die and their world here in the Cargo Hold would live on. Burt had no misconceptions though. As Jaime had said, they would have their turn in the spotlight of starvation. How would they fare? He found he didn't have the stomach to think about it.

DAY 97

FOOD AND WAR

1

"What do you mean they're banding together?" Rey yelled into Dante's face. "Speak plain man!"

"They're restless and there's nothing for them to do. They complain about being hungry all of the time. They complain about not having any female company, although Emma and Sarah have sided with Tony and his people. It's like the *Jets* and the fucking *Sharks* out there!" He paused for a moment and then plunged ahead, "And boss, they're mad because you have Kelly. I don't know...it's weird, but they're almost jealous."

This caught Rey off guard. He had anticipated this, but assumed they had more time before the men started acting like a pack of wolves. Regardless of whether he liked it or not, he understood their restlessness and anger somewhat. They had very little food and all the promises he had made to them about having their own women evaporated almost overnight. From this day forward, the only thing they could expect each day was a day similar to the day before and so on and so on. It would drive anyone nuts. This could be a problem if he didn't put a stop to it right away. "Who can you trust of the remaining guards," he asked Dante. "Who would you say is on *our* side?"

"Well, there's Jake Sandstone and Jason Wurther. They're solid."

"That's it??" Rey asked incredulously. "What about the others? The ones who left Soren?"

"As you know, Vince Eckels was killed outside the Cargo Hold and we've never been able to find Otto Helmut, although I'm almost certain that was his bloated body we saw in engineering. Tony, Al, Matt, and Rod Stigler have housed themselves in Med-Lab and Emma Pennington and Sarah Smith are with them. Whether they went there of their own accord or not is uncertain."

Rey was beginning to feel thin, almost transparent and not really *all there*. He'd felt like that before and it usually happened when he was faced with a seismic shift in his way of thinking. How had he not anticipated this? After their failure trying to blow a hole in the Cargo Hold, he should have expected the men to start turning away from him. He had promised them women once they landed on Europa and here they were, basically a dead stick in space *and* no women, save Sarah and Emma. He had no doubt that they were envious of him and Kelly. Envious of *his* woman. He was immensely grateful for his foresight in limiting Kelly's movement throughout the ship. In fact, he kept her locked in his cabin most times. Other times, he would bring her to the cockpit with him. He would have killed everyone on the ship if they had harmed Kelly.

"Boss?" Dante was saying. "You okay?" He waited for Rey to work out whatever thoughts had whisked him away. After a minute of silence, Rey reestablished eye contact with him. He continued on, "Now, as for Soren's old guards, Wade, Rich, Antony and Paul, they move back and forth between the cafeteria and the passenger quarters. They have Wayne with them." He glanced back at the cockpit and added, "I guess I can assume that Shelton is with us, but what about Soren sir? I know he's locked up in your old cabin, but..."

Rey interrupted him, "*But* nothing Dom. Consider Soren a prisoner of war. I don't want him out here mucking about trying to influence his old guards. He's right where I want him." Another thought struck him, "I want you to bring the remaining food to my cabin."

Dante looked at him curiously, "Why boss? I've been able to fairly ration out the food to the men. So far, they haven't ganged up on me and they're still somewhat respectful when it comes to the rations."

Rey looked at Dante closely. In the past, Dante would never have questioned him so openly. He began to wonder if Dante had plans on trying to keep all of the remaining food for himself. Maybe lock himself away somewhere while the rest of them slowly starved. No, he wasn't having that. If it came down to it, he and Kelly would be the last survivors, not a bunch of worthless guards. "You're doing a great job rationing the food Dom, but since you say the men are not listening to you, then I might need to be the one handing out the rations." He paused for a moment and then added, "I'm still the commander Dom...that has to count for something, right?"

Dante considered this and then slowly nodded, "Yes. Of course you're right sir. We'll get those rations to your cabin today."

2

Jake Sandstone was standing at the far side of the Commons. He had been waiting for Dante and Rey to finish their conversation. From where he was standing, he couldn't hear what they were discussing, but from

Rey's body language, he looked pissed...or something. He never could tell with Rey.

As Dante neared him, he asked, "What does the boss want now? I can tell he was upset about something, but these days, he's always upset. What was it about this time?"

Dante waved him off, "Bah...it was nothing, but he wants us to move all of the rations to his cabin."

"What?" Jake said, astonished. "Why? Does he think you're skimming off the top or something?"

Dante sighed heavily and said, "I don't know Jake, but I don't like the way things are turning out. The rest of the men are breaking away from us and we're no closer to landing on Europa then we were last month. If we could have gotten into the Cargo Hold, at least we'd have enough food to last a few more months, but even that's putting off the inevitable."

"So, what do you suggest?" Jake asked quietly, suddenly afraid of sounding conspiratorial.

"Let's get Jason and get this stuff moved to Rey's cabin, but let's set aside a little for ourselves, just in case." Jake shuddered when Dante said 'just in case'. It sounded desperate and reeked of despair. He tried, unsuccessfully to not think about their situation a month from now, but his mind went there of its own volition. What it saw was a dark and terrifying world on the *Cassiopeia* where each of them would meet their own demons face to face.

3

Sarah Smith snored softly next to Tony Hurt as he stared up at the ceiling in Med-Lab's largest patient room. Even though it had been several days since the rations were moved from Dante's cabin to Rey's, he was still irritated by it. He didn't care too much for Dante, but he was at least prompt in passing out the rations. He detested getting rations from Rey because Rey would only pass out the rations on *his* schedule, which was never consistent. And he was starting to notice that their rations were getting more and more meager. To this, Rey only responded that he was trying to stretch the rations out.

Sarah murmured something in her sleep and turned over on her side. Tony looked at her fondly and then thought about the rest of his 'team'. The day prior, he began to see their situation in a different light. They were on their own now. Rey, Dante, Sandstone, Wurther and even Hayes, were part of Rey's team. He hadn't seen Soren in ages and frankly, didn't give a fuck about him. Wade Smith and his folks were on their own too. He realized that eventually, they would have to go up against Rey to get the food they needed. He had no doubts that Rey would starve all of them out if it suited him. He wondered if he should get with Wade Smith and establish an alliance of some kind to get the food they needed and divide it amongst themselves. However, the more he thought about it, the more he realized that he didn't want to share the food with them either. There was only so much food remaining and he would rather have it all for him and his people than share it with Wade and his folks. They could starve for all he cared.

Before going up against Rey, they would first pay a visit to Wade's area. He knew they had all of the remaining potatoes under their control. They also had alcohol, which would make for some powerful Molotov cocktails that they could then use against Rey's stronghold. The more he thought about this idea, the more convinced he became they could pull it off. They wouldn't do it tomorrow or even the next day, but soon, very soon. With that thought, he turned toward Sarah and nestled up to her, visions of a bloody victory playing out in his head.

DAY 102

ARTIFICIAL GRAVITY GENERATOR

1

"Get those fuckers!" Tony yelled after the sprinting Dante and Sandstone. They were scrounging for more food in the empty passenger quarters, when they heard yelling and screaming coming from Wade Smith's area. Initially, they turned in the direction of the noise, but when they heard something that sounded like an explosion, they reversed course and started sprinting toward the Commons.

"Come on you guys! We can catch them!" someone yelled behind Dante. Running as hard as he could, he half-turned just in time to see something flying through the air toward them. He turned back and pressed himself hard against the corridor wall, just as something exploded behind him. There was immediate heat behind him, but he was far enough away that he didn't get burned.

They rounded the corridor leading to the Commons, where Jason Wurther was guarding. "Shut the bulkhead! Shut the bulkhead!" was all he heard as Dante and Sandstone came racing through. He was dumbfounded momentarily until he caught sight of several men racing toward them carrying fire. He was jolted out of his stupor by Rey behind him yelling for him to shut the bulkhead. He lifted the protective case covering the button that closed the bulkhead and slammed his fist into it. The closing mechanism was quick, but not before a Molotov cocktailed sailed through the opening. It hit the top of one of the chairs in the Commons and then bounced into the aisle in front of Sandstone, where it exploded. Luckily for Sandstone, only his leg caught fire, but he screamed piercingly anyway. Rey grabbed a blanket from one of the chairs and put the fire out.

Even with the bulkhead shut, they could still hear the muted threats coming from the other side. "Open this door motherfuckers! We need some of that food! We'll blow this fucker open if we have to!" Rey wasn't sure who was yelling, but it sounded like Tony Hurt.

They pounded on the bulkhead with their crude weapons, but Rey knew they would never get inside the Commons. The bulkhead was retractable, but could only be done from the cockpit. Hayes ran in from the cockpit carrying the cockpit's medical bag. Once he got Sandstone's burnt pants off, he began dressing his wounds.

"I guess that's it, huh boss?" Dante said to Rey. "We're pretty much on our own."

"Look at it this way Dom, at least we'll have more food for ourselves now, which means we'll last longer than them. And maybe by then, we'll have figured out a way to get to Europa."

"You mean there's still hope?" Wurther asked excitedly.

"Maybe," Rey replied. "We might be able to connect the guidance and propulsion system into the artificial gravity generator." He looked over at Shelton who was still busy dressing Sandstone's wounds. "We're still working out the details. Right now, you guys help Hayes get Sandstone to his cabin."

As they made their way toward Sandstone's cabin, Rey walked over to the bulkhead door. He couldn't hear Tony and his people anymore so apparently, they had given up trying to break down the bulkhead door. He turned back and looked out at the Commons. In the past, there was always someone in the Commons, but now, it was eerily empty. He found himself angry all over again at Doc's people holed up in the Cargo Hold. With them gone, he had no kingdom, no lordship. He was now the commander of the *Cassiopeia* with no one under his command except a bunch of treasonous ingrates. They stole his command...and his glory. He bristled at that. Instead of being the leader of the last of humankind, he was the *mob boss* of just a handful of guards in a busted ship going nowhere.

He turned and headed toward his cabin to look in on Kelly. If Hayes was unsuccessful in getting those two systems connected, then things here on the *Cassiopeia* could get very dire indeed. Their food was finite and it wouldn't take much to push their small, fragile group to a dangerous and homicidal edge.

2

Shelton Hayes crouched and half crawled through the huge, dimly lit conduits containing miles of cable and wiring that snaked and meandered throughout the entire ship. He was exhausted. For the past week, he had been working on reconfiguring the guidance propulsion system and adapting it to the powerful Artificial Gravity Generator hub. He had already reconfigured the software requirements for both systems to work together seamlessly and now he was physically repurposing modules and modifying connections for the new functionality. That functionality being the ability for them to pilot the *Cassiopeia* toward Europa.

The only thing left to do now was to reboot the Artificial Gravity Generator. Once it came back online, the guidance and propulsion system would be fully incorporated into the Artificial Gravity Generator system. The only issue he had was actually *getting* to the Artificial Gravity Generator hub. It was located at least three stories above the primary artificial gravity ring. Before he could even get to the ladder to make the climb, he had to half crawl almost five hundred feet through the gravity generator conduit first.

He crawled along, bumping his head occasionally on outcroppings of tubing and coiled wires. This trip would have been much easier if he could have accessed the hub farther back in the ship, but after the incident with Tony and his people, there was no way they would open the bulkhead door. So, he had to access the conduits through the heavy access door in the floor of the cockpit. Once inside, he heard the locking mechanism activated. In his earpiece, he heard Rey tell him that the access door would remain locked until Hayes confirmed he was alone when he returned.

As he continued crawling, he thought about their situation. There were now three factions, as Rey put it; Wade and his people and Big Tony's folks. And of course, their own. Three months ago, he would never have thought that Doc's people would be locked away in the Cargo Hold and that there would be essentially three "nation states" existing in an area that wouldn't even rank larger than a Home Owners Association.

At the onset of this turf war, things were cordial and civil, but as the food stores dwindled, Rey became increasingly harder to work with until eventually Tony grew tired of the meager handouts. At first, Rey told them that he was trying to stretch out the food, but eventually, he even pulled away from that reasoning. He completely stopped giving them food. His rationale was that he just didn't have enough food for everyone. And just like that, their barely civil détente evaporated. Tony, under the impression that Wade's folks still had pounds of potatoes left, considering how much liquor they had made, led a raiding party to Wade's area. Unfortunately, Paul Timmons was the only one there while the others were out scouting for food. Big Tony and his people took everything they had, including the liquor and beat Timmons senseless.

He wasn't worried about Tony getting into the Commons, because the Commons, like the Cargo Hold, only had one primary way to get in and it was now blocked because of the closed bulkhead door. There was the way he left, but like the bulkhead, they would never get through the floor access panel. It was only a matter of time though, he thought, before disaster struck their little group. Their food was finite and Rey was...unbalanced. What would happen when *they* ran out of food? He shuddered to think of it. If he could get the guidance system working, then all of what happened and what *could* happen would go away. At least that's what he hoped. He reached the junction where the ladder was and began climbing up. He glanced down before ascending, suppressing the sudden feeling of vertigo. Several stories below him were the platforms that housed the gravity rings. He could feel the power of the rings pulsing through the ladder as he climbed.

His legs began to burn as he made his way up the ladder. Sweat covered his face and the entire top half of his jumpsuit was soaked. He had gotten a late start, so it was already moving late into the afternoon. He cursed angrily. He would have to spend the night here because it would take him at least three hours to complete the reconfiguration process and he would be in no shape to make the long trek back.

He reached the top of the ladder and stood up in the Artificial Gravity Generator hub. It was larger here and he was able to stand up without crouching or bending over. He walked over to the hub and started typing in commands to reconfigure the systems. Two hours later, he was done. *Well, hold onto your butts,* he thought and laughed. He couldn't remember where he had heard the quote, but it had always stuck with him. He primed the Artificial Gravity Generator system and typed in the commands to activate the attached guidance and propulsion module. At first, there was no perceptible change, but the dim lights in the hub flickered, went out and then came back on. In the briefest of instants, he felt his feet rise from the floor and then there was a low grinding noise that got louder and louder until it was deafening. Shelton covered his hears and started screaming. He stepped back from the module involuntarily and found that he could barely move. In that terrible instant, he found it odd that a person's fear could be so real and so intimidating, that it had the physical power of disabling a person's ability to move. But as he stood there, he realized this was different. This was something totally different. He could barely move. He was nervous, yes, but he wasn't afraid. This was not fear. This was something else entirely. He tried walking toward the hub's system and found that he could barely lift his foot. All of a sudden, he fell to the floor, as if a huge weight pushed him down. Now he was afraid because he now knew what was happening.

3

Liz found herself staring at the monitors whenever she could. She had witnessed the attack on Timmons. She didn't care much for him, but was shocked and saddened when he was attacked by Tony and his people. Unfortunately for Timmons, his people had already left to scavenge for supplies and food when Tony and his folks arrived. What disturbed her the most was seeing Sarah and Emma on this raiding party. From what Liz could see, they no longer fought against their captors, they appeared to be part of the team.

When Tony's group found Timmons alone, they appeared to try to bargain with him, but Liz knew there were no more potatoes to be had because they had foolishly used them all to make alcohol. Timmons was unsuccessful in getting that point across, so they beat him viciously. Even Sarah and Emma joined in melee. They were laughing.

She glanced at the monitor in the Commons. It was always empty except when Dante would go in to see Rey or when the guards would play cards. This time, she saw them access the panel in the floor where Hayes disappeared into. She remembered Jaime talking about all of the access points to the Commons and he had told her that particular one led to conduits that eventually led to the Artificial Gravity Generator hub. Jaime felt that maybe they were trying to tie in the guidance propulsion system into the Artificial Gravity Generator, but warned that the gravity generator hub was designed as a standalone module, simply because of the amount of power that it generated. To recreate the gravity of earth was no small feat and any tampering with the system could have serious repercussions.

She only saw Kelly once or twice during this time. She was never alone and was always escorted to the cockpit and escorted back. And she was always escorted down the hall that led to Soren's cabin, not Rey's, so apparently, she was staying in Soren's cabin, which meant that *Rey* was staying in Soren's cabin. Since she hadn't seen Soren in weeks, she assumed he was either dead or Rey had him locked away in one of the other cabins. She had never seen Soren's cabin, but according to Finch, it had a huge viewport window. She sighed sadly and wondered how long Kelly would be able to endure her imprisonment.

Jaime joined her at the monitors and put his arm around her waist. She was about to turn toward him when all of a sudden, the ship began to shudder violently. "What the f..." was all Jaime got out before they were violently forced to the floor.

4

Shelton Hayes was terrified. He could feel the increased speed of the gravitational rings below him and knew he had somehow reversed the polarity of the huge gravitational rings. Instead of providing earth-normal 1g of force, the rings were slowly increasing that number. Already, he felt it was at 3g and rising. At this rate, it would tear the ship apart, but not before killing everyone onboard.

As he stared at the gravity generator module, his vision doubled and then trebled. He didn't have much time left before he passed out. He knew he would never be able to reverse what he did. Hell, he couldn't even stand up. But he had to do something before it was too late. Just then, he remembered that he had brought a stun gun with him for self-defense. He struggled mightily trying to get the stun gun unclipped from his belt and just as he felt himself about to pass out, it came free. He aimed it at the gravity generator module through blurry eyes. He wasn't sure that it would do anything, but he had to try something. He shut his eyes and squeezed the trigger, knowing that he was probably too close to it, but powerless to move away. The effect was immediate. He first heard the muffled sound of the concussion gun's shock wave slam into the module and then felt the resulting explosion as it propelled him across the floor. It hadn't occurred to him that he was sliding across the floor quickly and uninhibited until he felt himself crest the opening that he had recently climbed through. He frantically grabbed at the rungs of the ladder as he started falling, but the ladder was just out of reach for him to get a firm handhold. As he tumbled, he gritted his teeth for the pain to come and when it came, it wasn't the pain of slamming into the platforms above the gravity rings several stories below, it was his head hitting one of the rungs of the ladder during his plummet. Shelton could feel himself slipping into unconsciousness and almost welcomed it. He didn't relish the idea of the split second of excruciating pain he would feel as he slammed into the platform below, but he would be in La La Land by then. His last coherent thought before darkness overtook him was, *I would have loved to see Europa.*

5

Rey grabbed onto the cockpit console and pulled himself up from the floor cursing. "That fucking moron!" he shouted to Dante and Jake Sandstone. "He assured me he knew what he was doing!" He sat down in one of the cockpit chairs and stared at the Guidance and Propulsion System and Artificial Gravity Generator readouts. They were both offline. He couldn't make sense of it until he heard Dante weakly call out. "Boss…what's happening here?"

Rey looked at Dante and could see him slowly floating toward the ceiling of the cockpit. Sandstone was still sitting on the floor, but made a move toward Dante and found himself floating too. Rey hadn't realized their gravity was out because he was still nestled in the cockpit chair. He slammed his fist on the console and cursed again. This was it. He realized in no uncertain terms that they were now fucked. Hayes attempt at incorporating these two systems was their last option. He looked out at the huge image of Jupiter. Despite how large the planet looked, it was still thousands of miles away. He searched for Europa and at first couldn't find it, but eventually, he saw the pale blue planet close to the southern edge of Jupiter's space. It seemed to stare at them mockingly. So close and yet so far. Looking back at the massive Jupiter, there was no sense of mocking there. Eventually, Jupiter would claim them. He had no misconceptions that they would float helplessly past Jupiter. The powerful siren-song of Jupiter's humongous gravity would inevitably lure the *Cassiopeia* into its gaseous rocky shores. A casual observer would see an insignificant speck of a ship against the huge backdrop of Jupiter. It would be there one minute and the next, a barely discernible implosion of a life raft carrying the last vestiges of humanity.

6

It was chaos in the Cargo Hold. Only a handful of people had ever experienced zero gravity and they were doing their best to help the others control themselves. More than a few folks had bruises and bleeding scalps from moving around too fast and bumping into each other or the many pipes covering the ceiling of the Cargo Hold.

"Everyone, just grab onto to something and stay there!" Jaime yelled out. "If you try to move somewhere too fast, you'll end up breaking your arm or worse, so just remain where you are. Liz and I will help you get situated."

Burt looked around the room at his flying cohorts. Apart from the folks who were injured, he found it quite funny. When the gravity went out, he was sitting at one of the wall desks in the Cargo Hold. Since it was attached to the wall, it prevented him from floating from his seat. He saw Jaime and Liz frantically zipping around the room collecting the others like mother birds collecting their struggling babies. After about an hour or so, Jaime and Liz made their way to him.

"I knew they were going to fuck something up!" Jaime said, disgusted. "Unfortunately, for them to have made that attempt, it must mean that our guidance and propulsion system is gone." He looked at Liz and then grabbed her hand.

Burt sighed heavily. In a way, he had been expecting this, but to see it here at last, hurt his heart. They were blind in here and he had no sense of where they were in relation to Jupiter or if they had even passed it. But he knew that Jupiter would not so easily allow them to slide by. He knew that when the time came, they would be sucked into the gas giant. In a way, he felt that would be the best way for them to die, instead of starving to death as the *Cassiopeia* drifted out of the galaxy. He reached out grabbed Jaime and Liz's hands and thought ...*and what rough beast, its hour come round at last, slouches toward Bethlehem to be born?*

7

His head was throbbing, but Shelton Hayes was terrified to open his eyes. The last thing he remembered was the explosion and tumbling down toward the platforms above the gravity rings. He wasn't sure where he was because he no longer heard the gravity rings and he was...*floating!* With that realization, he yanked his eyes open and saw indeed that he was floating. He realized his stroke of luck that the ship lost gravity before he hit the platforms above the gravity rings.

Using the rungs of the ladder, he started to turn his body to head up to the gravity hub when he was struck by a horrendous odor. The smell was so strong, he almost gagged. Floating several feet above him was a badly mutilated corpse with long hair. The body was nude but had shreds of clothing still attached to it. Unable to control his ascent, he drifted into the mess and found his face pressed up against the rotted stomach of the body. His nostrils were assaulted with an even stronger odor and he did more than just gag. He violently vomited the meager food in his system, but it went as far as the body's swollen belly before splashing back in his face. He smacked at his face wildly for a minute and then felt himself pulled down by the ankle. His total look of surprise turned to fear when he saw Tony and Matt staring him in the face.

"Well, well, well," said Matt. "Are you yanking my pizzle? If it isn't little Shelton. Long time no see bruvver, what brings you to our neighborhood? You come lookin for Elsa, eh? Seems like you bloody well found her mate!"

DAY 106

THE WEAK ONES

1

"We spent half the day searching and only found this!" Reichart threw the two packets of dried vegetables onto the table and they bounced up into the air. Wade snatched them before they could float off too far out of reach and turned them over in his hand. They were in trouble. They had run out of food over a week ago and this was all they could find in the ship. Once they came upon Tony and his group, but they were in the same situation as them. They were all weak and starving.

"What are we gonna do?" Rich asked. "There is no more food left on the ship. Between our group and Tony's group, we've scoured the ship clean."

Wade pushed himself up from his chair and floated lightly above them all. Body odor and burnt equipment now took the place of the many delicious smells that once populated this space. "Let's face it guys, we're starving and these two packets won't do anything to help that." He pushed himself toward the front of the cafeteria, deep in thought. When he returned, he wore the look of unmistakable defeat.

"Are you guys familiar with the Donner Party story?"

Everyone but Wayne shrugged their shoulders. Wayne glared around the room in disbelief. "*What?* You want to resort to cannibalism?? Are you out of your fucking mind Wade?"

"Wait, what?" Rich said. "You want us to eat people? What kind of sick shit is that Wade?"

They all started talking at once and Wade let them. In the end, they would come to the same conclusion as he. Their fate was sealed and they would either die horribly as their bodies shut down or they would live. The choice would be theirs.

Reichart was the first to reconcile their predicament. "Hey guys, you know he's right. There's no food and no food coming. No help is coming either. We are the last of everything. I for one will do anything to survive...*eat* anything to survive."

"I'm not listening to this!" Wayne yelled out and floated out of the cafeteria as fast as he could. Rich was about to follow him, but Wade stopped him. "No, Rich, he needs to work it out for himself. We all do."

"What about Timmons?" Rich asked. "He's still not right after what Tony and his gang did to him. They paralyzed him and he still has headaches from the concussion. I'd be interested in his opinion on this."

"No," Wade said. "Don't tell Timmons about this."

"Why not?" Rich asked. "Why don't you want us to..." Rich stopped in mid-sentence. His face turned ashen and he looked visibly ill. "Are you thinking that we should start with Timmons?" Rich asked incredulously. "I kinda thought it would be *after* someone died."

"Come on Rich, think about it," Reichart said. "Even though we're starving now, it might take days for one of us to actually die. And by then, we might be too weak to do anything."

"So, what are you suggesting, Wade?" Rich asked. "Do we sneak up on Timmons and kill him? And then eat him? Shit."

"Well, that's the long and short of it, Rich. This is the hand that fate dealt us and we either deal with it or it will deal with us."

2

"Look here Hayes, either you tell us how to get there or you *will* die here on this fucking floor. Do you understand me?" Tony asked as he glared into Shelton Hayes' eyes. Hayes couldn't remember how long he had been here, but he knew he was in trouble. He knew the way back to the cockpit, but also knew there was no way Rey would let him back in through the access panel in the floor. Hayes was not a doctor, but he knew a paranoid schizophrenic when he saw one and Rey fit the bill perfectly. He wondered how in the hell they could follow someone with such a maladaptive disorder.

Tony pushed away from Hayes and then stopped himself with his feet on the other side of the room. He looked at Hayes' bloody body and knew that he would eventually lead them to the cockpit access panel. But that wasn't the real problem, was it? He believed Hayes when he said that Rey would never open the access panel for him, not unless he could prove he was alone. But Hayes had been missing in action for several days now and Rey's acute paranoia would not allow him to open the panel regardless of whether Hayes was truly alone or not.

But Hayes was an engineer. There may not be any other access panels, but Hayes would know a thing or two about the bulkhead door. He pushed off lightly from the wall and glided over to where Hayes was tied down.

"Hayes, I know Rey won't let you in, especially if he has an inkling that you're not alone. But what if you *were* alone? And you could prove that you were alone, would he let you in then?"

Hayes looked up through one swollen eye and said, "You're guess is as good as mine, Tony. You know Rey...he's fucking crazy. I would imagine by now that he won't let me because I fucked up the gravity generators and caused all this." He turned his head to the left and then to the right, indicating everything.

"So Shelton, why are you protecting him? You're out here with us and if we starve, you starve. But there's a caveat to you starving; I can guarantee that *you* won't starve before any of us, if you get my meaning."

Hayes' stomach hitched at the thought. Tony's group still had a little food left, but they didn't bite their tongues when it came to discussing what they would do to survive. Hayes knew that if he were still here as their captive when their food ran out, he would be butchered, bloodleted and packaged like some kind of human animal.

Tony smiled as he watched Hayes agonizingly visualize his own death and subsequent inclusion as the main ingredient in their future meal preparations. "Look Shelton, you're actually in the same boat as us now. We're on the same team now. Rey and his folks are safely tucked away in the Commons and they have abandoned you. We are your tribe now. Let's get in there and take the food that is rightly ours!"

Hayes lifted his head and looked at Tony weakly. Of course, he was right. Rey would never let him in. And Tony had Emma and Sarah on his team. Maybe if he played his cards right, he could lose his virginity before they plummet into Jupiter's Eye. He chuckled at this, but grew somber. "I think I can help you, Tony. I know I fucked up the gravity generator shit, but I'm very familiar with the bulkhead systems."

Tony moved closer to Hayes. "That's a good fellah, Hayes. You're one of us now. We share everything and if you prove yourself, then you can be included too." At that moment, Emma floated into the room and looked down at Shelton Hayes. "Shelton, have you ever had sex in zero-g? It's phenomenal."

All Shelton Hayes could do was shake his head and hope that he didn't soil his pants in that moment.

3

"Jaime!" Liz yelled. She had been watching the camera located in the cafeteria and saw the burgeoning horror happening before her very eyes.

At some point, she intellectually knew that this would be coming, but to see it in real time was particularly harsh to her civilized senses.

Jaime and Burt pushed off from where they were floating over to the where she was glued to the monitors. "What's going on Liz?' Jaime asked breathlessly. Even though there was no physical strain to get to where Liz was, her frantic cry was enough to cause his heart to start beating rapidly. He and Burt came to a smooth stop behind her, as did several others who heard her cry out.

"They, uh...they..." she started out, but was unable to complete the sentence. The only thing she could do was point to the screen. Burt and Jaime and several others who were crowded in behind them stared at the monitor showing Wade and his people in the cafeteria.

In the cafeteria, they could see Wade, Reichart, and Rich floating over Timmons' makeshift bed. Wade had a cloth and some sort of blade in his hand, but Reichart and Rich carried small blade-like instruments in their hands, presumably for cutting. They had all lost a lot of weight, but the fire and danger in their eyes belied the weakness their thin bodies seem to portray. They had all gotten adept at moving around in zero gravity and they floated up to Timmons hamper quietly. Liz wondered if maybe some part of Timmons' mind could sense a presence near him because he slowly opened his eyes. His brief smile turned fearful as he gazed on the no doubt demented faces leering at him from above. Liz could see him struggle, but he was tied down and could only be a spectator at whatever was about to happen.

"Paul," Wade said, "your sacrifice will save us". Paul Timmons' eyes grew wide and he was about to scream when Wade plunged a crude, homemade knife into his throat. In a similar situation, blood would have spurted into Wade's face and across the room, but in zero gravity, it simply spurted out about a foot and then began to spread out evenly in all directions. Timmons shuddered for a few seconds and then lay still. Rich did his best not to be in the path of the slowly expanding claret, but Reichart seemed to relish in it. In fact, Rich noted, Reichart opened his mouth and seemed to savor the slowly floating globules of blood. Rich clamped down on the rising bile in his stomach and waited for Wade's orders.

Liz turned toward Jaime and cried into his chest. Burt looked on dispassionately, knowing that it was only a matter of time before this happened. Jaime bit his lip and tried to console Liz as best he could. The others who were watching were turned away immediately, sickened by what they saw. He heard one person vomit and another person yell at him to collect his vomitus.

Burt made his way back over to the monitor after Jaime and Liz moved away. She was inconsolable. He saw them carve up Timmons' body and package it like it was cattle parts. He noticed that Wayne refused to participate, but knew in his heart that Wayne would eventually come around when the hunger got bad enough.

DAY 110

KELLY'S DARK HEAT

1

Kelly floated over to the wall unit in Rey's *new* cabin and pressed the open button where Soren stored all of his booze. Of course, she knew where everything was because she was here before...when she was being raped and abused by Soren. *Same place, different bastard*, she thought and laughed humorlessly. She grabbed one of the sealed pouches containing alcohol and pushed off the wall toward her normal spot in front of the huge window. Whenever Soren would drink, he would open up the tube and pour the contents into a glass. He once told her that he didn't like sucking down his booze through a straw. But now that there was no gravity, sucking the booze through the tube would have to do. Luckily, the majority of his drinks were already housed in pouches, so when they lost gravity, all she had to do was grab a pouch and go. She realized forlornly, that she drank a lot these days. Before this, the most she had ever drank was champagne on New Year's Eve and that was easily a few years before Lycos hit.

She looked out at the huge angry eye on Jupiter. She refused to call it the *Great Red Spot*. To her, it was an eye forever spying on her. She saw the eye at least once a day, sometimes twice if she were awake long enough. She hated it. To her, it was a swirling mass of hateful, dangerous energy. It reminded her of those eerily realistic paintings of people with preternatural eyes that followed you wherever you went. When she was younger, her parents had taken her to one of those avant-garde art shows. She remembered being terrified of one particular painting that portrayed an aging farmer walking off into the sunset with a shovel over his shoulder, like he was going off to war. He was walking away but had half-turned as if someone had called him. Years later, she found out that that type of *back figure* painting was called a *Rückenfigur*. It was supposed to "engage the viewer" and draw them into the painting, *thus creating a sense of shared experience with the figure in the painting.*

In the painting, the farmer was looking both at her and at something behind her. At least that's what she thought it looked like. She remembered moving to the left of the painting and then to the right, but his eyes never left her face nor the *thing* behind her. Even as she left the room with her parents, the farmer still stared at her and whatever nameless entity was behind her. That night, the only *shared experience* she had was one of pure terror. She woke up in the middle of the night *knowing* that those sad farmer eyes had followed her home and hid somewhere in her room, waiting. Waiting to hear her soft snoring. Waiting to slither out of its dark hole. Waiting to hop on her chest and burrow into her mind's eye and unleash its conscious-destroying malignancy, leaving her a hollowed-out husk, her vacant eyes staring at nothing.

But that was in another lifetime. A life where she was innocent and had the luxury of wondering who would be the man to rescue her from her virginity. Who would be the man that her future children would call father? She thought bitterly that that part of her life was gone forever. She wondered which bastard would father her first child. Would it be Soren or would it be Rey? She honestly didn't know. She sucked at her drink and allowed the strong liquor to soak into her and expand her horizon.

She looked out at Jupiter again, the alcohol slowly kicking in. They were so close to the huge planet that the swirling mass of clouds and gases took up almost half the viewing area of the window. She would sometimes stare at that constantly changing furious tapestry for hours. And when Rey or one of his few devotees would come for her, she would find her seat in the cockpit and stare some more at the massive planet. She once heard Rey say that it takes about three to four days for Europa to orbit Jupiter, so she tried to keep a schedule of when she might see the pale blue planet. It was her only companion. On the days she expected to see Europa, she found she was as giddy as a school girl. She would wake up and rush to the window and manically search the heavens for her little friend. One time, she was almost frantic when she couldn't find the planet. She began to think her schedule was off when she spied the planet directly in front of Jupiter, in bas-relief.

She realized then that her mood and her state of mind was tied directly to Europa's appearances, much like tides were tied to the movement of the moon. Her mother, one of those free-spirited new-age types, once told her that even women's cycles were tied to the comings and goings of the moon. She was just starting to have her own cycles when her mother told her this. She remembered the hurt in her mom's eyes when she guffawed and fell to the floor laughing. "What are we, werewolves mom?" she had asked and burst out laughing again. She thought about that time often, years after her mother had died. She would be racked with guilt every time she thought about her childish response and how the serious, earnest look on her mother's face would turn to one of horror and then hurt. Her mind floated back to the present where the eye was patiently waiting for her. Europa was nowhere in sight. When it was visible, she was, in a sense, visible herself. When it made its sojourn to the other side of Jupiter, her mood would be as dark as how she imagined the other side of Jupiter would be. Today was one of those dark days. The days that she would drink and allow herself to be consumed by her darkness and her anger. She no longer resisted Rey's fumbling attempts at being intimate with her. She simply lay back and stare toward the window, losing herself in Jupiter's swirling madness, waiting for him to crawl off her mad and frustrated. She listened to his ship woes with lackluster interest. She didn't care that they had to seal themselves inside the Commons and that the others were now on their own, fated to live as best they could in the foodless ship.

Her mind would sometimes make its way through the ship to Anton, Burt and the others safely tucked away inside the Cargo Hold. They would survive longer than her and Rey and his buffoons, certainly longer than the idiots trapped outside the Commons. The thoughts that saddened her the most were of Nola. She would cry inconsolably when she imagined Nola floating in complete darkness, slowly starving or freezing to death. By now, she would undoubtedly be dead. She knew that Anton was not *directly* responsible for Nola's death, but his cowardice certainly contributed to it. In a way, she still loved him, but knew she could never forgive him. She screamed piercingly and shoved away from the wall. As she floated to the other side of the cabin, she chided herself for screaming. Who was she kidding? She was locked in Soren's old cabin on the broken *Cassiopeia* in the middle of space. She could scream all she wanted to but she knew there was no help coming for her. No help coming for any of them.

She floated until her back gently bumped up against a hard surface. She stayed there for a moment and then turned, looked inside the container and grabbed a pack of peanut butter paste from the top case. She pushed away from the crates of food and looked at them disdainfully. There was probably two, maybe three weeks of food remaining. What would Rey do then? She didn't know, but she had a fairly good idea what he *might* do. Knowing Rey, he would lock the two of them inside Soren's cabin and allow the rest of his cohorts to starve. She bristled at the thought. She would rather die with them than to be one of the last two survivors, with Rey as the other survivor.

She looked at the crates of food malevolently as dark thoughts swirled in her head as furiously as the gaseous clouds on the planet Jupiter. She pushed herself over to the cabin's cabinet containing various kitchen-related items. She fumbled inside one of the small enclosures until she found what she was looking for. She also found the scalpel she had used to press to her throat. Rey tried hiding it, but she had found it the second or third day she was here. She smiled darkly and pushed herself back over to the crates of food, which she found were very easy to move around, thanks to zero-gravity.

2

"Don't you think we should go look for him?" Dante asked Rey. "He could be injured or something."

"Fuck him," Rey said emotionlessly. "It's his fault we're all floating in here like fucking sea monkeys in a kid's plastic toy spaceship." He looked up from the console computer screen and stared into Dante's nervous face. "Do you understand our situation Dom? I mean, do you *really* understand it?" Without waiting for an answer, he said, "We're fucked Dom. Up shit's creek. Downstream without a paddle. In deep kimchi. I don't care what idiom you want to use, but we're in serious trouble. Our ship is slowly moving toward Jupiter's space and we have no ability to slow it down or even turn it in the direction of Europa. In probably three, maybe four weeks, the ship will plunge into Jupiter. The last thing you'll feel will be your head imploding in on itself."

Dante, along with Wurther and Sandstone all looked at Rey with resigned fear in their eyes. They knew that Shelton's efforts were in vain, but since then, Rey had not really shared with them, whether or not that was their final attempt at a solution. Rey's open despair now unnerved them. This was the end. Truly the end. No last-minute heroics, no Hail Marys; only certain, painful death.

Dante looked over at Wurther. He was crying quietly in the corner. He turned away from him disgustedly. He wondered how it would be...at the end. Their food would most likely be gone by then. In the big scheme of things, he figured that they would be starving before the ship plunged into Jupiter. He considered his options and felt he would rather crash into Jupiter than to suffer the agonizing pain of starvation. He didn't like the idea of having his head popped like a zit though. He was about to ask Rey how long they would be able to stretch the food out, when one of the cockpit alarms started blaring.

"What the fuck is that?" Sandstone yelled over the strident sound. Rey looked down at one of the consoles and his eyes grew wide. "It's a fucking fire in the Commons!"

3

Sandstone floated out of the cockpit behind Rey and Dante. As he approached the fire, he stared in fascination. He had seen lots of fires on television shows and even a few big ones in person and they all had that same flickering, darting quality. This fire almost seemed to glow in place, but as it grew, the fire didn't jump or dart out, it rolled over itself until it made contact with an untouched surface. From there, it would continue to glow and burn until it rolled over another surface. Sandstone felt he would have stared into that dangerous beauty for hours if Rey hadn't yelled into his face. "The seats Jake! Get to the seats!" Jake glanced at the row of seats directly to his left and could see that glowing blob of fire roll over to several of the Commons' seats. They had all grabbed halon tanks before coming in and Jake aimed his at the seats. His first blast shoved him up toward the ceiling, but he was able to quickly recover and get back to the fire.

"This ain't working!" yelled Rey. "Don't just stand there gaping like an idiot Wurther, go hit the emergency halon activation system!" Wurther, to his credit, responded quickly and pushed off strongly toward the halon panel, where he yanked open the small door. He was so nervous that he pulled the door off its hinges, and it sailed quickly to the rear of the Commons, bouncing off the seatbacks of several chairs before finally coming to a spinning stop. He slammed the halon release button with his fist and the foam spray shot out of the nozzles located in the ceiling of the ship. The force of the foam being ejected was enough for the foam to make it to the fire and soon, all of the rolling flames had been smothered into submission.

Rey shoved past Dante, fearing that the fire had spread to his cabin. "Kelly! KELLY! Where is she?!" Sandstone and Dante floated directly behind him. They moved into the cabin quickly. The fire had not entered it, but Kelly was nowhere to be found. He zipped up to the bedroom on the upper level, but didn't find her there. The only other room in the cabin was the bathroom, but Dante was coming out shaking his head. Rey could feel himself slipping away, slowly losing his connection to himself, when he heard Wurther calling for them.

They pulled themselves out of the cabin and there in the Commons, floated Kelly, completely unharmed. She floated in mid-air, arms outstretched like the angel of death come to pronounce judgement. Her arms and hands were bloody and droplets floated around her like planets in a child's bedroom orrery. Dante and Sandstone could only stare at her open-mouthed.

She had one hand balled into a fist and the other gripped the scalpel tightly. Rey floated up to her and reached for her hands, hoping to retrieve the scalpel, but she snatched them away. "My God Kelly, where were you? Are you hurt? Why is the food out here? Were you trying to save it from the fire?"

She looked at him with disdain. She turned her head slowly and looked at each of them with disdain...and disapproval. She turned back to Rey and said accusingly, "You have all been judged and have been found wanting. The punishment for your sins...is death." At that pronouncement, she waved her hand toward the burnt remains of the food in the Commons. "The heat of God's fire has destroyed your greed. Not just greed of food, but greed of the flesh. We could have all lived together in peace on Europa. We would have eventually grown to trust and love one another and start families and start rebuilding the human race. But one man. One horrid man had to have everything to himself. And he passed that greed and arrogance on to you Rey, who passed it on to the guards, who abused the passengers whenever they had a chance. It was all of you who destroyed us. Destroyed the human race!" She pointed her finger at them, but at no one in particular. She glanced down at the smoldering food again. "I've destroyed the last of your food. You won't have two, maybe three weeks to wonder if there's a way to get down to Europa. You'll have several days, maybe a week, before real hunger starts tearing at your insides." She reached into her jumpsuit pocket and pulled out something small and bloody. "If you get hungry enough, eat this!" She flung the red thing directly at Rey and since he was still looking at the burnt food he didn't look up until the bloody pulp smacked him in the face. It stuck briefly and then slid down his cheek, leaving a bloody smear. He grabbed at the squishy thing before it had a chance to fall to the floor and looked back at Kelly. "What the fuck is this?" He turned the pulp over and examined it closely. "Is this a tongue?" He flung it away from him in disgust. The bloody thing sailed over Wurther's head and he cringed squeamishly.

They all looked toward Rey's old cabin in unison. It was no mystery who the owner of the tongue was. Dante and Wurther floated toward the hallway leading to Rey's old cabin. Sandstone turned to look at the food. It was completely destroyed. Because they had no gravity, the fire slowly burned and encompassed the whole mass of food before the sensors had a chance to register it. He dug through the burnt plastic, still warm, cursing and flinging clumps of charred mess. He was tempted to eat something that looked like food, but didn't want to take the chance that he would be eating plastic as well. He backed away from pile angrily. That was it. They had no food remaining. What would they do now?

4

Rey looked at Kelly coldly. He could feel himself reaching a breaking point and felt that sooner or later he would snap. He wasn't quite sure what he would do when that happened, but he knew it would be bad. It would be very bad.

Now, they would be forced to open the bulkhead and start foraging for food within the ship. But everyone locked outside of the Commons had been without food for over a week now. If there was food to be found anywhere in the ship, they would have found it by now. He thought about how easy it would have been if they had even one spacesuit, but Doc and Jaime completely and totally fucked him. They knew what they were doing.

Rey ran his hands through his matted hair. "Goddammit! Goddammit!" He realized he was losing it. Not long ago, he considered his situation quite good. He had confided in Dante of his plans to remove Soren from power and do away with this *First Father* bullshit. Nola or Kelly would have been his – he would never have allowed the farce of marrying Kelly and Finch to happen. He would have been in control of the *Cassiopeia* and Doc and his people would never have been allowed to lock themselves in the Cargo Hold.

He had still held out that while they had food, there was still a chance that they might figure out a solution to get to Europa. He just couldn't accept the fact that they would die here in the spaceship, within mere miles of life on Europa. He felt like a man dropping dead of thirst at the edges of an oasis. Now that the food was destroyed, he didn't quite know *what* they would do. He turned back to Kelly and grabbed her by her jumpsuit, "You've killed us Kelly. You've killed us all!" He shoved her away from him so hard that she floated toward the bulkhead door. She laughed crazily as her back slammed into the bulkhead door. She floated there with her feet pressed up against the bulkhead smiling emptily as Rey turned toward his old cabin.

Rey floated over to the door of his old cabin where Soren was. He was seeing red. Dante and Sandstone were attempting to bandage Soren's bloody stump of a tongue. Soren, still tied to one of the metal chairs connected to the floor, regarded him fearfully when he floated into the cabin.

Rey looked at him with pure hate. He thought about all the times he acquiesced to Soren's demands on the ship and back on the moon. He thought about Soren's ridiculous *First Father* philosophy. He didn't go along with that belief at all, so why didn't he say anything? Why did he allow Soren to shovel that tripe day in and day out? He knew deep down that he allowed Soren to dangle Nola over his head like a carrot. He was mad as hell but someone had to pay for their current predicament and it sure as hell wouldn't be him. A moaning, idiotic sound assailed his ears and he got even angrier. Soren was trying to speak to him over a mouthful of blood, gore and the ragged remains of his tongue. The moaning, whining pitiful sound was maddening.

"What are you saying?!" he yelled at Soren. "You know, this is all your fault you fucking fat man! All of it!" Rey spat into Soren's face. "You allowed us to get into this predicament. Maybe we *should* have brought everyone with us. At least we would have made it to Europa. Now we're a fucking dead stick *and* we've got no food!"

Soren could only stare up at Rey's hate-filled eyes. He thought back to his wife Katy and remembered *her* hate-filled eyes, except now, they were laughing eyes. Hate-filled laughing eyes, if that was even possible. It was almost as if she knew back then, when her life was draining out of her body that Alfred Soren would always lose. No matter how many tricks he played, no matter how many closed-door deals he machinated, no matter how many people he hoodwinked, he would always lose. And almost as if on cue, here he was losing in a big way. A loss for the ages. He and everyone on board would eventually die of starvation or murder, while their broken ship drifted aimlessly in the general direction of Jupiter.

He looked at Rey again and almost recoiled from his dark gaze. It was at that moment he had an epiphany; *this* was purgatory. There was no up or down, no forwards or backwards. No right or wrong. No chain of command. He had heard Kelly's pronouncement. She was right...they were all judged and were found wanting. He remembered watching some old television show and remembered some hapless, dying priest screaming at the top of his lungs that they had been cast down into the pit where every man will be measured by his own circumstances and his own deeds. This was true indeed.

Dante and Sandstone shrank away from Soren as Rey advanced toward him. He had relieved Kelly of the scalpel and now had it clinched in his fist. Soren, seeing the bloodlust in Rey's eyes began squirming and moaning, infuriating Rey even more. He floated up to Soren and placed the scalpel up against Soren's throat. A thin red line appeared almost immediately. "I could kill a motherfucker today you know that Soren? We may not be far behind you, but as long as I get to carve you up before I die, I'm okay with that."

Just as Rey began to press harder on the scalpel, a huge explosion shook the ship. Rey turned toward Dante, eyes wide. He was about to ask him what the hell had happened when he heard piercing screams in the

Commons. Dante floated to the entrance and was about to clear the threshold when a huge piece of metal rocketed past him.

5

By the time Rey got into the Commons proper, it was mayhem. Immediately, he could tell that something was different in the Commons, apart from the burnt-up food – there were a lot more people in here now. He thought he saw Big Tony sail through the air with some homemade-looking lance. Looking at him, he thought "Big Tony" was a misnomer; he was emaciated. He scanned the Commons and could see Emma, Sarah, Wade and his folks, and the rest of Tony's people. He even saw Shelton Hayes floating through the damaged bulkhead door. He couldn't remember how long it had been since he stopped giving them food, but from the looks of them, they were most likely starving. As he stood there, he saw Wurther flail uselessly in the zero gravity, trying to maneuver his body away from Tony's charge, but it was too late. Tony's lance gored his midsection and Rey heard what sounded like a cartoon grunt escape Wurther's mouth…*"oof!"* and then Wurther, Tony and the lance continued their journey together toward the front of the Commons where the lance stuck fast in the wall.

"Get those fuckers now!" screamed Wade. "Don't spare any of them!" He was wielding what looked to be a mace, but was having great difficulty controlling it and his body in zero-g. He swung at Sandstone but was too far away from him. His mace totally missed Sandstone, but his momentum threw him into an uncontrollable spin which caused him to let go of the mace. Like Wurther, he flailed helplessly in the air trying to reach the ceiling of the Commons.

When the fire alarm sounded earlier, they left the cockpit quickly and had not brought any weapons with them. The only thing he had was the scalpel he had taken from Kelly. Where was she anyway? A bolt of terror surged through him as he frantically looked around for her. When the explosion happened, he heard a scream but wasn't sure who it belonged to. Now he began to panic, thinking that it was Kelly who screamed.

It was slowly dawning on him that they were outnumbered and the sheer ferocity of their attack was unmatched. These were men and women on the brink of collapse. God only knew what they were living off of and this attack was probably their last hope before totally devolving into animals, killing one another off. He had long forgotten who was out there but estimated there were at least eight, maybe nine people total, including the two remaining women, Emma and Sarah. The women were converging on Sandstone and Dante like a pack of lionesses cornering a helpless zebra, with several men behind them. Sandstone and Dante fought as hard as they could, but there were simply too many. He saw Emma jab a jagged pipe into one of Sandstone's eyes. He screamed and grabbed at the pipe. Blood spurted out like a faucet, covering Emma's face and hands. Rey gagged when he saw her lick her fingers hungrily. Dante was able to push away from them, but someone grabbed his leg before he was two feet away. They clubbed him over the head and Rey could see the light go out in his eyes. His lifeless body slowly floated down to the seats in the Commons.

"There he is!" shouted Reichart, who had gone directly to the cockpit to look for Rey. Luckily, Rey had moved close to the destroyed bulkhead door while looking for Kelly. When Reichart yelled out, he turned and pressed his feet up against one of the Commons' chairs and prepared to launch himself out of the Commons. That was when he saw Kelly. She wasn't dead, but she was injured. She grimaced as she grabbed at her right leg, close to the ankle. From what Rey could see, both of her feet were injured and she was bleeding heavily. Her right foot hung at an awkward angle and he could see bone sticking through the left ankle. She glanced up at him angrily. He saw Shelton Hayes head in her direction and he almost pushed himself toward him. In his mind, he saw himself killing Shelton and then rescuing Kelly and getting the hell out of the Commons, but in reality, he propelled himself out of the Commons and out into the corridor. As he flew through the corridor, the only thing he could hear pursuing him was the sound of their laughter.

DAY 117

THE COMMONS LIFE

1

Soren was running faster than he ever had in his life! Somehow, he had fought off his attackers and had gotten away. Even though he could hear them clearly, they still seemed far away. There were no lights here, so he had to keep slowing down to prevent running into something or tripping and falling. Suddenly, he saw a faint light ahead and his heart leapt in his chest. He was going to make it! He was going to get out of here! Just as suddenly, however, he felt as if he were running in mud or quicksand. His legs didn't seem to work. Now he was sinking. He flailed his arms about, but his arms didn't seem to work. What was happening to him? He started to scream, but nothing came out. Those chasing him now seemed much closer. He began to panic, but the more he panicked, the more helpless he felt. As he struggled helplessly, an intense pain began blooming in his chest. Just when he thought he would explode, his eyes popped open and he found himself staring into a bright fluorescent light.

"Alright...we got him back!" Sarah yelled out, as she removed the defibrillator pads from Soren's chest. Of their remaining group, she was the only one who remembered anything about using the ship's automated external defibrillator. Soren stared wildly around him. Reichart, Wade, Rich and Tony were drifting around the large work table in the cockpit. It was the only flat space that was bolted to the floor and that allowed them to easily finish with Soren. They were all covered in blood. Soren looked around bewildered. The last thing he remembered was being locked up in Rey's cabin. They had been feeding him some rancid soup since he was not yet able to eat anything solid because of his shredded tongue. As he looked around, he could see that he was in the cockpit and for one wild moment, he thought they had brought him here to show him Europa. To show him that they had made it and would be starting landing procedures soon. He began to weep for joy, but it was short lived as he could feel slow, throbbing pain radiate from his legs and arms. It was weird at first. He initially felt an overpowering itch in his legs and forearms. The itch then turned into an intense burning. He struggled trying to sit up and angrily cried out, *"Hel meh uhp!!"* They stared at him curiously. He cursed within. He was trying to say *help me up*, but to his ears, it came out as idiotic mush. He calmed himself and tried as mightily as he could to make them understand him, *"Hel. meh.* UHP!!"

Sarah eyes widened as she caught on. "I think he wants to sit up."

"Hmm...I guess it's not a problem now," said Reichart. "And there's no real reason to keep him tied up." He glanced at Wade and Rich. "Untie him."

Wade and Rich floated closer to Soren and undid his ties. Immediately, he tried sitting up again, but he couldn't seem to make his arms work right. Now that he was more aware, the itching and burning sensation had gotten worse. He looked at his left arm, angry that maybe the rope had fucked up the circulation in his arm and what he saw caused his heart to skip a beat. He lifted up his left arm and almost gagged. Below the torn arm of the jumpsuit was a swollen stump with ragged shreds of flesh tightly bound with some type of surgical binding. He stared at the misshapen thing dangling from his shoulder in abject horror and disbelief. With immense trepidation, he slowly turned his head to the right and was met with another engorged abomination that used to be his arm. *"Wah uh fhuuck ihd u OO oo mee? Wah uh fhuuck ihd u OO oo mee!?"* Matt Valen was floating by the entrance and burst out laughing at Soren's *hellspeak.* Or *hellmush,* he considered and burst out laughing again. He yelled into the room, "He wants to know what the fuck you did to him!" and started laughing again. Without warning, Soren vomited violently into the nearest face. A stream of brownish liquid splashed into Rich's unprepared face. Even in zero gravity, the force was enough to envelop Rich's face.

"FUCK!" Rich Gebbons cursed as he pushed back from the table. He pushed so hard his back slammed into one of the high-back cockpit chairs.

"Someone sit him up before he chokes on that shit!" Reichart commanded off to the side.

Wade and Sarah drifted closer to the table, trying to avoid the stringy goo floating over their heads. Soren was coughing and spitting, trying to clear his mouth. After vomiting what little food he had in his stomach, he looked down at his itching and burning legs and beheld the final horror. Both of his legs had been crudely sawed off right above the knee. They both had the same surgical binding tightly restraining the escaping flaps of flesh still attached to his leg. His stomach hitched again, but his mind had reached overload. He felt as if he were looking down at himself. His breathing increased and he heard it coming in and out in huge gasps. Right before he passed out, he could see Tony Hurt, floating into the cockpit with a bundle in his hands. A bloody hand had escaped the covering and on the small finger, Soren saw the unmistakable shape of his pinky ring. He jerked once and slipped down into darkness. He thought he heard Katy laughing as he descended.

2

In the Cargo Hold, everyone stared in horror at the attack on Soren. Despite Soren's unpopularity, no one could actually bring themselves to cheer his demise. Burt noticed this and intuitively understood that what happened to Soren could easily have happened to any one of them. No one was safe in this craven new world and no one was immune to succumbing to its savagery, as evidenced by Sarah and Emma. As much as Burt wanted to turn away, he forced himself to watch every wretched minute of the butchery. Even though the system recorded everything, he wanted to see them in real time and to attest to the fact that they did happen, amongst so-called civilized men and women. If they all perished here on the *Cassiopeia*, then their *testimonial* would be space fodder and a sad, unfortunate, cosmic joke.

He looked at the camera mounted in the Commons, closest to Kelly. His heart went out to her. She was nearest to the bulkhead when Tony and Reichart were able to use whatever leftover explosives they had. Apparently, Rey had stashed a little in one of the unused passenger cabins and during their foraging, they had come upon it. If he were there, he believed he could have saved her foot, but there were no doctors or nurses out there and consequently, they had to amputate her right foot. She shivered violently for days, possibly due to a high fever. He thought she was going to die, but she surprised everyone by opening her eyes one day and asked for food. Her left foot was still bandaged, which gave him hope that there were no serious complications. Initially, she was tied down to prevent her from floating off in her state, but now that she was on the mend, they didn't fully trust her and so kept her tied down. He noticed that Al Treyborn spent a lot of time flirting with her. When the lights came on in the mornings, he would sometimes notice her jumpsuit barely covering her body. It infuriated him that he was helpless to help her.

Sometimes, he would look for Rey but could never quite pin him down. Rey seemed to always be on the move. Sometimes, like an apparition, he would see him floating across the cameras. One minute he would be there and the next he would be gone. Once, when Burt was staring intently into one of the monitors, he turned his head to cough. When he turned back to the cameras, Rey was there, his eyes boring into the camera. Burt felt his heart skip a beat...or two. Rey stayed at the camera for about a minute and then was gone.

Burt was beginning to think that maybe Rey had found some food somewhere until he realized that Reichart's group had sent Shelton and Rod Stigler out to look for supplies...any supplies. Only Shelton returned and he was bleeding badly. He also had a chunk of meat taken out of his arm. He told the group that Rey had bit him. "Rey's turned into a fucking wild animal" he had told the group. They didn't know what had become of Rod until they saw his severed head floating slowly through the Commons entrance. It was essentially Rod's skull because most of the flesh had been cut away. Everything was gone, the eyes, ears, tongue, everything. The Commons' group was shocked, but not really surprised. Burt was aghast.

Jaime had floated up to him, slightly startling him. "Sorry Burt. Well, I guess Rey is still alive and well in the bowels of the ship, huh?"

Burt kept staring at the monitor, watching one of the men retrieve the skull. He seemed to inspect it, pulled at something inside the skull and then popped whatever it was into his mouth. He took the skull toward the cockpit and put it inside one of the bathrooms there. All Burt could do was hold his head down. He didn't know if he was disgusted at the man or at their own situation. Would they be doing something similar a month from now?

"Yeah, he's still out there," Burt replied. "He's slinking around like some fucking missing link out there. He probably would put Bigfoot to shame." He leaned in close to the monitors, "It was hard to tell, but the last time I saw him, it looked as if he had long hair growing out of one of his armpits. Or somehow attached to his chest. Not sure now, but it was disgusting and disturbing."

Jaime moved closer to the screen, looking for Kelly. He spied her sighed sadly. "That's horrible what's happened to Kelly. To be so young, she's suffering enough for several lifetimes."

"I know Jaime and she's being molested practically every night by one, maybe two men down there. She's resigned herself to her fate, but...I don't know. I just wish we were able to get her in here with us."

"I know Burt, but that couldn't be helped. She made a strategic decision that allowed us to get inside the Cargo Hold and one that landed her in the predicament she's in now. It's definitely not fair, but actions have consequences." He paused for a minute and then added, "Anton is taking it very hard, you can be sure. It only took one viewing of the monitors for him to shut down. He hasn't looked at the monitors anymore, nor has he spoken to anyone. I think the men in the white coats have taken his marbles away."

"Shit," said Burt. "I may have to have a conversation with him." He looked out at the others in the Commons. They had ravaged Soren's body for food. Burt assumed that he was the most likely first target, since they all blamed him for their current situation. Luckily, the ship still had minimal backup power, so the refrigerator units in each of the crew cabins were still working. Any and all "food" was stored in the refrigerator units until it was time to prepare it.

He counted the remaining folks in the Commons. There was Reichart, Treyborn, Shelton, Tony, Matt, Wade and Rich. The surviving women were Kelly, Sarah and Emma, although he now saw Sarah and Emma as extensions of the crazy men they were with. Since he didn't see Wayne Kesk, he assumed he was "sacrificed" like Timmons was. Of course, out in the "wilds" was Rey and they had moved Soren to the cockpit to free up his cabin. Other than them in the Cargo Hold, there were only a handful of souls left in the *Cassiopeia*. He wondered how many would be alive a week or two from now.

DAY 130

THE BURNING FUSE

1

"Do you think this is safe being up here?" Sarah whispered nervously to Tony as they lay in their makeshift bed in the Med-Lab.

"Absolutely!" Tony replied enthusiastically. "It's been almost two weeks since we've seen or heard from Rey. There's no way he could have stretched out his food that long." He pulled her close to him. "I'm sure it wouldn't hurt to go look for him, but it doesn't matter now. If he *is* alive, he'd be so weak that one good punch would be enough to lay him out flat!"

Sarah laughed and nestled close to Tony. His body odor was strong, but not unpleasant. They had all decided to forgo taking showers. They weren't sure how long the water would last and to be honest, taking showers didn't really matter anymore. As she thought about it, nothing really mattered anymore. Body odors, showers, religion, good and bad, morality, God... This was a new world, temporary as it may be. She knew they would eventually run out of food. She also knew that as long as she was with Tony, she would at least be the second to last person to survive, if it came to that. She knew that Tony would protect her at all costs. They talked about it often. They had it planned out that if things got out of hand, they would rendezvous at a preplanned location.

She chuckled lightly as she saw a drop of blood making its way in the air above them. Even blood like that didn't bother her anymore. Nor did it matter. There was blood everywhere in the Commons...it couldn't be helped. Eventually, they got used to it, especially after they killed Shelton Hayes.

They had all lost a lot of weight and they were all bordering on malnutrition. All of them, except Shelton Hayes that is. He ate exactly what they ate, but for some reason, his body didn't succumb to the effects of prolonged starvation like theirs. She remembered Tony asking him why he wasn't as thin as they were and to his detriment, he responded that he was a fat kid growing up. "No matter how hard I tried, I could never lose the weight." He chuckled and then added, "Hell, I might be the last one alive by the time it's all said and done." Unfortunately for Shelton, it was an easy decision for the group's leadership, Reichart and Tony, to decide who would be next in line to prolong the lives of the others. Reichart convinced the others to keep Shelton alive, like Soren, so the meat wouldn't go bad as fast. They were finding that human meat went bad quickly, even when stored in the refrigerators. The freezers no longer worked, so they were forced to use the low-wattage refrigerators.

Thinking back on that time, she wondered if Shelton had a burst of clairvoyance the night he was "sacrificed," because he was ready when they came for him. He fought savagely, breaking Wade's wrist. In the end, Al Treyborn had to stab him repeatedly, but the final jab in the kidneys was what did him in. The screaming was unbearable and blood was everywhere. She remembered asking Tony later why they didn't just go after Kelly and he said that both Reichart and Al were infatuated with her and wouldn't think of it. Her time will come, she remembered him saying.

She snuggled in tighter to Tony and slid her hand into the waistband of his shorts. He moaned softly as she began caressing him. She smiled to herself feeling the growth in her hands and envisioned the ecstasy to come.

2

"Do you *always* have to cry? We've been doing this for several weeks now and you'd think that you would have grown to appreciate me."

Kelly opened her wet eyes. She was thinking of Nola, Burt and her pale blue friend out there all alone in front of the always angry Jupiter. As Al Treyborn clumsily undid her jumpsuit, she looked at him with disgust in the semi-gloom of the Commons. She thought to herself that this fucking moron was so selfish and depraved, that he had the nerve to think she was crying because of him. Weeks ago, but what felt like years, she had completely and irrevocably cast off any emotions that would make her appear weak. Early on, she had hoped to find some level of comfort and camaraderie with Sarah and Emma, but there was no love lost with them. Once Emma floated over to her to feed her and Kelly could immediately see the hate and disdain in her eyes.

She saw herself as an empty shell, no more, no less. She spat out any food they gave her, screaming at the top of her lungs, "I'm not a fucking cannibal! You can shove that shit up your asses motherfuckers!" After that, they simply poured soup down her throat. It was harder to not swallow the soup, so she knew that starvation would elude her until they decided to kill her and cut her up for skirt steak.

In Treyborn's clumsiness, he bumped up against her bandaged right ankle. She gritted her teeth, but did not yell out. She was in constant pain since the bulkhead explosion. The only thing she remembered before she fell unconscious was the odd way her right foot was hanging and the chickenshit Rey getting out as fast as he could move in zero gravity. She knew her right foot was damaged beyond hope. Maybe if Burt were here and had the full use of Med-Lab, he could have saved her foot, but not now. Not in this hellscape. She distinctly remembered looking at her left foot, though. It was bleeding, but she was able to move it easily. When she regained consciousness several hours later, she screamed out in anger and despair when she saw that her left foot had been amputated as well. They told her that her left foot had turned gangrenous and had to be removed. She cursed them bitterly, but in the end, it didn't matter. They were all going to die and it didn't matter if she had one foot or no feet.

She turned her head to look around the Commons. It was completely quiet, save for some distant machinery that still functioned and Treyborn's noisy petting. She guessed it was close to two or three in the morning – usually about the time when Treyborn would slip out of his dirty cubbyhole and pay her a visit. Most times she endured him, but something was different this time. She was ready to end this pitiful rendezvous. If it wasn't Treyborn, it was Reichart, who was worst.

As Treyborn slathered her neck, she cooed softly, "Let me have some fun too, Trey. I want to kiss on your neck too, baby. That gets me so excited!"

Treyborn stopped immediately and lifted his head from her neck. She could see drool sliding down the corner of his mouth and looked away quickly. "You *what?*" he said in complete surprise. "Oh God Kelly, I've wanted you to do that to me for so long!" Even in the pale light of the Commons, Kelly was able to see the almost palpable earnestness in his sex-starved face. The air was thick with it. He bent his head down to kiss her passionately and she allowed it for the time being. When he surfaced for air, she used that time to turn her head slightly to the side, exposing her neck. After a few minutes of him painting the side of her neck with saliva, she maneuvered her head to kiss his neck, alternatively kissing and biting at his neck. With her hands tied down, she wouldn't be able to apply any leverage to his head, but the harder she kissed his neck, the harder he pressed down into her mouth, moaning wildly.

Almost as if he could read her mind, he lifted his head up from hers and said, "I know I shouldn't do this, but I really want to feel your hands all over me." *This* is what she was hoping for. She had to dig down deep, but she forced up her prettiest, flirtiest smile and that seem to undo Treyborn. He quickly undid the ties holding her wrists pinned to her sides. He thought a moment and then undid the ties holding her legs down. He then rolled on top of her and pushed his head into hair as she began to kiss him passionately on the neck. Using both free hands, she reached up and grabbed his head, pulling him closer into her. She could feel him growing inside and was disgusted. He continued moaning as she kissed and bit at his neck. Kelly grabbed a handful of his greasy, matted hair and used all of her strength to pull him as tightly into her as possible. At the same time, she opened her mouth as wide as possible and bit deeply into his neck. His initial scream of pleasure quickly turned into a piercing scream of pure agony. Because his face had been buried deeply into her hair and neck, his scream was muffled.

As she expected, he pulled away from her immediately, but he had no real leverage in zero gravity. He repositioned himself to plant his hands or knees on the floor so he could jackknife himself up and away from the danger, but when she felt him reposition himself to push away, she readjusted her bite and was able to lock onto something more substantial in his neck. She felt him violently pushing away from her, but she chomped down as hard as she could, feeling a deluge of blood running down the side of her face and into her mouth. She held on and pulled until she could feel the tough skin and ligaments tearing free of their moorings. The next thing she knew, Treyborn had shot up toward the ceiling, trying unsuccessfully to scream, a river of blood trailing him as he went. She turned her head to the side and spat out the large chunk of neck-meat she had ripped from his neck.

3

Sarah awoke with a start, pulling her out of a dream that made her weep when she realized it was just a dream. She dreamed she was running in the woods with her cousin and they were laughing and singing. She realized it was the first dream she had of being on earth since she first arrived on the moon. She was running through the beautiful countryside with tall trees everywhere and green hills as far as the eye could see. This was how she imagined Europa would be, but she quickly pushed that thought out of her mind. It was all a moot point because she would never see Europa. She slowly swung her legs over the bed, trying to push the thought of Europa out of her head. She thought brutally, that the last thing she might see in this bleak and bloody world, would be a knife slicing her throat open. She shook her head sadly and wondered if things would have been different if Soren hadn't left the others. She was one of the women who gladly agreed to leave the moon. Sure, she felt icky leaving Tess and the others behind, but she was a survivor and knew she would do anything to live and at the time, considered Soren to be her best bet at life. She laughed, but there was no humor in it and thought, *Well, I guess I fucked around and found out.*

She pushed off from the bed and floated through the door. Even in zero gravity, she felt her bladder screaming at her for release. She thought she read somewhere that the urge to piss is less in zero gravity, but she felt like she was going to explode. She floated quickly to the bathroom in Med-Lab, cursing that it was all the way at the other end of Med-Lab. She reached the entrance and out of habit, closed the door. She hadn't thought much about it before, but realized that all of the bathrooms functioned as if they were in a zero-g environment, so they all pretty much got used to using the specialized vacuum toilets. She did her business, but sat there thinking about the folks on the moon again. She wondered if they were dead yet and how they died or would die. She knew that eventually, the power would go, but she wondered if they had enough food to even make it to that point. She wondered about that as she grabbed a medical pamphlet from a tray on the wall. She laughed as she opened it up; "How to manage UTIs in space."

Feeling refreshed, Sarah floated back to her room. She wondered if Tony was awake. She had stayed in the bathroom longer than she normally would have because she was hoping that maybe he would be awake when she returned – she was feeling frisky. As she reached the door frame of the room, she thought she heard a slight moan and smiled. Maybe Tony is up for round two, she wondered. She quickly slid in the bed and snuggled up to him. Like always, her hand reached down to cup his balls through the thin night shorts that he wore. She would always attempt to squeeze them hard and laugh her ass off when he would immediately yank her hand away in total fear. She knew he was awake because she heard him moan and she was tempted to squeeze them hard...just a little, but she only cupped them briefly before putting her hand inside his shorts.

She felt herself getting extremely excited when she felt the warm stickiness inside his underwear. *He's already getting ready for me*, she thought hungrily. She softly nibbled on his nipple as her hand continued to explore inside his underwear. She began to get slightly frustrated as she continued groping him. *Where the hell is his cock?* She asked herself. Once, when they were about to be intimate, he played a joke on her by shoving his penis between his thighs, while keeping his thighs closed tight, mimicking the sadistic killer in one of those old Hannibal Lecter movies. He came into the room screaming, "Baby! Space life is mutilating me! I think my penis slipped inside of me! Look!" She looked at his legs, expecting some awful, crass school yard humor, but the way he was holding his penis in looked like it was gone. Her initial shock and bewilderment turned into a hysterical laughing fit. After which, they made love furiously.

When she couldn't find his penis, she began thinking he was playing this joke over again. She chuckled slightly and began to more aggressively search for his penis. Since his thighs were closed, she had to force her hand between them to find his elusive phallus. Nothing. She began to get frustrated and was about to yell at him when her hand touched something rubbery and slightly stiff. She explored it with her fingers with mounting anxiety. "Fuck this! Come on Tony, what the fuck, huh?" She yanked off the covers and reached over to turn on the light in the room. It didn't take long, but when she started screaming, she knew in an instant that she had severely damaged her vocal cords.

4

Kelly kept her eyes on Treyborn hovering close to the ceiling. He was bleeding profusely and had abandoned any attempt to scream. The only thing he could do was try to hold in his torn jugular. *Good luck with that*, she thought. She could tell he was either going to die or pass out from blood loss – and then die. She undid the last of the ties around her waist, while still keeping an eye on him, in case he tried to come after her. But it was a false fear. He had lost so much blood that he no longer tried holding onto his damaged neck. He hovered there, close to the ceiling, his hands twitching, while he stared at nothing in the darkness.

Satisfied, she groped around on the floor near her pallet, where they had her tied down. She knew he always carried his weapon, so it was bound to be nearby. For one split second, she was about to panic when she spied it under one of the seats, probably pushed under there during their struggle. Treyborn used to brag about his jagged pipe, saying he could take on three, maybe four people at a time if he had to. Kelly always thought that he would most likely have impaled himself with it, if anything. The business end of the two-foot pipe had jagged shards sticking out in all directions. She imagined there must have been a powerful explosion to create this sepsis-inducing weapon of death. On the other end, Treyborn had used duct tape on the smooth pipe end, increasing its grip strength. She chuckled dryly and thought, *Duct Tape...truly the tape you can't leave home without.*

She pushed herself away from the cloud of blood hanging in the air above her. She had to use her hands because the brutalized nubs of her ankles, were still extremely sore. She thanked God that the ship's gravity was out because in her current state, it would have been impossible for her to function. Looking toward the bulkhead entrance, she could see the darkened corridor beyond. She could feel her excitement growing, despite the harsh warning she gave herself about getting too cocky. But now that the time had come, what would she do out there? She didn't know if they would come looking for her, but it was a big ship and she had no need to scrounge for food. She was focused on finding a safe and secure location, where she would stay until she died of starvation. Considering the folks she was with, that would be the more humane way to go.

She was floating quietly just above the chairs in the Commons and had made it to the hallway that led to the crew cabins when a piercing scream broke the solitude of the Commons. She thought maybe it came from Med-Lab, but she wasn't certain. She instantly froze where she was by grabbing onto the back of one of the chairs. *Goddammit!* She thought. Another two minutes and she would have been at the bulkhead door and out into the void of the *Cassiopeia*.

Just as she was about to move again, the lights came on in the Commons and she saw Reichart, Wade, and Rich come floating through the hallway entrance from their crew cabins. From the angle of the hallway, the first thing they saw was Treyborn floating toward the ceiling and they immediately shot toward him, totally missing her. Not so with Emma. When she came out, she just happened to be looking in Kelly's direction. Immediately, Kelly compressed her bootless legs against a chair behind her and rocketed toward Emma, grimacing in pain. Surprised, Emma opened her mouth to yell, but Kelly's speed had closed the distance in a matter of seconds. With all her might, Kelly swung Treyborn's jagged pipe at Emma's face. If Kelly had been a foot closer, she probably would have impaled Emma on the side of the head, killing her instantly. Instead, the jagged pipe edges caught Emma by the cheek and completely ripped open the left side of her face. The momentum of Kelly's swing sent Emma spiraling toward the other end of the Commons and her crashing into one of the walls bordering the crew cabins.

Even though Emma never got a scream out, the sound of Kelly smashing into the wall was enough to cause Reichart to turn around. He saw Emma spinning in circles and grabbing at strips of flesh dangling from the left side of her face, while Kelly fought to get her bearings in zero gravity. Both of her stumps were bleeding badly. "Get her!" he yelled to Wade and Rich. He turned back to Treyborn and grimaced. It looked like his throat had been ripped open by a goddamn vampire. Treyborn's eyes were open, but they were lifeless. And looking at the amount of blood floating in the Commons, he knew for certain that Treyborn was dead. *How in the fuck did he scream like that with his throat ripped open?* he thought. It didn't matter now. He could take care of Treyborn's body later. Emma needed his help now. He backed up against the wall at the head of the Commons and shoved as hard as he could in Emma's direction. He slowed himself down using the chairs in the Commons so he wouldn't hit her like a linebacker. Once he slowed down, then he lightly pushed off the chairs toward her. When he reached her, she was as pale as cottage cheese. "Come on Emma...hang in there!" he said to her. "You can't go into shock just yet. Let's get you fixed up." He pushed off toward the cockpit with her in tow. They kept all of the medical supplies and equipment there because it was easily the cleanest area in their part of the ship. The Commons was akin to a slaughterhouse, for all intents and purposes. Now, it would be downright toxic. There were all kinds of shit floating around out there; shit, for one, blood, strips of skin and flesh, a body part of two, and more blood. The cockpit had a door which essentially kept out all of the crap floating around out in the Commons.

Before he was fully in the cockpit, he could still hear Wade and Rich struggling with Kelly. To be severely injured like she was, she fought like a wild cat and was screaming like a banshee. He turned his attention to Emma and began treating her wound. As he worked, he wondered where the fuck Matt was. He knew Matt was a heavy sleeper, but damn! And who was it that screamed? It certainly wasn't Treyborn with his throat torn up like that.

5

Sarah had been instantly transported back to Earth. More accurately, she had been transported to a darkened movie theater showing three or four science fiction horror movies at the same time. Sarah loved the science fiction horror genre. She loved the entire *Alien* franchise, but the jury was still out on the prison one. The *Cassiopeia* was fully stocked with movie files from every genre, going back to the early days of television. She remembered thinking that a dedicated someone made a special effort to catalogue and create the huge database of movies. She only hoped the person who put so much effort into saving those old movies, was able to save himself or herself a spot on the moon, but that was a moot point now. As far as the movies, she thought it was one of the few things that made this godforsaken trip worthwhile...or at least bearable. The other thing was Tony. *Her* Tony. Their relationship started out badly at first, but she grew to love him and has it turned out, they realized they were made for one another. He knew her and she knew him. She knew everything about him. And in their lovemaking, she knew everything about his body...until now.

Now, as she hovered there shaking violently and screaming hoarsely, all she could do was stare down sickeningly at...the *evil* that was perpetrated on her man. It was all of the science fiction horror movies rolled into one. Before she had yanked the covers off and turned on the lights, the last thing she was doing was playing around his crotch area and naturally that's where her eyes went when the lights came on. She stared at the bloody mess where his penis used to be. In its place was...his tongue. It was huge and seemed to have been totally ripped out of his mouth. Fearfully, she looked up toward his face and saw the final horror and mutilation of her lover. He had something that looked like mushy Cornish hen eggs protruding from where his eyes had been. Her stomach hitched, but she held in last night's dinner. All she could do was sob. She looked at his crotch again and could see his ripped-open scrotum. Although she didn't consciously think this, deep down she intuitively knew that when she was rubbing on his crotch earlier, what she thought were his balls were actually his eyes. Apparently, she had dislodged one because floating near the bunched-up bedsheets near his feet was one of his brown eyes. Her stomach hitched again. She started when she heard a slight moan. Her head snapped toward him and she could see him struggling to breath. *Oh my God!* She thought. *He's still alive!* Something appeared to blocking his airway, so she moved close to him and opened his mouth. "Oh Tony! I thought you were dead! I'll go get..." was all she was able to get out. She suspected that if she were not in zero gravity, she would have involuntarily fallen backwards. As such, all she could do was shrink back in horror after she opened his mouth and stared directly at the head of his penis. She could no longer hold her dinner in. It launched itself out of her like wastewater from a broken toilet.

As she was bent over vomiting, she could see that his hands had been tied to the bed posts with wire. She wept bitterly when she realized he was alive while this was being done to him. He wasn't dead yet, but she knew they would never be able to save him. He had lost a lot of blood and was most likely in shock. She fought against this line of thinking and decided to get him to Reichart and the others anyway. They could help him. She lifted her head and began to wipe her mouth when Rey spoke up behind her. "I must admit, this was a masterpiece."

She whirled around as best she could in zero gravity. Even though her throat had been irrevocably damaged, she still managed to scream. Rey looked like a floating skeleton. His skin was stretched harshly on his gaunt face, reminding her of the ghoulish character in the movie, *Nightmare on Elm Street*. His eyes were soulless and lost in the cavern of his eye sockets. He was only wearing underpants, so she was able to see how hideously scarred he was on his arms, chest and legs. Some of the scars were healed lumps of keloid, while others looked fresh and angry. Sickeningly, she realized in an instant how he managed to stay alive so long: he was eating strips of his own flesh. As sickened as she was, she had to marvel at his indomitable will to survive.

Rey grinned at her coquettishly, "Hmm...you like what you see, eh?" He laughed when he saw the look of pure revulsion bloom on her face. "I'm sorry Sarah, but *Kelly* is my woman and there's no room for you." Sarah could only stare at him, her mind furiously working out a way to extricate herself from this situation. Rey stared at her a second longer, cocked his head to the side and jammed his scalpel into her stomach. Even as she looked down at the blood-smeared silver thing protruding from her navel, she couldn't comprehend what it meant. She only knew she had to get out of this room. She continued staring into Rey's ghoulish face as he grabbed onto her shoulder and pulled her close. He was rank and his breath was horrid. She stared at him, stared at his darkened rotted teeth and his thin cracked lips. All the while, she kept feeling distant tugs far below her. She didn't realize she was in pain until she heard a loud, sloppy wet sound and felt an immediate chill in her stomach. She looked down at her stomach and could see that Rey had disemboweled her. Her intestines noisily poured out of her open abdomen, while the remaining contents of last night's dinner drifted up toward her face. He reached inside her stomach like a street urchin stealing baubles and trinkets from an old woman's purse. He pulled out what looked to be undigested meat and popped it into his mouth. "Waste not, want not," he said hungrily.

At this, she wanted to scream again, but her body had begun to shut down. She sagged in his arms weakly, her head plopping onto his leathery hairless chest. "Kill me," she pleaded. "Please kill me."

He pulled back from her and held her head up. He looked almost bewildered and said tenderly, "I already have my love, I already have."

As Sarah's last clear thought drifted its way out of her consciousness, her eyes beheld Tony's torn and violated body. With the last of her will, she thought toward him, *Wait for me darling. Wait for me...*

DAY 130

THE HORROR

1

Burt was in the throes of a nightmare. He was being chased down a dark narrow tunnel and there seemed to be no end in sight. Someone called him and it sounded like Nola, but he wasn't sure. He heard his name again, but this time, it was right behind him. He turned around slowly and felt a hideous claw snatch him. *Noooo...,* he yelled out in the darkness. *Noooo...*

"Burt! Wake up man!" said Jaime. He was trying to keep his voice down since it was so early in the morning. He didn't want to alarm any of the others nearby. "You've got to see this Burt, they've lost their minds!"

Burt undid the belt that kept him anchored to his sleeping pallet. He felt very weak. They did what they could to try to exercise their muscles, but being in zero gravity with no specific exercise equipment did nothing to help with the atrophy of their muscles. He sat on the edge of his pallet for a minute longer and then pushed over to where Jaime, Liz and a couple others were clustered about.

As he floated over to them, he asked, "What's going on guys? You know it's almost four in the morning, right?

"I woke up from a nightmare myself," Liz said and looked at Jaime. "It was terrible. Somehow, Rey had gotten inside the Cargo Hold and was on a killing spree. After that, I didn't want to go back to sleep." She moved closer to Jaime and he put his arm around her. "I don't think I ever want to go back to sleep again," she added.

"She woke me up by accident, so I decided to stay awake also. I started looking at the videos to see what was going on out there and it looked to be a civil war of sorts."

"What happened?" Burt asked, suddenly very interested and very wide awake.

"At first, I saw Tony and Sarah head up to Med-Lab, where they used to stay. I've seen them go there before. They have their fun and then they go back and spend the night with the group. This time, they stayed there." Jaime took a deep breath and then continued, "I almost went back to bed, but then I noticed movement underneath the bed that Tony and Sarah slept in. I zoomed in frame by frame and saw the partial outline of a skull and part of a face peering out from underneath the bed." He shivered violently and then continued on.

"At first, I couldn't tell who was hiding underneath the bed, but I did a headcount of everyone else in the Commons and the only person it had to be was Rey."

"But I thought Rey was dead." Doc stated. "He's been out in the wilderness for almost two weeks, right?"

"That's what we *think*, Burt, but since Rey covered up the majority of our cameras out here, we're as good as blind to what's happening outside the Commons." He took a deep breath and prepared to continue when Liz touched him on his arm, "Just show him the recording. The recording is worth a thousand words."

Jaime stopped the real-time feed and found the Med-Lab and the Commons recording right before things began to happen. Burt leaned in closely as the recording began playing. While Tony and Sarah were having sex, Rey remained transfixed underneath the bed. Burt was amazed at his willpower. He remained under the bed until Sarah jerked awake and floated out of the room. Burt assumed she was going to the bathroom. Within seconds of her leaving, he saw Rey float out to the side of the bed and make his way toward Tony's face. When Sarah left the room, Tony never woke up.

Rey pressed the scalpel up against Tony's neck and whispered something in his ear and moved back while Tony positioned his hands so Rey could tie them to the makeshift bed posts. They were tightened so severely, that Burt could see blood dripping from the wrists. He saw Rey pull a syringe from his pocket and inject something into Tony's neck. At first, there was no discernible changes after the injection and then Tony began to shake violently. When he came to a stop, Burt could see that he was still breathing and still conscious – the only thing he was able to move were his eyes. Burt thought of the many drugs in Med-Lab that would incapacitate a patient, but not put them to sleep. He had to lock them up because soon after they left the moon, several vials of the strongest drugs came up missing. He brought it up to Rey at the time, but Rey dismissed it out of hand. Looking at Tony's frightened eyes, Burt now knew that Rey had stolen those drugs. He watched with mounting fear and revulsion as Rey violated Tony's body. Each time he thought the worse was over, Rey would surprise him with another monstrous act. Helpless to look away, Burt realized that looking at the tears of pain flowing from Tony's eyes, would forever be etched into his memory.

Once Sarah returned, Rey had already hidden again and it was only a matter of time before he was desecrating her body. He turned away as Rey began pulling Tony and Sarah's bodies through Med-Lab, down the stairs and out into wasteland of the *Cassiopeia*. Burt could feel his stomach doing flips inside.

Jaime laid his hand on Burt's shoulder. "That was rough to watch, I know," he said. There is more tape, but I can explain what happened in the Commons."

"Is Kelly still alive??" Burt asked, afraid to hear the answer.

"Yes," Jaime said, "but she's in a bad way Burt. She killed Treyborn when she bit out his jugular and she practically maimed Emma. She almost got away, but you could see that she was getting delirious, moving slowly. My guess is that she was losing too much blood from her amputations. Wade and Rich were on her in seconds."

Burt's heart hurt to hear that. Emma was a sweet woman. She was one of the young engineers who was assigned to Jaime's team early on. She was pulled later to work in the Reclamation Center. He was sad to hear that Kelly tried to kill her, but realized that Emma was now one of them. If Kelly was to survive, then she would have to think and act brutally.

"What's wrong with Kelly?" he asked. He already knew that they had to amputate both of her feet when the bulkhead door exploded. His biggest worry was that the badly performed amputations would result in some type of stump infection or even sepsis.

"If you're thinking she might have an infection, then you're right. It's hard to tell from the video, but both her legs are bleeding badly." He paused for a second and then continued, "They also beat her...badly. They didn't like the idea that she killed Treyborn and almost killed Emma. I think she's still unconscious."

Burt turned back to the monitors to see what was going on now out there. They had repositioned Kelly's pallet on top of the chair backs. It was wide enough that they were able to secure it firmly. This gave Burt a much better view of Kelly from the cameras. If it was still on the floor, he would not have been able to see her as clearly as he could now. Everyone out there was wide awake so the Commons' lights were still on. His heart hurt once again when he saw Kelly. They had re-bandaged her ankle stumps, but the bandaging was already soaked through with blood. Her face was swollen and both of her eyes were swollen shut. For some reason, she was dressed only in her underwear, as they all were. He began to wonder if the climate control system started breaking down out there. Since the Cargo Hold had its own climate control system, they were still fine. He wondered how long that would be.

Jaime floated over to his side and said, "Burt, we have to ensure that we don't fall into that same dark and tragic hole as them. We'll eventually run out of food too. What do you think will happen to us when we do? We have a lot of good, stable people here, but there are some who are beginning to lose their shit, even now."

Burt sighed, "I don't know Jaime, I really don't know. I think there is a transformation that happens in extreme situations. People essentially become different people when they're starving. The old 'them' is completely taken over by someone who is selfish, scared and willing to do unspeakable things in order to survive. In some situations, that might be an admirable trait, but here, with dwindling sustenance, that trait has the capability of turning monstrous." He looked down at the floor and shook his head, "God help us when that day arrives Jaime. God help us."

2

Seated in one of the cockpit chairs, Reichart stared out at Europa. He could see it serenely making its orbit around Jupiter, seemingly unconcerned by the swirling violent storms on Jupiter. He idly wondered how strong Jupiter's influence was on Europa. They had tons of science-backed information on Europa, but they all knew they wouldn't know the truth until they set foot on the planet. At this point now, however, they would never know the truth. He glanced at the computers in front of him showing various planetary readouts. He didn't know what the information meant, but he had heard that the readings showed that Europa was not as affected by Jupiter's massive presence as many scientists seem to believe. He already knew about the huge subsea caverns, but new information indicated that the surface was much more developed than they knew.

Reichart scoffed at the long dead scientists back on Earth and their never-ending arguments about Europa and whether it could sustain life. He was a simple man and simple ideas worked for him. What bothered him the most was the extreme confidence and arrogance that these scientists had about the planet. Despite the fact that they were millions of miles away, they would still say with *absolute certainty* that Europa did not have an atmosphere. Or that Europa *did* have an atmosphere. They could never agree and that disagreement made for great television. Based on his little bit of knowledge they gathered in the weeks and months since being this close, he knew things that the Earth scientists would never have suspected in a million years.

It didn't matter though, he thought sourly. It didn't matter to anyone. They were the last of the human race. The folks they left behind on the moon were most likely dead and if there were any survivors on Earth, then they would die soon enough when the Earth's orbit gets too close to the sun. Maybe after another billion years, a better lifeform will evolve *somewhere* that doesn't quite fuck things up like they did.

Emma moaned slightly and shifted on her pallet. It had been several days since their scuffle with Kelly and she was still unconscious. Part of it, he knew, was because she was in shock. The other part had to be because she was suffering severe malnutrition. They all were. That day exacted a heavy toll for them. Treyborn was killed, but it wasn't a very hard loss, since they were able to use his body to extend their own lifespan, limited as it was. And then there was the gory mess he found in Tony and Sarah's Med-Lab room. That had completely unmoored him. Based on what he saw floating in slow orbits about the room he knew that both Tony and Sarah had been gutted and disemboweled on the spot and the only person it could have been was Rey. How he was still alive, he had no clue. They let their guards down. They got comfortable, thinking that Rey *had* to be dead. It was two weeks with no food, for God's sake! But here he was, an apparition like a fucking male Baba Yaga boogeyman, floating around in the darkness stealing souls. He had dragged off Tony and Sarah's bodies like some fucking Wendigo and bada bing, bada boom, he's got food. It was only a matter of time before he came for the rest of them.

Emma was hanging on, but soon, they would have to make a decision on who to kill next. There was no doubt who that would be, considering all the trouble she just put them through. But after Kelly, it would have to be Emma, as much as he hated that. He had taken a liking to her and was just building up a relationship with her when all of this happened. In his late-night musings, he saw himself and her riding into the Great Red Sunset together at the end, kissing passionately until their heads burst like grapes underfoot. Unfortunately, he didn't think she would last that long considering the fact that she was still unconscious.

He cursed when he thought about Matt Valen. Initially, they thought Rey had gotten to Matt also, but they found him in one of the crew cabins, swollen, discolored and dead. Reichart thought he either couldn't handle the impending doom of the *Cassiopeia* when it hit Jupiter's atmosphere, or he didn't like killing off his friends and then eating them. Whether it was one or the other or both, Reichart didn't care. What pissed him off though, was the fact that Matt had taken the time to find cleaning agent fluids, hydraulic fluids and even some formaldehyde in Med-Lab – all of them toxic if ingested. All of the containers were empty when they found him. His body was so saturated with poisonous fluids that he was only fit for the Potter's Field. His spoiled body would provide no sustenance for them.

What made it worse was that it was actually his *intention* to not be food for anyone. He left a note that simply said, *I can't do this anymore and you can't have my body.*

DAY 142

INEVITABILITY

1

"That's my dried meatloaf pouch!" Ralph Valstok screamed into Eddie Chin's face. "I put it right beside me while I opened my saltines. Give it back or I swear, I'll break my foot off in your ass!"

"Fuck you man!" Eddie shouted back. "This is mine...I never touched your fucking shit!"

Both men turned toward one another simultaneously and grabbed each other by the fronts of their jumpsuits. They were about to come to blows when Jaime, Burt and several other men floated into the middle of the impending fight.

Jaime yelled at them both, "What the fuck is wrong with you guys? Are you fighting over *food*?"

Without looking at Jaime, Ralph said, "I put my food in my left pocket while I opened up another pouch. When I checked my pocket, it was gone. Fucking Chin here must have snatched it from my pocket when I wasn't paying attention. He must have been waiting for the opportunity!"

"That's bullshit Ralph and you know it!" Eddie retorted. "Why in the fuck would I steal your shit when I have my own right here?"

Ralph said, "I don't know your fuckin reason man! I just kn..."

"Ralph," asked Burt, "what's that floating by your foot?"

Ralph looked down and mixed in with some trash he had just thrown down, he saw his meatloaf pouch. He bent down and picked it up. He looked up at Eddie and the others ashamedly. "Goddammit! I wish I was out there man, instead of cooped up in here with you thieving fuckers!"

Burt whirled toward him, "What did you say? You'd rather be out there than in here??"

"Well, at least I wouldn't have to worry about someone eyeing my food all the time. Eddie didn't take it this time, bu..." Burt grabbed Ralph by the front of his jumpsuit and dragged him over to the monitors, pushing off the floor to do so.

"What the fuck man!" Ralph burst out. He tried twisting out of Burt's grasp, but Burt had a death grip on his jumpsuit. "You wanna be out there, huh? Do you see what the fuck is going on out there, Ralph? Do you see what the fuck is happening right now?" He shoved Ralph's face toward the monitor. "They're fucking eating one another, Ralph! And when they run out of food, they select another person to bludgeon and then eat! That's what the fuck is happening out there now, Ralph! They've devolved into fucking animals out there and that's where you want to be? I swear, if I could I would throw your ass out there in a heartbeat!" Several others near them looked up warily at Burt and Ralph. Burt released Ralph's jumpsuit and stormed over to airlock. Despite himself, he glanced through the window, where Larry and Allison still maintained their frozen vigil.

Ralph looked at Burt fearfully and then shuffled to the other side of the Cargo Hold. On his way there, he passed Eddie and Jaime, "Uh…sorry Eddie. Sorry guys." Eddie scoffed and sat down, angrily biting into his food.

Jaime floated over to the airlock where Burt looked to be in deep thought. Burt looked up as Jaime neared him and said, "Looks like our turn in the cold is about to start. Since we instituted this next level of food rationing the people are starting to feel it."

"Yeah, I know Burt," he said. "Where are we in terms of how much time before we're completely out of food?"

"We've gone as far as we can go to providing the bare minimum to people, which puts us at about seven to ten days away from being totally depleted."

"And what happens then?" asked Jaime. He thought he knew the answer, but he wanted to talk it out with Burt. "What do we say to everyone?"

Burt sighed long and exasperatingly. He didn't have all the answers, but they would have to have some answers soon or their somewhat peaceful village here might erupt in ways similar to what had transpired in the Commons. "We've got to talk to everyone Jaime. This is not a decision that we can just hand down to people. One thing is for sure; we will not allow someone to be killed for food. I draw the line there. I would rather starve before letting that happen."

"Same here Burt, but the people are rational now. What happens when they have low blood sugar or their stomachs are cramping so badly, they can barely think straight or they're so hungry, all they can think about is food? That's who we'll be dealing with in a couple of weeks."

"Yeah…I've been giving that a lot of thought, Jaime," Burt said. "I think our little society will have to transform from a democratic society to some version of a police state. We'll have to be very clear that we will not deal in cannibalism…period, and any intentional harm done to a fellow citizen will be dealt with harshly and swiftly. If we can't do that, then we'll have factions popping up like weeds and a burgeoning civil war in a space barely bigger than the Commons."

"This will be a difficult conversation to have Burt, but we need to have it soon. Ralph was just the beginning. If we don't come up with a plan, then we might have ten more Ralphs on our hands." He looked over at the monitors and sighed, "Once those idiots out there in the 'wilds' kill themselves off, we'll be the last of humanity. What a fucking joke," he said without any humor.

2

Reichart floated in the corner at the head of the Commons. He had been sitting in the cockpit when he remembered he needed to do something in the Commons. He pushed toward the exit, drifted out into the Commons and stared at the seats, trying to remember why he came out there.

"Goddammit!" he yelled to the empty Commons. He had been forgetting a lot in the last couple of days and his sleep patterns were off. Once, he woke up in the middle of the night and found himself floating in the corridor near the cafeteria. He could feel the blood pounding in his ears as he looked around the darkened corridor fearfully, half expecting Rey to materialize out of the darkness and pull his soul from his body. In a panic, he flew back to the Commons and hovered in the doorway between the cockpit and the Commons, eyes wide and heart pounding. He was so terrified by the experience, that he stayed awake for the next two days straight.

As bad as that was, it never got as bad as Rich's mental state. Lack of food seemed to have been the catalyst to Rich's mental decline. Several days ago, Rich started ranting about how weak Rey was. About how much of a lackey Rey was. He and Wade simply ignored his ravings, until one evening, he up and left the Commons. They followed him as far as the entrance to the Commons, calling after him, but all they heard was, "I'm gonna kill that fucker. I'm gonna kill that fucker. I'm gonna kill that fucker." He probably would have said it a fourth time, but in place of this litany, they heard a blood-curdling scream. It seemed to last for hours. When it finally stopped, all they could hear floating to them from the darkness was an almost soft, purring sound, "I'm gonna kill that fucker...tee-hee..." Reichart's skin crawled when he heard that giggle. They stared out into the darkness of the corridor, waiting for Rey to attack, but all they saw was something floating quickly toward them. It was too small to be Rey, so they remained where they were until Rich's head came floating up to them slowly. As the head floated past Wade, he could see a crazed and pain-stricken look frozen on Rich's face. His upper lip was shredded and barely attached. To Wade it looked as if it had been partially chewed off. They stayed awake the entire night, staring wide-eyed at the Commons entrance.

And then it was just he and Wade, but Wade made it known that he was not interested in carving up Soren or Kelly. He wanted Emma. He said Soren tasted 'off' and Kelly was dying. Wade knew that Emma was dying too, but in his mind, she wasn't as bad off as Kelly. Emma's wound eventually got infected and she simply lost the will to live. To Reichart, she was in a sort of wide-awake coma. Eyes open, but not responding to anything. Reichart became very protective of her and warned Wade not to lay a finger on her. Unfortunately, the next morning he went into the cockpit and saw a cloud of blood and guts floating in the air above Emma. He moaned forlornly and floated over to Emma's body reluctantly. He turned away disgustedly. Her body looked as if a wild animal had ravaged her overnight. Floating nearby was Wade, snoring loudly. Reichart went to his cabin and grabbed his weapon of choice; a five-foot pole with a kitchen knife firmly taped to the end. He went over to Wade's prostrate form and stared at him angrily. Caked blood filled his scraggly beard and he had blood smeared on his nose and forehead and on the sides of his cheeks.

Reichart stood over him for what felt like hours, but had only been minutes. He wanted Wade to be awake for this. When Wade finally stirred and slowly opened his eyes, Reichart said, "I told you not to fuckin touch her." Wade opened his mouth to say something, but Reichart didn't give him a chance. He jammed his spike into Wade's mouth, slicing open his mouth and pinning his tongue to the back of his throat. Choking and struggling to breathe, Wade tried removing the blade from his throat, but each time he grabbed at the blade, he did nothing more than slice open his hands. Reichart put as much weight as he could on the pole until Wade's hands floated lifelessly away from the knife. Reichart waited like that for five full minutes until he was certain Wade was dead. Movement caught his eye and he glanced over to where the armless and legless Soren was strapped to one of the cockpit chairs. He had a gag over his mouth, but his eyes were staring wildly.

"What the fuck is your problem fat man?" he said to him. "You know, I'm tired of all of this shit. Trying to stay alive for one or two days more. Losing sleep because I'm terrified of that demented Rey sneaking up on me while I'm sleep. Maybe I should put you and Kelly out of your miseries." He pulled his pipe out of Wade's mouth and prepared to advance on Soren, when he felt the slightest of touches on the back of his neck. For a second, he thought Wade was not dead and had snuck up behind him. He turned and prepared to jam his knife-pipe into Wade again, when he felt something hot slide into his lower back. He screamed and let go of his pipe.

"Don't you touch Kelly...she's *my* woman!" Rey spat at him as he jammed the knife deeper into Reichart's lower back. Reichart tried moving away from the knife, but had no leverage. It seemed the more he gyrated in Rey's grasp, the deeper the knife sunk in. He could feel himself shutting down, on the verge of passing out, but he had no energy to fight him off.

With a mouthful of blood, Reichart cried out, "Fuck you, Rey! You crazy fuck...just kill me!"

With the knife still embedded in Reichart's back, Rey turned him around slowly. Reichart shut his eyes tight. He found it odd that in his moment of death, he didn't want to face it. No, that wasn't right. He didn't want to *see* it. He didn't want to see the monster, the boogeyman that had terrorized them for weeks. At that moment, if he could have willed himself to die, he would have.

"Open your eyes Reichart," Rey said not more than two inches from Reichart's face. "Open your fucking eyes or I'll rip off your eyelids with my teeth!"

Reichart delayed for a minute until he smelled Rey's rancid breath getting closer to his face. "OKAY! Okay! I'll open them!"

Rey yanked the knife out and Reichart grunted painfully. He then felt Rey push away from him a little. He opened his eyes and beheld Rey's transformation. He knew then that he had already died and was now in hell. Rey floated in front of him with his arms outstretched like some religious martyr. Like all of them, he was suffering from severe malnutrition, but parts of his body were weirdly out of sync with the effects of the malnutrition. His eyes were deeply sunken into his face, yet his cheeks were full and almost healthy-looking. When opened his mouth, Reichart could see that he had lost a couple of teeth, as did they all, but Rey had somehow chiseled several of his teeth into sharp shards. When the coolant system ruptured a few weeks ago, the heat became unbearable, so they all stripped down to their underwear. So it was with Rey, but what Reichart first thought were strips of clothing, Rey had somehow attached hair to his chest. Dirty blond and brunette hair, dirty matted black hair, all of it attached to his chest. The hair floated around his obscenely huge potbelly stomach like some weird human jellyfish. His skin was littered with long thick scars. Reichart moaned partly in pain, but partly out of fear of this human monster. But who was he kidding...they were all monsters to some degree.

Rey looked at Reichart greedily. "You're wondering why I haven't finished you off. Don't worry, I will, but I've developed a craving since being out in what you guys called, the wilds. Truth be told though, this craving started some time back." He laughed, "Cute description though! *'The Wilds*...it might make for a good movie, if people were still making those types of movies." He stopped for a minute, absently scratching at one of the "hair things" attached to his chest. "The Wilds is a cute description, but not at all inaccurate. It is the wilds alright. Sometimes at night, I hear things..." He looked around fearfully, almost childlike. "There are things out there...I just know it!"

Reichart grimaced in pain again. Rey was always a little off, but now he was full blown crazy. He considered making a grab for the knife, but like all psychotics, Rey's guard never wavered. He waved the knife toward Reichart and wagged it back and forth. "No, no, no you don't," he smiled widely, showing his bloodstained and jagged eye teeth.

Reichart could feel himself getting sleepy, which meant he was on the verge of dying. As if from a dream or another world, he could hear Rey pontificating about one thing or other. He found that he was going in and out of consciousness. One moment Rey would be behind him, chattering on about something and the next he would be opening his eyes. He found himself dreaming about going to the dentist's office as a kid. He was terrified of this particular dentist because he was always smiling and he had bloodstains on his jagged teeth. He woke up with Rey yelling at him and crudely grabbing him by the mouth. "Not yet Jimbo...you don't get to die just yet. I told you, I developed a craving out in the wilds. I didn't realize it until I killed Tony. Well, at least I *thought* I killed him. The motherfucker was still alive by the time I dragged him and Sarah to my area. I must admit, it scared the shit out of me when he moaned loudly."

Reichart stared at him through glazed eyes. What the fuck was he getting at? He was so tired and could feel that he was very close to drifting into unconsciousness and never returning. He welcomed it, but when Rey would jam his knife blade into his legs that would send a fresh round of pain to his brain, waking him up. Out of anger, he made to swing at Rey's idiotic face and realized his arms and legs were tied down.

"Oh...just noticing the wire around your wrists? Yeah...I couldn't have you squirming away from me." He chuckled dryly. "Anyway, as I was saying, Tony was still alive and I was starving. I usually take my time when I'm cutting up pieces and storing them, but I was mad that he scared the shit out of me, so I cut out Tony's heart and ate it. Long ago, my grand-aunt was big on eating the hearts of animals because she felt you could absorb its strengths and qualities. She always did that to the critters she caught on the property and she was always trying to get me to eat them also." He looked off reflectively toward the large screen where Jupiter was swirling madly. "Yeah...she was crazy, but I took care of her."

He turned toward Reichart quickly, causing Reichart to jump. "But I digress my friend. I kinda feel sorry for the way that I left her because she was right all along! When I ate Tony's heart, I could feel his strength pour into me. I felt like I had the strength of ten men! I did the same thing with Sarah, but she was already dead and I think that made all the difference in the world. I wanted, no...*needed* that feeling once again."

Reichart could feel himself drifting off again. This was it he told himself. No coming back this time. He let himself go. Let himself float into the peaceful bright light that was beckoning for him. Just as he was about to drift off forever, he felt an immense pain coming from his chest. He opened his eyes and saw the top of Rey's head buried into his chest. Rey was tearing at the flesh with his jagged teeth like a fucking werewolf. Blood and chunks of skin floated in front of Reichart's face as Rey burrowed into him. He screamed in agony.

Terrified, Soren watched the monstrous scene play out in front of him. Watching the interaction of Rey and Reichart, Soren guessed that Reichart was ready to die, but hoped to die quietly, from the blood loss. But in the end, it wasn't quiet and it wasn't peaceful. Rey tore into him like a wild animal, just like Wade did. He closed his eyes tightly, but he couldn't close his ears to Reichart's bloodcurdling screams and Rey's grisly shredding. He could only hope for death to find him before Rey's appetite did.

3

Kelly lay on her pallet feeling the life drain out of her slowly. She knew she was dying and like Reichart, but unbeknownst to her, she welcomed it. During the incident with Treyborn and Emma, she had opened the wound in her left ankle and within days, gangrene had set in again. With no real medicine left, she had to endure another amputation while she was awake. She was in such immense pain that she passed out for almost two days after that.

From her position in the Commons, she really couldn't see anything going on in the Commons behind her. All she could do was listen. She heard Rich when he went crazy and floated out to take on Rey on his own. She heard Wade softly speaking to Emma, telling her it was alright. Telling her he would end her suffering. She heard Emma's soft voice pleading with him. She jerked awake when she heard Reichart speaking to Wade just as he drove his blade into Wade's mouth.

She was absorbing all of this in a sort of fog. Her eyes had gone cloudy. Sounds were becoming more and more muffled. She knew she had reached her end when she realized she could no longer feel the pain in her legs. She drifted in and out of consciousness and at one point, heard Reichart screaming at Soren. Her eyes slowly shut as Reichart's voice began to fade. When she opened her eyes again, she was shocked to find Rey floating silently above her. He pressed his finger up against his lips and floated toward the cockpit entrance.

If she had the energy to scream, she would have, but there nothing left for her. She began remembering being with her friends and her family. She remembered swimming at the local pool, laughing hysterically as they screamed and ran for cover during "Marco Polo". She remembered the local theater company organizing an outdoor theater evening for the little town she grew up in. One year, they played all of the *Lord of the Rings'* movies. She loved all of those movies, but there was one scene in one of the episodes, that always stuck with her. It was the one where one of the *Halflings*, as the Hobbits were called, was afraid that death was imminent and that he was afraid of dying. She remembered that the gray-haired wizard had responded by saying *"...the journey doesn't end here. Death is just another path...one that we all must take. The gray rain curtain of this world rolls back...and all turns to silver glass. And then you see it. White shores...and a far green country..."* There was more to the quote, but in her frazzled and depleted mind, she couldn't grasp it. All she knew was that she could feel herself floating toward those white shores. She thought of Burt and Jaime and Liz and the rest of her friends. She thought of Anton sadly. And she thought of Nola who was like a mother and a sister to her. If it wasn't for Nola, she felt she would have killed herself a long time ago. Tears rolled out of her eye that was not swollen shut.

With the last of her energy, she took the index finger of her right hand and probed the sharp end of wrist restraint that Wade had used on her wrists. When he had first tied her down, he tied her arms down at the elbow, harshly, almost to the point of cutting off her circulation. But he was careless with the wrist restraint. She was able to easily get her hand out of it and was now scraping the tip of her finger back and forth over the sharp end until her finger was bleeding heavily. She fought her impending unconsciousness with everything she had. This would be her homage to Nola Sykes, her mother, sister, friend and supporter. Kelly angled her finger as best she could to write her bloody eulogy. *Nola was a hero* was what her collapsing mind envisioned, but the neurons connecting her faltering brain to her fingers were no longer firing. When she finished, she peered closely at her handiwork and smiled. It was good enough for government work, she thought and closed her eyes. She felt her eyes were only closed for microseconds before she opened them again. She smiled again, this time more widely, as she ran toward two familiar figures waving at her, while they waited for her on white shores.

nola was there..

JUDGEMENT DAY

1

Rey floated through the corridors of his kingdom on wings of insanity. There was no one left but him and Soren...and Kelly. He refused to believe that she was dead. His mind simply wouldn't go there. After he finished with Reichart, he floated out to the Commons to share his victory and total dominion over everyone and everything and found her dead. He screamed desolately. He performed CPR on her lifeless body, seeming to think that he had the power to bring her back from the dead. After thirty exhausting minutes, he retreated back to the cockpit, where he took his anger out on Soren. He slapped him across the face and head and spat on him as best he could in zero gravity. When he got tired of that, he went screaming through the Commons and out into the rest of the ship.

Wherever he stumbled upon a camera he had covered up, he would yank the covering off, scream at the blinking red light and then move on aimlessly. One evening, he turned onto a corridor and ran headfirst into an almost completely intact skeleton. He screamed and shoved the stinking mess away from him as best he could. After that encounter, he decided he would "tidy up the place" and get it ready for Kelly, when she woke up. He couldn't remember how many days he spent rounding up skeletal remains. All he knew was that his days were blending in with his nights. All but the emergency lights had gone out and since then, he had no idea if it was daytime or nighttime. It was his mission to hunt down every piece of floating nastiness so Kelly wouldn't have to see it.

When he decided to sleep, he slept next to Kelly. He would whisper in her ear his darkest secrets and worst fears. He loved her. She never laughed at him or judged him. She listened to him, quietly...patiently. This excited him and he would sometimes find himself groping her body passionately, only to scold himself harshly to leave her alone and wait until she woke up. Only then, could they be together as lovers.

At some point during his existence within the ship, he realized that he hadn't eaten in days. He looked in the bathroom leading to the cockpit and saw only clean bones. He didn't know when it happened, but his ravenous hunger had just ebbed away. He wasn't even thirsty. He knew he needed to eat something though, so he made his periodic pilgrimage to the cockpit to visit Soren. Whenever Soren would see him, he would buck wildly against his restraints, to no avail. He would glare at Rey as Rey approached him with his cutting tool. But Rey was completely and totally indifferent to Soren. In Rey's mind, Soren only represented a fatted calf tied up in a barn, its only purpose to provide sustenance to the farmer and his kin. Whenever it would occur to him, Rey would sometimes take the time to feed his livestock. One minute, Soren would be screaming in pain from Rey's cutting tool, and the next, he would be clamping his mouth shut. He would shake his head from side to side, but Rey would effortlessly shove some Soren-tartare down his throat, with no more thought behind it than if he was forcing a child to take some nasty-tasting medicine. During these times, his sane mind would attempt to reject his actions with memories of fast-food places with logos of anthropomorphized chickens giving a huge thumbs up to the tasty chicken products inside.

Whenever he wasn't roaming the deserted corridors, he was lying next to Kelly, sharing with her things he had never uttered aloud. He began to notice that she was beginning to smell, but they were all in need of a shower, right? He filled a bucket with water one day and washed her entire body. He washed her red hair and then braided it as best he could. He floated back and looked at her. Even though Soren was tied down, he didn't want to take a chance that Soren would float out here and stare down at Kelly's naked body. He went to his old cabin and brought out a sheet to cover her with. To keep her *decent*. He had just covered her up when he felt a jarring within the ship. Despite the heavy and congealed miasma of his brain, he retained just enough self-awareness to understand that either a meteor had hit the ship or that the jarring was just a prelude to another explosion. A *ship-destroying* explosion.

2

"But this is not what we decided Ralph!" Jaime yelled. "You voted along with everyone else and the vast majority do not want to do this."

"Yeah, but in times like this, you can't leave it up to a simple vote. We're talking about survival here man!" Ralph turned to the few men and women floating behind him. They were nodding their agreement enthusiastically. Lindsey Murton, one of Jaime's engineers, floated next to Ralph. She used his shoulder to stop her movement.

"Jaime, you *know* that I have diabetes. You *know* what'll happen if I can't control it. I have no more insulin and we have no more food. What the fuck am I going to do now? Just die?"

Jaime stared at Lindsey. She was one of his junior engineers on the ship and so shy, no one could barely get a peep out of her. Now, she was frothing at the mouth, ready to incite murder. He and Burt knew this day was coming and they tried their best to convey to their comrades that it would be very difficult at the end. Almost ninety percent of them decided as group that they would endure starvation together and not resort to cannibalism. Even though the other ten percent were thoroughly disgusted by the idea of killing and eating their fellow passengers, they didn't want to rule it out completely.

He, Liz and Burt spoke to the group and did their best to describe how bad things were outside the Cargo Hold. They told them that things in the Cargo Hold would get very ugly at the end. They shared with them that the weaker, sicker people would be the first to fall to starvation. After that, there would be fighting and more people would die. If the ones who were not willing to resort to cannibalism survived the fighting, then they would be okay, until the next round of starvation deaths. However, they warned that if the folks who wanted to live and eat at all costs were to win, then their world in here would eventually turn into Rey's world, but much uglier.

"What if we were to just eat the folks who died of starvation?" asked Arnold Williams, one of the maintenance technicians. "At least then, we wouldn't have to kill nobody." A chorus of agreement rose up behind him and he nodded his head vigorously.

"I understand what you're saying Arnold, I really do," Burt said. "But how much time does that give you once the dead have been consumed? There are quite a few of us here. How many people do you think one body will feed? And for how long? Eating piecemeal like that simply prolongs the pain and the agony. Eventually, when all of the weak people here die off and there's nothing left, then what? At some point, we will reach a sort of equilibrium where the remaining survivors will each have the same level of endurance and survivability. What happens then? What happens when no looks to be on the verge of dying and you're all starving again? " Burt looked around defiantly. "Do you know what happens? I do. That's when the killing starts. It'll first start with rationalizations like 'Lindsey has diabetes, let's bash her head in because she'll be dead soon anyway.'" Lindsey's eyes went wide and she glanced around the Cargo Hold fearfully.

"I say all this because this is a slippery slope people. If we go down this path, we won't stop until there is only one or two of us alive." He pointed toward the monitor, "Like them out there now."

Ralph looked unconvinced. He nodded to several men in the corners and they pushed off toward him slowly, brandishing whatever they could scrounge for weapons. Burt and Jaime tried to secure all of the weapons in the Cargo Hold, but apparently, they didn't get them all. Burt looked toward Jaime, who motioned to a number of men and women alongside one of the walls in the Cargo Hold. They floated to where Burt, Liz and Jaime stood. Zoe and Elsa floated up to Burt...defiance in their eyes.

Burt considered their situation and wanted to cry. Here they were, the last survivors of Earth. The last of humanity. Yet here they stood or floated, about to cut one another down so that they could live for three or four days longer. It didn't make sense, yet they were their parents' children. The children of Earth. An Earth that would rather sentence its poorest inhabitants to agonizing starvation while the richest people wallowed in money they couldn't spend in multiple lifetimes. An Earth that, because of its lack of human unity, allowed a rogue planet to sneak up on her, allowing only a tiny fraction of its inhabitants a chance at life. An Earth that produced monsters like Soren and Rey and empowered them to snuff out the flickering flame of God's greatest creation. An Earth that produced weak and foolish men and women like Ralph and his minions in the Cargo Hold. Men and women who were ready to snuff out one another's life just to cling to this miserable existence for a day or two more, for there was no help coming. None!

Sensing that there was only one way this was going to end, Burt pulled the pipe out of his belt loop. Jaime, Liz and some others girded themselves for the melee to come. Ralph and his folks were sorely outnumbered, but their hunger pushed them forward over the cliff, like wildebeest following the herd. Ralph opened his mouth to yell something, when all of a sudden, they felt a tremendous jarring as if something had hit the ship. The odd thing was that it seemed to come from directly above them.

3

Rey zipped through the corridors. He wasn't sure what had hit them or what the jarring was, but he didn't want to be pulverized without knowing what was happening. He went to the artificial gravity generator rings, but they were still as dead as ever. He made his way to the bulkhead door showing the destroyed engineering section. Oddly enough, even with the humongous hole in the engineering section, there were still a handful of the emergency lights on. He craned his neck to look to his left and right, but he saw nothing. Nothing but Otto Helmut's frozen and bloated body. *Fucking moron*, he thought, as he pushed away from the bulkhead window.

As he made his way back to the Commons, he began to think that maybe what he heard was a rogue comet. It wouldn't have been the first. He was about to head back when he decided he would check out the hub where Shelton tried to connect the propulsion system to the artificial gravity generator. He had the wild hope that maybe the problem was self-correcting. He floated anxiously toward the tunnel leading up to the artificial gravity generator hub.

4

Once the initial excitement and nervousness over the jarring wore off, Ralph turned to several of the men amassing behind him. He whispered something that Burt couldn't hear. Burt gripped his pipe tightly in his hands. He hated this, but he couldn't allow this sickness and selfishness to breed within their little closed society. He felt that if he were to take care of Ralph immediately, then the others might fall in line. Maybe. Behind him, he could hear Zoe crying. He looked at her, but she was steadfastly focused on the group preparing to come toward them. Seeing her strength gave him the strength to utterly remove Ralph from the picture. He braced himself to launch into their group.

Off to Burt's left side was Walt Moore. He was terrified, but he was with Burt one hundred percent. Walt had told Burt earlier that day that he'd be damned if he gave in to his hunger and ate somebody. In fact, he thought he would actually be damned if he ate someone. This, more than any moral compunctions against killing someone and eating them, is what scared him the most. He had described to Burt that he could see himself standing in front of Peter at the pearly gates explaining why he souffléed Ralph's thigh meat. He chuckled to himself as he thought of his conversation with Burt. Despite the fact that Ralph was floating dangerously close to them, the thought of him in heaven explaining cannibalism to Saint Peter, struck him as funny. He turned his head to hide his grin and saw a face staring at him from the airlock portal. He nearly shit a brick. At first, he thought it was maybe Larry or Allison, but this figure was wearing a helmet. He floated over to the airlock, mumbling incoherently.

Burt heard Walt mumbling and did a quick turn of his head to tell him to focus. He looked toward Walt briefly and then turned his head back to Ralph, lest Ralph try to sneak up on him, but he had to turn back again. He felt his heart skip a beat. *Is that a man in there?* He asked himself? He dropped his fighting stance and floated over to where Walt was. Jaime, Liz and the others were now floating over to the airlock door.

"Oh my God," Walt exclaimed. "Who are you? Where did you come from?"

The suited figure pressed something on his helmet and his voice came through the speaker, "I'm from the *Orion*. What's your situation in there?"

Walt could feel himself bubbling up and starting to boil over. He was cold one second and then he was hot. He didn't know what to feel. There were a million things he wanted to say to the suited figure from the *Orion*, but the only thing that came to mind felt like he was telling his dad something bad his brother had done. "Oh God! Are you here to help us? These fuckers are crazy! Soren has gone crazy!"

Burt couldn't exactly hear what the suited figure was saying to Walt, but he could hear what Walt was saying and it was barely making sense. He moved up close to Walt and shoved him out of the way, "Get out of the way Walt! Let me talk to him."

Walt gave Burt a look of reproach, but pushed away from the airlock, just the same. Burt moved up close to the airlock door window, cleared his throat and said, "Hi, my name is Burt. Burt Stone. I'm a doctor." He immediately thought of all of the sick and malnourished people behind him. "We've got a lot of sick people here, and we're all suffering from malnutrition." He adjusted himself close to the door. "We lost gravity a couple of weeks ago. We need help badly."

Since the suited figure did not have his sun visor pulled down, Burt was able to see his face clearly. He looked vaguely familiar, but Burt's mental processes were not functioning at one hundred percent. Unfortunately, the man's face looked uncertain and Burt was terrified he was going to leave them to their fates. He was about to plead with the man when he spoke up again. "Burt, I wasn't with your original group on the moon, but Tess and Henry and others have told me..."

When Burt heard Tess's name, it felt like his heart did more than skip a beat, it felt like it completely stopped. *Tess? He knows Tess? And more importantly, he's WITH Tess?!* He looked at the man and could see the concern in his face. *"You're with Tess?"* he asked incredulously.

The man smiled briefly and said, "Yes...she's piloting the *Orion*."

5

After searching the artificial gravity generator hub, Rey was satisfied that there was nothing amiss there. He left the area and began making his way back to the Commons when he felt the jarring again. It was very slight, but for the deathly still *Cassiopeia*, it was enough for him to feel it. Now, he could feel deep in his bones that something wasn't right. He pulled himself down the tunnel away from the hub and made his way to the rear of the ship. He was about to head toward the Cargo Hold when he heard a slight clanging noise coming from the starboard side airlock, the one they used to go out to the Cargo Cabin. He pulled out his homemade half-glove and slid it on his hand. Once it was on, he depressed the blade eject button and six inches of gleaming steel sprang out. He looked at it lovingly. When he and his guys were confronted by Reichart and his people, he was not able to defend himself because he had left all of his weapons in the cockpit. He made it a point to never be weaponless again, so he created a sort of snug half-glove for his left hand. Scrounging around the passenger cabins, he found someone's switchblade, still in the packaging. Using duct tape, he secured the base of the switchblade into glove, so that while he was wearing it, he would be able to use the knife without fear of dropping it or having it knocked from his hand. He sharpened the blade religiously. He kept this half-glove and his regular, cutting knife in a strap on his side. When he heard the noise near the starboard side airlock, he quickly donned the half-glove and used his free hand to position his body.

He floated quietly toward the airlock, passing through the large semi-circular room that used to contain eight spacesuits. As he got closer to the airlock entrance, he thought he saw a light coming in through the small window set in the door. Immediately, he positioned himself near the ceiling of the short corridor leading to the airlock. From up there, almost ten feet above the floor, he would be able to see what demented space demon had wormed its way into his ship.

As he waited there, barely breathing, a suited figure came out of the airlock. It was actually walking on the floor, not floating! Somewhere in the deep jumbled recesses of his mind, he seemed to remember a thing or two about magnetic boots. He floated right above the figure, fighting the urge to descend upon it with his knife. The figure walked past him and headed down the corridor toward the Commons. He could see the figure looking left and right at items floating in the darkness. He seemed to remember cleaning up the place, but he also remembered he had a bit of a tantrum one morning. He had noticed there were blood stains dotting the sheet covering Kelly, so he wanted to put another sheet over her. A cleaner one. But when he removed the bloodied sheet, he saw bite marks all over her body. He was enraged. He stormed into the cockpit and beat Soren mercilessly. After that, he went into his old cabin where he had stored anything floating around the ship and started flinging them into the air. Some of them hit the wall and bounced back in the cabin, while a lot of them floated off into the Commons for all eternity in zero gravity. He cursed himself when he saw Kelly's foot floating lazily in front of the figure. He would have to remember to find it after he dispatched this creature.

Deep down in Rey's frazzled and starving consciousness, he knew that this was a person, a real person, but his mind had difficulty accepting that fact. As far as he knew, the only other people alive on this ship, other than he and Soren, were the folks in the Cargo Hold. He knew for a fact that they would never get out. The folks on the moon were long dead. Earth was long dead. So, who was this? He began to believe that his mind was playing tricks on him, making him see things that weren't there, but here it was, still walking toward the Commons. When the figure reached the end of the corridor, it opened a panel in the wall and flipped a switch. Rey had an almost physical reaction to the lights being turned on. He had turned off the emergency backup lights weeks ago. It made things look cozier and not so devoid of life. With the lights back on, it was a stark reminder of where he was.

The figure seemed to be taken aback once the lights were on and quickened its pace toward the cockpit. He would not allow it to go in there. He would not allow the creature to bespoil his clever efforts at animal husbandry. He slowly drifted closer to the suited beast. Soon, he would be right above it and that's when he would descend upon it like a knife slicing through butter. Just as Rey was ready to swoop down on the figure, it stopped short of going into the cockpit. To Rey's dismay, it had seen Kelly, resting peacefully underneath the clean sheet he placed over her.

Rey began seeing red. *How dare this space creature come into my home, disturb my peace, and now, disturb my woman?!* He watched from above as his breathing became more and more erratic. The figure had bent down to look at some bloody scrawls on the wall next to Kelly. He had never bothered to see what was actually there. As far as he was concerned, this area was sacred to him. He relaxed just a bit when the figure appeared to stand as if to move on, but it reached out a gloved hand and yanked her resting shroud from her body. The sheet flew across the room like a stork caught in a hurricane. Rey stared after it and then turned angrily toward the suited figure. He bunched up his knees and launched himself toward the mumbling creature, knife thrust out in front of him, lips pulled back in a snarl. The creature turned right before Rey hit it. Its eyes seemed to bulge out of their sockets, giving Rey a measure of satisfaction as he drove the knife deep into the intruder. The figure screamed, but Rey didn't hear it. All he knew was that if there was one, then there would be more. Let them come...he would be ready.

6

Rey turned the creature over and he felt something shift in his brain. This walking creature was actually a man! Rey's hold on his sanity was very tenuous. One minute, he would see a man, the next, a walking amorphous blob. It took him a couple of minutes to move the man-thing because of his boots. Distant, long buried memories of magnetic boots with settings floated up to his psyche. He moved the body to one of the bathrooms near the cockpit. The face in the helmet looked full and healthy. It might be exactly what Kelly...and he, needed to get their strength back.

Rey didn't have to wait long for the next interloper. Just as expected, he saw another suited figure making its way through the corridors and toward the Commons. He hid in the hallway, just inside one of the cabins. From here, once man-thing abomination lumbered by, he would be able to slip out behind it. He would have his blade buried deep in its guts before it knew what had happened.

Rey realized that this man-thing was more prepared than the first one. He carried a long pipe with slightly jagged edges, but that was of no consequence to Rey. He had the advantage of flight and would be able to use the suited figure's magnetic boots for leverage or to change his direction of attack.

Again, Rey's frazzled mind tried to put the pieces together that would help him understand that these were people, but his thoughts were so jumbled and sporadic, that all he saw was some type of man-thing space creature that had made it aboard his ship. But this one was different. He was being extremely careful. He was thoroughly checking the rows of the seating area in the Commons. Eventually, he turned in the direction of the cockpit. Rey pushed himself hard toward him with his half-glove knife slicing through the air. The man-thing didn't seem to notice him floating closer and closer...

Rey was almost upon him when he whirled around quickly. Rey had no time to adjust his angle of attack and was practically impaled in the chest by the pipe it carried. It hurt like hell as he floated down to the floor, but it didn't as much as break the skin. He raked the air in front of him with his half-glove knife. He realized his efforts would be in vain until he could get leverage again. As soon as his feet touched the floor, he prepared to jackknife himself into the man-thing's helmeted head, but it stepped on his wrist and slammed the pipe down on this half-gloved hand. The pain was immediate and immense and Rey screamed out like a trapped animal. Rey grabbed at the twisting pipe, but was not able to free his hand. Eventually, the glove and the knife were torn loose. He saw the man-thing kick the knife across the floor.

The suited figure then jammed the pipe into Rey's throat and started yelling at Rey. Rey could only look at it with hate-filled eyes. He could see the man – *Yes! It was a man!* his damaged mind finally admitted – yelling at him, but Rey couldn't hear a thing. Rey could see the revulsion in the man's eyes as he stared down at him on the floor, appraising him, judging him. Still pressing the pipe into Rey's throat, the man flipped on a switch on the side of his helmet.

Rey heard a woman's voice come through on the man's headset and for one, fleeting minute, thought he recognized the voice. His tortured mind attempted to make the connection, but it had receded just as quickly into the backwater marsh of his broken brainwaves. But none of this mattered to Rey. He was in charge here! This was *his* ship! In a scraggly voice, he yelled out, "*I am Rey, and I am in charge!*" For some reason, this statement struck his funny bone. He first giggled and then he laughed. His face immediately turned deadly serious as he stared at the man, "You want to take my woman too?" he purred.

Through the headset, he heard the woman's voice again. Something like *don't trust him.* Whoever she was, he couldn't help but agree with her. *Don't trust me*, he thought, as he wrapped his fingers around his cooking knife.

7

The man forced Rey to a standing position, presumably to walk him inside the cockpit. The man had his gloved hand on the back of his neck as they prepared to move forward. All of a sudden, the man stopped. Out the corner of his eye, Rey could see him checking his watch or some other readout. Without thinking, he whirled in the man's grasp while shifting the grip on his cooking knife.

Rey grinned, *Got you motherfucker*, he thought. Just as he was about to stab the man in his stomach, he saw the smooth arc of the pipe come up from the man's side. Before he could react, the man rammed the pipe into his face. Rey screamed and grabbed at his ruptured right eye. The knife he was holding drifted slowly from his hand. Angrily, he used one of his hands to grab at the man's air hose. He didn't know if it would do any good, but it was the only part of the smooth spacesuit that stood apart. Instead of trying to remove Rey's hands from the air hose, the man leaned in again hard on the pipe. Rey screamed again and let go of the pipe. He could feel tremendous pressure building up inside his brain as the man leaned forward on the pipe. He focused all of his attention on getting that pipe out of his eye. Nothing else mattered. No matter how hard he struggled, he simply could not be free of the pipe. Eventually, he could feel his strength flagging. He felt something tear in one of his arms and he could feel his bladder letting go.

And just like that, he felt no more pain. His arms fell to his sides and he could feel himself floating down to the floor. With his left eye, he could see Kelly's body, not more than ten feet from him. During all the fighting, her body must have gotten bumped around. She was at an angle on the floor in such a way that his eye met her eye that was still open. He flinched at the reproach he thought he saw in her eye. It laid bare every sneaky, dirty and evil thing he ever did. He wanted to say he was sorry. He wanted to say he was sorry for everything. Now that he was dying, his starved-out brain seemed to go into overdrive, as his memories came flooding back. If he could cry, he would have cried like a baby and poured out his soul in repentance. But that time was long gone. Like a whirlwind, names and faces came flooding back to him. *Tess! That was Tess on the microphone!* He coughed. A far away cough with lots of thick, phlegmy mucous. His crazed, bloody existence toward the end of his life came into clear focus too. It was almost unbearable. He wanted to shut out the memories before they drove him insane, when all of a sudden, he began to hear music. He couldn't believe it! Music! It was choppy at first, but it started slowly coming together. He smiled weakly. Music was good. He could feel the darkness coming for him, enveloping him. As the darkness closed in, so did the music. As he listened intently his smile first turned into a scowl and then to incomprehension and then to a frozen rictus grin. The choppy tune slowly and inexorably coalesced into the familiar *Mulberry Bush* ditty.

8

Soren sat staring at the stormy clouds on Jupiter. It was all he could do. His days and nights were one long nightmare. During the day, if Rey remembered, he would shove rancid food down his throat. He tried to pretend that he didn't know where Rey got the food, but he knew. He had always known. He looked at his scarred and massacred legs and arms and felt like crying. He didn't even know what the word was for someone who ate *themselves.*

He closed his eyes. *How in God's name did it come to this?* He had asked himself that again and again and again. But he knew how it came to this. Everything that was happening to him now and what was happening to everyone on the ship was the direct result of his actions. If he had controlled Rey early on, it never would have gotten to this point. Soren wasn't a religious man, but he often wondered if hell was anything like his life had been these past several months. That thought brought exquisite terror.

He heard Rey in some type of struggle, but he was not able to turn around to see who he was fighting. He had thought everyone, except for him and Rey were dead, but maybe someone survived out there in the ship. Or maybe Doc and his people were out making trouble for Rey. He doubted that. They were there to stay until they faced their own *Donner Party* challenge when their food ran out.

So, who was Rey fighting? He didn't know if he wanted Rey to win or not. If he won his battle, then his wretched existence would continue as it. If Rey lost, then who would he be at the mercy of? He tried turning his head, but he could see nothing but a part of the navigation room and the far side of the cockpit wall. As he was trying to look, he realized there was no more fighting. He waited for Rey to come in and boast about his victory, but there was nothing. All he could hear was Rey fussing around near the cockpit bathrooms. He turned his attention back to Jupiter and slowly dozed off again into an uneasy sleep.

9

Soren jerked awake to a bloodcurdling scream. He craned his neck again in a vain attempt to see anything, but he saw nothing. The fighting continued and he heard another scream and then silence. After what seemed hours, he sensed someone coming down the hall toward the cockpit. As the person got closer, he could hear voices coming through a microphone. He thought he heard something like *"You need to get out of there now!"* An old voice drifted up to him from the past. He wondered if it was Tess, but that was impossible. As he racked his brain trying to place the voice, the person walked into the cockpit and stopped at the navigation room. From the corner of his eye, he could see movement near the entrance of the navigation room.

He was straining with all his might to get a look at the person, when he heard, *"Tess, I'm here! Prepare for Cabin release!"* Soren's breath caught in his throat. She responded back unintelligibly, but Soren clearly heard *"...full control of the Cabin Stan, now get out, NOW!"* Soren was gobsmacked. Tess was alive! And so was Stan! In that moment, his mind couldn't comprehend how *any* of that could have happened. *How was Tess alive and how in the hell is Stan here now!?* He was still lost in his own quagmire, when he heard Stan say, *"You cut those tethers loose if you have to. Promise me you won't wait."*

Soren realized now that Rey was most likely dead. He sat quietly in the high-backed chair trying to keep as quiet as he could. He didn't know what Stan knew and didn't know if he would kill him on the spot. He could hear Stan move toward the cockpit entrance, but stop. He didn't know if he made a sound or not, but Stan came back and swung the chair around, facing him.

Soren didn't know what was worse, being killed here and now by Stan, being left here to die on the ship or the revulsion he saw in Stan's eyes. He didn't have a mirror and so didn't know how he looked. And it never crossed Rey's mind to show him a mirror, but when Stan faced him, he could see his reflection in Stan's helmet. The creature he saw reflected back at him was something he'd seen in horror films. His eyes were bloodshot red. His skin was pallid and pockmarked and filled with blood blisters. His lips had burst and healed so many times, they were unrecognizable. He couldn't see the rest of his body, but he didn't need a mirror for that.

He timidly raised his eyes back to Stan. Even if he still had his tongue, he didn't know what he would have said to the man. Stan looked at him evenly and said, "*Soren*. You deserved this Soren for what you did. And just so you know, Tess, my wife, and the others that you abandoned on the moon are in the *Orion* right now. *She'll* live. The *others* will live. And so will *you*, Soren. You'll live on this ship until it crashes into Jupiter."

Soren moaned and blinked his eyes wildly as if trying to communicate to Stan. He thrashed around in his chair, but to no avail. In his mind, he thought he was communicating that he wanted Stan to take him with him, but Stan turning his chair around to face Jupiter had the finality of the hangman pulling the lever on the *Cassiopeia* gallows. He stopped thrashing. Behind him, he could hear Stan saying, as if from a long distance, "*I found Chayton! We are leaving!*"

And then all was quiet, except the unavenged voices raging in his head. He thought about what Stan had said to him, "*...the others that you abandoned on the moon are in the Orion right now. She'll live. The others will live. And so will you, Soren.*" He glanced up at the gas giant. Even now, he felt as if the ship was moving faster toward Jupiter. Or maybe he was now attuned to it...he didn't know. *The others will live.* He thought about that and realized they must have rescued the others through an umbilicus portal connection between the two ships.

They had lost their gravity a long time and since he had been tied to the chair, he never got the opportunity to feel completely weightless. Now, as the *Cassiopeia* moved swiftly into Jupiter's incredible gravity well, he thought he could feel his weight being pressed down into the chair. Yes, the ship was definitely picking up speed. He chuckled dryly; the timing of the two ships meeting was flawless. If they had gotten here an hour or so later, it would have been too late for all of them. He closed his eyes as sweat began forming on his forehead as the temperature within the cockpit continued to climb.

FROM HELL TO THE *ORION*

1

"Copy that...thanks Julie. Tell Stan I'll be there in Med-Lab after I take a quick look at our *Cassiopeia* friends." Once Stan and Chayton were safely aboard and being cared for, she turned to Henry and said "Take the bridge...I'm headed down to the cargo area." Henry nodded and turned his attention to the console.

When she got there, she felt as if someone had plunged her headfirst into a cesspool. A human cesspool. The smell was so strong she almost gagged, but she quickly got herself under control. She glanced around at the motley crew of survivors from the *Cassiopeia*. They were all gaunt and moved about like old men and women. Part of it, she realized, was because of the lack of gravity on their ship. The other part was that they were severely malnourished. They had prepared and stuck with a harsh rationing schedule. She shuddered to think about what would have happened had the *Orion* not come along.

Her eyes fell on Burt Stone and she felt herself moving quickly toward him, her eyes filling up with tears. "Burt!" she yelled out, still moving in his direction.

When she called him, he was working on bandaging up one of his colleagues who had injured himself going through the umbilicus. He looked up sharply when he heard his name yelled out. For a second, he couldn't see who had called him and then his eyes fell on Tess. It just didn't seem real. None of them, while sealed in the Cargo Hold, would have thought in a million years that they would see Tess and the people abandoned on the moon, ever again. And here it was, they had actually been *rescued* by them. It was incredible. It was a miracle.

Doc stood up just as Tess made her way to him and hugged him fiercely. "Oh God Burt, I'm so glad to see you alive! I'm glad to see *all* of you alive."

After holding her for a minute, he pulled back and looked at her. "Not all of us made it. We lost a lot of people, Tess. A lot." His voiced hitched. "We tried to take over the ship when we were only weeks away from the moon. We wanted to come back to the moon for the rest of you. But...things fell apart." He looked away for a moment. Tess waited patiently for him to collect his thoughts. "We lost Nola. I...I lost Nola. After our failed attempt to take over the ship, Soren really came down hard on us. Severely reduced rations. Restricted movement on the ship. Entire areas of the ship were sealed off to what Soren saw as 'non-essential' personnel." He pulled up his jumpsuit, which hung on him like an oversized tent. "Something happened in engineering that compromised the entire lower-level decks. We didn't have enough food, so Soren selected a number of us to do a spacewalk to the Cargo Cabin. We were able to collect a lot of food, which was stored in the Cargo Hold." He paused again and rubbed at his eyes furiously. "We lost Nola on that mission." He looked at Tess's understanding face and added, "She changed Tess. I know you and she didn't get along on the moon, but she changed and wanted to go back to the moon for all of you. She...just...didn't make it."

"I understand Burt. I wasn't perfect either and I could have treated her better."

Burt nodded, "At some point during the trip, Soren, Rey and his men started acting erratically and dangerously, so we decided that we would lock ourselves in the Cargo Hold where all of the food was stored. We made a bet that we would be safe there until we landed on Europa. Little did we know we would never *make* it to Europa. Eventually, it became our tomb, but it was better than being brutalized by Soren, Rey and their guards."

Tess stared at him, imagining the horror that they endured. She glanced around the cargo area and saw a young man walking toward them. It was Anton Finch. She didn't know him well and had only interacted with him just a couple of times when they were all on the moon.

"Hey Doc. Hi Tess...it's great to see you." He gave her a cursory hug. "I don't know what we would have done if you guys hadn't come along."

"I'm just glad we got to you guys in time," Tess replied. "My guess is that the *Cassiopeia* was a dead stick and was slowly being pulled into orbit about Jupiter." She looked at him evenly, "We got here just in time."

"You're right. You got there just in time." He shifted uncomfortably and said, "It's great to see you guys. I'd better go and get checked out." He smiled nervously and walked toward the makeshift medical tent in the cargo area.

Tess looked at Burt curiously. "What the hell was that all about? He could barely look at me!"

Burt said, "Soren allowed him and Kelly, Masterston's daughter, to get married." Tess's eyes widened at that.

"Oh really?" she said. "That's not like Soren. He didn't share much about his personal thoughts on anything, but I remember him being dead set against marriages, at least this early on." She thought about the weird and honestly, disturbing vision Soren had of Europa. "He felt that marriages should be controlled once we landed on Europa. I told him that was ridiculous and we never spoke about it again."

Burt eyes bored into Tess's, "Tess, that's not the half of it. I'll have to fill you in on his *Europa Manifesto* one of these days, but regarding Finch, Soren allowed him to get married because Finch provided him crucial information on our attempted takeover of the ship." Tess snapped her head toward the departing Finch, a new, less positive impression of the young man beginning to develop. "Tell you what Burt, finish getting checked out here and then get yourself settled in your cabin and *get some rest!* We can chat about this over dinner in the next few days. I hope you like the cabin I have set up for you."

He came up to her and planted a kiss on her cheek. "To be honest Tess, even if I was sleeping on the floor, it would still be good because it's *here*, with all of you and not on that floating nightmare." He jerked his thumb upwards.

Tess looked at him kindly. Life had not treated him well on the *Cassiopeia*. In fact, it didn't treat *any* of them well. Burt and his people seemed to have aged a lifetime during their trip here. She laughed inside. If it came to that, they *all* had a rough time making it here to Europa. In the dark of night, with Stan softly sleeping beside her and Len noisily tossing and turning in the other room, she would think about the astronomical odds working against them – *all* of them. She often wondered if mankind was meant to live on.

DAY 150

TO THE CARGO CABIN!

1

To Burt, the next few days went by in a blur. After a few solid meals and some much-needed rest, he found that he was recovering well and fairly quickly. The first day, most of the survivors from the *Cassiopeia* stayed to themselves, but eventually, they began to seek out the others from the moon. There were many tears that day, Burt recalled. Soon, they started meeting the people from Earth. Thelma and a number of folks who got caught up in the prison nightmare. It seemed to Burt that Tess and her people had their own harrowing journey trying to get here.

Since both the *Cassiopeia* and the *Orion* had similar interior layouts, Burt was able to make his way around the ship easily. That was the *only* similarity between the ships. Life was different here. *Existence* was different here. He was amazed at the difference in demeanor amongst the passengers on the *Orion* versus when they were on the *Cassiopeia*. Here, there was laughter, stimulating conversations, children laughing and playing and eager, positive talk of the future. Twice a day, Tess would speak to the entire ship via intercom, updating them on their journey and now they were here, only minutes from landing on the planet. As Burt looked out at the planet, it occurred to him that it wasn't predominantly blue, as the old astronomy books depicted it. It was definitely bluish, but as they got closer, he saw more and more greenish areas. It almost reminded Burt of Earth, but on a smaller scale.

Tess made an announcement that everyone should be seated and prepare for landing, so he left his cabin and headed for the Commons. It was packed. He wasn't sure of the exact count of survivors, but there were a lot of them here in the Commons, looking out the windows in pure excitement. Tess had invited him to sit in the cockpit, but he wanted to be out in the Commons with the others, witnessing this miracle. He found a seat somewhere in the middle and after a few minutes, Zoe came over and sat down next to him, grabbing his hand as she did so. They both sat in silence as the ship made its way to their landing site.

Just like any airplane flight he took on Earth, there was turbulence as they entered Europa's atmosphere, but it was short-lived as they made their way to their designated landing location. Their entry into the Europan atmosphere brought them over an icy landscape. Huge mountains stood on either side of them. Everyone in the Commons laughed and shouted. Some were crying. He looked around and saw Anton Finch, sitting by himself, almost disinterested in the excitement all around him. Burt made a mental note to keep his eye on Finch in the days ahead.

They had released the Cargo Cabin several hours earlier when they were still in low orbit about the planet. Once they connected with its onboard guidance system, Tess released the clamps. As programmed, the Cargo Cabin's directional jets came on ten minutes after being released and then the rockets maneuvered it toward its entry point into Europa's atmosphere. Once it had safely made reentry, its direction-finder navigated it to its designated landing location. They were now following that route almost to the letter. The only difference being the exact location where the *Orion* would land. The Cargo Cabin didn't need as much space as the *Orion*.

The ship moved over a snowy landscape that slowly gave way to water, vegetation and trees. They even passed a huge waterfall that sent a ripple of awe through the group. He could hear people saying, "That's probably our best source of fresh water in this area." And others adding, "Not only that, but that's a great source of irrigation for crops!" There was laughter at that and much happiness that Burt could see. But more than that, he saw hope. On the *Cassiopeia*, they had no happiness, no hope. As he looked around the Commons, he found it incredible that *any* of them survived their ordeals. By all rights, he and his people all should have died on the *Cassiopeia*, but they were saved at the last minute by Tess, who should have died not once, but twice – on the moon when they were abandoned and when they went back to Earth for their needed supplies. The people left behind on Earth should have perished when Lycos destroyed the planet, but by the grace of God, they survived. He ran the scenarios over and over and over again in his head and each time he did, he was in total amazement.

He felt the ship bank to the left, toward the huge waterfall and could feel the ship descend lower to the ground. He actually began to regret that he wasn't in the cockpit to see this miracle, but he was happy just the same. Despite the well-insulated soundproofing of the ship, he could hear the huge jets underneath the ship, slowing their descent. The next thing he knew, he felt a slight jarring and then the ship was on the ground. The powerful jets underneath the ship allowed Tess to land vertically. It was perfect. Everyone in the Commons erupted in cheers.

When the ship landed, everyone was out of their seats and crowded around the windows. He and Zoe sat for another ten or fifteen minutes, just absorbing the energy and excitement here. Zoe turned to look at him and smiled. She leaned close to his ear and said, "Thank you for everything Burt." She kissed him on the cheek and then headed toward the *Orion's* Med-Lab. Burt smiled and headed to the cockpit to congratulate Tess. When he walked in, he saw Stan, Tess, Jaime, Liz and several others talking animatedly in the map room. Tess hugged him when he walked in and Liz grabbed his hand and squeezed it. Hanging in mid-air was a sky-blue holographic image of a large section of the planet. As he got closer, he could see a red line originating from the ship and after snaking its way through a couple of hilly contours, came to rest at a green marker; the Cargo Cabin.

Tess turned around at Doc's approach and smiled, "What do you think Burt? It's not New York City, but it looks damn nice to me!"

He laughed and gave her another hug. "Great job with sticking the landing." He looked out at the landscape. It looked inviting, but he wondered about the immediate area, air quality, animals? He had read some of the preliminary reports on Europa that they received from the Pegasus satellite, but it said nothing about the air...or the animals. He asked her shyly, "Uh...can we breathe here? I don't recall seeing any reports on environmentals."

She smiled at him, "I've already sent out a probe for that. Our only hope now is that the oxygen content is similar to Earth's. It should be close, based on reports we received very early in this process. If it comes back positive, then we won't waste time keeping everyone locked up inside. We'll send a team to the Cargo Cabin and then we'll get down to the business of living."

Burt liked the sound of that. He looked up at the holographic image again. Tess noticed and said, "We're mapping out the best route to the Cargo Cabin," she told him. "It landed about a mile or so away, just southwest of us near a heavily wooded area." She pointed to a pixelated grouping of small trees in the holograph.

Burt leaned in and squinted at the area near the Cargo Cabin. "Looks like it's very close to a water source too," he added. "It might be a suitable place to set up camp. When you're ready, let me know. In the meantime, I'll grab some water-testing kits to verify its potability."

2

The next morning, he and Stan were looking at an enlarged view of the area near the Cargo Cabin. "It looks like an easy walk from here," Stan said. "Mostly trees and a few open patches of land. As we get closer to the Cargo Cabin, the downslope gets a little rocky, but we shouldn't need ropes to traverse it, so I think we'll be okay."

"I'll have those Canadian adventure guys – what were their names? Curt and Dennis? I'll have them join us, just in case we need someone to tie off some rope harnesses," Henry added.

Joe laughed, "It's Curt and *Donovan* and I think that's a great idea. From what they've told me about their business idea, it sounds like they're very familiar with ropes and knots."

"That's great," Tess said. "Take whomever you need. Kyra and I will be working on mapping out this planet. There's a lot of information that we just do not have. For instance, we need to know where we can go if this area becomes unstable or is non-arable. We need a better understanding of the weather patterns here." She paused and took a deep breath before continuing. "And we need to know the long-term effects of Jupiter's low-level radiation on the planet."

Before they departed, Tess pulled Burt to the side. "Burt, I was speaking with Anton and he said something about Soren haranguing him for hours on end regarding some message that was coded just for me and my flight staff? Do you know anything about that?"

Burt remembered Finch complaining about how Soren was on him night and day to access some "secret" files in the system. He remembered that Finch did not have access to them. "Yes, I remember Finch telling me about that. He was never able to access the files and eventually, Soren gave up on it. But I overheard Soren and Rey talking about some information he received from the Pegasus satellite about some coordinates on Europa that were off limits. He didn't say why and I think it was because he didn't *know* why."

"Do we have those coordinates?" Tess asked, very interested.

Burt thought a moment and then said, "I only heard several numbers mentioned. I had them written in my journal, but that's long gone on the Cassiopeia." He seemed to remember something and then added, "Oh! I think I told Zoe. She was keeping a journal of our time in the Cargo Hold. I told her about the numbers and I saw her add them to her journal. And she actually brought hers with her."

"Okay, I'll have to check with her then. Thanks Burt...and be careful out there."

3

Two hours later, Stan, Burt, Henry, Joe, Curt and Donovan found themselves making their way through the densely packed forest separating them from the Cargo Cabin.

"This is amazing!" Curt exclaimed, for the third or fourth time. "I mean, I can't get over how similar everything is here compared to stuff on earth. I mean, these trees look just like the trees and leaves on earth!"

Burt exchanged amused glances with Stan. They were both just as amazed as Curt was, but they were better able to control their enthusiasm as they too stared around at the weirdly similar foliage. The oxygen content was slightly larger, but nothing serious. Gravity was a bit lighter and they found themselves almost running at times. At the head of the column, Henry whooped out loudly, "I found it! I found it! A couple of hundred yards ahead of us!"

They descended the hill easily and made their way to the Cargo Cabin, approaching it from the rear. All of a sudden, Stan looked around nervously. He couldn't shake the feeling that something was not right. He found himself regretting that they didn't bring any weapons with them. Being here felt as if they were on a deserted island and were the only ones here.

4

As they rounded the corner of the Cargo Cabin toward the front, Stan's fears dropped to the ground like a rock. The cabin looked undisturbed other than the surrounding grass, which was scorched black. Curt and Donovan walked around the cabin, whistling appreciatively. "Wow, this thing is impressive," Donovan stated. "So, it has everything we need to get our little colony started, huh?"

"Yes, it sure does," Stan replied. "It contains meds, long-term dried foods, fishing gear, if you can believe that, seeds, work tools and a helluva lot of other supplies."

"Does it contain any weapons?" Henry shouted from the opposite side of the cabin. He reached down and picked up the torn cable lying on the ground. A portion of it was trapped underneath the cabin. Stan, Burt and the others trotted to the other side and looked at the cable in Henry's hands. It looked as if it had been sheared off.

Burt reached for the cable tentatively, as if it might bite him. He turned it over in his hands a long time before dropping it to the ground. "Let's get this thing open Stan," he said. "Too many people have already died for it.

When we did our spacewalk, Finch had already opened it, so I'm at a loss as to how to open this thing."

Stan walked back to the front of the cabin. "There's a lever here behind this recessed area. He snaked his hand through a small opening in the main panel of the Cargo Cabin. Grimacing, he attempted to turn the handle, moving his feet back to gain leverage. "Shit! It's not budging. I don't understand it. Sometimes they get stuck, but you can usually feel some play in the handle, even when they're stuck. This bastard is holding tightly."

"Maybe it's broken," Burt said, his voice sounding small as he stared at the Cargo Cabin.

"Maybe," Stan said, "but it doesn't *feel* broken. It feels...like it's locked...from the inside. Almost as if..."

At that moment, they heard a dull, metallic clunk that seem to come deep within the Cargo Cabin. Almost in unison, they half jumped, half stumbled backwards, their eyes bulging out of their heads.

"What the fuck!" Joe yelled. Of the six of them, he was the only one who tripped and fell when they jumped back. "What the hell was that? It came from *inside* the cabin!" He looked around wildly as if he expected to be attacked. "Do you think an animal or something got in it?"

"No. Or I don't think so," Stan replied. "I don't think an animal could have gotten in it, if there are even any animals here. Maybe one of the mechanical tools inside activated during the trip here. I've heard of stranger th..."

At that moment, the handle made an unmistakable turning sound and then, as if commanded by an unseen magician, the entrance to the cabin slowly swung open. The men stood there, transfixed, not knowing what to say or do. They saw their own reflections in the dark spacesuit helmet staring back at them, getting closer as the lumbering figure moved toward them, arms outstretched.

Everyone, but Burt, took a half-step backwards from the oncoming shambling spacesuit. Oblivious to everyone, Burt actually took a step forward, his lips silently moving. Just as he reached the mouth of the cabin, the suited figure fell into his arms. They crowded around Burt as he settled to the ground, while Stan wrested the helmet off after undoing the helmet latch. They all stood there gaping, except Burt. He sat there, tears filling his eyes.

"Am I in heaven?" Nola whispered hoarsely and then passed out.

EPILOGUE

1

Today was the big day! Despite his excitement, Soren was terrified. This was the first time he was going to put his new prosthetic legs to the test. His fellow prosthetic wearers had also signed up for this event, so he was definitely looking forward to it. When he was first fitted with his two new prosthetic legs, he knew, absolutely knew, he would never walk again, let alone run. But after several months of falling, stumbling, shambling and then actually walking and running, he felt that there was nothing he couldn't do with his new legs.

He parked his large van directly across from the park where the runners were starting. After his accident, he was no longer able to drive the sporty corvette he spent a life savings to purchase. The money he got from Katy's will after her death, more than paid for the van. He got out and like each time before, surveyed his surroundings to ensure there was nothing that would cause him to trip or stumble. Satisfied, he walked from the parking lot over to where a large group of runners were stretching. When they saw him coming toward them, they all waved enthusiastically. "We're gonna knock this out of the park, eh Wil?!"

"Hell yeah we are!" he replied. He couldn't wait to get started. It was the local *Challenged Walkers Run* and they had all signed up together. He was very reluctant to participate, but they all cornered him and wouldn't let him move until he agreed to join them. As he looked around the venue, he was glad he did sign up, although something about this race nagged at him. Maybe it was the location? He couldn't be sure.

They all stretched and made their way to the starting line. One of his classmates nudged him and said, "Man, it's hot as fuck out here!"

Soren couldn't agree more! He had been sweating his ass off the minute he got out of his van. He looked at his classmate drearily, "I know! The weather service said the weather was supposed to be cool, with no hint of radiation on the forecast."

His classmate looked at him oddly and laughed, "Damn man, you say the weirdest shit!"

Soren looked at him and shrugged his shoulders. He thought to himself, *I hope he can finish the race in his state. He smells as if he's been drinking.*

2

They lined up at the start line, but Soren tripped and fell right before they got to it. A few folks moaned in sympathy, but when he gave them a thumbs up from the ground, they all cheered. That made him feel good. They only had about a mile to walk, but he felt he could walk to the moon. No, screw that, he felt like he could walk to Jupiter!

Now, back on his legs, Soren got into position. He looked to his left and right, giving his comrades another thumbs up. They cheered and waited for the sound of the starting horn. It seemed to take forever for the race starter to blow the horn. Here they were, sweating their asses off, while the starter stood over their flirting and jacking his mouth off. He was about to turn his head and shout at the starter when the horn blew. It took a split second for things to get going, but almost in unison, they lurched to a start.

To the casual observer, these walkers would have looked like a bunch of zombies shambling around for food, but upon closer examination, they would have seen the pure focus and exertion on their faces. A few folks had jumped ahead of Soren, but he was doing well. In fact, he was doing better than well. He was currently in fourth place and gaining on third and second quickly.

They had been walking for close to thirty minutes and Soren was in the lead. The person in second place was easily two hundred yards behind him. He could see the finish line. People were crowded around on both sides of the finish. They were all jumping up and down, cheering him on. He pushed on even harder.

As he got closer to them, he could see that they weren't actually jumping up and down...they were being bounced around, almost as if there was an earthquake happening at that very instant. He realized at the same time that his erratic and bouncy gait wasn't due to his legs, but to the ground. It was bouncing him around also! A few times, he almost fell, but he pushed on until he made it within ten feet of the finish line. By then, the jarring had gotten so bad that he could barely *see* the finish line.

He noticed that it was very hot here, close to the finish line. And the outrageous shocks of the earthquake caused his teeth to rattle in his head. He pushed forward until he stepped across the finish line. He looked around, expecting a huge chorus of applauds and cheers, but saw nothing. The people had gone, all replaced by walls and computer equipment. *What the fuck?* He mumbled, but it didn't actually come out the way he intended for it to come out. *"Wah uh fhuuck?"* he tried again, aloud. The reality of his situation jolted him wide awake. He didn't know how long he was out, but it felt more like he passed out, instead falling asleep. He raised his eyes to the cockpit window and took in the panoramic view of the monstrously huge planet of Jupiter, but now it took up the entire cockpit window. He couldn't be sure how long it had been, but the *Cassiopeia* was orbiting Jupiter and the heat he was feeling meant that the *Cassiopeia* was getting very close to Jupiter's deeper atmosphere. As much as he wanted to, Soren couldn't close his eyes. His morbid curiosity baited him to keep observing the final destruction of the *Cassiopeia*…and himself.

Soren was grateful that he was actually tied down to the chair, otherwise he would have been bounced all over the cockpit. As he sat there clenching his imaginary hands, he felt a tremendous wrenching and violent twisting. This time, he closed his eyes tightly. He kept repeating in his mind, *This is almost over. This is almost over.* When the ship didn't implode, Soren opened his eyes and could see…stars! Before that could fully register, the pressure and the heat began to get worse and he was just about to close his eyes again when he caught sight of Europa. The sight of it filled him with intense remorse and loss. It was only there for a moment before the *Cassiopeia* dropped like a rock into the belly of the beast. Soren shut his eyes and started screaming. He could hear parts of the *Cassiopeia* collapsing in on itself and tremendous groans throughout the cockpit. The crew bathrooms leading into the cockpit broke open and spilled their dreadful contents into the ship. Skulls and bones sailed out in all directions. In the Cargo Hold, shoes, dirty laundry, and several books floated around crazily as the ship bucked and jumped in the violent gasses on Jupiter. The last of Burt's carefully rationed food exploded throughout the Cargo Hold when the container broke open against one of the Cargo Hold walls. In Med-Lab, the bloody bed covers that Tony and Sarah used flitted around the room like crazy caged birds. Burt's carefully maintained logs of everyone aboard the ship were unceremoniously shaken out of the cabinets. Deep within the ship, Elsa's remains floated silently and angrily in the darkness. Clutched in a partially eaten skeleton fist were the remains of a jumpsuit nametag. The only letters visible were "R" and "e".

As the ship continued squeezing and then expanding, Soren's body felt as if a huge mythic beast had plucked him up and began squeezing him slowly. Soren opened his weary eyes and screamed again. Floating around the cockpit like a warped child's mobile, were skulls and a variety of human bones; tibias, femurs, ribs, pelvises and countless others he never knew existed. And floating amongst them was Rey. He was dead, of course, but the one eye he still had was open and for some ungodly reason, it was looking right at him. He closed his eyes and prayed. Even though he didn't know God, he prayed to Him anyway. His prayer was cut short when he felt his bowels let loose, practically exploding through his ass. He screamed again just as his stomach began to force out anything that hadn't been digested. It happened so forcefully, that vomit exploded out of his mouth and nose at the same time. Just as he was disgorging the contents of both his stomach and his intestines, he could feel tremendous pressure on his head. At first, it was just a slow buildup, but soon, the pressure became so intense, Soren forgot who he was and what was even happening to him. What was left of his brain before Jupiter's immense gravitational forces ground it into a miniscule sample of organic molecules, was a bunch of lost, disconnected and random thoughts, memories and expressions swirling around his head – all in chaotic fear.

The End